Mystery Mer
Merkel, E. L. (Earl L.)

Virgins and martyrs : an Aria
Quynn novel

VIRGINS AND MARTYRS

AN ARIA QUYNN NOVEL

VIRGINS AND MARTYRS

E. L. MERKEL

FIVE STAR
A part of Gale, Cengage Learning

GALE
CENGAGE Learning™

Detroit • New York • San Francisco • New Haven, Conn • Waterville, Maine • London

GALE
CENGAGE Learning™

Copyright © 2008 by E. L. Merkel.
Five Star Publishing, a part of Gale, Cengage Learning.

Set in 11 pt. Plantin
Printed on permanent paper.

LIBRARY OF CONGRESS CATALOGING-IN-PUBLICATION DATA

Merkel, E. L. (Earl L.)
    Virgins and martyrs : an Aria Quynn novel / E.L. Merkel. — 1st ed.
      p. cm.
    ISBN-13: 978-1-59414-635-0 (hardcover : alk. paper)
    ISBN-10: 1-59414-635-7 (hardcover : alk. paper)
    1. Women detectives—Florida—Fiction. 2. Teenage girls—Fiction. 3. Florida—Fiction. 4. Terrorism—Fiction. 5. Religious fiction. gsafd I. Title.
    PS3613.E7565V57 2008
    813'.6—dc22   2007041781

First Edition. First Printing: April 2008.

Published in 2008 in conjunction with Tekno Books and Ed Gorman.

Printed in the United States of America
1 2 3 4 5 6 7 12 11 10 09 08

For my family, once again—especially for Linda, Jeff and Steve, and for my mother Mary

ACKNOWLEDGEMENTS

This book could not have been written without the help of the dozens of women who shared with me their own experiences related to the circumstances which form the storyline of *Virgins and Martyrs*. Neither could it have been written without the assistance of people of both genders, who took pains to fill in the gaps in my own knowledge in the fields of law enforcement, medicine, trauma counseling, and religion. People in both these groups patiently answered my questions, corrected most of my mistakes, and (in many cases) courageously re-lived experiences that most found terribly painful to remember, yet alone to relate . . . but did so anyway.

Perversely, *Virgins and Martyrs* would also not exist—at least, not as the book that you read in the following pages—had the publisher which *originally* purchased the manuscript not balked at much of the content, largely on grounds that sounded much like political correctness. Without this resistance, I might not have discovered how much I cared about the characters and their stories. Admittedly, *Virgins and Martyrs* would have been published at least two years earlier. But it would not have been *this* book.

Many thanks go to the people at Five Star Publishing and Tekno Books who *did* recognize the story I wanted to tell, and graciously helped me to do so. Foremost among these are John Helfers (who bought *Virgins and Martyrs*) and Deni Dietz (whose incisive-yet-tender editing was a writer's dream). As always, I also am grateful to my agent, Kimberley Cameron, whose tireless efforts on my behalf are always greatly appreciated.

CHAPTER 1

The uniformed Sheriff's deputy waved me forward, and I edged carefully around a Lexus that partially blocked the oncoming lane. Its driver's-side door was winged out, left open as if in a careless discourtesy.

As I passed, I could see that it had locked bumpers with the car in front, a blue Toyota that was itself angled hard against the street's curb; apparently, the impact had come at a slow speed, given the relative lack of damage to the Lexus' grillwork.

But as I drove slowly forward, I could see the fan of blood spatter on the Toyota's side windows.

It was a variegated pattern that grew heavier and darker as it moved toward the back of the passenger compartment, until it appeared that some vandal had spray-painted a streaky, red-brown curtain across the inside of the unbroken rear window. I braked alongside the vehicle, noting that the Toyota's wind-screen was completely missing; where it should have been, black loops of weatherproofing dangled amid twisted strips of chrome.

In any other circumstances, my first assumption would have been that the driver had been ejected, violently and lethally, by the force of a head-on collision. It is a scene not uncommon to anyone in law enforcement. In Spanish Bay—where the Northwest Florida sun and sugar-white beaches drew heavily from map-distracted vacationers, the college-aged on spring break and laid-back locals whose disregard for their own blood-alcohol level was legendary—it was a regular occurrence.

But here, no torn and bloody torso protruded through the empty windshield; even stranger, no blood or pebbles of shattered safety glass glittered on the Toyota's hood.

"Sweet Jesus," Tara Kinsey muttered from beside me.

She had twisted in the seat, craned her head for a better look; the hair that brushed her shoulders—currently, the color-of-the-month was a vivid scarlet that did not exist in nature—hung at an awkward angle. From her vantage point in the passenger seat, she could see deep into the interior of the ruined auto, inches away.

Then Tara swiveled wordlessly and stared forward, her face the impassive mask they teach at the police academy. Only the muscle in her upper jaw, knotting restlessly as if she had been working at a stubborn bit of gristle, hinted at what she had seen.

I pulled diagonally in front of the Toyota, noting that its headlights too had been shattered, and parked where the deputy indicated. I had the tinted windows up and the air-conditioning cranked high against the late-afternoon sun. When I shut down my engine and opened the door, the heat rolled over me with an almost physical weight. It was a dead-air heaviness, not unusual for Northwest Florida in August. But now it carried a sickly-sweet, smoky tang that stung the back of my throat like an astringent.

"Straight down th' driveway, Lieutenant Quynn," the deputy said, an odd huskiness in his voice. "They waitin' for th' two of you, down there." He turned away before I could reply, but not before I saw the track marks where tears had washed lines in the soot on his face.

Further up the street, Mars lights from an army of various emergency vehicles painted a rotating pattern of reds and blues against the windowless vehicles that lined the curb. On a number of these, the hoods jutted skyward. It might have been another result of the blast, or merely an attempt by the first-responders to quiet the din from dozens of car alarms triggered by the concussion. If the latter, it was a futile effort: two or three still squalled and warbled, discordant in what otherwise was now a shell-shocked silence. Not even a single bird chirped from the trees that arched over the pavement.

As we stepped from the car, the reason for that was obvious. The ground was covered with leaves and fragments of palm fronds that had been stripped away, suddenly and violently.

Tara glanced at her wrist.

"Ninety-six minutes. That'll teach you to take a long lunch hour, partner."

I did not respond. I was divorcing Ron again. This time, I had retained a different lawyer, one whose reputation gave me hope that he would be a match for Donald, the attorney through whom Ron always filed his countersuit.

I had driven to Pensacola earlier today for a late-morning meeting at my new lawyer's office, a *faux*-antebellum building on the fringes of the city's historic district. It had stretched into the lunch hour, and he had suggested that we continue our discussion at a café across the square.

To that point, all had seemed encouraging; he had been all business, commenting neither on the summer-weight suit I had selected for the occasion nor the amount of thigh that my worsted skirt exposed. It was a relief, given my previous experiences with divorce lawyers. The most recent had begun with a hand placed too casually above my knee. It had ended when the thumb-lock I turned on him had dropped him to his own.

Alarmingly, at lunch my new counselor had showed a marked appetite for Glenlivet and soda. He was just starting on his fourth when my pager went off. I had half carried him back to his office, and cursed the impulse that had made me wear heels for the occasion.

By the time I had threaded my way through the tourist-season traffic and sped east along the coast toward Spanish Bay, the bombing was already being carried on every news-radio station from Mobile to Tallahassee.

Tara was still speaking.

"By now, it's probably a *real* cluster-fuck at the crime scene."

"Beaulieu caught the call."

"That's what I mean." I caught her sideways glance. "You okay with this? Getting sent out here to baby-sit that jerk?"

"Why wouldn't I be?"

She snorted. "Yeah, right. Well, let me do the talking when we see him, okay?"

I glanced at her profile, guessed at what she thought. "He left Beaulieu in charge because he knows it won't last long. Not with this target. The FBI will take it over faster than you can spell 'Federal jurisdiction.' "

Tara nodded, curling her lip. "Yeah," she said. "Well, working with the Feds is always like Christmas and Mardi Gras wrapped up in one. We get to root around in the dumpsters, they get to handle the press conferences. I'd almost rather leave it in Beaulieu's little mitts. He might be an incompetent prick, but at least he's *our* incompetent prick." She shrugged, a cynical resignation in the gesture. "Oh, hell—let's get this over with. I got my hair appointment after work. Want to know the color for next month?"

"Surprise me."

"Don't I always?"

As we picked our way down the driveway, I felt the crunch of glass and other debris underfoot. Once again, I wished that I had selected footwear more appropriate to the event. For the devastation I was surveying, that would have meant steel-toed workboots.

The blast had been indiscriminate, seemingly haphazard in

the level of damage it inflicted on the largely residential neighborhood. Some buildings appeared virtually untouched, at least structurally. Others displayed exterior walls caved in or peeled back to show the inside furnishings. But the most universal effect was to the windows. Few had survived intact, and none that had been facing the blast site. As the bomb sent out its concussive force, the ring of its shockwave had immediately transformed most glass into fast-flying shards of razor-edged shrapnel.

Unbidden, into my mind came an image of a woman—a young mother, perhaps—passing in front of her picture window when the room lit up with an intense, dirty-yellow flash. Depending on the distance, her mind might have had just enough time to register this curiosity when, almost simultaneously, the sound and the pressure wave would have arrived.

For her, and for any others doomed by proximity and the flukes of wave mechanics, it would have been the last conscious thought they ever experienced.

We edged past one of the several ambulances that remained on-scene, parked at random angles along the curbs. Above the low murmurs of the first responders tending the walking wounded, a woman's voice rose.

"You. Miss. You're a police officer, are you not?"

She was physically small, even shorter than I. Her fine-boned face was grimed with soot, and drying blood matted her dark, shoulder-length hair. A latex-gloved paramedic was swabbing at a gash on her cheek that appeared painful and deep. But even in her current situation there was an unmistakable intensity in the eyes that looked past the paramedic to focus first on the badge I had affixed to my blouse, then on my face.

"Are you in charge?" she demanded. "I want to know about my husband."

Tara answered before I could speak.

"We've just arrived, ma'am. You need to let these people—"

The woman shook her head angrily. She pushed away the hand of the paramedic, an action that seemed more than slightly imperious.

"I am Susan DeBourche," she said. "*Doctor* DeBourche. My husband is David DeBourche, and that is our clinic. I want to know if he is still alive."

"You were in the building, Doctor?" I asked. My voice surprised me. As if of its own volition, it had slipped into the impassive monotone that allowed me distance from the pain of people I encountered on the job.

"No. No. I have an office downtown, a private psychiatric practice. I counsel women here on Tuesday and Thursday afternoons. I was parking when . . . when the explosion . . ." Her voice sharpened again. "I asked about my husband."

"Are you certain he was in the clinic?"

"As necessary, I perform procedures here. Today I had a scheduling conflict. He offered to—" Her words stopped abruptly, as if they had caught in her throat. "David is dead, isn't he?"

"I'm sorry. We have no information yet." Tara's eyes flickered significantly to the paramedic, and he resumed his ministrations as we moved away.

"Parking her car," Tara muttered, her eyes down as she picked a path through the fallen debris. "Lucky woman."

"Probably not," I answered, and something in my voice made Tara look up sharply.

We had turned the corner, stepping through the looking glass into a surreal world. On the street, the damage merely had resembled a war zone. Here the devastation was virtually complete.

The clinic had once been a private home, a three-story summerhouse constructed in an unflinching opulence typical of the robber barons who had been the first wave of Yankees to invade Spanish Bay a century ago. Part of the green-shingled roof still stood at a crooked angle, though much of the top floor had collapsed into a yawing gap where the front entrance should have been. What was left of the upper balcony's wrought-iron railing now corkscrewed crazily, dangling over the blast-shattered void.

The initial detonation had created a vacuum behind itself, and the return wash of superheated air had vomited great chunks of shattered redbrick out onto the circular drive. Paramedics clambered over the mounded debris, checking the vehicles beneath for additional victims. Nearer the clinic, teams of firefighters directed streams of water into the still-smoldering ruins.

A number of cars had been parked here; now they were upended and twisted, toys strewn randomly in a giant's tantrum. One was upside down, wrapped half around the trunk of a massive live oak where a knot of men conferred. There, a thickset man, red-faced and with a shaved pate shiny with sweat, watched with ill-concealed hostility as Tara and I approached.

"Just don't start up with him," Tara warned me in a low voice. "Let's not get stuck here all day, okay?" Then, louder, "Hey, Beaulieu. What's the score now?"

I leaned my back against the trunk of the live oak, which was as wide as a double doorway. It did nothing to ease the ache in my feet. But I said nothing, and Beaulieu did not look at me.

"Two dead, both inside the clinic," he said, "including the doctor who actually does—did—the abortions. Guy named De-Bourche. Bodies still in there. The bomb squad and the evidence technicians gotta do their thing first."

"Injuries?"

"Four from the building," he said. "We've carried out three more so far from houses around the neighborhood—a woman, a retired guy maybe in his seventies. And a four-month-old kid who was taking a nap. Bedroom faced the clinic."

"You come up with any witnesses—anybody who might have seen who set this thing?"

"Yeah, witnesses. Maybe we'll find somebody who's still alive that saw something." Beaulieu looked disgusted. "Okay, they had a surveillance camera hanging on their building—hell, these days *everybody* has one of the damn things. Except the clinic had theirs feeding into a recording system at a security station just inside the entrance. Between the blast and the fire—" He shook his head, his message clear.

"The G-men show yet?" Tara's tone was carefully neutral.

Beaulieu's head jerked in the direction of the street. "Half dozen of 'em, more on the way over from Mobile. Probably comin' from Atlanta, too. I'm using 'em as support manpower. 'Til Cornelieus says different, it's still my crime scene."

I spoke up, despite my earlier resolve.

"You have people exposed all over the street, Beaulieu. Whoever set this just might know what he's doing. If there's a second bomb waiting—"

"There *was* a second bomb," he interrupted, though his gaze did not leave Tara's face. "Smart-ass bastard set it to detonate at maybe twenty minutes after the one that took out the clinic."

He nodded at a shredded Subaru the blast had pushed hard against a jumble of other vehicles, a dozen yards from what had been the clinic's entrance. "My guys found it in there, out on the front seat. Disarmed it in place. Six minutes left on the timer."

His words triggered an alarm somewhere inside my head. I opened my mouth to speak, but Tara shot me a warning glance.

"Good going." Tara glanced over her shoulder at the activity around us. "You got it all under control now, I'm sure."

"Hell, it's comin' up on two hours since the damn thing went off. When the rest of the Feds arrive, I'm gonna be up to my ass in people steppin' on my evidence."

"Cheer up. They show, it won't be your headache anymore."

Beaulieu grunted. "We'll see 'bout that."

"Uh-huh. I don't guess you're going to need Quynn or me here?"

"Nope." His voice was flat. "Tits on a bull, the pair of you hangin' around." He kept his expression deadpan as he looked at Tara steadily. "No offense, of course."

"Okay," Tara said. "We're going to take a quick look around, then get out of your hair." She smiled without humor at his expression. "No offense, of course. C'mon, Quynn."

She turned and walked off, so abruptly that it took me by surprise. By the time I pushed myself away from the tree trunk to follow her, Tara was a half dozen paces away.

At that instant, her scarlet hair flared out like fire that has been fanned by a sudden gust of wind.

My mind had not yet begun to process that oddity when the main part of the pressure wave reached us, traveling at a supersonic speed that outstripped the flat reptilian roar of the detonation itself.

I had the sensation of a massive impact, as if I had been struck from the side by some speeding truck, enormous but unseen. Then I was weightless, my world a cartwheeling maelstrom of light and blurred color and formless sound.

I can summon no memory of my impact with the earth. There was only the realization that I lay facedown, partially covered with twigs and smoking leaves. More fluttered down, torn from the oak tree that had shielded me from the full force of the blast. There must have been noise, a chaotic tumult that is the aftermath of such events. But as I lifted my head I heard nothing but a vague rushing, like swift water over rocks.

Everything was bathed in an eerie lemon light that turned the world into a stark and unreal place of blacks and primary colors with nothing in between. Figures moved on the periphery of my vision, like fairies in an enchanted woods. But they too were unclear, indistinct in form or purpose.

All that was clear was a strangely familiar figure that struggled to rise, hauling itself hand-over-hand up a crazily angled auto—a scorched form trailing tattered strips of blackened flesh and topped by a smoking mane of tangled scarlet.

Swaying slightly, it stood upright as if in victory.

But only for an instant.

Then Tara Kinsey pushed herself forward on her single remaining leg and tumbled back to the ground. My last conscious memory, before a darkness blacker than night closed around me, was of the bright red blood that pulsed in a rich, unstoppable flow from the stump of her charred thigh.

CHAPTER 2

A hospital bed is less a place than it is a span of time, a confinement that defies measurement by calendar or clock. Instead, I had found, it can only be calculated by what the fortunate uninitiated would dismiss as minutiae, the minor indignities of any enforced routine.

But that realization came later.

For the first two days, amid the ebb and flow of people who smelled faintly of iodine and disinfectant, I fumbled for a sense of place that had been stripped from me by the force of the blast. Strangers appeared, usually dressed in greens or whites or multihued patterns incongruous in their implied cheeriness. These people would engage me in conversation as if addressing a longtime friend, and I found myself trying to respond in kind.

I also found myself unable to compose a sentence consisting of more than a disjointed jumble of incoherent sounds, a fact that should have alarmed me. Instead, I was inordinately pleased to find myself among so many smiling people whose names I was utterly unable to remember.

That they too appeared to accept this as normal was oddly comforting.

It was only gradually that I began to realize that the ceaseless stream of visitors were hospital staff members, tasked to keep me awake lest I slip into a slumber, deep and potentially permanent.

By the end of the second day, the extended twilight of my

concussion was replaced by a dawning awareness of my situation. By nightfall, I was judged far enough out of danger to be allowed sleep.

Perversely, permission did not equate to ability.

Strangers still entered my room, now in a pattern that was just irregular enough to ensure the low-grade sleep deprivation common to all hospital patients. It gave me a chance first to discriminate between the various footfalls in the hallway outside, then to assign them to specific faces that materialized moments later. Hands touched me, some gentle and some less so, to check my pulse rate or temperature. In the half sleep between those events, the electronic chirps from my bedside monitors competed with the other noises of the endless institutional night.

By the afternoon of my third day, when I was finally permitted visitors, I was well along toward earning a reputation among my caretakers that was as uncomplimentary as it was well-deserved.

Tito Schwartz eyed the door through which another nurse had just exited, her posture stiff and disapproving.

"You have a real smooth way with the staff here, Quynn," he said, nodding sagely. "What happens now? I mean, after she uses her fingernail file to blunt down your next hypodermic needle."

I grunted, irritably. Tito pulled the hospital-issue chair close enough to prop his shoes on my bed, and settled back. On the television mounted near the ceiling, the Braves were in the top of the fifth at Houston. It was 7–1, Astros, a fact that did little to improve my humor.

Tito picked at the box of Whitman's he had brought me, intent on the game.

"Gina sends her best. Her and Vic, both," he said absently. "Says she'll try to get over to say hello, if you're still here in a day or two." When Tito had been my partner as Spanish Bay police detectives, I had been a frequent fourth at dinner with his wife and daughter, learning to enjoy what Tito claimed was "traditional Hebrew/Cubano cuisine."

But that was two years ago, before he had beat an addiction to games of chance that had twice bankrupted him and that, in its last taunting incarnation, had led him, moth-like, too close to the fires of his personal hell.

A winning streak gone sour had left him hopelessly indebted to the Italians who still operated out of New Orleans; in turn, they had sold his marker to the Russians who had taken over much of the gambling racket from Tallahassee to Biloxi. A policeman on a short leash was perceived by the Russians as an asset, both in real terms and in the entertainment value these grinning thugs would extract at every opportunity.

But in Tito Schwartz they had acquired more than they had bargained for; as a pet, he proved impossible to housebreak.

In the end, Tito had been true to his own nature. He had turned himself in, cooperated undercover with the Federal probe that broke the ring, and escaped jail time.

But he had not slipped punishment entirely.

Tito had been forced to retire, quietly. He had never discussed it, but I knew the experience had left him with an abiding distrust of Federal law enforcement and scornful of any promises they might make.

It had also broken his heart.

He had surprised me, both by remaining in Spanish Bay and in the teeth-gritting determination he had brought to his new vocation. In just two years, the private investigation firm he had started as a one-man operation had grown into a thriving business, expanding into event security and crowd-control services for the various clubs and venues that catered to the seasonal tourist and spring break crowds. Tito had prospered, even bought the vintage Cadillac of his boyhood dreams, a '67 Eldorado as big as a freighter; to keep it running, he spent enough in parts and mechanic's services to support a second family.

But I knew material success was scant consolation for Tito.

He was an enigmatic man, subject to dark moods and the occasional outburst of barely contained violence that never failed to alarm even those who thought they knew him. I suspected he did not understand them himself. But I knew three indisputable facts about Tito Schwartz. He was the best partner I had ever had, and the smartest cop I had ever known.

He was also my best friend.

I looked at him now, saw him anticipate the question I was about to ask.

"Gina says she heard that Ron's out of town," he said. "Left a couple days before you got yourself blown up, she said."

He wouldn't meet my eye, and I knew he was as aware as I that Ron had not traveled alone.

"Some people might think a husband should be with his wife," I said, "particularly when she's in the hospital."

Tito pulled a face.

"Maybe he's just forgot that you two are currently married," he retorted. "Simple enough mistake, the number of times you two have split up. Hell, sometimes *I* get confused." He rolled his eyes at the look I shot him. "Chrissakes, Quynn. Ron's in Bimini or Bermuda or some damn place, okay? Maybe he doesn't even know what went down here. Give it a rest."

We were silent for several minutes, pretending to watch the game.

"Tara's parents had her body sent back to California," I said. "Sacramento, she came from. I never knew that."

"Yeah," Tito said. "I heard. I also heard that the department is gonna have a special service for her here."

"Day after tomorrow."

From the corner of my eye, I saw him nod.

"I'll drive, if you want."

"Thanks," I said. "My car's scrap metal now."

Again, we were silent. On the television, a left fielder with massive biceps and a salary that could retire the national debt hit into a double play, ending the Braves' half of the inning.

"Listen real close, okay?" Tito's voice was quietly exasperated. "Who could have figured on a third bomb? It wasn't your fault. Look, you want to blame somebody, blame Beaulieu. It was *his* damn crime scene, Quynn, not yours."

It was a rationalization I had ached to make, during the long hours of the previous night. Beaulieu, I had learned, had escaped the blast with hardly a scratch. But I could not escape the facts as I knew them to be.

"Beaulieu's too dumb to blame. He said they found the second bomb on the front seat of a car—in plain view. The bomber made it easy to find. Too easy. I knew it, and all I did was prop up a tree instead of . . ." I stopped short, suddenly without words.

"Then blame Chick Cornelieus, for leaving an incompetent asshole like Beaulieu in charge out there." Tito bored in hard. "Or blame the damn Feds, for taking their own sweet time getting on-scene. Or, better yet—blame the sly motherfucker who decided God wanted him to close down an abortion mill with five kilos of Semtex." He snapped his fingers. "I got it, Quynn. You go right to the top with this. Blame *God* for not warning you and Tara Kinsey that the bomber had enough shit to plant *three* bombs. Yeah. God's the dirty bastard here—that's the ticket."

His voice had risen now, but despite his heat I could feel no effect from his words. Once again, we fell into an unsettled silence. This one lasted a long time.

"She was a funny kid," Tito said, finally. "What was it with the hair, anyway?"

23

"She got it dyed once, about a year ago," I said. "The head of the city's personnel department was a real jerk—son-in-law of one of the courthouse gang, so he thought he could walk on water. He told Tara that she had to have a new ID issued, just because she had changed her hair color from brown to blond. Said rules were rules, no exceptions. He made a big issue out of it, finally got Cornelieus to order her to go along."

Tito arched his eyebrows, looking more interested than the anecdote called for. I had a sudden suspicion that he already knew the story, and was milking me more for my sake than for his edification.

"You had to know Tara," I said, nonetheless. "Her philosophy was 'get mad *and* get even.' So right after she went in and got her new photo-ID card, she dyed her hair coal-black. Bingo—another new card. Three weeks later, strawberry blond. She came in lime green the next month. Personnel guy went ballistic, tried to get the chief to make her stop. Rumor is, Cornelieus laughed and told him rules were rules. No exceptions."

By now, I was grinning like a Cheshire and Tito was laughing out loud.

"She even set up an office pool," I said, and suddenly realized tears were wetting my cheeks. "Called it her 'color of the month' lottery. Buck a month ante to get in. Once—I think she was kidding—Tara offered to let me know in advance, if I'd split the winnings with her. I pointed out that the squad room was full of people who had paid their dollar, and they all carried guns."

Tito roared with mirth, and I joined in.

The door opened, and I saw the expression on the face of the nurse. Then her features softened, and the door again closed.

"Don't stop now." Tito grinned. "Got any more stories? Maybe we can get you thrown out of here today."

He checked his watch.

"Time to let 'em give you an ice-water enema," he said, standing. "I gotta go check on a security detail I got running over on the east side."

"Anything interesting?"

He twisted his lips.

"Yeah, as if. Last job I had that even came close to boilin' my oats was a month ago—identity theft. This guy has his house creeped. Next thing he knows some bunch in the Ukraine is using his ID and credit rating to run an Internet scam in Italian real estate."

"Sounds like a job for the police, not a PI firm."

"Uh-huh," Tito said, and winked. "Unless the client's a bookie who doesn't want law enforcement looking into his finances. We ran it all down, turned over the . . . uh, *relevant* stuff to the Feds and Interpol." He snorted. "Made me feel like a cop again, 'cept now I get to pull credit reports and banking files without bustin' my balls trying to get a warrant."

"God bless the Internet."

"Yeah. Well, opened my eyes, I'll tell you that. These days, every new client, running your basic credit check is only the *first* step I gotta take." He shook his head. "Downside of runnin' my own shop."

"So what's the deal today?"

"Real big-time stuff," Tito said dourly. "Crowd control. We're coordinating with your people on the force, doing grounds security for this guy. Keep everybody on the sidewalk, make 'em pick up their Taco Bell wrappers, that sort of thing. Makes the neighbors happy, or at least keeps 'em from siccing the hounds on the crowd."

"Must be something, if he needs grounds security."

He shrugged. "Just the size of the crowds. Started out a few days ago with a handful, but now it's up to a couple hundred a day standing outside his house."

"What's the problem?"

"No problem," Tito said. "It's just that word's out on this guy's daughter. According to her, she's talking to the Mother of God. The Virgin Mary, live and in person. Shows up every afternoon at four, on the dot."

He grinned at whatever he saw on my face.

"That's the upside of things," he said. "Never a dull moment."

CHAPTER 3

I awoke on the morning of Tara's service while it was still dark outside, and I could not remember where I was. For a moment, I stared wide-eyed into the darkness, my heartbeat racing and my senses quivering.

Then, as if they were light through a curtain suddenly pulled aside, the memories returned. It took several moments for my breathing to slow and my pulse to steady. When it finally did, I reached out, instinctively feeling for my watch on the captain's shelf that ran alongside the vee-berth where I had fallen asleep.

It was just after four a.m., almost twelve hours since I had been released from the hospital, freeing my bed for patients with better attitudes and worse maladies than half-healed abrasions and multicolored bruises. The insurance agency had arranged for my rental car, a GrandAm the color of a fire engine that was waiting in the hospital parking lot. I had driven myself here, to the houseboat I currently called home, and surprised myself by falling asleep almost immediately upon arrival.

I went topside to stare over the still waters of Spanish Bay Harbor.

I do not know how long I stood against the railing, nor can I recall whatever dark thoughts must have shouldered against each other in my mind. But when I next looked to the east, a thin line of light the color of a dying rose had stretched across the horizon.

With a strange reluctance, I drew myself away from what felt like the brink of a precipice and went below. I dressed in running shorts and a faded crimson-and-gold T-shirt with SPAN-ISH BAY MATADORS lettered across the front, and tied on my Reeboks. Topside, I stepped onto the wooden quay and—without waiting even to stretch—began to run.

I cut across a construction site at the top of the harbor overlook, where a multimillion-dollar beach house would someday soon block this access. I trespassed along the property line of a high-rise condominium sited on what had, until only a few years ago, been a protected sea turtle nesting area. I pounded along, the sweat itching between my breasts, until I reached the low dune that rose and sloped down to the waters of the Gulf. Then I was jogging along the shoreline, the sugar-white sand packed hard and damp beneath my shoes.

Occasionally I passed other early risers, but mainly it was a solitary run toward the orange disk that rose above the sharp slate line of the horizon. I pounded on and on, not understanding why I was pushing myself but knowing that it was somehow essential that I did.

Near the breakwater jetty, I slowed to a walk, my hands on my hips as I waited for my breathing to return to normal. By the time it did, the sun was higher, and I could already feel the sting in it. I pulled off my running shoes and socks and peeled my T-shirt from my sweaty body. Then, in shorts and sports bra, I turned and ran into the water, a splashing dash into water that was the cool, pale green of a Coke bottle.

I dove under a curling breaker, swimming seaward underwater along the sandy washboard until I could hold my breath no longer. When I surfaced, I was surrounded by millions of sparkling diamonds, the light chop gently slapping against me.

I swam in a fast crawl against the tidal current that ran parallel to the shoreline, once doing a surface dive into a school of shiners that parted as if by magic to allow me passage. I kicked down to within an arm's length of the sandy bottom, feeling the pressure against my eardrums. Bubbles trailing me, I angled away from a faint delta depression in the seabed. As I porpoised by, it exploded into a boil of sand. A southern stingray, true to its shy nature, sped in the opposite direction, its wings a rippling undulation above the sun-dappled depths.

I swam hard against the tide for a half mile, then rolled onto my back and floated easily in the current until I saw my shirt on the gleaming shore. I stroked lazily back until my feet found the bottom and waded ashore.

Then I walked back to the harbor under a sun that was hot and bright in a robin's-egg sky; it was a cloudless morning, except for those I carried within myself.

The memorial service for Tara was covered by the media like the Second Coming.

She was only one of the three fatalities in and around the clinic that day, but she was also the only non-civilian to die. That cast her in the pre-packaged role of hero for the print reporters and TV newscasters tasked to cover the service. It was big enough to draw the national media; these were recognizable by the undisguised disdain they showed for their regional and local counterparts, like Brahmin mistakenly paired with the teeming Untouchables.

For the most part, the accredited reporters were forced to watch from the sidelines, itchy in an uncharacteristic silence, as a Presbyterian chaplain led uniformed police and firefighters in prayers. People lugging cameras on their shoulders, themselves an underclass in the media hierarchy, wandered the aisles, oblivious to the dark looks they received in return.

Still, only once was there anything close to a scene. It occurred when one of the TV crews—looking for the cutaway footage and background shots that producers euphemistically call "B-roll"—roamed to where Tito and I sat. As the camera operator leaned close to Tito's shoulder, my erstwhile partner pressed his strikingly large thumb firmly on the middle of the lens.

"Oops," Tito said, in what for him passed for a whisper. He stared without expression into the eyes of the startled videographer. "My bad."

Afterward, as Tito and I moved through the mid-morning heat toward where he had parked his vintage Caddy, we pushed past a knot of cameras, both still and video. They had gathered around an angular figure whose dark, suit-cut outfit appeared designed to look simultaneously humorless and authoritative.

Tito snorted, his lips twisted sourly.

"Gotta hand it to the FBI," he said, not bothering to lower his voice. "Show 'em a camera—bingo! Instant press conference. Must be something Bureau people learn at Quantico, during rookie training." He pretended to study the scene. "Showing lot of polish there, Quynn—Osterholm almost doesn't come across as a headline-hungry harpy at all. Got a real TV presence, too."

I did not reply, though several heads turned to look our way. One of them belonged to a tall man improbably dressed in Dockers and a dark pullover that read MILLIKIN UNIVERSITY. He shifted the TV camcorder he held on his shoulder, and leaned to murmur something to a trim-looking man in a blue-gray blazer who stood alongside.

We were at Tito's Eldorado, its cruiser-scaled hulk riding stately at curbside anchor. As usual, to ensure against scratches, Tito had parked so as to take up two spaces; this time, it was in front of one of the ubiquitous monuments to modern American culture, a curbside automated teller machine. I stepped around the queue of the cash-poor that the ATM was busily serving, and had just opened the passenger door when a voice spoke from behind.

"May I have a moment, ma'am?"

He was compact, shorter than he seemed on the television screen. Gone was the trademark silver-blond mane I remembered from when I could still afford cable TV. Now it was close-cropped and preppy, the hairline razor-edged above the collar of his oxford-cloth. But the face was the same that had once been featured as a rising star at the Atlanta-based news operation where he had worked.

Tito muttered something I could not catch, and stepped from the curb to the driver's side without a backward glance.

"You're Lieutenant Quynn, aren't you? My name is Jack—"

"I know who you are, Mr. Reagan."

His smile was practiced and professional. I knew it, and was still surprised by my reaction to it; I felt myself want to smile back.

"Lieutenant Quynn, I'd like to videotape a few of your reflections on Officer Kinsey."

"I'm sorry."

"But you worked with her, Lieutenant. You were present when she was killed. Your insights would help the public better appreciate the sacrifice that—"

I shook my head. "Mr. Reagan, Tara Kinsey was a fine officer and a good friend. You were at the services; you heard what the chaplain had to say. There's nothing to add."

His smile dialed itself down several degrees.

"Think of it as a tribute, then. To her memory."

I shook my head without speaking. By now, his camera operator had left the crowd around Moira Osterholm. He stationed himself to my right, the three of us forming a rough triangle. There, with minimal effort he could cover a shot that would include both me and Jack Reagan.

Jack Reagan glanced at him, making a slight circular motion

with the index finger of the hand not holding the microphone. His voice dropped in timbre.

"This has to be a deeply emotional event for you, Lieutenant Quynn. How long had you worked with Officer Kinsey?"

I stared at Jack Reagan, aghast and for a moment speechless. Then I turned to the camera operator and said, "Turn that off, please."

Instead, intent on his task, he pressed a button that ratcheted the lens into a closer focus.

I looked at Jack Reagan, knowing I should hold my tongue, that I should just turn away. But the up-swell of anger from deep inside me would not be restrained.

"I once admired your work, Mr. Reagan," I said, tightly. "When did you turn into a vulture? Was it while you were in drug rehab?"

Immediately, I felt ashamed of my words.

The newsman's face froze, and for a moment he paled under his tan. Then his eyes narrowed and his color rose with heat.

"Keep rolling, Jimmy," he said, an aside to his cameraman.

I turned and slid into the passenger seat. But when I reached to pull the door shut, I found it blocked by the bulk of Reagan's cameraman, who bent to put my face into close focus. At the same moment, the newsman thrust the microphone into my startled face.

"Why won't you comment, Lieutenant? Is there something to hide, something that you don't—"

Before I could react, from the corner of my eye I saw movement coming fast around the side of the Cadillac. Then a beefy hand grasped the projection of the camera lens, jerking it upward and off the shoulder of its owner as if it was weightless. Tito stepped back, popping a black-plastic videocassette from the camera and pocketing it.

"*Fuck* you think you're doing?" the cameraman began, then

stopped as Tito held the Betacam to the side in his left hand, at arm's length. "Jesus! Be careful, man! Those things cost thirty thousand—" He advanced toward Tito, hands outstretched.

"This belong to you? Some dickless asshole was sticking it in my car," Tito said, and flung the videocam into the photographer's chest with the contempt of a drill instructor discarding a recruit's uncleaned weapon.

The cameraman caught it awkwardly, and his feet danced madly as he fought to find his balance. At the same instant, Reagan moved forward protectively, a fierce grimace on his face.

Tito spun toward him. In the past, I had seen the expression he wore now; I had watched men considered dangerous back away from it.

To his credit, Jack Reagan held his ground.

"Take it easy, for God's sake," he said angrily. "We're just doing our jobs, man."

"Then find yourself another job, asshole," Tito said. "The one you got makes you act like a cheap piece of crap."

As Tito circled back to the driver's side, Reagan turned to me. "That tape is station property, Lieutenant Quynn. Do you really want to start a war with the news media?"

"I'm not starting a war, Mr. Reagan," I said, as Tito dropped the Eldorado into gear. "I'm merely ending this conversation."

But as we drove away, in the side mirror I watched Jack Reagan glare after us. Beside him, the cameraman had his eyepiece pressed close to his face, panning with us as we turned the corner.

Since September 11, 2001, virtually any criminal activity can be interpreted so as to fall under one or another provision of various legislation that collectively has come to be known as the Homeland Security Act. Whenever authorities elect to exercise that option, an immediate Federal response was mandated by what some now see as an overenthusiastic Congress. Some of these interpretations have been motivated by expediency or politics or simple bureaucratic ambition, and subjected to second-guessing in both the media and the courts.

But crimes involving high explosives—particularly as part of an organized campaign of systematic violence—tend to turn the decision into a no-brainer.

To the surprise of nobody, the FBI had assumed absolute jurisdiction for the abortion clinic bombing. It was an act that had occurred simultaneously with the arrival at the bombing scene of Moira Osterholm, assistant Special Agent in Command out of the Bureau's field office in Mobile, who made the sixty-mile trip to Spanish Bay in record time.

I am told that she arrived scant minutes after the explosion that killed Tara Kinsey, part of a convoy of vehicles crammed with personnel drawn from the alphabet soup of Federal law enforcement. Osterholm had thrown a single disgusted glance in the direction of Beaulieu, who was pressing a handkerchief to the gash above his left eye. Then she had begun barking a series of orders.

One pulled the uninjured firefighters and paramedics back behind cover, several of them dragging injured comrades in tow. Another sent into action a special ATF squad. These were dressed in blast-resistant body armor and equipped with blackbox technologies to sniff out unexploded ordnance, even through the acrid air that roiled skyward in evil clouds.

Only with the all-clear from the senior ATF technician were the rescuers freed to swarm forward to the aid of their fallen comrades, I among them. We lay sprawled, broken and moaning, in a fan-shaped pattern that radiated from where a white-and-blue mailbox had recently stood. By then, of course, what had remained of the mailbox was torn and twisted metal, centered on a smoldering crater. Even so, it had been a far smaller bomb, one that appeared designed more to avoid immediate detection than for the sheer destructive power of the first.

By some miracle, only Tara Kinsey had been killed by the second explosion. It was an irony she would have appreciated.

I learned much of this in the hospital, and the rest after Tito dropped me off at the Spanish Bay Municipal Center. There, a parade of officers stopped by my desk for a quiet word; a few shook my hand, a gesture that seemed to embarrass them as much as it did me. Nobody mentioned Tara by name, a fact I understood too well.

I cooled my heels for an hour, working through the backlog of case files that had sprouted in my absence; they were uniformly minor in nature, and I suspected that the more demanding cases had been parceled among my peers. I flipped through a pile of get-well cards and personal notes, some of them ribald. I did not expect to see anything from Ron, and in that found myself prescient. I booted my desktop, found little of significance in the e-mails that had come in while I had been hospitalized. With nothing better to do, the remainder of my wait was spent going through the jackets and mug shots, routinely sent to me by parole officers, of felons recently released back into Northwest Florida. As always, there seemed an inordinate number of them.

By the time I finally was summoned by my boss, the depression I had tried to fight down since dawn had rekindled itself into an anger fueled by my own frustrations. The delay had done my mindset no good. If the wait had been intended to calm me, to lull me back into the *realpolitik* by which all bureaucracies live and die, it failed dismally.

Somewhere during our conversation in his office, my command superior gave up any attempt to derail what I clearly was broadcasting in face and feature.

"You saw the scene," Chick Cornelieus said, his eyes steady on me. "It was a mess—rubble and wrecked cars, half the place still on fire. It was simple luck that they found even *one* of the bombs before it blew. Suppose Jesse Beaulieu did have enough people for a thorough search—and he didn't, not by a long shot. It's still not likely they could have found the other one in the mailbox. Not in time."

"When Tara and I arrived, nobody was looking anymore. Beaulieu was too busy trying to think up a way to keep the Feds off his turf. That, and come up with the right quote for the television crews."

"Nobody's to blame in this, Quynn." It sounded like a warning.

"You don't believe that any more than I do."

Cornelieus sat back in his chair, his eyes still fixed on mine. He had been a slender man to begin with, and the disease that we both knew feasted unrestrained within his body had pared him to a wraith-like gauntness. The failed chemotherapy had reduced him even more, leaving his complexion the color of weathered canvas. But the voice was still deep and resonant, the tone of a man accustomed to command.

"I can't do anything about Beaulieu. Not yet; maybe not ever. If I tried now, within a week he'd be back on the force. It would give them an excuse to retire me now, rather than wait until—" He stopped, then shrugged. "Very likely, by the end of the month he'd be sitting in this office, given his . . . *family* connections. And I don't think you'd enjoy working under Jesse."

"Maybe the Congressman doesn't want a lot of publicity, either."

"Give it up. Blood's thicker than water."

I was silent for a moment. Then: "I want the case."

"You're not hearing me. It's not our problem anymore. It's

Federal." He turned to gaze out his window; on the far horizon, a thin sliver of the Gulf of Mexico glittered in the late-summer sun. "If you want to complain to Agent Osterholm, I can give you her office phone number."

I bit back the first words that came to my lips. Then I said, "There's something else. After the services, a reporter from Channel Twenty-two tried to—"

"I know. Their news director already called. He wants a videotape returned. Immediately." Cornelieus raised his eyebrows in inquiry.

I shrugged, remembering how the handfuls of Mylar had glinted in the sunlight as Tito, laughing hugely, pulled the tape from the cassette as he drove.

Cornelieus seemed to read my mind, and nodded as if confirming something to himself. "Okay, let me hear it. *All* of it."

I told him what had happened.

"I might have overreacted," I conceded.

"Somebody did." Cornelieus turned again to the window, his hands clasped casually behind his head as he leaned back in his chair.

"Reagan's news director demanded a public apology—from you, to Reagan. He also wanted Schwartz prosecuted for assault and theft."

"That's ridiculous."

"Fortunately, I was able to make the case that it could also be bad publicity. For *his* station. I reminded him that Schwartz is a private citizen—that he just happened to be accompanying an injured officer, as that officer paid her respects to a partner killed in the line of duty. If the station wanted to file a complaint, I told him it would become a police matter we would investigate, in detail and in the full glare of the public spotlight. We would get the full story of who did what to who." Cornelieus paused, and pursed his lips. "Or is it 'whom'?"

"And?"

"He declined the opportunity."

We sat in a silence that was something less than comfortable. After a few seconds, Cornelieus spoke.

"Concussions can be tricky," he said, still not turning from whatever insights the window offered him. "They can make some people act in . . . *inadvisable* ways. You're limited to light duty, until I'm convinced you have recovered fully. Get some sunshine, a little fresh air. Stay away from the office for the next few days." He swiveled his chair, and his eyes locked on mine. "And stay away from Beaulieu."

He pushed a case folder toward me.

"Department liaison; crowd control—no, I talk and *you* listen. I'm in no mood to argue." He turned to the window again, and his eyes focused at the far horizon. I picked up the folder and walked stiffly toward the door.

As I left, Cornelieus spoke once more.

"Tell your *paisano* Schwartz he owes me one."

In a town other than Spanish Bay—or a neighborhood other than this one, in the city's old-money district—the Shepard residence would have been considered genteel, perhaps even elegant. A well-cared-for expanse of lawn led down to a small boathouse at the water's edge; oaks and transplanted palms shaded large sections of it, stonework portals guarded the driveway, and a gleaming white ironwork fence paralleled the sidewalk. Elsewhere, all this would have marked the property as an abode of privilege, a residence where prosperity was an accepted part of life.

Here, it was merely comfortable.

On either side, masonry walls as tall as a man flanked the property, shielding densely wooded estates for which Roger

Shepard's Tudor-style home would have been considered little more than a modest outbuilding. But to the crowd of perhaps two hundred who milled on the sidewalk or gazed at the structure through the ironwork fence, it might have appeared, fittingly, like paradise.

A polyglot Babel of languages and accents filled the air, some in excited conversation and others in the syncopated rhythms one associates with group prayer. Most of them were women; a surprising number of these carried infants and napping toddlers, dangling light blankets that had been new long years before. Some had brought home-packed lunches, or purchased fast-food in garish wrappers. There were a few guitars. Children of vastly differing skin hues ran weaving through the throng, their voices shrill in the universal language of play.

"Must give the neighbors a *bad* case of the shit-fits, all these people standing out here," Tito said, and chuckled. "Gotta feel for them. The Mother of God moves in next door, and *bang!*— property values all go in the crapper."

I did a quick head count.

"With a dozen of your people here, it feels like a waste of public resources to assign five cops too."

Tito looked at me. "You're kidding, I hope. You *seeing* this circus? Somebody decides to jump the line, it'd be nice to have people with badges to make it all legal."

"Your guys are bonded," I said, only half in jest. "Or wouldn't your client pony up to pay for liability insurance?"

Tito snorted. "He's paying top dollar, don't sweat that. Guy can afford it, too. I ran his credit history on the computer. Hell, I'm only sorry I didn't goose up the bid I gave him."

His voice rose a notch.

"Jesús!" he shouted, and a number of heads snapped to stare in our direction, wide-eyed, before pivoting just as quickly to where Tito was looking.

A trim, dark-haired man in a forest-green uniform turned at Tito's voice. He spoke briefly to another security guard, then trotted to where we stood under leafy boughs that shielded us from a white-hot sun.

He grinned broadly at Tito, mopping perspiration from his forehead with the heel of his hand.

"Hey, boss—you wanna be careful, yelling something like that around *this* crowd," the young man said. "They could, like, take it literally." He held out a hand to me, and I shook it. "Jesús Castile. I've seen you around places, Lieutenant Quynn. They got you directing traffic now, or you just stopping by to check out the carnival?"

Tito spoke before I could respond.

"More of them out here today, looks like."

"Getting bigger every day, Mr. T," Jesús agreed. "Wish I was selling tickets."

"They seem pretty well behaved," I said. "A little noisy, maybe."

Jesús nodded.

"It's coming on four o'clock—that's showtime, so everybody's kind of getting themselves all worked up," he said. "But it's still mostly hymn-singing and praying. If the kids get too loud, the parents take care of it right off. Hey—I've worked rock concerts, political rallies; I'd take these folks over that *any* time. And compared to college kids on spring break, this is nothing."

"Anybody try to get through the lines?" Tito asked.

Jesús grinned broadly.

"Ten minutes ago, guy dressed like a priest comes up, tried to talk himself past security. Didn't work. Takes more than a fake collar to get past my guys." He looked at me and winked. "We let your people take care of him, ma'am. Turned out he was a photographer from some crappy supermarket tabloid. Mr. Shepard already signed the trespassing complaint."

"Shepard's pretty pissed at the noble Fourth Estate," Tito said to me. "Yesterday, we caught one of 'em trying to climb over the fence in back. Another was up a tree down the block, trying to use a telephoto lens to shoot into the daughter's bedroom."

"How did word on this get around so fast?"

Tito snorted derisively. "The girl had her first 'vision' in a goddamn shopping mall, Quynn. With about a hundred people watching. Hell, these days, all it takes is one zealot with a link to the Internet, and you're world famous."

At that moment, a light-colored Ford pulled into the driveway forty yards away. One of Tito's green-uniformed security guards and a Spanish Bay patrol officer I did not recognize converged on it, and bent to the window that rolled down. After a moment, the security man straightened and I saw him raise his hand to his face.

The handheld on Jesús Castile's belt crackled to life.

"Car down here, want to see Mr. Shepard," a voice said from the speaker.

Jesús frowned, and pressed the "transmit" button.

"Yeah, well—folks in hell want a glass of ice water," he said, winking at Tito and me. "They ain't likely to get that, either. What you got, another news reporter?"

"Got two people, one of 'em a lady," the voice said. "They got badges, Jesús. The lady's ID says she's with the FBI. She don't look happy, neither."

CHAPTER 4

Moira Osterholm had changed from the clothes she had worn to Tara's services earlier in the day, having exchanged the somber black skirt-suit for a pearl-gray pantsuit. If she was trying to lighten her image, it was a wasted effort; she could have made a cheerleader's costume appear tailored and severe. It was less her attire than the reserve she broadcast through eyes as cold as they were intelligent. With Moira Osterholm, you knew immediately what you could expect.

But it was her companion who was the surprise. He was leaning against the car when I arrived, a short man with the classic Han features that are as common in the medical profession as they are rare among lawyers. As I approached the two of them, I noticed Osterholm glance in my direction, lean toward him and speak in a low voice. He shook his head, a hint of impatience in the gesture.

"Howard Zhang-mei, Department of Justice," he said, and reached inside his jacket for his identity wallet. He flipped it open-and-shut like a television actor playing a detective, and looked delighted with the effect. "You know Assistant SAC Osterholm already, or so she tells me."

I nodded and shook the hand he extended. The strength in his grip was another surprise.

"What's this about, Mr. Zhang-mei?"

"Howard," he corrected me, and smiled. "That is, if I can call you Aria."

42

From behind me, I heard Tito snort.

"I don't use my first name very often, Mr. Zhang-mei. How can we help you?"

"Tell you what, Lieutenant. Why don't you come along, see for yourself?"

He appeared not to notice Osterholm's unspoken reaction to his suggestion.

During the walk, Zhang-mei talked nonstop, a steady monologue of minutiae that might have been carefully selected so as to require no response or even participation from others around him. He was unlike every other prosecutor I had known—so much so that I immediately felt a sense of wariness.

Inside the high double doors, we were met by a short, middle-aged woman whose attire did not fit with the rest of the environment. It might have been the stethoscope that bulged the pocket of a starched lab coat, or it might have been the coat itself, several sizes too large for her frame. Far more likely, it was the gray-and-black nun's habit she wore beneath it.

If he was surprised, Zhang-mei showed no sign of it.

"Good afternoon, Sister," Zhang-mei said, and held his identification card for the nun's inspection. "We're here to see Roger Shepard."

She nodded as though we had been expected, and looked at a man's wristwatch she wore on her right wrist. The numerals were oversized, and even looking past the prosecutor's shoulder I could read the watch face. It was a few minutes past four.

"Mr. Shepard is upstairs with his daughter. I'm sure he would ask you to wait." The nun led the way to what looked like a study, and nodded toward a pair of chairs that, despite their overstuffed cushions, somehow succeeded in looking uncomfortable. "If you would not mind." As Zhang-mei opened his mouth to speak, she stepped outside and closed the door firmly behind herself.

We waited for more than an hour, during which both Howard Zhang-mei and Moira Osterholm murmured into cell phones that seldom left their hands. I alternated between watching them and pacing the room in which we were confined.

Occasionally, I peered through the drawn curtains that shielded the room from the outside. The best view was through a set of hinged windows that overlooked the crowd seventy yards distant. If anything, it had grown during the period since I had left it. Several times I saw Jesús Castile sprint across the front lawn to cut off a particularly enthusiastic trespasser, and I tried to convince myself that I was still as agile as the young security guard.

Zhang-mei appeared to share my own impatience with inactivity. At one point, he rose from the couch abruptly and left the room. Through the open door, I saw the nun who had greeted us materialize, intercepting him like a falcon homes in on a pigeon.

The prosecutor tried his boyish grin, but by the skeptical expression she gave in return, the nun was having none of it. They spoke for a few minutes more before he pulled something white from his pocket. The nun took it with no change in her expression, and waited impassively as he returned to our confinement, his face sheepish.

He saw me watching.

"Tough woman out there," Zhang-mei said, and reassumed his seat next to his companion, whose cell phone had not left her face.

It was another half hour before the door opened and two people entered—one the nun who had met us at the door, the other a man in tan dress slacks and an obviously expensive lightweight sweater. He was broad-shouldered and trim, and looked to be fit. His face was made up of sharp angles, even to the clean lines of his razor-cut hair.

"I'm Roger Shepard. What do you want?"

Zhang-mei went through the rituals of introduction, and Shepard nodded to us in turn. He did not introduce the nun at his side. Instead, he looked at me and frowned slightly, as if searching his memory.

"Lieutenant Quynn is a Spanish Bay police officer," Zhang-mei said. "She is supervising the police detail protecting your house."

Roger Shepard studied my face closely.

"Okay, I know you now. I saw you on the early news. You're the cop who told off that reporter—what's-his-name, the guy from Channel Twenty-two, the one who got caught with all the cocaine couple of years back. Schwartz was with you." He snorted. "When Schwartz grabbed the camera, I thought the guy was going to club him with the damn microphone."

I felt my face redden. "I didn't think Channel Twenty-two had tape of it."

"Hell, you *know* they didn't. But Channel Five sure did."

He chuckled at my expression. "Guess you didn't notice Schwartz parked his car in front of an ATM. Can you believe it?—those things have a video camera aimed at the street. Somebody at Channel Five must know the guy who runs the bank security."

Shepard broke into a thin smile, his own expression one of hard satisfaction. "Damn media vultures. I hired myself one tough Jew, eh? When I put Schwartz on the payroll, I figured him for a guy who didn't take any crap."

Shepard stepped to a large red-leather chair and sat. He waited until the rest of us had settled, then turned back to Zhang-mei.

"Okay. Once again, Mr. Chang—what's this all about?"

"Zhang-mei. How is your daughter, sir?"

Shepard looked surprised, then rolled his eyes.

"Is *that* it? A thirteen-year-old girl thinks she's seeing things, and somehow it's the business of the government?"

Moira Osterholm spoke up, addressing Shepard's companion.

"With respect, Doctor—" she began.

"Sister," the nun corrected her. "Sister Marie-Vincent Benedicta. I am a physician, but I prefer the latter form of address, please."

"With all respect then, *Sister*," Osterholm said. "What is your role here, please?"

"I am . . . let's just say, I'm assisting Mr. Shepard and his daughter."

The FBI official nodded, obviously unimpressed.

"Your presence during this interview may be inappropriate, Sister."

"She stays," Shepard said.

"No." Osterholm shook her head firmly. "Sir, we are here on a Federal inquiry. You do not set the ground rules."

"Then you can go to hell." Shepard fixed her with a glare. "Okay, I didn't ask for any of this . . . this *bullshit*. Look outside. Do you think I enjoy having strangers harass my daughter and myself? Maddie is my only child. If she's having some kind of breakdown, what do I—" He closed his eyes tightly for a moment. "The hell with it; the hell with you, too. All of you. Do you have some kind of a warrant?"

Howard Zhang-mei raised his hand, a placating gesture.

"Let's all take a deep breath and start over," he said with a smile designed to encompass us all in the warmth of institutional comradeship. He turned to Osterholm. "Moira, if Mr. Shepard doesn't object to the presence of Sister Benedicta—or Lieutenant Quynn—I think we can accept it."

Zhang-mei did not wait for a consensus. He leaned forward to rest his elbows on his knees, and an earnest look came to his face.

"Mr. Shepard, does anyone in your family have occasion to access the Internet?"

Shepard's brow furrowed. "Of course. All the time."

Zhang-mei nodded, encouraging Shepard to continue. But if the lawyer expected any unprompted elaboration, he was doomed to disappointment. Shepard sat wordlessly, as if he had closed the subject.

Had it not been for Zhang-mei's patiently genial expression, the silence that followed would have been awkward. In the event, it was only extended, long past the point where an interviewer less experienced would have felt compelled to fill it himself. Finally, it was Moira Osterholm who spoke.

"Mr. Shepard, this will go much more easily if you cooperate."

"I thought that's what I *was* doing, Agent Osterholm. What, you want it in a complete sentence? Yes, I use the Internet frequently, for research, for my investment and personal-finance information, for sending e-mail to various friends and colleagues."

"Does your daughter?"

"Maddie's a normal thirteen-year-old. She has her own computer, and an account with AOL. I'm sure she is as computer-literate as any girl her age."

"Do you monitor the Web sites she visits?"

"There had better be a point to this," Shepard said.

It was Zhang-mei who spoke. "Mr. Shepard, are you familiar with an entity called 'The Centurions of The Lord'?"

By chance, I was looking toward Sister Benedicta when Zhang-mei asked the question. I thought I saw the nun's eyes widen slightly, as though startled. If so, it was gone before I could be certain, replaced by the thoughtful expression she had worn since the interview began.

"No. Who are they?"

Zhang-mei glanced briefly at Osterholm, then answered. "The Centurions are a quasi-military organization that opposes abortion-on-demand. It also advocates what it terms 'active measures' against individuals who perform or assist in abortions. You understand what that entails, do you not?"

"What I *don't* understand is what this has to do with my daughter, or with me."

"Has Maddie talked about abortion or abortionists?" Zhang-mei looked apologetic. "During her 'visions,' I mean."

"Perhaps I should address that, Roger," Sister Benedicta interrupted. "Mr. Zhang-mei, the Catholic Church has rigid protocols that must be followed in situations such as those involving Maddie Shepard. Perhaps I should be somewhat more clear in my own role here. I am a delegate from the Sacred Congregation for the Doctrine of the Faith. Are you familiar with us?"

"Only in general," Zhang-mei said. "Not so long ago, you were called the Papal Office of the Inquisition. These days, you and your people decide what is a miracle and what is not."

Benedicta smiled, as if amused. But her eyes held steady on those of Zhang-mei, and I could detect no humor in them.

"The Inquisition. It certainly invokes awful images—the darker stories of Poe, or perhaps Stephen King. Very evocative; far more so than describing our role as the more mundane task of investigating matters of faith. Or is it merely more prejudicial?"

She arched her eyebrows, but Zhang-mei did not rise to the bait. Benedicta shook her head, a self-deprecating gesture that seemed to me too practiced to be sincere. "But as far as your latter statement, I'm afraid you have given me and my fellows more stature than we deserve. We make no such decisions, sir."

"Really. Then who *is* in charge, Sister?"

"Due to the high visibility this matter is receiving by the

public, overall responsibility for the investigation has been transferred from the local diocese directly to the Curia. In its wisdom, the Vatican assigned it to the Archbishop in Atlanta. In turn, His Eminence asked me to come here."

"What does that make you, then?" Moira Osterholm interjected.

"I represent the Archbishop—or, if you prefer, I'm the delegate of the Vatican, once removed." She laughed. "Don't worry, Agent Osterholm; I won't impede whatever secular inquiries you may wish to make. I'm not exactly a novice at this."

"I'll ask again, Sister. Precisely why are you here?"

"Actually, we are in the same sort of business: we investigate, and present our findings to a higher authority for a decision. My assignment is quite straightforward: to investigate all aspects that relate to the . . . *alleged* apparition Maddie Shepard is claiming to experience."

"Ah. Pardon our ignorance," Zhang-mei said, and his own smile was somehow feline. "Agent Osterholm and I know very little about supernatural matters. That *is* what you're looking for, isn't it? Some kind of miracle?"

Benedicta tented her fingers. "A number of possibilities exist here, Mr. Zhang-mei. Trust me, a supernatural explanation is only one of the *less* likely. Simple self-delusion, a physical or mental pathology manifesting itself in hallucination, a young girl's need for attention, or even—" She shrugged, and smiled. "Well, we cannot dismiss the possibility it *is* authentic. That's why we investigate, is it not? To make such determinations?"

"And what has your 'investigation' determined?" Moira Osterholm's voice held a challenge, though her face was impassive.

"Not much," Benedicta said. "At least, thus far."

"Let me be more specific," she said. "Has Ms. Shepard made you—either of you—aware of any message or instructions she has been given during these apparitions?"

Shepard made a noise from deep in his throat, and looked disgusted.

But when Benedicta spoke, she appeared careful in her choice of words. "Any reputed 'messages'—from the Holy Mother, or from any source, supernatural or other—would certainly not be communicated or circulated outside of a very small circle of prelates. Certainly, not at this stage of our study."

Zhang-mei's look of interest was not feigned.

"This 'small circle' you mention. Who would they be, Sister?"

"Church officials. The Archbishop, in Atlanta, a select number of officials and priests in Rome."

"What did you report to them?" Zhang-mei asked.

"I have not yet made a report," the nun retorted, and nothing in her tone indicated that she suffered fools gladly. "But I can assure you, had I done so it would remain confidential—under pain of mortal sin, sir. Those of us who are assigned to such tasks take a vow to that end, Mr. Zhang-mei."

"So I understand. That is why I find this so . . . confusing."

Zhang-mei fished a single sheet of paper from the briefcase at his feet. He half rose to hand it to the nun. He waited until Benedicta had finished reading before he spoke.

"Do you recognize those words, Sister?"

Benedicta's voice was level. "I cannot answer that. Not without permission from my superiors, in Rome."

Zhang-mei drew in a deep breath and exhaled slowly, for the first time showing the exasperation he must have felt since the interview began.

"Then I suggest you obtain that permission immediately," he said. "Because I don't want to direct Agent Osterholm to arrest you for obstructing a Federal investigation."

"You'll do what you must do, Mr. Zhang-mei. As will I. And as will those much higher than either of us in the chain of command. Yours and mine, both."

"Is that some kind of a threat, Sister?"

"Not unless you choose to take it as such. You have the only response I can give you, sir."

"Excuse me," I interrupted. "Exactly what are we talking about?" I did not expect an answer, and was surprised when I received one.

"The words on that paper were taken from an Internet Web site run by the Centurions of The Lord," Zhang-mei said, his eyes still on Sister Benedicta. "It purports to be a message from the Virgin Mary, as delivered four days ago to one Maddie Shepard of Spanish Bay, Florida. In it, Ms. Shepard says—"

"This is the dumbest fucking—" Roger Shepard broke in, but Zhang-mei cut him off as if he had not spoken.

"The day before an abortion clinic in her town is bombed, Ms. Shepard—here, in this house—gets a message she insists is straight from the Mother of God. 'Chastise the baby-murders and all who support them.' " Zhang-mei's voice was now icy. "Within an hour, it's posted—verbatim, unless I am misinformed—on a Web site run by a radical organization that encourages the murder of those who disagree with it."

"Whatever happened, this has little to do with Maddie Shepard," Sister Benedicta said.

"Correct me if I'm wrong," Zhang-mei retorted. "In essence, she's told all the crazies in the world that it's open season out there, that Heaven's telling them to go for it."

He settled back in the chair, and once more his face settled into a mask, calm and reasonable. Deliberately, his gaze shifted toward Roger Shepard.

"I don't really care where your daughter is getting her information, Mr. Shepard," he said. "But I am very interested in knowing where the Centurions of The Lord get theirs. I'd like to know before more people get killed because of it."

51

"Okay, that's it," Roger Shepard said, his voice tight. "My daughter is *my* daughter, and *I* decide who she talks to and what she does. No one else. Get out and leave us alone."

"Not much chance of that," Zhang-mei said.

"Actually," Sister Benedicta said, her voice carefully neutral, "that remains to be seen."

On the walk back to their car, neither Zhang-mei nor Oster-holm had much to say to me. The cell phones were out again, and from what I could overhear, Roger Shepard's life was about to become even more complicated. It seemed overkill for a man whose only child was already beset by complications both earthly and divine.

At last, Zhang-mei snapped his phone shut and turned to me.

"You know why I let you come along, don't you?" he asked. "Aside from the fact that I enjoy the company of good-looking women, that is."

"Why don't you enlighten me?"

"The fact is, the nun in there has a point," he said. "This thing has 'career-killer' written all over it. Conceivably, I could have the pro-choicers, the pro-lifers, the religious Right, the ACLU, every radio talk-show host in the country, not to mention the entire Catholic church, all of 'em chewing on my poor, overexposed Asian-American butt."

"So?"

His smile was frosty. "So I spent the last three years where the most exciting part of my job was tracing deadbeat dads who had fled across state lines. I don't intend to get stuck doing *that* again."

The prosecutor walked on another few steps, brows knit as if weighing his options. "But I can't dodge this thing, either. It's too high-profile. The Justice Department can't look like we avoid cases because the politics are too hot. And I really can't expect Moira and her FBI people to take any of the heat; they're as career-minded as me. Probably more."

He did not lower his voice during the former statement, but I could detect no change in Moira Osterholm's attitude or posture. Had she been asked, she might even have agreed with her colleague's assessment.

I nodded, sensing what was coming.

"But *you*, Lieutenant Quynn—well, you've made it pretty clear for a long time that you don't give a rat's ass for your career." He winked to take the sting from his words. "You seem to favor . . . let's call it 'direct action,' shall we?"

"And that means what, exactly?"

"Just that your record makes for interesting reading, Lieutenant. Some might say you've racked up an impressive tally of incidents that border on insubordination. Especially for a female officer." Zhang-mei waved off the response I was about to make. "That's a matter of perception, and sexist as hell, am I right?"

"Mr. Zhang-mei, I don't worry much about what people perceive, sexist or not. A police officer has to deal in accurate information. If you've seen my record, you know the word 'insubordination' isn't used, even once."

"I stand corrected. Still, according to what I've seen in our case files, you do take a particular pleasure in sticking it to the FBI. You like to do things your own way. That might be of use in the present circumstances, wouldn't you say?"

"Is this going somewhere, Mr. Zhang-mei?"

He shrugged. "Clearly, you have a reputation as a pretty competent investigator. Even Agent Osterholm here thinks so. Isn't that so, Moira?"

She gave no reply, but it did not appear that Zhang-mei had expected one.

"Are you asking me to work this case with you, Mr. Zhang-mei?"

Zhang-mei looked amused.

"Wouldn't *that* be fun, having my own personal loose cannon crashing into everything on deck. No, Lieutenant. Even if I wanted to watch the pretty fireworks up close, how would having you on the team solve my job-security problem? If you were actually working for me, it would only make them worse."

Zhang-mei opened the car door. Then he turned to me, and before I could react he pushed something white into my breast pocket. I fished it out as he slid behind the wheel, and noticed the telephone number printed under the Justice Department seal.

Zhang-mei winked. "In case you ever feel the need to keep in touch."

"I can't imagine why I would, Mr. Zhang-mei."

"Ah, well—you're probably thinking that it's too bad all this comes under Federal jurisdiction, aren't you?" he said, not as if it was a question. "Otherwise, you might have wanted to maybe poke around the edges of this thing."

"I can't imagine why I'd do that, either."

"Sure. I'm probably thinking about another kind of person entirely. You know—the kind of woman who'd maybe want to see if there's some kind of connection between the Shepard kid and the Centurions of The Lord."

He nodded judiciously.

"Woman like that might want to prove that Little Maddie's faking it, maybe, before our friend the Sister gets her declared a saint. A woman like that might even want to know if a bunch of religious fanatics actually did get the word from on high. To blow up Tara Kinsey, I mean. In fact, a woman like that might even feel a *need* to get involved, to find out the facts for herself. You know—just to put all that 'accurate information' on the record, maybe keep everybody honest."

He slid behind the wheel. But before he pulled away, he looked up at me once more. This time, there was no bantering in his tone.

"Might be," he said, "the only way a woman like that could find some peace. Have a good day, Lieutenant."

CHAPTER 5

"Wasn't much, as trauma cases go." The speaker shrugged, unimpressed. "Irrigated both hands, bandaged 'em, popped in a broad-spectrum antibiotic, intramuscular. Would have given her a tetanus booster, but the admitting nurse checked with the father, and the kid was up-to-date. Treated and released to the parent. Wrote out a script for ampicillin."

On the pocket of the emergency room greens he wore, a laminated card identified him as MELVIN SHENKER, M.D.—RESIDENT. Below it, in black marker, someone had hand-lettered the word SUPERDOC.

It was almost seven o'clock, more than two hours since I had watched Howard Zhang-mei interview Roger Shepard. I had avoided Tito Schwartz's questions and dodged an invitation to dine with him and his wife. Instead, I had motored off, Zhang-mei's parting words echoing in my mind.

Somewhere during my aimless drive, I had decided that I wanted no part of Zhang-mei's attempt to plant a seed, to manipulate me into a course of action that suited little more than his own purposes. A few miles later, I had convinced myself that Zhang-mei's motives did not matter; certainly, not if the course of action he advocated was one I wanted to follow, anyway.

I had persuaded myself both ways half a dozen times. I was still not certain of which argument had won, not until I found myself turning into the circular driveway of Spanish Bay Memorial Hospital. Here, perplexed ambulance EMTs had rushed Maddie Shepard on a Saturday afternoon less than a week before, after a trip to the mall had taken an unforeseen twist.

Admissions sent me to Billing, which in turn directed me to the Emergency Care department. There I had worked my way through several layers of health-care professionals, until I found Shenker.

We were seated in a cramped space that apparently served as a sort of office-cum-sanctuary for the resident medical staff; half-filled paper cups of coffee long cold littered an untidy desk where Shenker perched. I sat on a cot that had been shoved against a far wall. Shenker had taken the opportunity to check out my legs, without being overly obvious about it. After a glance at the stains on the hotplate carafe, I had declined his offer of coffee.

"How was she injured, Doctor?"

His eyes regarded me with something akin to caution.

"Paramedics reported she had collapsed at a shopping mall. Possible seizure—still, no history of epilepsy, nothing on the EEG, and no loss of consciousness involved. Kid presented here alert and responsive." He shrugged in a noncommittal way, but his gaze did not leave my face. "I guess she got herself cut when she fell to the floor."

I raised my eyebrows.

"An unusual sort of injury, wouldn't you say? Her hands, I mean."

Shenker snorted. "For the ER? Oh, yeah." He pulled a foam plastic cup from a nearby stack and reached over to the carafe. I noticed he seemed to take his time pouring.

"A year back, I had a rotation in the Psych unit here," he said, finally. "Off the record, okay?"

I nodded.

"The injuries to her hands might not have been so unusual up there."

"Self-inflicted?"

"Looked possible to me."

"You wrote it up as 'accidental.' "

"I talked to the father first." Shenker shrugged. "Hell, no kid that age needs a psych tag on her record. Even your so-called 'normal' teenagers—those years, the nighttime monsters move out of the bedroom closet and into the cranium. Part of growing up, for most kids."

"Do most kids cut themselves, Doctor?"

"More than you'd think. I can show you the stats. Anyway, I talked to the two of 'em, gave ol' Dad a couple of names he could call."

"Did he?"

"He promised he would. I was planning to follow up this week, see if he really did."

I let it pass. "A self-inflicted wound like that. Wouldn't it have been painful?"

"It would have hurt like hell," he said, and lifted the cup to his lips. He sipped, grimaced, then raised his voice to carry to the outer office. "I wish *somebody* in this damn place would learn how to make decent coffee. This stuff still tastes like formalin."

I waited, in an attitude I hoped would pass for patience.

Shenker rummaged through the stacks on the desk beside him. He selected a sheaf of paper, a metal clasp at one corner, and pushed it across the desk to within my reach.

"Okay, check out the diagram—third page in. The wounds—they're slits, actually—are a little more than six millimeters in length. That's like a quarter inch, okay? Center of each palm, more or less; they're through-and-through, which means whatever the hell was used penetrated the width of her hands."

I winced, involuntarily, and Shenker chuckled.

"Yeah. *Big*-time 'ouch.' Lucky, though. Missed major blood vessels and nerves. *Double* lucky, doing it to both hands like that."

"How sure are you Maddie Shepard did this to herself?"

"From a medical point of view? Nothing I could swear to in court. But the anecdotal evidence kind of rules out everything else. If not her, who else? She was in a shopping mall, Lieutenant. Sure, lots of people around, but the closest one was on the other side of a table. Anybody walks up and stabs the kid through her hands, somebody would have noticed, right? So, one minute the kid's eating mu-shu pork, or some damn thing; the next, she's on the floor, twitching and bleeding like a stuck pig. You tell me who did it."

"Can you think of another possibility, Doctor?"

He examined my face closely. "Aw, come *on!* Tell me you're not asking me what I think you are."

I was silent.

"Look, I'm a physician. I don't believe in voodoo, or demon-possession, or the goddamn poltergeists. And I don't believe in stigmata, either, okay? You want that kind of crap, go buy yourself a copy of the *National Enquirer.*"

"Nobody saw her cut herself," I said, and was surprised at the contentious tone I heard in my voice. "Nothing in the reports about finding any sharp instruments, either at the mall or the hospital."

"So our little Ms. Shepard's got a knack for sleight-of-hand. Look, lady—my opinion? You got a kid here who wanted attention, and chose a pretty damn stupid way to get it." Shenker twisted his lips as if he had tasted something sour. "Guess it worked, huh? TV last night, they showed the crowd out there. Poor superstitious shmucks."

"People believe what they want to believe," I said.

The irony was lost on Shenker.

"Yeah, well," he replied, as if we had found a common ground. "You got that right."

"I already told all I know about it," Wendy Kramer said, her face an improbable combination of acute boredom and a dawning awareness of her own importance. "To the television people."

I nodded, and tried to look impressed. We were seated in a well-appointed living room, across from each other. Behind the girl, a floor-to-ceiling glass wall provided an emerald-and-blue panorama of the Gulf that would have rendered an agoraphobic short of breath. The associated price tag of beachfront property would have done the same to anybody else.

In the far corner, the slim woman who had ushered me in paced as if she was running laps, and spoke into a cell phone. She was conversing with animation, and seemed to have forgotten my presence. I noticed that her pastel tennis outfit played nicely against the carefully tanned skin and streaked blond hair. It also matched the attire worn by the girl on the sofa.

"I don't get a chance to watch much TV," I said. "But I'd like to hear your story."

"It was pretty gross."

"Good," I nodded solemnly. "I like gross stories."

Wendy regarded my face for a moment, making certain that her carefully arranged attitude of skepticism registered with me. Then she shrugged, and began to speak.

This, with only minor prompting, is the story she told me.

They had been having fun, though neither of them would have dreamed of describing it that way: two girls, of perhaps twelve or thirteen years, part of the crowds that thronged the shopping mall. They were pretty, innocently worldly, dressed in fashion carefully chosen to look like an afterthought—in short, indistinguishable from the other girls of similar age, all of them enthusiastically engaged in acquisition as a Saturday afternoon's entertainment.

Had anybody been observing them—and aside from the occasional knots of passing boys their age, no one was—the pair would have drawn scant attention. There was certainly nothing to suggest that either were other than what they appeared. There was even less to indicate that one of them was about to be brushed by the supernatural, and possibly the divine.

They had passed a Victoria's Secret without a sideways glance, in an agreement that was neither spoken nor acknowledged. They had lingered briefly at the display counter of a chain store jeweler's, carefully examined the small-print disclaimer taped to a kiosk called THE PIERCING PALACE. They had let the swirls and eddies of the crowds carry them through the mall—alternately cavorting like the much younger girls they recently had been, or striking haughty attitudes worthy of much more experienced sophisticates.

Finally, they had found themselves in the central court, where all three of the mall's wings joined in a miasma of overheated oil and frying meats.

"Taco Casa?" Maddie Shepard had suggested.

"Grease heaven," countered Wendy Kramer. "Last time, gave me zits. Plucky Chicken?"

"Salmonella city," Maddie retorted. "Last time, gave me cramps." Both girls convulsed in laughter at the double entendre.

They had settled for stir-fry from a faux-Chinese stand named THE SMILING PANDA, and found a table in the crowded food court. There, Maddie fished a cell phone from her shoulder bag.

Wendy had pulled a face.

"You're checking in again?"

Maddie had shrugged, not meeting her friend's eyes.

"Dad gets ticked if I don't."

Wendy had sighed, a deeply theatrical exhalation.

"It's just . . . like, so intrusive. What does he think you're doing, buying drugs or something?"

She had watched her friend press the speed-dial button, and forked a water chestnut into her mouth as Maddie spoke into the telephone. It was, typically, a one-sided conversation: Maddie would report her current location, who she was with and what she was doing—as if, Wendy thought, she was on a leash or something. She had shaken her head, though whether in sympathy or scorn she would have been hard-pressed to decide.

At that moment, Maddie had looked up directly into her companion's eyes. Wendy was surprised, then annoyed, at the expression of abject hurt—*even,* the thought flitted across Wendy's mind, *shame*—that she saw cross Maddie's face. She had covered the moment by concentrating on her tempura until Maddie snapped the phone closed.

The two girls had eaten in silence for several moments. Then, tentatively: "Parents can be so lame, you know?"

Maddie had nodded, as much in gratitude as agreement. "Totally. Fathers can be worse than moms."

"None of them get it. It's so . . . infuriating."

"Absolutely. They're clueless."

Oppressed sisterhood reestablished, they had chattered on through the stir-fry.

Maddie had checked her watch.

"Walk through the Gap?"

"That'd be okay," Wendy had said, hoping she looked more enthusiastic then she felt. "Then, if you want to, I'll get my mother to drive us over to—" She had stopped, puzzled at the expression on her friend's features. "Maddie, what's the . . . Maddie?"

For an instant, Maddie's features had become fixed, frozen. Then, as Wendy watched, her eyes had slowly rolled back until only the whites remained visible. At the same time, Maddie's lips had begun to move, forming soundless words that came, faster and faster. She had started to tremble violently, her head whipping madly back and forward.

It's what—epilepsy? Wendy remembered thinking to herself, in alarm. *Oh, Jeez—she must be having a seizure and—*

Abruptly, the convulsions had stopped.

And slowly, Maddie's features calmed. Her eyelids had closed, and a beatific smile lit her face.

Wendy was suddenly aware that all sound had ceased around her. She had chanced a glance at the tables in the teeming food court, where patrons were looking in their direction, some of them staring wide-eyed, others with annoyed expressions at the disruption.

"Maddie," she had hissed, though her tone was desperate. "Stop it. Stop it now!"

It was enough. As she watched, Maddie's eyes had fluttered open. The ecstatic smile faded from her face, replaced by a look of confusion.

The first shout had come from somewhere to their left.

"Oh, my God! Look at her!"

Maddie's head was down—staring, Wendy had thought, at her own lap. Then Maddie had looked up and raised her hands slowly.

They had been covered with blood.

Oh, gross, Wendy had thought. *Now she's having her period, right here in—*

The thought had died even as her mind gave it words. Maddie's eyes were wide in a face suddenly ashen. As Wendy had watched, she had turned her hands palm out, either in display or to push away some unseen horror.

In the middle of each palm, a clearly defined slit wept crimson.

"Wendy, I—"

Then Maddie had begun to scream, a high-pitched keening noise that only rose in intensity until it had seemed to Wendy that her friend's throat would burst. It stopped only when Maddie had pitched forward, crashing to the floor and curling into a tight fetal comma.

I nodded again, and made my voice serious.

"I'd like you to think about this for a minute, Wendy," I told the girl. "This is pretty important. Could Maddie have been . . . well, *exaggerating* what was happening?"

Wendy frowned. "You mean faking it?" She shrugged, but not in a gesture of doubt. "The blood was real."

"Do you think she could have cut herself?"

This time, the girl regarded me as if I had tried to give her fashion advice, then shook her head, slowly and firmly. Not for the first time, I considered how fortunate I was not to deal daily with children more worldly than I.

"I have a date to play tennis now. Mother–daughter doubles. Are you done?" she said, and despite her age it did not sound like a question. She looked at her mother, and her voice took on the tone of the unjustly aggrieved. "*Mom*, we're going to miss our court time."

I showed myself out.

CHAPTER 6

As was my practice, I bought dinner that night in the white take-out cartons familiar to anyone whose personal life tended toward the chaotic; this night it was Mongolian beef from a storefront restaurant, operated by an extended family who lived above the place.

I don't cook—not well, and not often. Throughout our marriage, that fact had been a source of ongoing friction between Ron and me—though, relatively speaking, it had ranked as a sapling amid the tall sequoias.

While I waited for my order to be bagged, I had winked at the dark-haired child in pink pajamas who had stared at me through solemn eyes.

If I had expected the gesture to reduce her to giggles, I would have been disappointed. It might have been some learned sense of caution or reserve; possibly, she might have detected an absence of maternal instinct in me. It may even have been the product of the intrinsic dignity of certain young children. Whatever the reason, she had merely turned and toddled back through a beaded doorway into the brightly lit kitchen.

Suitably rebuked, I collected my purchases and headed for the harbor, to a place I had not yet learned to call home.

Ron still lived in the house we occasionally shared on the far side of town, the one he had owned when we wed. When we divided our assets in the first of our divorces, Ron had kept the house, if not the memories we had shared there.

After the divorce, I had moved into overpriced quarters that rented to the cynically single, to the chronically solitary, to an eclectic variety of other too-cheery unfortunates. All of us had somehow lost our way; maybe we had never found it in the first place. But if we socialized, it was seldom with each other. Aside from the occasional nod as we passed in the corridors, we were an encampment of well-dressed loners.

For all that, it had helped me discover that I was not unique, except in the particulars that defined my own specific circumstances: few of my neighbors were embittered, and perhaps slightly lovesick, police detectives.

Late at night, I had found myself going for long drives that seemed to take me past the darkened house where my ex-husband lived, sometimes by himself.

On occasion, there would be a car I did not recognize parked in the drive or at the curb. More than once, hating my own weakness, I had jotted down the license number, knowing that I could invent some pretext to run the tag on the department computers. But through some grace I still did not understand, I had always found the strength to pitch the balled paper into the darkness after driving a few more blocks.

That initial divorce lasted almost six months. Then Ron and I had remarried, a tacit acknowledgment of the strange addiction that held both of us in thrall.

It was the first in a series of estrangements and reconciliations that formed a pattern as unhappy as it was unhealthy. There had been several subsequent separations, bookends to another divorce decree that lasted three months before we reconciled. Ron and I were like asteroids spinning in parabolic orbits that coincided at irregular intervals. During these periods of overlap, we would come together with an intensity that was almost violent in its combination of needfulness and remembered passion. But inevitably, we would whirl apart again in equally intense pain and acrimony.

I was determined that, this time, the cycle would end.

This time, I had left of my own volition. This time, instead of finding shelter in rental apartments priced to gouge the Spanish Bay tourist trade, I had opted for a solution I saw, paradoxically, as both more permanent and more transient.

I had tapped out my savings for the down payment on a secondhand houseboat, complete with an unreliable diesel below deck and enigmatic electrical problems throughout. Mooring expenses at the marina proved a fraction of what I had paid for land-based housing. I had even purchased the essential furnishings and utensils and small luxuries of day-to-day life.

All of those actions defined the permanent in my living arrangements. As for the transient, I found a strange mix of relief and apprehension whenever I looked at the lines that held me to my moorings—in aspect, mere threads which I could break at need or at whim. For the first time since my adolescence, I felt a frightening freedom of action without the need for immediate decision or long-term resolve.

It was all meant as an affirmation of my own rehabilitation, of a commitment to a Ron-free life; but privately, one which I feared I was proclaiming too loudly, even to myself. Late at night, during periods of the involuntary introspection that insomnia brings, I would question the wisdom of my choices. I did not dare to examine the permanence of them, not yet.

And now I stepped aboard, balancing my bagged dinner as I fumbled for the key to the salon door. It slid open and a wash of air, stale and superheated as if from an oven, greeted me.

Inside, I coaxed the air conditioner into operation, feeling it start to wring the humidity from the cabin air. I waited a minute to make sure the load had not overwhelmed the circuit breaker, feeling the sweat itch between my breasts. I stowed my handcuffs and 9-mm Smith & Wesson automatic in their usual drawer, then showered under tepid water for a quarter hour. When I emerged in running shorts and a Florida State T-shirt, my hair pulled back into a damp, dirty-blond ponytail, the cabin had cooled to a bearable temperature.

I had just started my dinner on the galley's folding tabletop, forking the savory beef morsels into my mouth and reading from the book I propped against the bulkhead, when I felt the vessel dip slightly. Footsteps clocked across the topside deck.

I glanced at the digital clock-radio: 11:34, too late for either a misdirected Jehovah's Witness or the random social call.

My book was in my hand as I crossed the salon, pausing only to pull the Smith & Wesson from its drawer as I passed. The privacy curtains were drawn across the sliding doors off the salon. When I pulled them aside, I was anything but prepared for the person who stood on my threshold.

Jack Reagan had shed the station-logo'ed blazer he had worn to Tara's service. It was a savvy fashion decision. The blue cotton shirt fit him well, accenting an understated masculinity that needed no added emphasis. The shirt was tucked neatly into khaki pants that, no doubt, had been fitted by a tailor. Reagan stood on my houseboat's deck, his eyebrows raised in a genial greeting. Part of my mind registered that his body was trim and athletic, more compact than he appeared on television.

I must have been staring at him, because when he spoke it came as a minor shock.

"Is this a bad time?" The words were muffled through the double-panes of thermal glass, and I grappled with the latch briefly before I could tug the entryway open.

Jack Reagan stood on the deck outside, but there was nothing awkward in his posture or attitude. His gaze fell to the book I held, or perhaps to the pistol in my other hand.

"I've interrupted your evening, Lieutenant; I apologize." He smiled. "I see you read Stephen Ambrose. I'm a bit of a history fanatic myself."

I found my voice. "What can I do for you, Mr. Reagan?"

"May I come in? I mean, I *did* drive all the way back here from Pensacola."

I stepped aside, catching a hint of whatever scent he wore as he passed. It smelled expensive and was more than slightly disturbing in a way I did not want to examine. Perhaps in self-defense, an irritation as involuntary as it was irrational rose within me.

He walked to the middle of the salon and turned to face me.

"I didn't know you lived on a boat, Lieutenant Quynn. It must be a marvelous—"

"It's very late, Mr. Reagan. Perhaps you should get to the point."

"What happened today, Lieutenant." He hesitated, as if trying to form the words in his mind. "I want to . . . I was up against a deadline, and I thought I needed the interview with you. You were within your rights to decline." He took a deep breath. "I lost my temper. What I did was unprofessional and unwarranted. What happened was my fault, entirely."

"Your news director may not agree," I said. "He told my boss he wanted an apology from me."

"I think he was only sorry that Channel Five had tape of it," Reagan said.

"So am I."

"At least those ATM videocam systems don't record audio."

"I'm sorry for what I said. It was uncalled for; the crack about rehabilitation, I mean."

Jack Reagan smiled, but it was not the high-wattage version I had seen earlier. This one was, I suspected, a private stock. It seemed a little too worldly wise, maybe a little too bruised, to have been put on display regularly.

"Nothing to apologize for, Lieutenant. Everybody knows I

was in a drug program. It was big news, for a while." Then he looked at me, his expression serious. "But not everybody knows I still go to meetings. It wasn't just to make the plea bargain look good."

"I still had no right—"

"Neither did I."

We stood silent for a moment, both of us looking at the other. Then he smiled again, and this time it was the full-strength version.

"This is going to go nowhere if we both keep apologizing to each other," he said, and held out his hand. It felt right to take it, and to smile back.

"I'm glad we settled this," he said. "After our little problem this afternoon, I went back to the station and looked up what we had about you. I don't think I'd enjoy being on your bad side, Lieutenant."

I was not certain how to respond. After a moment's hesitation, I decided to take it as humor.

"You're in no danger, Mr. Reagan. Unless you're a serial jaywalker. We're pure hell on jaywalkers in Spanish Bay."

"You're not one of those people, are you?"

"What people?"

"The kind who pretend to be humble and full of 'gee-whiz' clichés. Particularly when they know I've already done the research on them."

"No," I said. "I'm not."

Reagan nodded judiciously. "I'm glad. A . . . *colorful* career is nothing to be ashamed of." He grinned suddenly. "Look at mine. How many people go from anchoring *News@Nite* to serving as assistant librarian at a minimum-security penitentiary?"

"You made it back, Mr. Reagan."

In a less composed person, I would have called the noise he made a snort. As it was, there was no doubt as to Reagan's reaction to my observation.

"My current employer is third in local-news ratings at four, six *and* ten o'clock," he said. "Plus, they hired me to work general assignment, which now makes me the lowest of the low."

He arched his eyebrows, as though inviting comment; but I had nothing of value to contribute.

Then his eyes became steady and intent. "At present, I'm good for the novelty value. People tune in to see what I look like after six months on a prison farm. But a few good stories— real rating magnets—and I could be back on top, Lieutenant."

Again, I knew no words to add. This time, the silence threatened to turn awkward.

"I'm putting together a special report, Lieutenant Quynn, one that will examine the violent role that radical-religious groups are playing in opposing social policies. I think the bombing of your abortion clinic here is a very timely hook for the story."

I kept my face as impassive as I could, and waited.

"I already know a little about the Centurions of The Lord," he said. "I've seen their Web site, too. And I don't mean all those detestable photos they publish of women going into family planning clinics, or even what they had about the Shepard girl's 'visions.' I'm talking about the most recent content."

Reagan paused a beat, as if inviting a question. Then, despite himself, his voice took on the professional tone I had heard him use on-camera. "Do you think there's a connection between the Centurions and the clinic bombing here, Lieutenant?"

"It's an FBI investigation, Mr. Reagan. Ask them."

"The Centurions updated their Web site this morning. Would you be surprised to hear that a man named Bobby Teasdale is quoted on it? That he threatens to start killing people if they're involved with abortion clinics?"

"I've heard Teasdale's name before. But unless you know something I don't, I'm not aware of any connection to the bombing we had here."

"The bombing occurred two days after the Shepard girl had her first episode, in the mall. Doesn't that make the connection pretty clear?"

He waited for my response for a moment, then grinned.

"C'mon, Lieutenant. I won't quote you. I'd just like to hear your opinion."

His voice was conversational again, and I felt a little foolish at my reluctance to answer.

"It's a valid question," I conceded. "I would want to look at that angle. *If* I was investigating the case."

"Let's say there is a connection, just for the sake of discussion. That would mean that somebody close to the Shepard girl is feeding information to the people who run the Web site, doesn't it?"

"I don't know what you want me to say."

"What does Roger Shepard say?"

"How would I know that, Mr. Reagan?"

"You were in the Shepard house today with Moira Osterholm and her little Justice Department friend. We had a remote truck out there. I saw the live video feed when it came in at the studio."

I regarded him carefully. "Exactly why did you come here, Mr. Reagan?"

"To make sure everything was okay between the two of us," he said without hesitation. "But I also want an interview with Maddie Shepard, Lieutenant Quynn. I think you can help me get it."

I looked at him, and resisted the urge to whistle softly.

"You're good," I said, not making it sound like a compliment.

"I already have an hour of tape with the Kramer girl," the

reporter countered, impatience in his tone. "I've located a half dozen people who were in the mall when Maddie Shepard had her first . . . well, her first whatever-it-was."

"You've been very busy, Mr. Reagan."

"I have other leads, too. Look—I know you can track down the same people. But why should we duplicate the effort, Lieutenant? We're both after the same thing, aren't we?"

"No, Mr. Reagan. I don't think we are."

Now he looked frankly exasperated.

"We both want the truth about Maddie Shepard, about the Centurions of The Lord—about the bombing that killed your partner. And please drop the 'Mr. Reagan,' Lieutenant Quynn. My name is Jack."

"You want a story, Mr. Reagan. A few minutes of juicy details that you can arrange any way you want, to tell any story you think will play best with your viewers."

"I want the story, yes," he said. "Of course. But that's not all I want."

"No," I agreed. "Maybe you want to impress a station manager in New York or Los Angeles. Or perhaps some network news director."

I stood. "I appreciate you coming here. But you really don't have anything I want."

"I have one thing that you don't," he said.

"And what would that be, Mr. Reagan?"

Jack Reagan smiled again, but this time I felt no desire at all to smile back.

"I have a name and a telephone number," he said, "of the person who heads the Centurions of The Lord. M. C. Mason has agreed to talk. To *me*."

CHAPTER 7

At about the time that Jack Reagan was knocking at my door, less than a dozen miles away another scene in what had become a lethal morality play was nearing its own denouement.

There are still estates in Spanish Bay that are left largely wooded, a tribute as much to the ego of the property owner as it is to any environmental enlightenment. Palmetto and tangles of clinger vine rise from the sandy soil, competing with sand-spurs and ground sumac for the scant nutrients left after the thickets of towering loblolly pines have taken their fill. Here and there, the occasional live oak spreads wide its limbs, as if offering an embrace; from them, dense clumps of Spanish moss hang like tattered rags. Where the grounds of several like-minded landowners adjoin, to the random trespasser it can seem a vast forest primeval, far from the sounds and light of the city itself.

In these unlikely woodlands, the late-season insects still fill the sticky warmth of the night with their lovesick murmurs. This must have provided a soothing background soundtrack for the figure who rested prone on the pine-needle carpet. They had not ceased their song during his long, slow belly-crawl to his position, not even for a moment's instinctive wariness at some unfamiliar sound; he would have been that quiet, that stealthy.

Occasionally he might have sensed a larger movement in the patch of night sky visible above. Perhaps he was even lucky enough to have seen the darker shadow of a bat corkscrew through the blackness in silent pursuit of some doomed prey.

If so, perhaps the irony would have made him smile.

Or perhaps not. Perhaps his attention had been focused completely on the single rectangle of yellow light more than three hundred yards distant. At that range, it would have been little more than a pinhole of light fringed by the boughs of the trees that lined his shooting corridor. If his naked eye could see any movement at all, it would have been the false twinkle of refraction, an optical illusion he would have known signified only the relative humidity of the night.

But through the ten-power scope of his weapon, it would have been a different story entirely.

Through it, the picture that would have leaped into sharp-edge focus would have appeared as if he was standing at the windowsill. When a figure crossed the window, moving left to right, he would have had no difficulty identifying the back-lighted profile as female, though so petite in stature as to appear little more than an adolescent. His sight-picture would have filled from the top of her auburn hair to the slight swelling of her breasts against the blue-silk pajama fabric.

Now he would have been sure, would have known for a fact that his target was there, and had but minutes to live.

He would have made his final adjustments: calculating that the effects of the slight downward slope would have required perhaps two, certainly no more than three clicks of the elevation knob. Then he would have eased the bolt back, feeling the double *snick* as the top cartridge rose to alignment. With a similar care, he would have pressed the bolt back into battery— quietly, but firmly enough to ensure the round was seated and engaged.

Had he then waited? Had he again eased the butt stock of the rifle back onto the pine needles, the spring-loaded bipod elevating the muzzle slightly in rest?

It appeared so, when evidence technicians examined the site a few hours later. Then, indents left by the bipod legs would form the base of a long, narrow triangle to an apex scuffmark that might have been left by the weapon's shoulder piece; in length, it would approximate the dimensions of a Remington Model 700 hunting rifle.

But that is pure conjecture, of course.

What we do know for certain is that at 11:47 p.m., whoever was looking through the telescopic sight settled into a shooting position, bone locking against bone to ensure stability. He would have taken one or two deep breaths. Finally, with a conscious effort, he would have willed all tension from his body, feeling himself settle into the pine-needle carpet like a deflating balloon.

Then the figure had again come into view, this time moving right to left as she entered one side of the lighted window.

He would have shifted slightly, unconsciously making whatever minute adjustment was necessary to center the crosshairs on the tip of the target's nose—leading her in precise compensation for the caliber-.308 bullet to travel three hundred yards.

When the weapon fired, lancing a bright tongue of fire that for a moment would have dazzled his night vision, it would have been anticlimactic, perhaps even without any emotion other than a craftsman's satisfaction of another job well done. Despite the reverberation of the gunshot—a report loud enough to startle neighbors blocks away and subsequently allow us to precisely determine the time—there was no sign of haste in his retreat. He had slipped away into the darkness, where most of our monsters reside, as if it had been commonplace, part of a routine.

As it was.

For this was not, we were to be told when the forensics tests were completed, the first time Robert Matthew Teasdale had killed this way.

CHAPTER 8

I heard of the shooting just after dawn, when I flipped on my department scanner even before I fumbled for the coffee grounds.

I had slept only fitfully after Jack Reagan had left, and only partly because thoughts of sacred apparitions, armed religious radicals and Web sites calling for holy war competed on my mental movie screen. I told myself that it was only my insomnia threatening to become chronic, but the truth was that Reagan's visit had left me troubled in ways I did not care to examine. Not all of them involved his proposal that I accompany him to an interview with the leader of a shadow army convinced it had a mission from God.

When I realized what the scanner was reporting, I had waited neither for coffee nor to shower. I scribbled down the address and drove across town into the rising sun.

It was yet another neighborhood of mansions shaded by tall oaks and maples. I went inside the house first, passing without challenge two uniformed officers flanking the double doors that winged open, wide and yawing. Other officers and several persons in civilian clothes were inside the large foyer. I did not recognize any of the latter, and their presence puzzled me. As I passed, one of the civilians pointed a digital camera up the stairway and triggered a blue-white flash. From the corner of my eye, I noticed one of the uniformed policemen shake his head in what looked like disgust.

Upstairs, in a bathroom connected to the master bedroom, I arrived in time to watch two gloved and gowned technicians spread out a heavy-gauge body bag next to a form that, from the neck down, was still recognizable as a woman.

The technicians ignored me as I bent to examine what the bullet had done. The mushrooming impact, behind and above the left eyebrow, had shattered the crown of its target's head. The hydrostatic shock had turned what was left of her facial features into something less than human—even partially peeling back an adhesive bandage to reveal a deep gash along one cheek. Then the bullet, by that time deformed and tumbling, had exploded through the far wall of her skull. Opposite the window, the tasteful alabaster tile work had been painted a lumpy collage of crimsons and grays.

Death, mercifully and obviously, had been instantaneous.

As the medical examiner's team had lifted the mutilated body, I turned away to the bathroom window. The slug had drilled a neat, dime-sized hole in the glass; its supersonic speed had left the pane in the frame, though spider-webbed to a creamy opacity. The morning sun prismed along the radiating cracks, dancing and sparkling as if alive.

I stood on tiptoe and sighted down the hole, pretending to estimate the trajectory the bullet had followed. It was unnecessary. Downrange, figures already were grouped around the spot where the shooter must have lain. But I remained at the window anyway, a sham attempt to distance myself from the sights and the smells that accompany all violent death. I stayed there long enough to be certain that the body bag—from the corner of my eye, it seemed unbearably still and impossibly heavy for its size—had been bundled away. Then, with a heaviness of my own that felt much like guilt, I walked the three hundred yards to where the sniper had fired.

A tall man with coffee-colored skin watched as I approached.

"Hey, Loot. Heard you got farmed out to direct traffic—or something worse," he said. "Cornelieus put you back on full-duty status already?"

"I'm a fast healer, Linc," I said, not quite lying. "Thought I'd lend a hand here."

"Uh-huh." Lincoln Jabbar regarded me for a moment through thoughtful eyes.

"You sure you want to be here, Quynn?" Jabbar asked. "On-site bossman supposed to be Beaulieu. He don't seem to enjoy sharing, know what I mean? 'Specially with *you*. Be pure hell to pay, he comes up and finds you cuttin' in on his turf."

I made a show of looking around. Milling among the trees and thick underbrush that lined the small clearing were more than a half dozen evidence technicians, at least as many uniformed police and a handful of Spanish Bay detectives. Some of the latter, like Lincoln Jabbar, were occupied with the various tasks associated with crime-scene investigation; others were studiously trying to appear so. It was quite a show, and only management was conspicuous by its absence.

I stitched on my most beguiling smile. "Let's risk it. So where is he?"

Jabbar arched his eyebrows, eloquently. " 'Round somewhere, I guess. Uncovering clues, meetin' with the medical examiner, holdin' a press conference. Something important like that."

"I didn't see Beaulieu inside the house. I don't see him out here."

"Could be he's been studyin' to be a master of disguise. Help him take that next step up the career ladder, if y'know what I mean." He shook his head mock sadly. "Here I be, caught smack-damn in the middle. What to do, what to do?"

"One thing you can do is shit-can the Uncle Remus act, Linc. You put in for night-school tuition reimbursement, remember? I've seen your transcripts. You're majoring in political science, not ebonics."

A conspiratorial smile tugged at the corners of Jabbar's mouth. "Point taken, Lieutenant. I've found it makes life easier not to mention my educational aspirations to Jesse Beaulieu. Flies in the face of the prevailing wind, if you get my drift." His voice shifted back into dialect. "Hell wit' him. You willin' to risk the shit-fit, it's 'tween the two of you. Go 'head—look 'round, knock yourself out."

He started to turn, then leaned in to examine my features.

"By the way, Lieutenant, you look like hell."

"That's what a girl wants to hear. Thanks a bunch, Linc."

"Not my business, but you certain you're ready to be back at work?"

I pretended not to hear the question. Instead, I squatted at the perimeter of the yellow crime-scene tape that marked the shooter's stand.

A few hours before and three football fields downrange, a bullet fired from this spot had cored through flesh and bone and brain. It had extinguished a life as abruptly as if a switch had been thrown, and did so at a distance where the act itself might even have seemed clean and antiseptic—perhaps even eloquent in the statement it was intended to make.

Now, from behind me, Jabbar again spoke.

"Susan DeBourche," he said as if reciting from a textbook. "Forty-two. Says here she's a doctor."

"Psychiatrist," I said, still squinting down the path the bullet had taken. "But psychiatrists are fully qualified M.D.s. She doubled at that family planning clinic, in the surgery. Performed obstetrical-gynecological procedures there."

"Woman's doctor," he corrected himself. "At the abortion clinic. Well, that fits, doesn't it?"

"Fits what, Linc?"

"There's some bunch of religious nuts out there. Word is,

they've declared war on anybody in the abortion business. So first it was the clinic, now it's this one." He snorted. "You don't watch TV? It was on the news last night. Channel Twenty-two."

I nodded as if it was just one more piece of information to consider; but the news surprised me. Apparently, Jack Reagan had been busy, even before his decision to pay me a nocturnal visit. He had not mentioned that this part of his story was already being aired, and I did not believe it was by oversight. I wondered what that meant.

But not for long.

"What the *fuck* you think you're doing?"

By the time I straightened and turned to face him, Jesse Beaulieu had pushed up so close that I could feel his breath on my face. He was a head taller than me and his body was thick and solid, still the torso of the light-heavyweight wrestler he had been twenty years before at Auburn. Whether for reasons of fashion or to mask a receding hairline, he had taken to shaving his scalp. The effect somehow made his head appear even larger than it was. Now, a single strip of adhesive bandage gleamed starkly on the expanse of his forehead. His scowl arched it downward, a crinkled third eyebrow centered over a face tight with anger.

"Nothing got touched," Jabbar said. "I was watchin' all the time."

Beaulieu turned his anger to the detective. "You were *watching*," he repeated. "You mean you *let* her wander around out here?"

"Get off his back, Beaulieu," I said. "This isn't where your problem is."

"Nobody asked for your advice, Quynn."

I nodded in the direction of the DeBourche residence. "C'mon, Beaulieu, you can see it from here. People are walking in and out like there's a sign on the lawn that says 'open house.'

For all you're doing about it, they could be chipping pieces of the bathroom tile to auction off on eBay."

"Everybody there is authorized. You're not."

I frowned at him for a moment before the realization came to me.

"You're astounding, Beaulieu. Who are they? Friends? Political supporters, here to watch you play Sherlock Holmes? Wise up—this won't help you get Cornelieus' job."

"Somewhere you picked up a real bad habit," Beaulieu said. "You keep giving advice that's not wanted. Let me give you a news flash, Quynn. People do fine without you."

"What happens when one of those yahoos contaminates the scene? Be smart. Clear them out before the reporters catch on."

"What's going to clear out of here is *you*, Quynn. Start walking, now. Or I'll have you escorted off by one of these officers."

"That might be hard to defend, Beaulieu."

"Really? I think you're unstable, Quynn. Isn't that why Cornelieus put you on limited duty? Oh, I don't mean just getting your head scrambled with that bomb. Way I hear it, you're under a shitload of . . . *emotional* pressures."

"What the hell are you talking about?"

"I'm worried about you, Quynn. We all are. A messy personal life can spill over into the job, fuck your judgment all to hell." He smiled through lips thin and cold. "You've been through a lot, your girlfriend getting herself killed like that."

I felt my jaw drop. "Tara Kinsey wasn't my girlfriend."

"That so? I guess I shouldn't listen to rumors. About you, about Kinsey. About your husband, even. By the way, is he back in town yet? Heard he took a little vacation. Group tour, was it? Good rate for double-occupancy rooms that way."

The heat rose in my face, and a sensation not unlike that of balancing on an undulating footbridge rocked my legs beneath me. As if from a distance, I heard my voice respond.

"What's that supposed to mean, Beaulieu?"

I realized that my voice had risen; all activity around us had ceased, and faces were turned in varying degrees of curiosity or anticipation.

"You're such a hot-shit investigator," Beaulieu said, and jabbed his forefinger hard into my sternum for emphasis. "Figure it out."

My reaction was automatic, and as far outside of my conscious control as was the ability to stop my heartbeat.

I slapped his hand away and stepped forward, my focus so narrowed that it felt as if I was moving in slow motion. My right hand balled into a fist, and I felt fabric bunch in my left hand as I pulled Beaulieu toward me.

But simultaneously with the realization, the cloth was ripped from my grasp, and suddenly Lincoln Jabbar was between us, his chest a solid bulk against mine.

"Use your damn head," the detective said, his voice in my ear pitched low and placating. "The fucker is pushing your buttons on purpose."

He stepped back, palms up and careful to keep them from touching me. "C'mon, Loot," Jabbar said, in a voice intended for a wider audience. "People are watching this. Don't make a fool of yourself."

I let him walk me away from the clearing; my hands hung stiffly at my sides, trembling with the aftereffects of the adrenaline rush.

When I spoke, my voice sounded hoarse.

"What Beaulieu said. Are other people saying that, Linc?"

He had the grace to look uncomfortable.

"I don't know. Yeah. Maybe some of them." He glanced at me, sidelong. "Look, Loot—what did or didn't go on between you and Tara Kinsey, I don't know, or want to. People talk, and sometimes they talk pure shit. But it's no secret you and your husband have had problems, you understand what I'm saying?"

"That's none of Beaulieu's—"

"Not unless you start taking swings at him over it. C'mon, Lieutenant. You know how that makes things look. And if somebody wanted to, they can make that reflect on Cornelieus' judgment in keeping you on the street."

We walked on silently the rest of the way to my car.

"This isn't about you, Quynn."

"It's me he's using to slur the memory of a friend. I'd say this is a whole *lot* about me, Linc."

"It's not you he's after," Jabbar said, his voice insistent. "Not directly. You know that."

"He's ambitious."

"Damn right. Smart money has Cornelieus gone before the end of the month."

"Don't count the man out too quickly."

"Problem with being in an appointed position is you can get *un*-appointed, too. Ol' Jesse's been lining up his ducks for the past six months, ever since word got out that Cornelieus was sick. Beaulieu's got his brother-in-law; more to the point, he's got the man's organization behind him. Political machines always like having one of their own running the cop shop."

"What are you saying, Linc? They've already cut a deal?"

He would not meet my eyes.

"City here has a tradition of making deals, Loot. Lot of people made a lot of money 'round this town, cutting deals with each other. Guess some people think it's time to start again."

"Cornelieus came in as a reformer. He cleaned up a dirty department. This place owes him."

"This is still Spanish Bay, Loot. You're the last person I have to tell what that means. You remember what it was like before Cornelieus."

"So do a lot of people. Nobody wants that again."

"Wish you were right," Jabbar said. "I just don't think so. Too many people have a stake in seeing the man go down. Beaulieu's going to be the next chief, real soon. He gets there faster by stepping on your face, that's just the cherry on top."

CHAPTER 9

I left a message for Jack Reagan on the voice mail at his TV studio, hoping my inflection no longer carried the tight hoarseness I had heard in the immediate aftermath of my encounter with Jesse Beaulieu. Then I drove for a half hour, keeping mainly to residential side streets. But not even the placid tree-lined thoroughfares gave me a sense that the world remained on a steady axis.

The balance of the morning I spent parked at the curb outside the Shepard house, occasionally talking with one of the skeleton crew of Spanish Bay police present at that hour, and trying not to look completely useless.

Tito Schwartz checked in once, the call coming through to Jesús Castile. Jesús found me sitting in my rental car, and grinned in commiseration.

"Don't worry, Lieutenant," he said. "Morning's always real slow. Folks start showing around noon. By quarter to three—that's when things start poppin'." He handed the cell phone through the window. "Boss wants a word."

"You had an exciting morning, I hear," Tito's voice said in my ear. "Word is you went postal on that asshole Beaulieu. Did Lincoln Jabbar really have to pull you off the bastard?"

I grimaced, wondering how that particular image was playing with Chick Cornelieus.

"Not quite. But I didn't do myself any favors, either."

Tito laughed. "You so *smooth*, girlfriend. Wish I had your

charm." His voice turned serious. "Cornelieus in the picture yet?"

"Uh-uh."

Tito's silence was both extended and an admonition.

"Tito—I know, okay?" I took a deep breath. "Are you going to be out here soon?"

"Wasn't planning on it. Some new stuff on a client just came over the Net. Screwy shit. I'm trying to puzzle it out."

"You need to handle it right away?"

"Probably not. More of those damn deep-background credit reports. Supposed to help keep my paranoia under control. As if."

"Look, Tito—I need you to cover for me here for a couple of hours. I'm sure Jesús is good, but I'd feel better if—"

"No prob. But tell me something, Quynn. You just trying to duck Cornelieus, or is something else going on?"

I hesitated, and once more it said far more than I would have wanted.

"Oh. Okay, partner. I get the picture."

"Tito, if I could—"

"Fuck it. I'll be out there to cover your ass inside an hour. You tell Castile it's no reflection on him, okay?"

"Dammit, Tito—"

"Whatever. You go be the cop, Quynn. Keep your damn secrets, I'll keep mine. Me, I'm just a glorified crossing guard anyway, right?"

The phone went dead in my hand.

The newsroom studios of Jack Reagan's television station were located a few blocks east of the Pensacola Civic Center, an area I once knew as a mismatched collection of pre-war buildings, cinderblock houses and the occasional crab shack restaurant that catered less to tourists than to knowledgeable locals.

In one of the latter, more years ago than I cared to remember, a high school boy two years older than I had plied me with pitchers of beer, a seduction that hadn't taken an undue amount of persuasion. His name was Paul, and I remember being terribly flattered by his attentions, and terribly hung-over the next morning. Not for the first time, I marveled at how so many of us survive our high school years.

Certainly, this district had not. In less than five years, it had been largely razed, taking down with it most of my more tawdry adolescent memories. The streets of my sinful youth were now a bustling commercial district, the relentless tangle of traffic an inevitable byproduct.

By prearrangement, I met Jack half a block away from the television studio. He was waiting in a recessed delivery doorway when I pulled up, and we were rolling again almost before I had completely stopped.

"Place called 'Harold 'n Nita's,' " he said. "In the county, back where the armadillos go to become roadkill. We'll meet Mason's representative there."

Jack settled into the passenger seat, studiously avoiding my eyes.

"You know about this Teasdale person?" he asked.

"I do now."

Sometime during the morning hours, the State Crime Lab in Tallahassee had tied the weapon that had killed Susan De-Bourche to two other sniper attacks over the past three years.

The first had been a near-miss of a gynecologist who volunteered his time to an abortion clinic just outside Raleigh. The round, a .308 Winchester, had starred his windshield as he drove, passing harmlessly between the physician and the retired Air Force colonel who had been riding shotgun in the passenger seat. Neither man was injured, though the Kevlar vests both had been wearing would have scarcely slowed a more accurately aimed shot with the high-powered round.

The second attack, a week later, had involved a nurse who had worked part-time at the same abortion mill. The shooter had targeted her in the parking lot of her apartment building, and this time had not missed. The bullet's point-of-entry was not unlike that which killed DeBourche: a head shot that was horrific even in the black-and-white of the faxed images I had reviewed. It was here, in the second sniper attack, that a spent brass casing had been found. The partial print it had carried had been insufficient for a positive match. Nor had informants from inside the various groups done more than provide a list of names—some plausible, others less so. But it had all been tossed into the evidentiary mixmaster anyway, becoming grist for the speculation mill, both in law enforcement and in the media.

More conclusive evidence was needed, and to the delight of North Carolina authorities it arrived in the form of a signed letter to the largest newspaper in the state, replete with misquoted Scriptural passages of a vaguely threatening nature. Added to everything else, it had been deemed enough to make a tentative identification of the suspected shooter as one Robert Matthew Teasdale.

But Teasdale had proven difficult to locate, despite the running commentary he kept up with letters to the media. Several highly publicized forays into the rugged Carolina backcountry had turned up little more than additional mailed taunts from the quarry, unless you counted the newspaper editorials decrying the ineptitude of the hunting parties.

Now it appeared that Teasdale had branched out into Florida. As usual, it had been decided to withhold that information for the time being. As usual, it had been leaked, almost immediately, to the news media. I had heard the details over my car radio on the drive into Pensacola.

Jack Reagan had nodded, too casually. "We had it on *News at*

Noon," he said. "This is the first time Teasdale has been involved in a bombing."

I looked at him, examining his profile.

"What bombing?"

"Come on. Don't act as if you didn't suspect he was involved."

"Who says he was?"

"Sources," Reagan said in a tone not designed to elicit elaboration.

"Ah," I said. "Sources."

We drove on in silence for a few blocks.

"You sound skeptical."

"Teasdale's a shooter, not a bomber," I said. "I can't say he hasn't decided to mix methodology. But it's unusual for a man like that to change his signature so radically. Particularly when he switches back a few days later."

"Consistency is the hobgoblin of small minds," he said.

"Most murderers *have* small minds," I countered. "That's how we catch them. But it becomes a harder job when people muddy the waters."

Again, we fell into silence.

"You puzzle me, Mr. Reagan," I said, finally.

"There's nothing mysterious about me, Lieutenant." He laughed, once, and there was a hard-edged, almost bitter element in it. "My life is an open book these days."

"I used to watch you on television. Often. You always seemed to be . . . I don't know. A different sort of reporter."

"Did I?"

"Was I wrong?"

"Lieutenant, journalists are pretty much all the same," he said. "We're professional spectators. To succeed, we have to hitch a ride on someone else's bandwagon."

I arched my eyebrows, but kept my eyes on the road.

"That doesn't sound like a resounding endorsement of your profession."

"Doesn't it?" he asked. "Perhaps not. But there are advantages to riding the bandwagon—at least, a reporter is never stuck out there all alone. All of us are after the same story. That's why we tend to hunt in packs."

"You didn't. Once upon a time."

He nodded, as if in agreement.

"Once upon a time," he repeated. "Once upon a long, long time. Look, I came up-market when I was a kid, Lieutenant—twenty-four. That was eight years ago. In television journalism, that's ancient history."

"I've heard good things about you, Mr. Reagan. Are they true?"

"Depends on what you heard," he said. "The past year or so, probably not."

He turned toward his window, the conversation obviously closed.

But since his visit the night before, I had called in a few favors—mostly from reporters, particularly those with a reputation for usually knowing more than ever saw print. I discovered that I was not alone in my puzzlement about Jack Reagan.

For a few years, it was considered a given that Reagan was bound for the major leagues. I was no judge of journalistic talent, but even I had sensed something different, something special about the man I saw on the screen. He had a quality that fascinated, that compelled people to pay attention. That quality had, in less than four years, propelled him from an ABC affiliate in Decatur, Illinois, to a cable-news network in Atlanta that put his talents on a national showcase.

In his on-air interviews, Jack Reagan could be, by turns, cool in his detachment, warm in his approval, outrageous in his humor, sincere in his interest. He could also be fiery, as on the occasion when I had seen him confront an unrepentant celebrity wife-murderer as the former gridiron star swung through Atlanta to promote a book on his acquittal. In addition to the in-studio interview, where the responses had been carefully scripted by publicists and lawyers, Reagan had convinced his news director to let him try a different approach. The journalist had waited in a thicket of trees that lined the eighth hole of a nationally known golf course just outside the city, and emerged as the startled celebrity lined up his approach shot.

The result was anything but scripted, and turned into a classic of ambush interviewing when it aired that evening.

Jack was widely held to have had the best of the exchange. The incident was extensively publicized, even receiving the modern version of immortality: references in both the *Letterman* and *Leno* monologues.

"So he's still looking for the *real* killers," Letterman had quipped in a gibe destined to be repeated at water coolers across the country. "But it looks like he's closing in on them. See, if you saw the interview he did with this Jack Reagan fellow, apparently the main suspects are *caddies.*"

But just when you were ready to dismiss Reagan as just another stunt-crazy, tabloid-TV, talking head, he could also show a stubborn sensibility. According to media legend, in one of his first on-air stories for a ratings-rich report called *News@Nite,* Reagan had been reporting live from a spectacular public housing blaze. The newcomer was in the middle of interviewing two young children who lived in the building when he stiffened, pulled out the earphone that connected him to the station's control room and abruptly concluded his report. The on-air anchors had to scurry frantically to intro the next story. The station's general manager had been especially furious.

Reagan might have been disciplined, perhaps even fired— except that someone leaked the intercom tape to the *Atlanta*

Constitution, and from there to the wire services that fed it nationwide. On it, an idiot of a producer was ordering Jack, repeatedly and with mounting profanities, to inform the two children, live on-camera, that they had just been orphaned.

The resulting furor made Jack Reagan an overnight celebrity, and in some quarters a hero.

In the very public turmoil that followed, the producer was the one who was fired—run out of town, all the way to Chicago. There, *The Jerry Springer Show* knew a kindred soul when it saw one.

For himself, Jack was promoted to five o'clock news co-anchor.

It was the first of a string of high-profile accolades and awards. And indirectly, perhaps it was the first act in the Greek tragedy that would, only a few years later, cost him everything he had gained.

When I was younger, a place like Harold 'n Nita's would have been called a roadhouse, or worse. Located a dozen miles inland, it squatted amid a dusty expanse of tire-rutted gravel, surrounded by the piney woods and sandpits and rusted-out house trailers abandoned alongside the potholed county macadam.

It was a beer-and-a-shot place, where the product came in long-necked bottles or the kind of thick-bottomed cheater glasses that boosted house profit margins at the tap. Kids wearing high school letter jackets would flock to it on Friday nights, after the game: here, an ID so obviously fake as to make a blind man snicker passed muster without a word. Here, bikers and hard-luck farm workers and truck drivers with a few too many points on their licenses would bring their women, or someone else's, with the reasonable expectation of two or three parking-lot knife fights.

I had never been here before, but I knew it well even at first sight.

Inside, the decor tended toward promotional bric-a-brac supplied by beer distributors to high-volume establishments. Everywhere I looked, equine forms strained in harness, enormous barrels of beer stacked high in the massive vehicles they hauled.

It seemed an unlikely place to meet anyone who professed a belief in salvation, at least the kind that did not pour from a bottle. When Reagan and I had entered, a shaft of sunlight had illuminated the room. A chorus of groans and shouted curses had greeted us before I had pulled the metal door closed behind us. It was as if we had uncovered a nest of Morlocks.

As directed, Jack had approached the dour woman behind the bar.

"Is Harvey here?"

"Does it look like he's here, honey?" The bartender had ducked her head briefly, and when her face came back into view there was a cigarette in her mouth. She had studied the two of us for a moment. "Take a table. Anybody named Harvey comes in, I'll send him over."

Now, at the table where Jack Reagan and I waited, a dented and scarred *faux*-brass lamp cast a circle of pale lemon light. On the painted metal shade, a team of the giant horses strained at an overloaded sledge, condemned to endless circuits against a backdrop of what passed for a wintry landscape.

I made the mistake of vocalizing that observation.

"Wow—you're a cheerful date," Jack Reagan replied with a sidelong grin at me. "Do you get depressed when you see the Energizer Bunny, too?"

"If I see him hanging out in a bar. Particularly at two in the afternoon."

He picked up his glass of club soda and sipped at it.

"At my twelve-step meetings," he said, "we'd call that a definite danger sign. Seeing giant pink rabbits, I mean."

I started to reply, but stopped short as his eyes focused on something over my shoulder.

"Don't look now, but I think it's showtime," he said.

I waited long enough to make it appear casual, then scanned the room as if bored. At the bar, a thick-chested man was listening to the bartender, who nodded in our direction. The visitor glanced at us, and his lips moved in reply.

Then he ambled over, a hip-rolling gait designed to signal to the world an arrogant contempt for either its opinion or its indifference.

Biceps and pectoral muscles strained against the fabric of his shirt, the kind of hyper-development that health clubs promise but seldom deliver. The edge of an India-ink tattoo vined and twisted along the left side of his throat, as if unwilling to be contained beneath the unbuttoned neckline. His attire seemed out of place here. The shirt was a burgundy Polo, tucked into ash-gray slacks that had been cold-pressed into a knife-edge crease. The cuffs of his pants broke with tailored care over tasseled loafers that matched his shirt. The overall impression was of someone who had been dressed by a particularly attentive mother.

He ignored me, standing so that his bulk loomed over Jack Reagan where he sat.

"I'm Jack Reagan," the newsman said, thrusting out his hand as if looking for votes. "Your name is Harvey? Is Mr. Mason going to meet us here?"

"You," he said. "You wanna come with me."

"Great. My friend and I are eager to—"

"Not her. Just you."

Reagan shot a grin up at him; it was the version designed to charm wild boars. "Oh, Quynn's okay," he said. "C'mon, Harvey, I can't leave a lady in a place like this. Besides, in TV news, we *always* work with a producer—you understand, to take notes for the reporter and so on. I'm afraid it's a union rule, Harvey."

His response stumped Harvey; his expression could not have been more perplexed if Jack had spoken in Esperanto. His eyes flickered toward the back of the room and lingered there for a moment. When I followed his glance, I found a thin, tight-featured man standing almost motionless in the near-darkness. He leaned with his back against the wall, studiously looking elsewhere as he spoke into the cell phone in his hand.

Somebody at the other end must have responded, because after a few seconds Thin Man shook his head once, a hard negative.

"Just you," Harvey said. "Or nobody goes."

Jack looked at me.

"Well, I suppose she can wait in—"

"Hey, Harvey," I interrupted. "Tell me something. How long have you been out?"

He turned to me full-face, as if noticing my existence for the first time. For a moment, he measured me, up and down, through hard, unblinking eyes.

"Chicks with smart mouths usually get a big surprise around here. You looking for a surprise, lady?"

"I bet you know all about surprises, don't you? I bet you're the world's biggest expert on the subject."

"You trying to get in my face?"

"Just making conversation. I'm guessing you've been back on the street four weeks—maybe six, right?"

I turned to Jack, and spoke as if I was discussing a specimen at some exotic petting zoo.

"The tattoo is one clue—notice how amateurish it looks? See, some con used a sewing needle and the ink from a Bic pen. In the joint it's considered high art, even if it makes our friend look like a freak out here in the world. But the real tip-off is the weightlifting. A good-looking guy like Harvey here goes in the slammer, right off he starts getting all kinds of . . . let's call it *attention*."

"Quynn, don't you think it would be wise—"

"No, this is interesting stuff; for your story, I mean. See, ol' Harvey comes in as fresh fish—anybody's punch, sexually speaking. Gives new meaning to the term 'hard time,' as you'd imagine. Makes the first few months a definite eye-opening experience for our boy here. So he starts to spend all his free time pumping iron. It's self-defense, you see. Keeps those visits to the shower room less stressful. Problem is, takes a while to really bulk up."

I paused, then looked up to meet Harvey's eyes. "Any of this sound a little too familiar, Harvey?"

Harvey was staring at me. It was the kind of fixed look which precedes extreme violence, and which was ancient by the time Cain turned it on Abel. But when he spoke, his words were for Jack.

"You going with me or staying with the bitch? Decide, now."

Jack looked at me and shrugged. "I'm going with you," he said to Harvey, and stood.

I also started to rise. But I was only half out of my chair when a hand jammed against my breast, and my bottom bounced back hard against the seat.

Then Harvey leaned over close to my face, his hand still on me, and smiled. It was a toothy smile, shark-like in its assurance of its own position on the food chain.

"You must *want* to get hurt, smart mouth," he said. "You one of those pain freaks? Get off on a good beating?" His hand flexed against my chest, suggestive and rich with contempt.

"Let's all be friends," Jack said, dialing the smile to its most soothing setting and widening its focus to include both Harvey and me. "I just want a TV interview. Nobody wants to offend anybody."

"No offense taken," I said. "But it might be a good idea to remind Harvey here where he stands. He's just a messenger boy. My guess is that he's also out on parole. That complicates Harvey's life. For instance, being caught in an establishment that sells liquor is a parole violation."

I pulled aside my jacket to show the badge clipped to my belt. "Bad luck, Harvey. I'm a cop."

Harvey's eyes narrowed. The hand still on my chest stiffened, though whether to attack or to push its owner away I could not tell. Perhaps Harvey did not know, either.

But I did not give Harvey an opportunity to make the choice.

I seized his extended arm just above the wrist and stood, using the leverage of my movement to twist his hand palm-up in my grasp. Harvey bent at the waist and stumbled forward into the table, falling over it as I half turned and smashed my offside forearm against his elbow. The combined effect of the arm-bar hold and the momentum of his body threw him over the table, which splintered beneath the impact. His face smashed into the wall behind, with enough force so that the room shook.

Still holding his wrist, I kicked the shattered table aside and levered his arm high against his spine. I snapped the cuffs around both wrists and turned him, easing Harvey back against the wall. His legs splayed awkwardly on the floor and his head lolled.

I tilted back his chin to examine his face. The blood that streamed freely from an ugly gash above his left eye mingled with the gore that dripped from his pulped nose. I felt the fury inside me, and something else too, but whatever it was I knew was not directed at the man slumped on the dirty floor.

I looked up to the back of the tap room; Thin Man had not moved, except to continue speaking into the cell phone.

But I had his full attention now.

"You want to help your boy here?" I called to him. "He's going to need stitches."

For a few seconds more, he held the cell phone to his ear. Then he approached our ruined table.

I took the phone from his hand.

"My name is Quynn, and I am a Spanish Bay police lieutenant," I said into it. "Harvey can go back to serve out whatever time he had left, plus what I can get tacked on for assaulting a police officer. Come to think about it, Harvey here is probably looking at attempted rape. I can take him in, or you can spend a few minutes talking to Mr. Reagan and me. *Both* of us. It's your choice, Mason."

"Please give the phone back to the man you took it from," a voice said. "I have an office upstairs. I am looking forward to meeting you, miss."

The voice was a surprise; soft and amused, and with the slight quavering quality one associates with age or infirmity.

It was also, unmistakably, the voice of a woman.

CHAPTER 10

"You appear surprised, Lieutenant," M. C. Mason said, when she had waved us into what would have, in an earlier day, been called a parlor. The antiquated furnishings were in sharp contrast to what stood along the far wall.

There, two oversized computer monitors dominated a floor-to-ceiling wall unit. I counted six computer servers stacked on the utilitarian aluminum shelves, linked by a dangling tangle of cables to a bank of at least thirty modems. Everywhere, LEDs blinked and flickered, pinpricks of green and red like the startled eyes of nocturnal lizards, automatically fielding what appeared to be a constant flurry of incoming log-ons.

I should not have been surprised, given the nature of what the Centurions were now posting on their Internet site. Still, I wondered if the volume of people accessing the Web page had been as high when the site's most controversial content had been the less-than-candid photos of the women running the gauntlet of protesters to enter abortion clinics around the country.

Somehow, I doubted it.

"What a sweet puppy," Jack was saying. "What's her name?"

Mason shuffled ahead of us, moving as if her feet ached from some ancient malady. As she did, a black and tan form wiggled and twisted in the crook of her elbow.

"Missy is not a puppy," Mason said perfunctorily, and I heard the slight quavering in her voice again. "She is a mature miniature pinscher. And she knows better than to act in such an inappropriate way, particularly around guests." Mason muttered softly to the animal. Immediately it calmed, its black-marble eyes steady on its owner.

Mason settled into a winged armchair across from Jack's position on an undersized sofa. I pulled up a spool-legged wooden chair closer to Mason than custom dictated, and the three of us formed a rough triangle.

"I didn't expect you to be a woman, Ms. Mason."

"I prefer 'Miss Mason,' if you please. If you consider that honorific too politically incorrect, my given name is Margot."

She waited until I nodded.

"There's nothing in Scripture that bars a woman from holding a leadership role," Mason said. "Certainly, there is nothing in the bylaws of the Centurions that does so, either." She smiled. "I should know. I wrote them."

"What does Scripture say about people like your friend Harvey?"

"It says that he who is without sin should cast the first stone. If I am correctly informed, Lieutenant, *you* chose to do exactly that."

"Uh-huh. Are many of your Centurions ex-convicts, Miss Mason?"

"I've known the person in question for more than six years, Lieutenant. His incarceration came as a result of human weakness. He has paid the debt for his actions, and we have accepted him back into our fold."

Her gaze suddenly changed, became sharp and unyielding. "But since we speak of debts . . . hypothetically, aren't you concerned that he, or an interested party on his behalf, might file a brutality charge against you?"

"Not particularly, Miss Mason. For one thing, Harvey outweighs me by about seventy pounds. Not many pumped-up ex-cons want it known they've been bitch-slapped by a woman, even if she's a woman cop. As for an 'interested party' lawsuit, any organization that might do that could find itself under a pretty bright public spotlight."

"The Centurions have nothing to hide, Lieutenant. Nor do I."

"Of course not; I was answering a hypothetical question. Still, you go by your initials instead of your name."

She nodded. "I *choose* to, Lieutenant. Just as I have chosen to meet with Mr. Reagan. To talk with him, and possibly to allow him to videotape an interview with me."

Jack's head snapped up. " 'Possibly'? You told me you *wanted* to talk."

"Yes. To talk. That does not commit me to an on-camera interview. That decision will come later, after our discussion."

"Things have changed since you and Mr. Reagan spoke," I said. "You know about the shooting last night?"

Mason nodded, and there seemed more than a touch of smug satisfaction in her expression. She stroked the dog's head with her free hand.

"Doctor DeBourche," she said. "It was on the news." She nodded at the electronic equipment. "I have already updated our Web site."

"I see. Do you have any thoughts on who might have pulled the trigger?"

"Of course," Mason replied. "So do you. DeBourche was on Bobby Teasdale's list."

"You know that for a fact?" Jack interjected. "That Teasdale intended to shoot her?"

Mason looked at him.

"If you mean did I have foreknowledge that she would be killed," Mason said, "then I did not. That would have made me an accomplice." She gestured at the television console across the room. "I heard it from you, earlier today."

Jack leaned forward and nodded, and I wondered how long he had practiced the look of intense interest, focused but fascinated, that his expression conveyed. "Of course. But you were not surprised, either."

"Susan DeBourche and her husband had been doing abortions for more than twenty years," Mason said. "Between the two of them, they personally have murdered tens of thousands of babies, and the clinic they established at least as many more. For her own part, she is—*was*—also very well known among those who support abortion, both here and around the country. It is logical to believe Bobby would have seen her as a person whose death would serve his purpose. He has developed a well-planned strategy, you see."

"I've looked at Teasdale's file, Miss Mason," I said. "He dropped out of high school at sixteen. Until the past few years, he specialized in burglary and the occasional convenience store stickup. He doesn't strike me as a master strategist. I'm having a bit of difficulty trying to believe he thought all this up on his own."

"Believe what you will."

"People are being murdered, Miss Mason."

"Yes. It's horrible, isn't it? We live in a culture of death today, Lieutenant Quynn. As a people, we have abandoned our God and dared Him to chastise us."

" 'Chastise.' Interesting word. You used it when you published what Maddie Shepard supposedly heard from the Virgin Mary. Are you Catholic, Miss Mason?"

"Church of God." She smiled, too sweetly. "River-baptized not five miles from here when I was fourteen. Many people are not overly concerned with the Pope of Rome or what he has to say about anything. I am one of them. But if God wants to send a message from the Mother of His Son—even if through the mouth of some poor Catholic girl—who am I to act as censor?"

"Who told you the Shepard girl actually said anything like that?" I asked.

"Like Mr. Reagan, I do not divulge my sources," Mason said. "I will say only this. Since *Roe v. Wade* became law, more than forty-eight million abortions have occurred in this country. No plague, no holocaust in human history compares to this death toll. Is it surprising that the Deity would at last condone the idea of using death to prevent the continuation of systematic, mass murder?"

"You acknowledge no difference, Miss Mason?"

"This is a tired debate, Lieutenant. It is not murder to use violence—even extreme measures, including the death of the other—to defend one's life, or that of another innocent party. You are a woman as well as an officer of the law. What could be more innocent than an infant's life?"

"We're not talking about an infant . . . or a fetus, or an embryo. We talking about a woman who was living and breathing and thinking one moment, and had her skull blasted apart the next."

"Interesting, Lieutenant. You have just described what occurs in a partial-birth abortion—a procedure Dr. DeBourche performed on a regular basis in her clinic."

"Whatever her politics—or yours, Miss Mason—this was a viable human life that—"

" 'Viable'?" Mason interrupted. "At conception, an embryo grows, reacts to stimuli, consumes nourishment and expels wastes. It cannot live outside the womb, admittedly; nor can many other humans live outside the hospital rooms where they are connected to life support. Do the latter meet your definition of *viable*, Lieutenant Quynn?"

"I'm not equipped to debate the pro-choice position, Miss Mason."

"Then I suggest you not make the attempt, Lieutenant. What some choose to call 'potential' life is merely an intellectual conceit. A metaphysical concept."

"I would have thought metaphysical concepts a little beyond a man like Teasdale."

"Bobby Teasdale may talk like a rustic," she answered. "In large part, that is an act. He is a very intelligent man, and you would do well to remember that."

"Do you know where he is?"

"At this moment? No. Three nights ago, he was here."

"In Spanish Bay, you mean?" Jack asked.

"Actually, Mr. Reagan, right there on the sofa where you're sitting." She crossed her legs at the knees, and underneath the thin trousers she wore they looked like sticks laid atop each other. "Missy heard a noise shortly after midnight. When I came down to investigate, Bobby was already making coffee for the two of us. We spoke for several hours before he left."

"What did he tell you, exactly?" Jack asked. "Did he make specific threats, or mention specific individuals?"

"He said—and this is a direct quote—'I'm going to stop them. I've already stopped a bunch and I'm sure as hell going to stop more.' Close quote."

Jack looked doubtful. "Those were his *exact* words?"

"I made notes. He was adamant that he be accurately quoted."

"Who had he already stopped?"

Mason shrugged. "I assumed he was talking about the clinic bombing. He said nothing to indicate anything else."

"Did he specifically state that the bombing was his work?"

"No."

"You didn't feel an obligation to notify the police?"

"I am completely in sympathy with his aims," Mason said, "if not his methods."

Jack nodded, as if recognizing logic in the woman's reply. "But why the warning this time? Why would Teasdale let anybody know what he's planning, let alone allow you to post it on your Web site?"

"He didn't 'allow' it—he *asked* me to do so," Mason said. "Bobby told me he was giving them one more chance." She chuckled, softly. "I suspect his motives went far deeper. Pride is one of the deadly sins, a weakness that is difficult for even the righteous to avoid. Bobby had planned a grand stroke against every abortionist in the country, and he wished it to be widely known."

She twisted, and with the hand not holding the dog rummaged among the heaps of paper on the tabletop. She selected a sheet of lined yellow paper, discarded it and found another, and studied it as if for some hidden meaning.

"Here it is. He said, 'I know I can't kill them all. But I got me a list of twenty-seven baby-killers and people who help 'em do it. This warning is addressed to them twenty-seven. I know where you live. I know what car you drive. I may not actually know all your names, but I got your license number and I've followed a lot of you home, so I got your street address. I got it all.' "

Jack Reagan had been scribbling madly in his notepad. Now he looked up with a frown.

"Twenty-seven people? Here, in Spanish Bay?"

"I asked the same question. He just smiled."

"Twenty-seven is a lot of people to stalk in a single community." Jack Reagan looked at me. "If it's all local, he'd have to hang around for a while."

"Bobby Teasdale's been on the loose for a long time," I said. "Long enough to avoid that kind of dumb mistake."

"Make up your mind, Lieutenant." Mason's voice was

107

amused. "A moment ago you had a far lower opinion of his intellect."

I did not respond, but she had made a telling point.

"So he's probably targeted people all over the country," Jack continued. He thought for a moment, and despite himself his face brightened. "That makes this story a natural for the network."

"Too bad," I said. "They'll give it to Diane Sawyer."

"Not if Miss Mason agrees to help me," he retorted, then looked at our host. "I can tell this story fairly, Miss Mason. You can count on that."

I tried to keep my face impassive. "You appear pretty determined to give this fanatic national attention."

"If he kills twenty-seven people, he's going to get *worldwide* attention, Lieutenant Quynn. It might as well be my story as somebody else."

"Oh, he doesn't have to kill all of them, Mr. Reagan." Margot Mason wore a serene expression on her face, and scratched behind Missy's ear. "He just has to kill a few, enough to prove he's serious and has the ability to carry through. Imagine if you worked in an abortion mill, or perhaps for a referral service that sent women to one. Would you wonder whether you were next on Bobby's list? What might you do? Consider a change of careers, perhaps?"

"Obviously, he didn't tell you who's on his list."

"That's the beauty of it, of course," she said. "The very uncertainty he creates leverages the impact exponentially. Mr. Teasdale is quite a clever man."

I kept my voice level. "Do you want to see more people die, Miss Mason?"

"On the contrary," Margot said. "It is my heartfelt desire that no human life is destroyed. You see, there is no doubt in my mind that Bobby Teasdale is quite ready to demonstrate how deadly serious he is. My sincere hope is that every baby-killer would—at the least—immediately consider taking a *very* long vacation. That will save their lives, and those of the babies they would otherwise murder."

"Teasdale is a murderer and a terrorist," I said, "and you are abetting him."

"Oh? Do you now wish to accuse me of participating in a terrorist plot?" She laughed, a modulated expression of simple amusement. "Is dissemination of this information illegal, or even actionable? Well, Lieutenant Quynn, perhaps you should ask yourself this: Let's assume I hadn't published. When Bobby began to kill the people on his list, would their blood be on my hands?"

I forced myself not to engage in her debate. She waited, her eyes frankly mocking. Finally, she answered her own question.

"Regardless of what anyone might like to think, we Centurions of The Lord do not relish violence." Mason shrugged; to my eyes, it appeared as if in mild regret. "I am actually giving twenty-seven baby-murders an opportunity. They are slated to die by Bobby Teasdale's hand. If they will not repent, they can at least prepare."

"If that's what you really want, I can spread that message much more effectively than an Internet site," Jack pressed.

"Perhaps."

"Do you know how to get in touch with Mr. Teasdale?"

Margot Mason cocked her head at the newsman. "If I had that information, that would make me legally complicit, wouldn't it? As it is, I am in the same position as those twenty-seven on Bobby's list. He knows how to find me, whenever it serves his needs to do so."

"Would he talk to me?" Jack asked. "If he contacts you again, will you ask him?"

"I will not participate in setting a trap for him, Mr. Reagan."

"No traps, Miss Mason," Jack said to her.

"No promises," I said, intending it for each of them.

"I will give you one piece of advice, both of you," Margot Mason said. "If you ever talk to him, don't tell him any lies. He has no tolerance for liars; none at all. Trust me. You would not want to antagonize him. Nor would I."

"You're afraid of Teasdale," I said, not as a question.

"It would be wise to fear him," Margot Mason agreed.

She was looking down at her dog, and Missy was answering with adoring eyes. Mason spoke as if she was addressing the animal, and her voice was still serene.

"Despite all that he is, Bobby is a very uncomplicated man. To him, people choose the side they are on. If you lie to him, you are one of the enemy—and you have seen how he deals with his enemies."

CHAPTER 11

It is no understatement to say that, as Jack Reagan pitched the interview to his news director over his cell phone, he was as calm, as coolly professional as any veteran journalist could have been.

I eavesdropped as he negotiated for the resources that would have done a Superbowl broadcast proud: a crew and microwave relay truck, priority editing resources for the recorded feed, a guarantee of three-and-a-half minutes—more, if the day's news was light—for the live stand-up segment that would accompany the story.

It was only after he snapped the cell phone closed that he let loose with a victory cry, startling birds from the trees we were driving past. Reagan twisted in the passenger seat to mock-punch my shoulder, playfully enough to leave a bruise.

"Why the long face, Quynn? By the way, I intend to call you 'Quynn' from now on. No more 'yes, ma'am, Lieutenant, ma'am.' I don't even care if you drop the 'Mr. Reagan' business or not. Say, when my crew comes out for her interview, how's this? What do you say I roll some tape of you playing with her little dog?"

His excitement was contagious, perhaps intentionally so. I did not take the bait.

"Oh, come *on!*" he pressed. "You got what you wanted, I got what I wanted. What's the problem, Quynn?"

"Maybe I'm worried that M. C. Mason got what she wanted, too."

Jack pulled a face, but it did not dilute the self-satisfied energy in his tone.

"She has a point, Quynn. What—you'd prefer Bobby Teasdale to kill two or three people, and *then* let the rest of his targets get the word about his list? He's a force of nature, Quynn, like a tropical storm. Hurricane Teasdale is out there, maybe coming onshore. It would be irresponsible *not* to broadcast the storm warnings."

"He has an agenda," I said. "So does Mason. Are you comfortable advancing their agenda, simply because it happens to fit yours?"

"So I have my own priorities. Good God, Quynn—who doesn't? You? I saw what you did to Harvey's face. You're dying to punish somebody for killing your partner."

There was a moment of complete silence. I kept my eyes on the road ahead, and my hands firmly on the steering wheel.

"Oh, man—I am so sorry, Quynn. I can't believe I said that."

When I spoke, I was relieved to hear my voice sound almost normal.

"Mason and Teasdale are terrorists. They want to impose their philosophy through the use of death threats as a terror tool. Teasdale, at least, has proven he's willing to take it to the next level. We know how far he's prepared to go."

I turned to look the newsman full in the face.

"But here's what I don't know. How far will *you* go to get what you want, Jack?"

He looked at me as if I held secrets he did not wish for me to share.

"I have to answer that right now, Quynn? What if I don't know, myself? Not everybody knows himself that well. Or wants to."

I shrugged, conceding the point. But I could not escape my own conviction that, at least in his own mind, that decision had already been made.

At that moment, Jack's cell phone sounded, a soft electronic whir that to certain driven souls is more compelling than the sirens' song. Jack listened intently, spoke into it in a low voice.

Once again, the phone snapped shut.

"We'll have to postpone our little analysis of my wants and needs," he said, staring directly to the front. "We need to get to the Shepard house, as fast as you can drive this thing."

"Why? Has something happened?"

"Not as of two minutes ago. But my cameraman says things could go ballistic any time. It seems the pro-choice and pro-life people are there in force, and they're about to declare war. How close are we?"

"Five minutes. Maybe less. Hold on."

By the time I arrived with Jack Reagan, his microwave relay truck already had arrived. It was extending its tall antenna, an intrusive metal finger telescoping heavenward as if to poke, with wry irreverence, at whatever it might encounter there.

"You pick some funny ways to make your life interesting," Tito Schwartz said, his voice a low, cautionary growl. He glanced past my shoulder, and his lips twisted as if he had tasted alum. "I hope you know what you're getting into there, Quynn."

A dozen yards away, Jack Reagan was speaking intently with his camera operator and the broadcast engineer who had been dispatched from the newsroom.

"Please tell me the two of you didn't—"

"Give it a rest, Tito."

I studied the scene before me. Without being told, most of the Spanish Bay police detail had already donned the protective headgear they carried in the trunks of the patrol cars.

"We need more manpower here."

"Oh, you think?" Tito said, peevishly. "I already called Cornelieus. You got the cavalry on the way. Five minutes, maybe less. He wanted to know where you were. I told him you were up to your ass in crowd control, too busy to talk."

"Thanks."

"Yeah, sure. This is a fuckin' riot looking for an excuse to happen." Again, he looked toward Jack and his crew. "Now that all the media is here, that's just the excuse these numb-nuts need."

"Can your people keep the lid on until we get more cops out here?"

"Get serious, Quynn. We do your garden-variety crowd control. These assholes want each other's blood. This gets ugly, we're going to need hickory sticks and tear gas. That's your department."

I took a deep breath. "Okay. Give me your radio."

Moments later, I had the police detail formed into a cordon that lined the concrete Jersey barricades blocking Roger Shepard's driveway.

Along the sidewalk, Jesús Castile had arrayed the personnel Tito had on-scene. Castile alone appeared composed, though careful not to turn his back on the crowds as he moved along the security line. Not so the men he commanded. They appeared skittish and tense, and no longer even pretended to keep the mass of humanity from spilling onto the roadway.

It would have been fruitless to try. Already, the numbers had grown so large that the sidewalks could no longer accommodate them all.

But it was not merely the size of the crowd that had changed. There was a raw tension in the air, the kind of restless unease that signals the thunderstorm's approach. It turned the crowd edgy and unsettled, a herd of horses that senses the cougar upwind.

Nor was there now homogeneity among their number. A smaller but far more organized contingent had gathered, forming itself into a salient whose point lanced aggressively into the larger mass. These latter carried poster-board placards and the occasional bullhorn; periodically, they chanted slogans and waved the hand-printed signs they carried.

RIGHTS OVER RELIGION, one said. WE WILL NOT BE INTIMIDATED! OUR BODIES ARE OUR OWN, another read. I heard shouting, threats, curses from both sides. Somewhere, voices rose in what sounded like a hymn, and others joined in. A bullhorn replied in amplified electronic rasp: "Hell no, Roe won't go!" over and over.

The Shepard house was no longer merely a shrine, whether of the devout or the misguided. Now, politics had mobilized, arraying itself against whatever force, power or delusion it had come to represent. It was now a symbol, controversial and under siege by both sides.

Then, as I watched, a small knot of men breasted through the crowd, angling directly toward the newcomers. For a moment, each faced the other calmly, as if sizing up its opponent.

Then one of the men leaped forward and snatched a placard from the hands of a protester. He ripped it in half, once. Before the pieces struck the ground, one of the protesters had leaped forward, fist cocked.

"Oh, shit," Tito said, and keyed the handset of his transmitter. "Schwartz here. The dumbshits are starting to fight each other, guys. Pull back to the property line. Let the cops handle the rough stuff, but keep these assholes away from the client's house. And watch each others' backs, people."

He turned to me.

"Hope your reinforcements are almost here. Or else your

new boyfriend is going to have a really good story for tonight's news."

All attention was on the two knots of angry protesters converging on each other. For that reason, or perhaps because of the direction it came from, nobody noticed the slim form that slipped by my police cordon. The first sign that something unexpected was happening came when the tumult faded. The back-and-forth press of the crowd slowed, then froze as if in mass paralysis.

A moment later, from the fringes inward, a corridor opened like the Red Sea parting.

"What's going on down there, Jesús? Talk to me, damn it!"

In response, Jesús Castile's voice crackled over Tito's handset.

"Holy shit, Mr. T. I think it's—keep them *back*, guys—I think it's the Shepard girl. She's trying to—"

Castile's voice drowned in a banshee howl of feedback. Then there was only the mad crackle of static.

Tito looked at me, his face tight. Without a word, he wheeled and thrust his powerful bulk through the throng like an infuriated snowplow. I followed in the wake he left, hardly noticing as the gap refilled behind us.

It took almost half a minute to reach the mass of humanity's innermost ring. Tito was a few feet in front of me when he broke through, and I saw him pull up as abruptly as if he had hit a wall. I pushed alongside, and peered past his shoulder.

Standing alone was a girl of perhaps twelve or thirteen. Incongruously, she was barefoot and dressed in white pajama bottoms and an Oakland Raiders T-shirt. Spotless white gauze swathed both of her hands, leaving only her trembling fingers bare. I had never seen her before, but I had no doubt of her identity.

"Stop," Maddie Shepard said, in a voice so thin that I marveled at how clearly it carried. It did not seem the voice of a girl so young. Her eyes were open wide and fixed in their focus on a distance I doubted could be gauged in any earthly measure.

"Stop. Please. Stop this . . . *hatred* . . . it hurts so . . ."

Maddie's voice faltered, and she fell silent. As we watched, her eyelids drooped and her slim form swayed. She was trying to raise one arm, as if to ward off some unseen assailant, when her knees buckled beneath her.

But before Maddie could strike the ground, Tito leaped forward. He caught her in his massive arms, scooping her up as if she were a bride. Her right arm hung at her side, as if lifeless, and her head lolled against his neck.

"Clear a fucking way out of here, Quynn," Tito growled. "Move your ass, damn it!"

I shook myself and pushed back into the eyewall of the stunned crowd, forcing open a path before us.

But not before I had seen what those ringing us saw, and what Jack Reagan's videotape would show countless skeptics and believers alike over the next few days.

As if by its own volition, the bandage had unraveled from Maddie Shepard's hand. As the tag end fluttered to the ground, there was an instant when her hand hung as if unclothed for all to see—clean and fresh and seemingly unmarked.

Then the blood began to well from the back of her hand like a rosebud blossoming. As Tito carried her through a crowd now stunned and awed, it fell in rich red drops to the pavement at his feet.

CHAPTER 12

Tito glared out the window of the same study in which I had last waited with Howard Zhang-mei, his only movement a muscle twitching high on his jawline. In stony profile, he looked like a furious pagan deity; nor did he turn when he spoke, as if he recognized that his potential for violence was still un-quelled.

"What moron lets a thirteen-year-old wander into a goddamn riot?" Tito demanded. "Fucking idiots . . ."

"If you need to blame someone for Maddie's actions today, Mr. Schwartz," Sister Marie-Vincent Benedicta said, "go ahead and blame me. I was here. I was responsible."

"Yeah, I'll send a nasty note to the Pope."

Benedicta raised her hand, as if in mild rebuke. But it was as effective as trying to flag down an angry rhinoceros.

"Where's her father? Why the hell isn't he here?"

"Mr. Shepard is at an airport in Detroit. His flight leaves within the hour, and he will be here before seven o'clock tonight."

"Good of him," Tito growled.

"Mr. Shepard was meeting with an associate whose business he may lose—largely because of the time he has spent trying to help his daughter through all this. Put yourself in his place, Mr. Schwartz. He's trying to function under difficult circumstances. As for Maddie, she's not a prisoner. No one believed there was a need to lock her in."

"Oh. Sure. That makes sense. Kid thinks she's getting express mail from heaven, nothing unusual there. No need to maybe protect her from herself."

Tito turned from the window and looked hard at me.

"Why are you being so quiet?" he demanded. "You got nothing to say about all this?"

"I don't know what 'all this' is, Tito. I don't know what made the girl go out there. I sure as hell don't understand what happened when she did."

"She got herself in the middle of a damn back-alley brawl, that's what happened. She could have—" Tito stopped, and stared at me strangely. "For God's sake, Quynn."

I could not meet his eyes.

"Worry about things that are real, partner," he warned.

"The blood on your shirt is real."

"So the cut on the kid's hand opened up again. Big fucking mystery, okay?"

"Maybe. Let's see what the doctor says."

Tito rolled his eyes.

"Cryin' out loud, Quynn," he said. "What is it with you? Why try to turn this into a damn miracle? Are you *that* hard up for something to believe in?"

"Be careful, Tito," I said.

Our eyes locked for a long moment. Then Tito wheeled to the window again, as if what he saw through the glass might provide whatever resolution he sought.

"No one was injured," Benedicta said. "It could have been far worse."

Tito's face reddened, but I spoke before he could respond.

"Why are you here, Sister?" I said. "What makes Maddie Shepard so important to you?"

"That should be obvious, Lieutenant."

"It should," I agreed. "But I'm starting to find that the obvious explanations don't quite answer my questions. For instance,

I'm having difficulty understanding your new role in the Shepard household. The father goes on a trip and leaves you in charge. Why?"

"Maddie's mother lives in Los Angeles. I'm told there has been little contact with her since she . . . left. There are no other relatives. Had I not offered to stay here last night, Mr. Shepard would have been unable to deal with his business situation."

"You're still a stranger to the Shepards, Sister."

"I'm also a nun, and they are people in need. As for the proprieties, there is another member of my staff present, sir. He is a priest. While his specialty is psychiatry, he is of course also a fully qualified medical doctor." She took a deep breath. "I'm humoring you because I believe you have the girl's best interests in mind. But I'm running short of patience. Have I adequately answered your questions, Lieutenant?"

"You could end all of this," I told her. "That is, unless you truly believe that Maddie is having a religious experience."

"Excuse me, but I don't believe that is a question."

"Sister, we were lucky today. But the people outside—whatever side they are on—are not going away. Neither are the people who murdered Susan DeBourche last night. They are using Maddie's situation to incite more violence."

"Precisely what do you expect me to do?"

"I don't know. Like I said, walk away, maybe. Put out a press release that there's no evidence of divine intervention here. But don't turn that girl into some kind of religious icon. Don't let the crazies on either side use her to justify their violence."

"I can't walk away, Lieutenant. Nor can I control the violence. All I can do is condemn it."

"Yeah, how's that working for you?" Tito muttered, still staring out the window. "Think maybe there's still a kink or two you gotta work out of the plan?"

"Come off it, Mr. Schwartz," Benedicta said. "Abortion-related violence is endemic across the United States. There's been a dozen or more physicians killed in just the past five years. This man Kopp may have been responsible for at least four in the northeastern states. Eric Rudolph was setting off bombs everywhere, until he was caught. Now there's a half dozen of his wannabes at large. I've lost track of the number of clinics that have been firebombed."

"We read the newspapers, Sister," I said.

"Then you realize that abortion's become a lightning rod, Lieutenant. Every part of the political spectrum—from the neo-Nazis to the ACLU—is lined up on one side or the other."

"How does it help to put the ramblings of a troubled girl into the public domain?"

"I don't know how the Centurions knew Maddie even exists, let alone what she said. Do you think I *wanted* to see her words emblazoned on their Web site?"

"Somebody did, Sister. And there's not a long list of candidates who were present."

She did not respond, and after a moment's pause I let it pass.

"Who benefits from the situation?"

"Well, let me think, Lieutenant," she said. "Say, how about the extremists? You remember, the idiots on both sides."

"That makes the rest of you what, exactly? The moderate majority?"

"Is there a middle ground when it comes to abortion? You saw the answer outside, today. Either you believe an embryo is a human life or you don't. I know what side I'm on, Lieutenant. Do you?"

"I'm on the side that's against bombs and sniper rifles."

"The extremists are only more violent in the means they employ. But make no mistake. Each side views the other with horror—revulsion, even."

"And each side has a social agenda."

"Or maybe a moral one, Lieutenant Quynn," Benedicta said. "The Church is crystal clear in its teaching. An embryo is a human life. The innocent unborn must be protected as a matter of the highest morality. Call it natural law, if you know what that is."

" 'The law that is indelibly written in the heart of man,' " I recited. " 'Good is to be done and evil avoided.' "

"So you've read your Aquinas. I'm impressed." She lifted her hands, then let them drop in frustration. "Then you realize we're trapped in a contradiction. The Church condemns terrorism, bombings, vigilante violence. But—" She stopped abruptly, as if she had triggered some internal fail-safe mechanism.

"But what, Sister? But 'sometimes prayer alone isn't enough to combat an evil'? That every now and then it might take a few pounds of high explosive, or maybe a hunting rifle?"

"Do you ever wonder, Lieutenant, what would have been prevented if someone had shot Hitler when the first extermination camp opened? Or Stalin, *before* he began his murderous rampages? God forgive me, but perhaps we are supposed to make our *own* miracles happen."

"What about Maddie? Is somebody making that 'miracle' happen?"

"Are you asking me to answer as a nun, a physician, or as a professional skeptic?"

"I'm asking for an honest answer."

"Very well. I don't know what is happening—with her, to her. But I see all too clearly what is happening *because* of her, Lieutenant. And I don't know what I—what any of us—can do to stop it."

"This doesn't have to be part of some holy war, Sister Benedicta. You don't have to use Maddie Shepard to fan the flames. You can't believe that's what your God wants."

For the first time since I had met her, the measured demeanor

Benedicta wore as a mask slipped, and what I saw surprised me. Instead of the anger I had expected, perhaps had even hoped for, what I saw could have been weariness—even pain.

But before I could do more than register that fact, the door to the study opened and a balding man in a Roman collar beckoned to her. He and Benedicta conferred in low voices; after a minute or so the visitor withdrew, leaving the wooden door ajar.

Benedicta turned and spoke.

"Maddie is unharmed, thank God," she said. "The doctor has examined her, and found nothing untoward."

Tito grunted, brusquely. But I saw the tension leave his expression, and marveled again at the unplumbed depths to the enigma that was my friend.

"I want to talk to her," I said, knowing as I spoke that it was useless.

"Maddie is asleep, Lieutenant. But I'll pass your request to her father."

"I just want to see her hands, Sister. I won't wake the girl."

"They would show you little," Benedicta said, revealing nothing in her features or body language. "They are both bandaged now. But if it helps you, the doctor said the wounds appeared fresh."

CHAPTER 13

I was not allowed to see Maddie Shepard, nor was I given an opportunity to appeal Benedicta's decision at long distance by talking to Roger Shepard. No crime had been committed. Any breach of the peace that afternoon had been quelled, not inflamed, by Maddie's dramatic appearance. I had no foundation for forcing my way to see the girl. We all knew it, and my insistence only ended up embarrassing everyone concerned. After a quarter-hour of arguing my point, even Tito was unable to meet my eyes.

Finally, he took me aside.

"Give it a rest, Quynn," he said, his voice an undertone. "Maybe tomorrow you can talk her father into giving you a thumbs-up on the face-to-face. But it's not going to happen today—not now, not with Benedicta calling the shots. Get out of here, get some rest. Call me later, okay?"

By the time I left the house, shortly before six p.m., most of the crowd outside had dispersed. I rounded up my police detail, selected a volunteer to remain for the balance of mid-watch, and sent the rest of them home. Jesús Castile stood at an embarrassingly respectful distance until I was finished; only then did he gather his own guard force for a debriefing. I could tell the young guard was curious, perhaps even troubled. He wanted to talk; but instead I started my rented car and backed into the street, lifting a hand briefly as I passed but not meeting his eyes.

I used my cell phone to check in, more from habit than from

any expectation that I would be needed, or even wanted. I left my number with the police dispatcher, told him I was heading for an early dinner and where, and imagined him stifling a yawn.

But at the restaurant, midway through my amberjack sandwich, I looked up to see the always-imposing form of Moira Osterholm standing over me. Before I could invite her to sit, the FBI agent pulled out the chair across from me and did.

"The DeBourche shooting has been federalized," Osterholm said without preamble. "It is no longer a matter of concern for the Spanish Bay police force. I assume that comes as no great surprise, but I wanted to tell you face-to-face."

"Why tell me at all? I assume you know that Jesse Beaulieu is the primary on it—*was,* I suppose, now."

"Yes. I have also heard that your attempt this morning to involve yourself in his case almost resulted in a fistfight. Now that it is no longer a local case, it is even more inadvisable for you to force your way into the investigation. Or, for that matter, into the matter of Maddie Shepard."

I nodded.

"Uh-huh. I expected that you had another reason for tracking me here," I said. "I was invited in, remember? You were there when he did, Moira. I don't recall hearing you raise any objections at the time."

"I have never considered you a foolish woman, Quynn. But if you are seriously considering Zhang-mei's proposal, you are indeed a fool. You do not want to be involved with this. Had I a choice, *I* would not choose to be."

"Because it's too hot a potato?"

"Because it can do little except to further Howard Zhang-mei's own career. He sees you as a way to shield himself from any controversy. You would do well to remember that, Quynn."

"I'll take it under advisement. As long as we're being candid, who is Zhang-mei, Moira?"

She did not answer immediately, as if parsing each word before she decided to speak it.

"He has been with the Justice Department for somewhat more than eight years," she said finally. "Zhang-mei has acquired a reputation for . . . I have heard it termed 'personal ambition.' He has acute political instincts, without doubt. Immediately after the 9/11 attacks, I have been told, he lobbied rather intensely for assignment to the World Trade Center investigation. Later he pulled every string he could pluck at the Hoover Building for a liaison posting with Homeland Security."

"Ah-ha—the career fast-path these days," I said. "Whether you're a Justice Department lawyer or in the Bureau."

By her expression, Osterholm might not have heard my words.

"He was passed over for both positions," she said. "That is when he shifted his attention to all other available areas related to domestic terrorism. He was in the Raleigh office when the name of Robert Matthew Teasdale initially came to the attention of the Justice Department." She sat back in her chair and watched me with steady gray eyes.

"I think I'm beginning to understand," I said. "Zhang-mei worked the sniper attacks in North Carolina. The ones attributed to Teasdale." I shrugged. "And?"

"Even today, in his office in Mobile," Osterholm said, "he keeps a framed copy of Teasdale's wanted poster on his desk. A month ago, when Teasdale was placed on the 'Ten Most Wanted' list, Zhang-mei insisted on taking several of us to dinner. To celebrate. Am I being clear here, Quynn? Do you still wish to play in this particular game?"

"As I said, I'll think about it."

"Do as you wish," she said, and stood as if to leave. "I have said what I came to say. My conscience is clear."

"Is it? Or was this little heads-up your version of atonement for past sins?"

Osterholm's lips tightened to a single thin line. She started to walk away, but stopped suddenly and turned to face me.

"In all likelihood, Tito Schwartz would be in a Federal penitentiary had we decided to press the issue," she said. "I believe he received fair value for his contribution."

"He brought you your case, wore a wire into situations where doing that was tantamount to a death wish," I said. "His testimony put a half dozen Russians in Marion Penitentiary. In return, he lost the only thing he valued aside from his family."

"You cannot seriously believe that the FBI should have left a crooked cop with his badge."

"I believe people should honor the promises they make."

"There were no guarantees given to Schwartz."

"He thinks differently. So do I."

"Oh, grow up, Quynn," Osterholm snapped, and I realized that I was witnessing history of a sort. The Ice Queen demeanor had slipped. I was seeing a side of Moira Osterholm that I had not heard discussed even in rumor. She was furious. Even more astounding, she was not concealing it.

"Schwartz put himself into a bad situation because of his own gambling problems," Osterholm said, her face crimson and her words clipped and tight. "He compounded that by waiting more than a month before coming to us."

"But he *did* come to you, Moira."

"Not because of shame or guilt over what the Russians were telling him to do. Oh no. He did so because his ego was offended. Schwartz simply could not stand the thought of taking orders from them, or anyone else, for that matter. He came within a hair of torpedoing the investigation a dozen times by ignoring the direction that I—that *we*—gave him."

"Maybe Tito isn't the only one with an ego problem, Moira."

"Or the only one incapable of understanding where his best interests reside, Quynn. He still doesn't, as a matter of fact."

"What's that supposed to mean?"

She leaned over the table. "You might want to advise Schwartz against violating Federal privacy statutes. Is he too stupid to realize that we track activity on those snooper sites on the Internet? Schwartz's name has crossed my desk a half dozen times in the past month."

"Credit checks are illegal now, Moira?"

"They are when you use a site that hacks into nonauthorized databanks. Tell Schwartz to stick to Equifax or TRW. If he continues on his current path, the least that will happen is he'll lose his PI license."

"*Seig heil,* Moira. Authorize any illegal phone taps lately?"

"Insult me all you wish, if it makes you feel better. No matter what Schwartz was promised, and however Schwartz chose to misconstrue it, he still benefited more than he deserved. He betrayed his badge, never forget that."

I shook my head, but my eyes did not leave hers.

"You're wrong," I said. "His trouble was that he was incapable of betraying his shield, or anybody who carried one. It never occurred to him that they might be capable of betraying *him.*"

"We all do what is necessary, Quynn. We do what is needed to make the case."

"Is that what you tell yourself? I mean, so you can sleep at night?"

"I've said all I care to. Have a good life, Lieutenant."

And she pivoted on her heel, leaving in an unremorseful stride that appeared timed to a military cadence that only she heard.

But I could not resist having the last word.

"Ask yourself this, Moira," I called to her retreating back. "Aren't we supposed to be better than the people we arrest?"

I spent most of the evening in the library, amid the corps of senior citizens and adolescents who, for their own vastly differing reasons, constituted the facility's prime-time population while the world overstimulated itself with Must-See TV.

By showing my badge, I managed to get a reference librarian intrigued enough to keep a steady stream of annotated books, magazine articles and newspaper clippings flowing to the carrel I had claimed. For almost three hours, I scanned and made notes in the spiral-bound tablet I bought from a vending machine in the library's lobby.

Finally, the librarian laid a laser printout on the desktop before me. It was a wealth of cross-indexed Internet Web sites.

"I put this together for you," he said. "Might be something in a few of them. We have some Net-connected computers available to the public. I think one or two of them may actually be working today."

"I appreciate the time you're taking on this."

"I majored in library science 'cause I liked to read and I enjoyed research." He shrugged. "So now I don't have time to read, and most of my research involves pointing high school kids to the right shelf. Trust me, Lieutenant, this is a nice change of pace. Interesting subject, stigmata. I'm Geoff, by the way."

He held out a hand, which I shook.

"Quynn."

"Mind if I sit?"

He pulled up a chair.

"People aren't usually here to look up the history of stigmata," he said, then arched an eyebrow. "This have something to do with that Shepard girl? I saw it on TV during my supper break. Weird, don't you think?"

"Not something you see every day," I said. "Made me wonder."

He glanced at the stacks of materials piled high in front of me.

"You have a healthy curiosity," he said. "You finding what you need?"

"A lot of it seems to contradict itself. I'm not seeing much hard information."

"The whole issue of stigmata is pretty dicey," he said. "It's none of my business, but are you a religious woman?"

"I try to keep an open mind."

He nodded, as if to agree. "The reason I ask, stigmata is one of those areas where the theological and the temporal worlds supposedly coincide—a physical manifestation of a spiritual experience. It's one of the few areas of religion that doesn't depend solely on faith, on blind belief. You can actually examine some evidence." He smiled, a self-deprecating gesture. "I minored in comparative religions, in case it doesn't show."

"How does the evidence hold up for stigmata?"

"Not so good, I'm afraid. Take the Five Wounds thing, for instance."

"I don't follow."

"Traditionally, in the Gospels and other Christian literature, they talk about Christ's wounds. There's the crown of thorns, first; then you have a nail wound in each hand and one through the feet—they count that as one wound, for some reason. Finally, a Roman soldier did the *coup de grâce* with a spear to the heart. Five wounds, okay?"

I smiled. "The math works."

"Right. But most instances of alleged 'stigmata' report only two wounds. Almost inevitably, in the palms of the hands. Not the feet, not the chest, not the head." He shook his head. "Pretty half-baked job for a miracle, don't you think?"

"I guess I hadn't thought about it that way."

"Okay, and how's this—why the palms at all? I mean, have you seen an X ray of a hand? The bone structure is pretty flimsy in there. Put a nail through it, try to hang the weight of a human body . . . well, it would rip right out!"

Geoff did not require a response, and perhaps not even an audience; he spoke like a man engaged in a debate with someone whose inner conflicts he knew far too well.

"The Romans were experts in this stuff. They had a lot of practice before they got to messianic Jewish rabble-rousers in ancient Palestine. When they nailed somebody to a cross, they went through the wrists. See, there's a band of ligaments there strong enough to handle the load. *That's* how they would have done it. It's an historical fact."

He nodded earnestly, warming to an argument that I already had recognized was not directed at me.

"So why do these so-called 'miracles' put the wound in the wrong place? What, are we supposed to believe that God missed his own memo on anatomy? I mean, how much faith can you put in a supernatural event that can't even get the details right?"

"I don't know."

"That's right! That's exactly right—you *can't* know, nobody can, because there's nothing that really explains it. That's what's so infuriating. Now, this Maddie Shepard girl—you say you saw the videotape on the news? Okay, so here's the thing. The blood was coming from her hands! The wrong place *entirely!* So it *can't* be—"

The librarian must have realized that his voice had risen with the last word. For an instant, he looked even younger than he was.

"I didn't mean to . . ." he said and smiled thinly. "I've been watching too much television. Perhaps I've gotten a little too caught up in this subject. I should probably be more impartial, don't you think?"

"It's hard to be impartial about some things," I said. "You've been very helpful, Geoff."

After a moment, he rose.

"Well," he said, as if searching for something more to say. "I'll leave you to your reading. Let me know if you need anything. Other materials, whatever."

"Thank you," I said, and gestured at the books on the desk. "I'm sure I'll find an answer in one of these, somewhere."

"Wouldn't it be nice to think so?" he said.

It was already after midnight when I walked up the flagstone pathway and stepped onto the porch. I knocked, softly, and leaned against the pale gray brickwork while I waited. High above, the stars were blue-white pinpoints beyond count, spilled madly across a lonely black abyss.

No lights came on inside, but after a few moments the door cracked open and I heard a voice, deep but subdued.

"Come on in, Quynn. I'm gonna have a drink. You want one?"

"I know it's late, Tito."

"Gina's upstairs sleeping. Vic is in Los Angeles. Job interview. So it's just me, and I'm thirsty. You coming in or not?"

I followed Tito as he padded in bare feet through the darkened house and into a room that, back when he had been eased out of the Spanish Bay police force, I had helped him convert into an office.

There, I told him everything: my conversation with Howard Zhang-mei, the late-night visit from Jack Reagan, M. C. Mason—even about the damage I had done to Harvey's face.

"Uh-huh. You just *guessed* this Harvey was a con?"

"No. I recognized him from the monthly probation reports."

He snorted. "You explain that to the TV guy?"

"Never pays to say too much, Tito."

"Let me ask you something, Quynn," Tito said. "You've put yourself in all this up to your neck. Exactly what do you expect to get out of it?"

I took a deep breath. "What have you heard about me and

Tara Kinsey? Straight dope, Tito. I'm not going to clutch at my heart or pull a faint on you."

"Somebody said the two of you were an item—more than just partners on the job. Implied that was why Ron ran out on you. I told him it was a load of shit. I might have offered to re-arrange his nose if he said it again."

I chuckled softly. "Thanks."

"Thanks, hell. We partnered for three years, Quynn. I kind of know you, okay? Besides—how do you undercut anybody's cred-ibility, 'specially if it's a woman? Simple. Spread bullshit about her sex life. Oldest dirty trick in the book."

"Still."

"So answer my question."

"People want to believe I'm out for revenge. As if all this was some kind of stupid comic book. My partner gets blown away, so I must want to track down her killer." I shook my head. "It's been a hell of a year, Tito. I've watched Cornelieus get sick, then had to stand by while Beaulieu set himself up to take his place, to turn everything back the way it was when we couldn't tell the cops from the robbers."

"I know. I was one of the robbers for a while, remember?"

I shrugged his comment off. "And then there was this thing with Ron—well, you know that's an old story. We've been down that road before. Except this time it feels different, like the tank is empty, somehow. No anger. That's the scary part. I wish there *was* anger. It just feels . . . I don't know. Over.

"So here I am, and I don't seem to feel my feet touch the ground. I almost punch out a moron who'll probably be my boss soon. When that falls through, the first chance I get I goad a half-wit punk until he comes after me, just so I can put his head through a wall. What does that make me, Tito?"

"Hell, you're asking me? Human, maybe."

"And now this business with the Shepard girl. Maybe you're

right. Maybe I'm just looking for a place where my feet touch something . . . solid. Maybe I *am* working overtime trying to believe there's something supernatural going on. Except then I pick an argument with anybody who says that maybe it *is* real." I lifted my eyes to his. "I may be pretty messed up, Tito."

"You think too damn much, Quynn."

"Maybe," I agreed. "I've been thinking about how things might have turned out if I had made a different decision about a dozen years ago."

"Yeah," Tito said, his voice gruff. "Wondered if you were beating yourself up over it again."

"She would have been about the same age," I said. "Or *he* would. Seems we're short of a pronoun when it comes to a few grams of tissue, you know? Anyway, it's a bit late for regrets."

But Tito refused to be drawn into my well of self-pity.

"Bullshit, Quynn," he said again. "Was it the right decision for a sixteen-year-old kid?"

"At the time, I thought it was the only decision."

"So put it away. Focus on *now*, partner. Hell, focus on your job."

"Hard to focus these days, Tito. I'm not sure there's a lot to focus on."

"You're trying to see answers before you're done puzzling out the damn questions. You want to call it messed up? Maybe that's what it is, but it keeps you looking. That's what solves cases, particularly when they're as fucked up as this one."

"I wish you were right."

"You want my opinion? Stop staring at your damn navel. Stick to simple questions."

"Such as?"

"Such as, how long you plan to keep ducking Cornelieus?" Tito asked, and took a long swallow from the bottle of Rolling Rock he held. "Sooner or later, you're gonna have to cop to taking off with Reagan this afternoon. And my bet is he's gonna want to know more about your little tiff with Beaulieu, too. If you try to lay this oh-I'm-so-confused bullshit on him, he'll put you on medical suspension faster than you can say 'nut case.' Probably make it permanent."

I stared into the tumbler of vodka and ice Tito had poured for me, and from which I had sipped only once.

"Jesus. Is that what you want, Quynn?"

"I don't know. I really don't."

"Oh, pull your thumb out of your ass," Tito said, and there was real anger in his voice. "You know how lucky you are? You're a cop. You can still *do* something about the situation. Instead, you pull this damn breast-beating bullshit. Just say it, for God's sake. What do you want?"

"I want to believe in . . . something. I want to have one single thing that I can say: this is *real;* this is—I don't know. True, I guess. That would be good. Or maybe I just want to fucking *care,* Tito."

He rolled his eyes in an unveiled impatience.

"You care, you dumbshit. I listened to you interrogate Benedicta at the Shepard house. I saw your face when you tried to get her to let you see the girl. Maybe you want the kid to be part of some damn miracle. Maybe you want God to do all the work, give you all the answers, nice and neat. If you want to feel sorry for yourself when He doesn't, that's fuckin' up to you." He took a deep breath, blew it out hard. "Just don't try to say you don't care, okay?"

"Sure."

"Sure? *Sure?* Fuck that. I want you to show me some goddamn balls."

There was silence for a moment. It hung in the air like smoke after a gunfight, thick between where we both now found ourselves. I realized we were both waiting for the other to speak, and sensed that we both feared the words that might be said. Oddly, with that very realization I felt the tension slip from my body.

Then I spoke.

"Okay, when do we get back to talking about what *I* want?"

Slowly, a smile tugged at the corner of his mouth.

"What you don't want is to get me started. Stop trying to get answers from God, Quynn. And stop looking for redemption. You're not going to get it, because nobody does."

"So, let me hear it straight up. What am I supposed to do, Tito?"

The look he gave me was less than sympathetic.

"Look—it doesn't matter if Maddie Shepard is living in a miracle or not. What matters is that some very bad people are using that poor kid to do some very bad shit. She knows it, too. Jeez, you can see it in her eyes."

"I can't be her mother, Tito. And Maddie already has a father."

"Hell, her old man's no help. He's an arrogant prick who thinks he ought to be fuckin' dictator of the world. Probably screwed the kid up as much as this so-called miracle thing has."

"So? What am I supposed to do?"

"So you keep it simple. You got a job to do. *Do* it. Don't let anybody use that girl."

He glared at me, fiery and magnificent in his passion.

"You were a hell of a cop, Tito. Best case investigator I ever knew."

The comment surprised Tito; he hid whatever pleasure it brought him behind another long draw of his drink.

"You weren't a complete nitwit yourself," he growled. "That is, once you stopped beating yourself up over every damn thing."

He studied me for a moment.

"I should probably keep my mouth shut," he said.

"Never worked for you before, Tito."

That brought a rueful half smile to his lips.

"Okay, you asked for it," he said. "You may not know what you want, but I damn well do. You want to fuckin' *save* everybody, Quynn. It's probably why you became a cop. You see somebody you think needs saving, and you turn into fuckin' Mighty Mouse, cape flyin', coming in to save the damn day."

I felt my face redden in embarrassment, but I said nothing.

"When we partnered, you always were looking to rescue somebody. Hell, you did it when I was all fucked up with the gambling. You probably tried to rescue Ron on a daily basis, for God's sake."

"Nobody ever needed rescuing less than Ron."

"Uh-huh. My guess, that's why you two are always paying divorce lawyers."

"Cheap shot, partner."

"Yeah," he said. "I said I should shut up, didn't I? But don't tell me I'm not on the money with your damn save-the-world complex, either."

We drank on, mostly in silence. But it was no longer an uncomfortable silence.

A little while later, Tito walked me out. He stood in the open doorway, regarding me through eyes that concealed far more than they revealed.

"Nobody gets everything they want, Quynn. Try to keep that in mind."

I opened my mouth to reply at the same instant that he flung himself forward into me.

Tito smashed into my chest with a force that took my feet from beneath me, the two of us a tangle of flailing limbs. My back thudded hard against the trimmed lawn, the impact a vivid white flash across my vision, familiar to anyone who has taken a punishing body-blow.

Or so I believed it to be, even as my ears registered the evil flat blast of the first gunshot.

"Car, Quynn," Tito rasped, and there was pain in his voice. "Asshole's got a shotgun."

I rolled hard from under Tito's weight, my right hand clawing at the pistol holstered at my belt. Before I could clear my weapon, another flash like a photographer's strobe lit the night and the turf exploded a foot from my head.

And then I was up on one knee, both arms extended and the Smith & Wesson bucking wildly in my hands as I fired, again and again, at the dark sedan double-parked alongside my own vehicle, forty feet away. The chain lightning of my own muzzle flashes dazzled my eyes, but not so much that I could not mark the impact of my shots; an irregular line of clean-metal blotches gnawed into the driver's door, each centered on its own bullet hole.

But even as I fired, the dark form behind the wheel made its own decision. The rear tires spun and screamed as the driver stamped against the accelerator. In an instant, the sedan was fishtailing away, picking up speed.

I stood then, centering my sights between and above the twin crimson beacons of his driving lights, still pulling the trigger even after the slide locked back on the empty magazine.

But the car reached the intersection, and skidded around the corner as it fled.

For a moment I stood stock-still, smelling cordite and burned rubber and what might have been my own fear.

Then Tito groaned, a sound that seemed to carry as much rage as it did pain, and I felt myself shake off the dread that had frozen me. I turned toward where Tito lay, his left fist pounding rhythmically against the ground.

Lights were coming on in houses along the length of the

street as I knelt in the cool grass beside the man who had just saved my life.

CHAPTER 14

If I were a character in a novel, the close brush I had survived would have filled me with an immediate, terrible resolve; in a book, the fact that my closest friend had been a victim of the ambush intended for me would only have served to underscore that grim determination.

But this was real life.

What I felt, even before the squealing of tires faded in the distance, was an overwhelming disbelief that I was still alive. It mingled with equal parts of confusion and a wholly inappropriate tendency to break into uncontrollable laughter.

Then Tito groaned again, jolting me back to a cold sobriety.

I bent close over Tito. Now, he was rocking from side to side with knees drawn into a tight fetal coil. His eyes were slits behind a face twisted in agony.

"Son of a bitch," he hissed through clenched teeth. "Mother-fucker . . ."

"Where are you hit, Tito? Come on, talk to me, man."

"Hit . . . *hell*, that hurts! Your knee . . . when we fell . . ."

"My knee? I'm okay, Tito. He missed—"

"Dammit, Quynn! I *fell* on your damn knee. Caught me . . . square in the family jewels . . ."

It took me a moment to process what Tito had said.

And then I fell back onto my haunches beside him, helpless to stifle the peals of laughter that burst full-born from deep inside me.

Through the blur of tears that streamed from my eyes, I saw Tito look up at me in astonishment, followed closely by indignant outrage. Finally, the absurdity of the situation hit him, too. In a moment, we were both caught up in laughter, hysterical and relieved. For Tito, it was also somewhat pained.

There is no telling how long we would have lay there, our howls rising into the night sky, had Gina Schwartz not found us like that. She stared down at Tito, whose hands still gingerly clutched his groin.

"Hi, baby," Tito said, his voice shaking with unrestrained mirth. "Don't worry. Bastard missed."

The comment sent us both back into paroxysms.

Gina looked from her husband to me, and I saw her eyes register the empty automatic pistol that was still clenched tight in my hand.

"I forgive you, Quynn," she said. "Every now and then, I've felt like shooting at him myself."

But nobody was laughing forty minutes later, when Chick Cornelieus pulled past the patrol car parked diagonally at the same intersection where my assailant's car had skidded to escape. He drove slowly down the street, past houses where the revolving red and blue Mars lights danced across their walls. He seemed not to notice the residents, who stood arms folded in robes or hastily donned street clothes to watch the action.

Already, yellow crime-scene tape stretched from my rental car's front bumper all the way to Tito's front door. There, the first shot had chewed away a splintered chunk the size of a dinner plate. Criminologist technicians were at work at various sites on the property, invoking their own brand of scientific wizardry. In the street, another group of them measured and photographed the twin black stripes of skid marks that serpentined down the pavement.

I watched Cornelieus' approach, as he stopped every few feet to confer with one or another of the officers on the scene. He spent a long time with Elle Kvamme, the sergeant who had been among the first to arrive. She had taken firm charge, directing and delegating with a calm competence as the troops had rolled in.

Finally, Cornelieus walked to where I waited at the paramedic's van. In the harsh illumination of the crime-scene searchlights, his complexion appeared even more pallid than usual. Not for the first time, I wondered if he slept at night; were his hours spent listening to the tick of the clock, subtracting each from the column of those remaining?

"Quite a crowd," he said. "You must have most of the third shift out here."

"It's not as bad as it looks," I said. "A lot of these people were off-duty, from middle watch. The county deputies, too. Somebody put it out as an 'officer needs assistance' when I called in the shooting. People heard about it on their scanners and came running."

He nodded.

"A little unorthodox," he said, "the target of an attempted shooting working her own investigation."

"Sergeant Kvamme is the primary, Chief. I'm giving her the benefit of my wisdom and experience."

"She says you're okay. You and Schwartz, both."

"Tito knocked me clear. I wouldn't be here if he hadn't."

"You were the target? You're certain of that?"

"The first shot could have been at either of us. The second one was definitely aimed at my head."

"Any theories why, Quynn?"

"Way too early to speculate, Chief."

"Lieutenant, I'm trying to stay reasonable here," Cornelieus said. "I want to give you the benefit of the doubt. So if you want to stay off suspension—let alone in any supervisory role, in this investigation or any other—I need to hear what is happening. With you, with all of this. I advise you to start speculating. Right now."

"I was drawing my weapon before the second shot. That's one possible reason; the shooter wanted to eliminate me as an armed threat. It does not rule out Tito as the actual target."

"But it makes it less likely. In your opinion."

"Tito doesn't make friends easily. But since he left the department, I don't see him getting anybody upset enough to use a shotgun."

Cornelieus' grunt could have been agreement, or not.

"A few hours ago, I had a disagreement with a parolee. Things got a little physical. It's possible he holds a grudge."

"Make sure Kvamme has all the details," Cornelieus said, and then he looked at me closely. "Is there something more, Quynn?"

"I also had a conversation with a lady named Margot Mason. You might know her better as 'M. C. Mason.' "

Cornelieus said nothing, but his expression was not intended to ease any employment-related concerns I might have had.

I plunged into deeper waters.

"I was there with Jack Reagan."

"Oh," he said. "That's different, then. As long as it's all going to be on TV, how could I see a problem?"

"Chief, I—"

"Did your conversation involve an ongoing *Federal* investigation, in which you have no jurisdiction? Or did you limit yourself to talking about the DeBourche murder? In which, I hasten to add, you have no standing, either. Beaulieu is the supervising officer. But at least it's merely a local case, for now." He saw the look on my face. "What?"

"Moira Osterholm made a point of finding me at dinner.

They've taken jurisdiction. The paperwork is probably already on your desk."

"Perfect."

"Mason is a link to Bobby Teasdale and the threats he's made. Her Web site put them on the Internet, just like it published Maddie Shepard's so-called message before anybody else knew about it. Add to that, the Centurions of the Lord have to be near the top of any list of domestic terrorist groups."

"You have a point here, Lieutenant?"

"So why is a Spanish Bay cop the only person from law enforcement who's bothered to talk to Mason? Where have the Feds been hiding?"

"Once the FBI gets around to it, they'll make the official determination that the bombing and shooting are linked," Cornelieus said. "When they find out what you've been doing, you'll be lucky to avoid prosecution yourself."

"Howard Zhang-mei already knows, Chief. He all but invited me into the investigation."

That brought him up short.

"The FBI agreed to that?"

"Moira Osterholm was there. She heard Zhang-mei; technically, he's her boss."

Cornelieus frowned, and I could see the wheels turning inside.

"They're both worried about the political fallout they could catch," I said. "I'm somewhat more expendable."

"That's one possibility. Okay, give me everything, now."

I filled him in on my activities over the past two days. Given the situation, he took it remarkably well.

"Have you talked with Zhang-mei since his . . . invitation?"

"I assume he'll contact me, when he's ready."

"I want to know when he does. Is that clear?"

"That could be a problem, Chief. Zhang-mei doesn't—"

"Remember who you work for, Lieutenant."

"What do I do until then, Chief?"

His gaze was steady. "Leave your weapon with Kvamme, so ballistics can do a test firing. You can have it back tomorrow. Officially, you're still on light duty. That should give you time to . . . let's say, to *assist* in the investigation of tonight's incident." Cornelieus' voice had not been warm, but now it cooled several degrees more. "But there will be no more off-the-books freelancing for the Justice Department, Quynn. You will report any relevant progress to me. *Only* to me, unless I tell you differently."

I opened my mouth to object, then merely nodded. Cornelius eyed me as if he read tea leaves on a regular basis.

"Okay, what else?"

"You haven't asked me about Beaulieu."

"Ah. Is there a reason I should?"

"Earlier today, I—"

He raised a hand. "Earlier today, you offered Lieutenant Beaulieu the benefit of your—how did you just put it? Your wisdom and experience. Something about preserving the integrity of the crime scene, I understand."

"Something like that."

"Good. Because if it was anything else, I would be forced to take action—very probably, in a way I neither want nor need. Am I being sufficiently clear?"

"Sure. Okay."

"It's possible that the . . . banter that occurred during this exchange might have crossed a line. My understanding is that the conversation included some back-and-forth of a sexual nature. I'd advise against anyone taking too much offense, of course. Questioning a co-worker's sexual orientation is one of the oldest tricks in the book—and, when it is patently untrue, one of the least effective. But it *is* actionable, which re-opens the can of worms I'd like to avoid. Unless everybody concerned agrees it was a poor attempt at humor, that is."

"Beaulieu was kidding around," I agreed. "That's all he intended, and that's how I took it. No harm, no foul."

Cornelieus nodded abruptly, then turned to leave.

"For the record, I want my officers to assist each other," he said. "With all appropriate enthusiasm."

I had to strain to hear his final words—which, in any account, may not even have been intended for my ears.

"Just try not to leave any visible marks," Cornelieus murmured, and I could swear that I heard a wry satisfaction in his voice.

The next three hours were filled with the routine, mundane but essential, that makes up the bulk of all police activity. Elle Kvamme handled the lion's share of the supervisory role with a cool, single-minded proficiency that left me envious.

First, she dispatched uniformed officers to canvass the neighbors on the off chance that the shooter had been inept or unlucky enough to provide some means of identification. Area hospital emergency rooms were alerted, in case my own luck had been better than my marksmanship deserved.

Every quarter hour or so, Elle requested an update on the hunt for the shooter's car. The all-points already had people in three counties looking for a midsized, late-model sedan. It was a thin description indeed, but the bullet holes that now peppered the driver's door and the trunk were a distinguishing feature that would be hard to miss, even in rural Florida. The odds were good that the shooter would know this, too, and trade up to less conspicuous transportation as soon as possible. Any stolen vehicles reports that were called in would also come to Elle immediately.

As I watched Elle Kvamme coordinate the weaving of the net, the awareness of my own redundancy weighed on me. The crime-scene technicians required no guidance from me, even if I had been expert enough to provide it. Nor did the detectives working under Kvamme; I had already provided a hand-written report of all I recalled about the ambush and submitted to their follow-up questions.

I was not needed, not even to advise on the care and feeding of the news media. Unlike Beaulieu, Kvamme had little inclination to curry their favor or court their attention. She glanced only once at the pack that had been drawn by the scent of fresh blood, and ignored the questions they shouted at her. A uniformed Sheriff's Deputy—selected by Kvamme, I suspected, largely on the basis of his intimidating size and demeanor—was tasked to ensure that the reporters stayed behind the yellow tape marking the perimeter.

I was standing alone, surveying it all, when a voice spoke behind me.

"Don't see your little playmate in there," Tito observed. "What—he hear Elvis is having an affair with E.T.? Rush off to grab the interview?"

"Shouldn't you be resting?"

"Yeah, right. Rest always helps a knee to the goodies."

"Tito . . ." I hesitated, trying to find the right words. "Thanks. You saved my bacon. I mean it."

"Sure, sure. You can cut my grass for a few weekends, make it up to me. Or wash my car sometime, maybe."

"Whatever."

"So where is he? I don't see that one missing the biggest show in town."

I grunted. But inside, I was puzzled, too.

I had not seen Jack since Maddie Shepard's performance— that is, not in the flesh.

Along with most of the region, I had watched him earlier in the evening on the ten o'clock news. Jack had opened the broadcast with a live studio intro to the latest miracle. Then they went to the videotape. It was a masterpiece of frenetic editing, intercutting shots of the nascent riot in a way that made the conflict appear more violent than it was.

The highlight, of course, was the sudden appearance of Maddie Shepard. Jack's production staff had somehow managed to zoom in, digitally enhancing the portion of the shot that showed Maddie's hand. It made the frame-by-frame slow-motion all the more dramatic.

Church officials had declined comment, but Jack had dug up an Atlanta-based "expert" in "spiritual phenomena," and the live phone-in interview had been a showpiece of speculation and hyperbole. In the end, Jack's wrap-up had been of the "nobody knows for certain, but one thing is clear" variety, though to the discerning viewer the alleged clarity might have seemed conspicuous in its absence.

But no one could deny that it was effective television, presented in a way that undeniably showcased Jack's abilities. Better still, certainly for Jack, it ran just under seven minutes in length—encyclopedic, in TV time.

Jack was on his way back, clawing up the ladder again. I probably should have been happy for him, but all I felt was an unfocused dismay.

"You look like hell warmed over, Quynn," Tito was saying. "Gina says she'll fix up Victoria's room for you."

"Tell her thanks," I said. "But I better head home."

"You too good to go slumming here?"

I shook my head, as if to commiserate. "Frankly, I'm just not too keen about your neighborhood, Tito. I don't know how you get any sleep around this place, all these guns going off."

The marina was quiet, though it might not seem so to anyone unaccustomed to the rhythmic clanking of sailboat halyards or the regular slap of wavelets against boat hulls. A handful of my neighbors still showed lights, but most of the sloops and cruisers and other craft moored around me were dark and still. My footsteps sounded loud on the wooden planking of the pier.

I stepped onto the deck of my houseboat, feeling the craft rock slightly under my weight. Directly overhead, a moon just shy of full cast a cold, blue-white light not quite bright enough to read under. It foreshortened my shadow as I moved aft along the railing.

I half expected to find Jack Reagan waiting for me. But there was no sign of him, and I could not decide if I was disappointed or relieved. It was too late for an unannounced visit, but even in the brief span of our acquaintance I was becoming accustomed to his particular brand of unpredictability. Jack moved by clocks and calendars and an agenda that seemed to defy conventional measures, and which were as indecipherable to me as were the other compulsions or necessities that drove him.

Occupied with such thoughts, I unlocked the sliding door to the main salon and stepped inside, fumbling until I found the wall switch. But when I clicked it on, nothing happened. Neither the shore-side power nor the boat's battery supply was functioning, a fact that should have given me pause. Instead, I muttered darkly and slid the door shut behind me. The circuit panel was on the far bulkhead. I felt my way across the darkened cabin, waiting for my eyes to adjust.

I was midway across the space when from my left I heard a voice, low and with an accent that spoke of pine woods and backcountry hollows.

"Right there, girl. Don't you move, hear?"

I froze, and told myself not to think about the Smith & Wesson, its weight missing from my belt. I cleared my throat, not quite trusting my ability to speak. It was just as well; before I could, the voice continued.

"You make any noise, I'm gonna make a bigger one. Put them hands up, real slow."

A figure moved with a wiry caution from the shadows where he had waited. He was short for a man, if a head taller than I—slight and almost adolescent in form as he stepped close. But there was nothing undersized in the pistol he held, unwavering, in his right fist.

He stopped a few paces away, his features still in the shadows. But, by an odd fluke of positioning, the revolver was illuminated by a shaft of blue-white moonbeam from the overhead skylight. It had the unmistakable raked profile of a Colt Python revolver, and the .357 Magnum rounds it fired had been designed to perforate cast-iron engine blocks.

"Lace them fingers behind your head. That's it; real slow."

The revolver was lightly burnished with oil, and the reflected moonlight softened the blued steel to the texture of dark velvet while eliminating none of the weapon's hard-edged lethality. From my vantage, I could even see the flattened copper-clad noses of the bullets that filled each chamber.

"Easy, friend," I said, and marveled at how reasonable my own voice sounded. "Take what you want and leave. Neither of us wants this to become a worse problem, do we?"

"Nuthin' you can do make me worse off'n I already am," the stranger said. "You don't want to move that hand none, girl; not if you want to keep it. You know who I am?"

He moved forward, just enough for his face to be illuminated by the ray of moonlight.

The mug shot I had seen was three years old, and the man before me had cultivated a thin goatee-style beard since police in Jacksonville, North Carolina, had arrested him for a botched burglary. Both the beard and the tangle of hair that fell from under the baseball cap now were dark brown, a dye job that showed more enthusiasm than competence. But there was no mistaking the nose and cheekbones, or the distinctive ridge of his brow line.

"Yes," I said. "I know who you are."

"Good," said Bobby Teasdale. "Then you know why I'm here, you lyin' piece'a shit."

Before I could react or respond, he stepped forward.

His hand was already moving before he finished the epithet, the pistol he held a blur in the semidarkness.

I tried to duck, instinctively, and felt the impact, a blinding pain high across my crown. Then, somehow, I was on my elbows and knees, my forehead brushing the cool teak of the deck. I strained to push myself upward, finally managing to raise my eyes to ankle level. Two feet, sock-less inside frayed canvas boat shoes stained with old fish blood, filled my vision for an instant. Then a second hard blow knocked my head down again.

"You're making a mistake," I said, and this time my voice was little more than a croak that came from some arid recess deep inside my chest.

"Wouldn't be the first time, girl," Teasdale said, his voice coming soft and indistinct, as if from some unfathomable distance. "The last neither, I 'spect."

My final memory is the cold finger of the revolver jabbing hard against the crown of my skull. That, and the flat mechanical click of a hammer being thumbed back to full cock.

And then the world lurched sharply and exploded into a crazy pinwheel of sparking colors.

I pitched forward into the void that suddenly opened wide, as if to welcome me to its bottomless depths.

CHAPTER 15

I swam slowly upward, finning my way through warm salt waters toward a quicksilver ceiling dappled by the sheen of the moon. The sea around me was dark in comparison, and indistinct shapes flitted in and out of the periphery of my vision.

My breath came easily and regularly; but, oddly, no bubbles rose from my scuba regulator to flutter against my dive mask. The rubber of the mouthpiece tasted sour, and my throat was painfully dry. I forced myself to swallow once, then again. I briefly considered making one more try before deciding the result was unworthy of the energy expended.

I thought to raise my hand, expecting to see the phosphorescent halo I had encountered in other night-diving sessions; but I found myself unable to lift it. This should have disturbed me; it did not. Instead, I closed my eyes and reveled in the weightless disconnect of the ocean's embrace.

"You ain't hurt none," a voice said. "I didn't hit you all that hard. Open your damn eyes, *now.*"

I complied. The world swam for a moment, and then I found myself staring into the face of Bobby Teasdale.

Teasdale bent, and I felt a tug at my wrists. As if in a stupor, I looked down. Handcuffs that might have been my own were laced around a stanchion bolted solidly to the bulkhead. Then Teasdale stepped behind me, and propped me into a seated position on the teak sole. He dragged up one of the galley chairs, and I noted that the Python was tucked into his waistband.

"Reckon I got your attention now," Teasdale said, and with the satisfaction of a famished man bit into the sandwich he held. He gestured with it, grandly. "Hope you don't mind. Made me up a little something."

I shook my head, and winced at the pain. Teasdale grinned.

"Betcha thought you was one dead woman," he said. "Did—am I right, girl?"

The lights were on now, both literally and figuratively. I could feel my reason returning like a disk drive spinning up. One moment I had absolutely no idea what Teasdale meant; then, not in a rising flood but as if a switch had been thrown, the remembered horror of a pistol against my skull was fully alive in my mind.

I swallowed hard and spoke my first words.

Teasdale knit his eyebrows, puzzled. "Hell'd you say there, girl?"

I licked my lips and tried again.

"I said, you can stop calling me 'girl.' "

He laughed and it did not sound like a threat.

"Well, you got some grit, I guess. *Loo*-tenant Quynn."

"What do you want?"

"Well, for starters, I want somethin' more to eat. Got anythin' 'cept for sliced-up ham? And hey—where y'all keep the beer on this tub?"

He had shifted moods entirely. His voice no longer carried the edgy, on-the-brink quality that had earlier made me doubt my own longevity. Now, as he gnawed at his sandwich, it sounded cheerful, almost jaunty. As if reading my thoughts, he grinned and kicked playfully at my ankle.

"Cat got your tongue or sumptin'?"

"This is a dumb play, Teasdale." I was surprised; my voice was almost normal again. "You have to know that. You're asking to be caught."

"Three years, ain't nobody caught me yet. Weren't for lack of tryin', neither."

"Why are you here?"

He snorted. " 'Cuz you got a number listed in the phone book—least, your ol' man does."

I stared at him, suddenly chilled.

He shook his head, as if I had spoken aloud.

"Naw, I didn't do nuthin' to him. Hell, he ain't even there. I found out 'bout your boat here cuz your lawyer sent him a letter, copy to you here. Found it with the other stuff in his mailbox." He shrugged. "Mebbe you don't care none, divorcin' and all. But I got some professional advice you oughta give your man. You go outta town, git the post office to hold the mail."

"Thanks. Am I going to be around to tell him in person?"

Teasdale looked suddenly disgusted.

"You and that lyin' sum'bitch on TV," he said. "Y'all have me kidnapping the damn Limberger baby 'fore you're quit with it."

"I don't understand."

"You sayin' I'm here to kill you. I ain't. And that stuff he said on TV? It's bullshit, 'cuz I ain't done it."

By now, the patent absurdity of having survived two apparent attempts on my life over the space of a few hours was having its effect. A perverse exhilaration grew inside me, unwisely manifesting itself in sarcasm.

"Exactly what ain't you done, Bobby?"

"I ain't shot nobody. But you start mockin' me, girl, I might jus' fix that 'fore I leave here."

I studied him closely and the puzzlement I displayed was only partly a sham.

"Let me get this straight. You deny killing Susan DeBourche?"

"See, that's your problem," Teasdale said. "You don't lissen' worth a damn." He leaned forward, so close I could smell the mustard on his breath. "I . . . ain't . . . killed . . . *nobody*. It git

154

through that time?"

"Where were you earlier tonight, Bobby?"

"I been here since sundown. Watched your TV. Saw that damn Reagan bastard prob'ly tellin' lies about that kid, one with the hands." He squinted at me, suddenly suspicious. "Why? You got something else you tryin' to put on me?"

"Here's my problem, Bobby. A while back, somebody used a Remington .308 rifle to shoot an abortion clinic nurse in North Carolina. They found a spent cartridge, and took fingerprints off it. People are saying they're probably yours."

"Yeah, I heard that. *I'm* saying it ain't true."

"That's going to be a hard one to sell, Bobby. Especially after all those things you said to M. C. Mason, on the Web site. Unless you didn't do that, either."

Teasdale rolled his eyes.

"Sure I said it, but it didn't mean nuthin'. Them damn people, murderin' all them poor little babies—I just wanted to mess with 'em. Look, I ain't *got* no damn list. Worse I ever done in my life was a stickup or three. That, and bust into a coupla places."

"Then let me take you in. Look, if you're telling the truth, you have nothing to—"

"Take me in," Teasdale repeated. His single laugh could have curdled milk. "That ain't gonna happen, no ma'am."

"Then what do you expect from me, Bobby?"

"I want you to tell that Jack Reagan to stop makin' me look like Bonnie Clyde or somethin'," Teasdale said. "I don't have to take that bullshit. I'm tellin' you, just like I told Miss Mason. It ain't right."

"What did Miss Mason say?"

"She said she didn't like the way Reagan sat there, pretendin' to be all friendly, when all he wanted was—" Teasdale stopped abruptly.

He rose and moved quickly to the circuit panel, then ran his hand down the row of switches. The cabin went dark. By the time my eyes had adjusted to the level of moonlight that fell from topside, Teasdale was already at the sidelight porthole, peering through the small gap he had pulled in the blackout curtain.

He stood like that for at least a minute, his face grim and his eyes flickering like a metronome. Gradually, his features relaxed and he let the curtain fall shut again. He turned to look at me, and his lips twisted in scorn.

"You think you could git much flatter down there? Best sit up, 'fore you cut off the blood runnin' to your hands."

I untwisted myself from where I had tried to find whatever cover the salon's sparse furnishings might have offered.

"You spook pretty easy for a cop."

"Maybe you don't spook easily enough, Bobby. Maybe you're too dumb to see where all this is going."

The joviality disappeared from his face.

"Don't think I won't beat you like a rented mule, you keep goin' that way."

"Look, Bobby, it's one of two things here," I said. "You've either been roaming around the country shooting abortionists, or somebody else has—and fixing things so it all falls on you. Are you still with me?"

"Go blow y'self. Yeah, I'm lissenin'."

"You have the FBI and half the police in the country chasing you. You're either very good, or there are people helping you stay ahead of the manhunt. That's fine for you, but what if they're the same ones who are setting you up?"

"People I know wouldn't do no such thing."

"Keep telling yourself that, Bobby. I'll make sure they carve it on your tombstone."

"I suppose y'all got some bright idea 'bout how—"

This time I heard it before Teasdale. But just barely.

"*Ho*-ly shit," he had time to say, and then he was on his feet and moving fast—but forward, toward the seldom-used hatch that opened onto my small sundeck.

Had the cabin lights been on, Teasdale would have had no chance; his silhouette, either as he ran across the salon or for the instant that he was jack-lighted in the open cabin door, would have been more than enough of a target. And had the tactical team been properly equipped—a portable spotlight that would have turned the night into noon, or night-vision sights on their weapons—the result likely would have been equally as lethal.

But as it was, they had neither.

And when Bobby Teasdale kicked through the wrong hatchway, only the bright disk of the moon above illuminated him as a target. He hit the forward sundeck in a tight roll that would have done a gymnast proud. By the time the riflemen had shifted their aim from the sliding doors aft, he was already on his feet running.

One of them did get a shot off, a single wild round that whanged off my radio mast and ricocheted, screaming, across the marina.

But by then Bobby Teasdale had vaulted the railing. He hit the water in a slicing dive that took him deep into the murky water of the harbor. I am told the shooting team rushed down the wooden pier toward the sound of the splash, finally training their weapons on the concentric ripples that had already spread to an inscrutable diameter.

But neither they, nor the Harbor Patrol and Coast Guard who crisscrossed the harbor with the proper spotlights and night-vision devices for the balance of the night, found any trace of Bobby Teasdale. He had disappeared as if he had never existed at all.

CHAPTER 16

"I had a tip," Beaulieu said, his voice the sullen monotone of a schoolboy far too familiar with being called to the principal's office. "So I assembled a tac unit and went to investigate."

"A tip." Cornelieus nodded, though probably not in encouragement.

"It was called in to my phone," Beaulieu paused, and corrected himself. "My cell phone. I was home, in bed."

"Called in by who?"

"No name. It was an anonymous tip."

"I see. And exactly what information did this anonymous tipster give you, Lieutenant Beaulieu?"

"Said if we wanted to catch up to Bobby Teasdale, he was at the marina in back of Conquistador's Landing. Hiding out on a boat. Gave me the number of the boat slip and hung up."

I sat in the corner of Cornelieus' office, working overtime to maintain a professional demeanor. It was a hard fight, but it would have been harder had Cornelieus not already taken the trouble to warn both me and Jesse Beaulieu that he would brook no foolishness this morning.

"Of course, you took the time to confirm that the call wasn't a hoax?"

"The tip seemed credible to me."

"So you stormed out to a public marina with a group of four officers, all of you armed with assault rifles."

"I wanted the additional firepower. Teasdale's wanted for

multiple homicides."

"A dangerous man," Cornelieus said; I noted that he did not specify the subject of his observation. "Why didn't you call for additional backup? Enough officers to, say, secure the perimeter."

"We had enough, I thought. Nobody expected Teasdale to bolt like he did."

"Who fired the shot?"

"It's in my report," Beaulieu muttered.

"I know."

Cornelieus sat back in his chair and tented his fingers as if musing over a particularly difficult dilemma. He studied Beaulieu for a long moment before speaking.

"Jesse, I have a problem here. On one hand, what you did early this morning could be seen as a complete fiasco; a masterpiece of mismanagement. At worst, it was utter incompetence. At best, very poor judgment."

He tapped Beaulieu's signed report on the incident, on the desk before him. "There might even be a case to be made for public endangerment, against you individually. You were in a crowded harbor, and the bullet you fired could have gone anywhere."

Cornelieus shook his head. "But it could be argued that you did rescue a fellow police officer who was being held hostage—" with a raised hand, he silenced the comment I had started to make "—and, thank God, nobody was injured by a stray round."

Beaulieu locked his gaze on Cornelieus; he made no comment, but his expression was wary, like a man calculating odds.

"By law, we have no grounds to withhold the details of this incident. If we get an inquiry from the news media, we'll have to provide them with the report. I'm afraid it wouldn't stop there; you know how the press can be when it smells blood. But none of us want to see a . . . misinterpretation of the actions you took. It could reflect poorly on the department. And, of course, on you personally."

Finally Beaulieu spoke.

"So," he said, and despite his situation it came out with a hint of challenge, "what are you going to do now?"

Cornelieus looked at him, a guileless expression on his face.

"I'll get back to you on that, Jesse. I want to be certain I'm making the right decision."

I waited until Beaulieu had left, closing the door with ill grace behind himself, before I spoke.

"What the hell was that all about? The man's a walking disaster area, and you allow—"

"Think before you say anything more," Cornelieus interrupted in a tone I recognized as indicating he had reached his zero-tolerance point. "Consider your next words very carefully, Lieutenant."

"That was me in there with Teasdale. I don't like thinking about what could have happened if Beaulieu was any better at noise discipline."

"You think I'm being too lenient."

"I think you're passing up an opportunity to make the world a safer place."

"Is that your only consideration, Quynn?"

"You know it's not."

"I appreciate your concern, Quynn, both for public safety and for whatever job-related issues I might have. But let me worry about personnel matters in this department. That's my job."

"I'd rather you kept it, Chief. I won't work under Beaulieu."

Cornelieus nodded.

"I'll take that as a vote of confidence in my judgment," he said, and it was clear the subject of Beaulieu's ambitions was closed. "Sure the head's okay?"

I touched the lump, hidden mostly under my hairline; it hurt. "I'm fine."

"Anything on Teasdale's whereabouts?"

"We have people still looking. I don't think they'll find anything."

"Why?"

"There are maybe three hundred boats moored in Spanish Bay Harbor," I said. "Even if you figure that maybe a third of them are live-aboard, or too far for Teasdale to have reached before the search started—well, that still gives him a lot of places where he could have climbed on board and waited out last night's search. He finds a change of clothes on one of them, sits tight until morning, mingles with the charter fishermen and the pleasure boaters and the tourists. You get the picture."

"What's the next step?"

"Teasdale didn't strike me as the sharpest pencil in the box. Okay, he says he didn't kill DeBourche or the other abortionists. Whether we buy his story or not, he had to have help or he'd have been caught a long time ago."

"The Centurions?"

"Teasdale mentioned something Margot Mason said to him, about Jack Reagan sitting in Mason's parlor, pretending to be nice."

"So Teasdale talked to Mason after the two of you visited there."

"And then came looking for me," I said. "I want to talk to Margot Mason again. This time, without the media along."

I took the long route, circling the bay while I picked at the thoughts and musings that filled my mind.

U.S. 98 is the coastal highway on the mainland. It steps, awkwardly, across the waters of Spanish Pass before regaining its balance on Okaloosa Island, a barrier island that shields the mainland almost to Pensacola. For more than forty miles in either direction, the Pass is the only natural corridor between the estuary called Spanish Bay and the Gulf of Mexico. The protected anchorage it opens into is the reason the city called Spanish Bay was founded in the early 1800s.

At the apex of the state bridge that arches over Spanish Pass, an incautious driver can gaze seaward far into the distance— past the emerald waters that parallel the bands of white beaches, out to where the deep cobalt of the Gulf surrenders to the more complex tones of the horizon. It is truly mesmerizing, a view described by one local poet as not unlike staring into eternity.

But the most startling sight is still to come.

Near the foot of the bridge is a stretch of sprawling sugar-sand dunes, one of the few remaining relics of the barrier wall that for so many years stretched the length of the island.

They are striking, magnificent. Under the uncompromising orb of the Florida sun, these gleaming white dunes resemble nothing so much as snow-covered promontories, flanked by moguls and rippling drifts left in the wake of some wind-driven blizzard. Even in mid-summer, they give the sense that you have dropped into a wintry scene pulled wholesale from a Currier and Ives lithograph—that is, so long as you keep your car windows closed and your air-conditioning cranked to high.

Only a relative few of these gleaming white mini-Matterhorns survived Hurricane Opal, which registered a direct hit on Spanish Bay in the mid '90s. In the fury of that storm, the intricate sand castles that took nature decades to construct were consumed in a few terrifying hours. Since Opal, a series of near-misses by Ivan and Katrina and others among her seasonal brothers and sisters have mocked the expensive, federally funded programs to replenish the protective wall to even a shadow of its former grandeur.

But here, as wherever some meteorological fluke has spared

any, these impassive guardians stand tall and proud. Flecked with necklaces of ivy and stands of graceful sea oats, they gaze out over the Gulf waters as if they possess some secret knowledge—perhaps contemplating their own inevitable fate, or that of the mortals who mourn them in passing.

Soon I was in the backcountry, where the only mounds were the indistinct shapes of fallen-in cabins and barns, shrouded by their feral overgrowths of kudzu. I tried to find the poetry in it, also; but mostly, until I pulled into the dusty lot, I wondered if Bobby Teasdale had recently passed this way, too.

This time I bypassed the entrance to Harold 'n Nita's tap room, instead going directly to the rear stairway that led directly up to Mason's lodgings. It was still before ten in the morning, and I was in no mood to see what manner of patrons populated the bar at this hour.

I knocked on the door, hard enough to make the frosted glass panel rattle in its frame. Immediately, all hell erupted on the other side. It was an unlikely combination of howling alarm and mournful wail, punctuated by a shriek pitched high enough to shatter crystal. At the same instant, a frantic scratching came low on the frame.

I waited half a minute for the clamor to bring Margot Mason to the door, then knocked again. No response, and I cursed my decision not to call ahead.

Why I did it, I cannot say; perhaps it was frustration, or my need to react to the klaxon alarm that Missy was still sounding on the other side of the door. For whatever reason, as I half turned to leave my hand fell to shake the doorknob. It turned easily in my hand, and the door opened a crack. Immediately, the glistening jet-black tip of Missy's muzzle wedged into the opening, sniffing madly. I reached down, and gingerly eased the wet protuberance back inside.

But when I took my hand away, my fingertip was stained

with a faint rusty smudge.

Without thinking, I spun out of line with the door, flattening myself against the brickwork alongside the jamb.

I pushed my jacket aside, unsnapped the thumbbreak of my holster.

"Miss Mason, this is Lieutenant Quynn of the Spanish Bay police. Your door is not locked, Miss Mason. If you are inside, please respond."

There was no answer, no sounds from inside except for those Missy was making. That could mean nothing, or everything.

There were any number of possible reasons Missy might have blood on her muzzle, I told myself. She could have climbed onto a counter, drawn by the pot roast Mason was thawing for dinner. She could have ambushed an itinerant Bible salesman, caught a trespassing rodent. I had heard that Mini-Pins were a highly intelligent breed; she may have injured herself while opening a can of Alpo. As for the lack of response from inside, Mason might merely be a heavy sleeper. Even more likely, she might not be at home at all.

There were many reasons for me to ponder the advisability of entering, pistol drawn, the office abode of a woman who headed a group of fanatics who spent their weekends firing Mini-14s and Chinese AKs. I had no desire to be misunderstood by anyone who might be inside.

But if a mistake was to be made, I wanted it to tilt in my favor. I eased my Smith & Wesson from its holster and thumbed the safety up into firing position. Then I cleared my throat, suddenly dry and tight.

"I have reason to believe that you may be injured, Miss Mason. I'm coming inside now."

And then I pushed through the door before I—or anyone inside who might be drawing a bead on the doorway—could reconsider.

I entered in a low shooter's crouch, arms extended, sweeping the foyer and hallway. It was intended as serious business, but Missy—after an instant where my abrupt entrance had startled her almost to flight—took it as an invitation to play. She bounced around me almost to the height of my nose, yipping in what I took for delight, her stump of a tail wagging wildly to and fro.

That is how we searched Mason's abode, a ludicrous room-to-room parade that was equal measures of stealthy caution and a yapping announcement of our approach to anyone who might have been there.

But no one was.

Instead, what I found was the jumbled debris that had been the hardware behind the Centurions' Internet presence. The entire wall unit had been tumbled to the floor and the equipment it held smashed, with a methodical intent that ensured complete destruction. The winking lights and LED displays I had seen on my previous visit were dead, extinguished.

Across the room, something else caught my eye; at the edge of a faded throw rug, the hardwood slats of the floor seemed asymmetrical, the parallel lines somehow askew.

I edged nearer for a closer look. One of the floorboards carried the marks of a tool, perhaps the blade of a folding knife, that had been used to pry open what I was certain was a hiding space below. I left it for now and continued my room-by-room search, still accompanied by my canine partner.

In other rooms I found brochures protesting abortion-on-demand, placards calling for reversal of *Roe v. Wade,* and a collection of political and religious books and pamphlets that would have done a small library proud.

But of Margot Mason I found no sign, unless you count what I encountered when Missy and I entered the small kitchen. There I found two dark-red smears on the wall next to the back door. They were long tracks, starting at shoulder height and running almost to the floor.

Missy was strangely subdued now, and her earlier frolic had faded to small, fretful sounds. She stayed behind me as I edged around the counter to read whatever the stained wall might reveal.

It was then that I stopped abruptly, for I had almost stepped into a thickening pool of red that spread wide across the kitchen floor. Undersized paw prints dappled its surface, but it was something else that drew my eye.

On the margin of the pool nearest the door, a single shoe print was preserved in the congealed blood. Even at a distance, I recognized the odd, flat pattern of zigzagging lines, machine-razored into the soft rubber sole.

It was made by a boat shoe, the kind of footwear I had most recently seen on the feet of Bobby Teasdale.

CHAPTER 17

Officially, since Harold 'n Nita's was outside the municipal limits of Spanish Bay, it was a county case. Or would have been. But somebody at the Okaloosa County Sheriff's Department either read the newspapers or had been briefed thoroughly enough to contact the FBI, probably within minutes of my telephone report.

The first Sheriff's Deputies had scarcely arrived when, as if by a conjurer's trick, Howard Zhang-mei was standing at my shoulder.

He flashed his Justice Department credentials at the county detective whose questions I was fielding; then, with a hand on my elbow, he walked me out of the man's earshot and into the ravaged parlor. Already, evidence technicians were dusting and tagging and placing the ruined components into evidence bags. We stepped around the floorboard hiding space I had noted. It was now open, a yawing cavity that, on close examination, had proven itself empty.

"I've been kind of waiting for you to call," Zhang-mei said, affably enough.

"Nothing to tell you," I said.

He grinned. "Of course not. You've been shot at, held hostage, and stumble into what looks like a scene from *Texas Chainsaw Massacre* at the office of a woman who may have set a killer on your tail. The woman—or her body, more likely—is missing. So is the most plausible suspect, who happens to be Mr. Teasdale, your erstwhile abductor. Did I mention he's already wanted for murder and sundry other terrorist acts? I'm willing to bet we're going to find his prints all over this place."

Zhang-mei arched his eyebrows, waiting.

"You wanted information on the bombing of an abortion clinic, Mr. Zhang-mei," I said. "You wanted to know if Maddie Shepard's situation was somehow connected to it. I don't have any answers to those questions—not yet."

"Fair enough," Zhang-mei said. He looked around the room and sighed. "Since I think there's an obvious connection, I'm going to have to declare this under Federal jurisdiction. So I'll settle for what you can tell me about the involvement of Robert Matthew Teasdale in the . . . well, we'll call it the 'disappearance' of M. C. Mason. At least until we find the body."

"Aren't you getting ahead of yourself?"

"There's a lot of blood in there," Zhang-mei noted.

He had a point. Margot Mason had not been a large woman, and the volume of blood that was coagulating in her kitchen indicated wounds that could easily be life threatening. Neither could I fault Zhang-mei's logic as to the most plausible suspect. Even if I had not noted Teasdale's preference in footwear, the sheer weight of other circumstantial evidence would have made him a prime candidate for the deed.

But neither could I shake the sense that, in the past few days, little I had encountered was explicable by logic alone.

Zhang-mei seemed to read my mind, or perhaps my expression.

"Maybe Teasdale didn't do this," he said agreeably. "Could have been somebody from the pro-choice contingent, tired of having Mason post instructions on what doctor to murder next." He shrugged. "But it would make my life less stressful if Teasdale is our man."

"Do I sense a touch of bias, Mr. Zhang-mei?"

Zhang-mei chose not to respond; that, or he intended his lack of comment as the answer to a self-evident question.

I pressed harder. "What about Maddie Shepard? Is a girl having religious visions less of a political problem than a red-neck with a hunting rifle?"

Zhang-mei shrugged again. "I'm not ashamed to admit I overreacted there, Quynn. As it turns out, all the publicity about her 'visions' seems to have defused any political fallout she might have caused."

I frowned. "Exactly how do you figure that?"

"She's become the stuff of trash TV and supermarket tabloids. The girl's not much more than a mildly interesting sideshow now. Anything she might have to say has the general credibility of an Elvis sighting, unless you live in a trailer park." He waved a hand dismissively. "Ms. Shepard's a distraction, and that's something I don't need to concern myself with now. With Teasdale out in the open, I can draw a pretty solid line between the Centurions and the clinic bombing."

"About Teasdale—do you have any real evidence, Mr. Zhang-mei? Aside from what you've heard on TV or read in the news-paper, I mean."

"I have his military record, Quynn, which says he was a pretty good shot. So good, he was recommended for the Army's sniper school. He would have been sent there, too, if he hadn't been caught trying to stick up a convenience store just outside the base. He's a screwup, and a mean little piece of work. I have a copy of his dishonorable discharge after he went AWOL. I have subsequent police reports, witness statements, the case file from a woman's sniper death in North Carolina. I have pretty much the whole sorry record of Teasdale's stupid little life. How much more do you need, Lieutenant?"

When I did not answer, Zhang-mei smiled as if we were friends.

"Tell you what, Quynn. If it makes you happy, I'll have the records run again. We have a shooter who can blow a woman's head off at long distance. We have a guy who has some familiarity with explosives. Okay. To me, that all says ex-military. So I'll see if the computers can come up some candidates in addition to Mr. Teasdale who fit that bill. Will that satisfy you, Quynn?"

"I'll be satisfied when I know you've arrested the right man."

"Oh," he said, "don't worry about that, Lieutenant. One way or another, we'll get by. We usually do, you know."

The standing security at the Shepard residence had been beefed up considerably since the previous day's revelry. Now I had almost a dozen Spanish Bay uniformed officers assigned to me, and Tito had increased his company's contingent to at least twice that number.

It was still early for too much of a crowd; only a token force stood sentinel at the driveway entrance. Most of those tasked to guard Maddie Shepard had found a shady place to sip soft drinks and watch while others labored in the heat.

When I arrived, I saw Jesús Castile talking to a man in hard hat and overalls, both of them studying a clipboard Castile held. Nearby, a truck-mounted crane was positioning additional concrete Jersey barriers on the sidewalk and into the right-of-way, creating a series of maze-like corridors and cul-de-sacs. Then Castile saw me and crossed the street to my car.

"The latest in crowd-control strategy," Jesús Castile explained. "Supposed to channel the crowd, make it harder for 'em to get at each other, in case of trouble." He shook his head, doubtful. "It'll probably just give 'em someplace to take cover, if your people have to start shooting rubber bullets."

"Tito around, Jesús? His wife says he's out here somewhere."

"Checking the rear of the property. Want I should get him on the radio?"

I waited while Castile keyed his handheld unit. He spoke in an undertone to the microphone clipped on his forest-green shirt. It was only late morning, but already two darker patches had begun to spread under his arms. The humid air shimmered as it rose from the sun-heated pavement.

While I waited, I surveyed what I could see of the Shepard residence. There was no sign of activity, at least none visible from the outside. Maddie's appearance yesterday may well have quelled a nascent riot, but it also had sparked a furious media feeding frenzy. My guess was that neither Roger Shepard nor Sister Benedicta would chance another encounter.

Tito appeared at my window. He looked as he always did on the job: as if he had just heard bad news and anticipated that worse was on the way. He bent to speak, then peered past me.

"Who's your little friend?" he said.

Missy looked up at him, then back to me, her stub-tail a tentative semaphore.

"Mason's lapdog," I said. "The crime-scene techs thought she had walked through the evidence once too often. It was me or the county animal shelter."

"I've been on that tub of yours. Probably kinder to send her to the pound. They find Mason's body yet?"

"Still listed as 'missing,' " I said. "Zhang-mei took over the case, turned it Federal. He likes Teasdale for it, as well as for the bombing and the DeBourche murder."

Tito studied my face closely.

"But you don't," he said, not as a question.

"I swung by my office after I left Zhang-mei at Mason's place," I said. "I've spent the past hour taking another look at the case file from the first shooting, the one three years ago in North Carolina. The only physical evidence linking Teasdale to it was a partial print, on an ejected cartridge casing."

"We've gone to the mat with less than that, Quynn. What's

the problem?"

"Susan DeBourche was killed with the same rifle. On that point ballistics have a lock."

Tito was silent for a moment. "Huh. On the run for three years, all over the country. And he still had the *same* rifle? That's pretty hinky, even for a dumbshit like Teasdale."

"There's a lot of people trying to turn Bobby Teasdale into a one-man crime wave," I agreed. "He fits as a suspect in the shooting, but only if you work overtime on *making* him fit. Factor out the print in North Carolina, and everything else linking him is conjecture or circumstantial. Same with the clinic bombing. Mostly, he only looks good because of the quotes he gave to Mason's Web site. And Teasdale told me that was mainly an act to scare the abortionists and their staffs."

"What does Zhang-mei say?"

"He says Teasdale solves all his problems."

"Doesn't solve how Maddie Shepard is connected."

"He's not all that interested anymore. Apparently, all she does is complicate his case."

"He's got that right."

"It's all a little too convenient, Tito. For everybody concerned. Except maybe Teasdale."

"Yeah, I saw the news at noon on TV. Now they have him painted as a master assassin, a real-live Davey Crocket with a sniper rifle."

I was surprised, and showed it. "That was fast. I only heard it this morning."

"Your friend Jack Reagan had the story. Said the Feds were pulling records on anybody who ever went through military sniper training, and Teasdale's name jumped out." He pulled a face. "Trust the media to get it wrong."

"The part about the record search is true," I said. "I heard Zhang-mei give the order." I frowned at his expression. "What?"

"Trained sniper, my ass," Tito snorted. "Look, when I was in the Corps back at Lejeune, I knew people who were Scout Snipers. Those guys are *serious* shooters, Quynn. You said this woman doctor was shot at from—what? Three hundred yards?"

"About that, from where we have the shooter sited," I said.

"Well, there you go," Tito said. "You got a guy trained by the military as a sniper, he thinks in terms of seven, eight hundred meters—hell, a *thousand*-meter shot. Look, those people are elite, specialists. Three hundred yards? With a scope, any halfway decent meat hunter could knock that down without breaking a sweat."

"What are you saying, Tito? You think this is some kind of dodo dance?"

"I'm just saying, they limit the search to trained shooters, somebody's making a dumbshit mistake." He shrugged, intending it to appear a careless dismissal of a stranger's problem. His eyes were hooded, but even though I could not fully read them, what I saw in them was neither cynicism nor indifference.

"So, what's the big plan now?" Tito said. "Assuming there *is* one, I mean."

"I'll let you know," I said, "when somebody tells me."

After a moment, I gestured at the activity around us. "How are we set for today's mob action?"

"We're just peachy, now that you're here with your killer canine." He wiped the perspiration from his face. "Seriously? I don't know, Quynn. We got more troops out here now, between your people and mine. Those damn concrete barricades might do something, I guess. But if we get a shit load of pissed-off idiots going at each other for God or country or some other damn thing, it's a crapshoot, far as crowd control goes."

"What's your best guess, if we have more trouble?"

Tito shrugged, but not carelessly.

173

"Even money that we can keep 'em from hurting each other. Or us."

As it turned out, all of Tito's concerns and preparations were wasted effort. Nature intervened, in the guise of a phenomenon typical for Spanish Bay in mid-summer; it was unusual only in the intensity with which it visited us this day.

At two-forty, only a handful of people were on the sidewalk, most of them more curious than contentious. But then, what had started an hour earlier as an ineffective breeze began to rise, pulling and tugging at the palm fronds over our heads. The skies were still clear to the south, over the Gulf, but overhead the wispy clouds of morning had given way to towering cumulus formations that boiled ever higher, until they brushed the stratosphere. There, high-altitude gales tore their tops flat, forming a classic anvil configuration. Chain lightning pulsed blue-white inside the darkening mass, like a strobe behind lace curtains.

On the ground, I felt the sudden deep stillness that precedes the tempest. Then the trees began to sway again, this time with an urgency that felt like they were spreading the alarm. Even as I watched, the light died, collapsing in on itself until nothing remained but a shadowless, ominous cast. A sudden wash of air that felt cold by comparison swept fallen leaves from the gutter, and pinned them hard against the Jersey barricades before releasing them to spin off into the troubled air.

"We may be in for some luck," I said to Tito, as the first drops began to fall fat and heavy from a charcoal sky.

In less than a minute, the full force of the squall line was upon us. Torrents of water filled the air—not falling, but driven sideways as if from an overpressured fire hose. Bright flashes crackled low overhead, followed almost without pause by the chest-rattling concussion of thunder.

174

The storm's fury washed the street clean of all human interlopers, irregardless of their politics or theologies. It also sent those of us assigned as sentinels into retreat, for the most part chasing us into squad cars or personal vehicles. Only a few, the foolhardy or the stubborn, took shelter in the lee of the stonework portals that flanked the driveway.

There, soaked to the skin and our hair plastered flat, Tito and I grinned at each other. It felt as if we had been granted a reprieve, a last-minute pardon that was neither expected nor merited. Missy, equally wet, squirmed and lapped and shivered in mad excitement from the crook of my arm.

Then Tito looked past me, and when I turned I saw the white van inching its way down the street, through the maze of barricades. Its headlights were swallowed in the downpour, against which the windshield wipers flailed ineffectively.

"Company's calling," he said, and looked at me sidelong. "Maybe you better handle this one."

By then, I had already seen the lettering on the vehicle. As the van drew to a stop opposite the gate, I stepped into the full force of the storm and rapped hard against the passenger window. In response, it cranked down partway.

"What's this about?" I demanded, as the wind-driven rain pelted me like small lead shot. "Why are you here?"

"Hello to you, too, Quynn," Jack Reagan said. "I have an appointment in the house. I'm going to interview Maddie Shepard."

CHAPTER 18

Compared to the darkness we had just escaped, it was almost preternaturally bright inside the Shepard residence. Every lamp and fixture was lit, as if the intensity alone could form a bulwark against the tempest that raged outside.

Sister Benedicta had admitted us, her face showing no apparent reaction to Jack's video crew or the equipment it carried. I buried my face in the thick towel I had been handed. The towel felt warm, as if it had just been taken from a clothes dryer. But it might have been only the contrast. In my waterlogged clothes, the chill exhalation of the house's central air had raised goosepimples on my flesh even before the door closed behind me. The fact that my rain-soaked blouse had turned virtually transparent did little to increase my comfort level.

As I blotted my dripping hair, I glanced at the nun. One of her arms was close across her chest, and with her free hand she was vigorously rubbing and massaging another bath towel. A small black nose burrowed from its folds, sniffing furiously. Then two eyes emerged, blinking, and Missy craned her neck to peer up at her benefactor.

"Careful, Sister," Tito said from beside me. "Treat that beast too good, you'll have a new recruit following you back to the convent. And I don't know if she's even Catholic."

"Mr. Shepard will be down shortly," the nun said. "If you don't mind, I'll find something for your dog to eat."

Missy either understood English passably well, or was possessed of psychic abilities. As if on cue, she squirmed in delight in the nun's embrace.

"Don't go to any trouble, Sister," I said, but she was already heading down the hall. I could hear the nun talking softly to the animal as the door to what I assumed was the kitchen closed behind her.

A few paces from us, Jack Reagan was engaged in low conversation with his video crew. He had the full complement with him for this visit. In addition to the camera operator and sound engineer, a man in faded dungarees and a Black Sabbath T-shirt was assembling lengths of tubing into light stands; at Jack's elbow, a thin-faced woman I assumed was a producer held a clipboard on which she scribbled furiously.

The windows lit up for an instant, and thunder rattled the glass in its frame. Simultaneously, the lights flickered throughout the residence.

"What happens if we lose power?" Clipboard Woman asked Tube Man.

He screwed up his face. "We can go on battery, just light with the mini-floods if we have to." He thought for a moment, then grinned. "What the hell, might just give us that *Blair Witch* look. Record some ambient audio from the storm outside, frame a shot showing the lightning through the window, whatever. Could even be cool."

I took Jack by the upper arm, walked him a few paces from the assembly.

"Are you sure you want to do this, Jack?"

He pulled his arm from my grasp and looked squarely into my eyes.

"I don't know what you mean, Lieutenant."

We were back to using formalities. I noted the fact, but did not comment.

"Don't put that girl on camera. Don't make her the star in a geek show."

"I talked to the father. He doesn't feel that way."

I was taken aback; I had not envisioned Roger Shepard in quite that light.

"How? What could you say that would convince him this is a good idea?"

"Ask him. Perhaps Shepard understands how important this is, how many people Maddie's experience has touched, deeply and profoundly."

I opened my mouth, but swallowed the words I had been about to say.

"Mr. Reagan. Jack. You know this is wrong."

"I'm sorry you think so," he said, his voice level. "If you'll excuse me, I have work to do."

Jack walked back to his crew, and all I could do was stare after him.

"Trouble in paradise, Quynn?" Tito rubbed the towel vigorously, and when he took it away his hair was spiky and disheveled. But his expression lost its humor when I told him what Jack Reagan had said.

"What about the nun?" he said. "Maybe she can talk this dumbshit out of letting the world see his daughter as a brain-meltdown."

"I don't know, Tito. I don't see Benedicta allowing this. But I didn't think the father would buy into it, either."

"I can't figure the man out," Tito said. "Every time you look at him, something different is in there looking back. Guy operates with his own rules, on his own schedule and—oh, *crap.*"

"What?"

He glanced at his wristwatch and scowled.

"Almost ten after three, Quynn."

The meaning of Tito's words escaped me for a moment. Then I realized the import of what he had said.

Tito read my expression and nodded dourly.

"Yeah," he said. "Unless somebody's taking a celestial rain day up there, little Maddie's scheduled for her afternoon playgroup-from-heaven in less than an hour. Except this time it's gonna be on TV."

Officially, I suppose, it was Tito's job to stop me.

He had a contract with Roger Shepard to provide security for house and grounds, and to ensure that only those with an expressed invitation were allowed anywhere on the Shepard property. In the absence of any legally enforceable writ or warrant, I had no special privileges here; certainly, I possessed nothing that could be interpreted as permission to search out Shepard in his own house.

But there are times when such formalities are irrelevant.

I found Shepard on the second floor, just as he was closing the door to what appeared to be a bedroom. I caught a brief glimpse of a framed Zak Efron poster against floral wallpaper before he pulled the door shut.

"What's your business up here, Lieutenant Quynn? I assume you have a reason for wandering through my home. If not, wait downstairs."

He started down the hall toward the staircase, then pivoted to return to where I stood, unmoving.

"Okay, you are starting to seriously piss me off, Lieutenant."

I tried to look apologetic, or at minimum reasonable. If the darkening expression on Shepard's face was an indication, I failed utterly.

"There's a television crew waiting in your front hallway, Mr. Shepard. I wanted a chance to talk to you and Sister Benedicta before things were too far along to stop."

"The good Sister has nothing to say about this. See, Lieutenant, she also seems to think that I don't know what's right for my daughter and myself."

"Mr. Shepard, I'm trying to say . . . you don't want to do this, sir. You don't want to let these people use your daughter for their own purposes."

"If you believe that I'm enjoying any of this, you're sadly mistaken."

"Tell them you've changed your mind."

Roger Shepard glowered at me.

"Lieutenant, I've changed my mind about this a dozen times in the past six hours, okay? But there are people out there who have decided that there's something miraculous about these delusions Maddie is suffering. They're drawing the fanatics from the other side, and now they're determined to kill each other in front of my house."

"Putting her on television is throwing gasoline on the fire."

"They need to see that my daughter is ill," Shepard said hotly. "They have to know that she is only a teenaged girl who needs psychiatric help, not some latter-day Joan of Arc. She has no messages for them from God, or God's mother, or anyone else. She's *sick,* Lieutenant. If they can see that with their own eyes, maybe they'll stop this nonsense and leave us alone."

"Mr. Shepard, right now the television people are downstairs, debating ways to make their videotape look like a horror movie. How is that going to help end Maddie's problems?"

Shepard's voice was stubborn. "Mr. Reagan assures me he won't sensationalize this. I have his promise on that."

I threw up my hands in frustration.

"These people are not your friends, or Maddie's," I insisted. "They have their own agenda, sir. You'd better realize that, before you do something you will surely regret."

"There's nothing about this damn mess I don't already regret," Shepard said, and shook his head. "You think you're helping, Lieutenant. You're not. This has to be done."

"Then at least do this, Mr. Shepard. Before you let the TV crew in there, let me see Maddie. A few minutes, just the two of us talking."

He frowned. "To what end, Lieutenant?"

"Call it insurance. If the television people decide to portray her as something she is not, I can say that I interviewed her just before they did. I can talk to other reporters. They will quote what I have to say; I guarantee it."

Shepard glanced at the closed door, then back to me.

"If I agree to this, I'd have to be present."

I shook my head firmly.

"If you're in there, they could say that you influenced what Maddie says to me. Alone, I'm an independent witness to her mental state." I heard my voice soften, become sincere and earnest; I wondered just how different I was from Jack Reagan and his peers. "What do you lose by doing this my way, Mr. Shepard?"

I saw the indecision in his eyes; I could only guess at the doubts, and even suspicions, that fueled his hesitation. For a moment, I was certain he would refuse my request, and waited for him to order me from his house.

Then he spoke, as if he had lost a debate with himself.

"You can have five minutes with Maddie, Lieutenant. I'm trusting you not to do her any more harm."

I knocked once, and waited until a voice inside answered. Then I opened the door and stepped in.

I could hear the wind and rain outside, a million insistent fingers flailing and rattling and probing against the windowpane, trying to find a fingerhold to use to their advantage. The curtain was drawn, and the window shade, too, but neither were proof against the pulsating incandescence of each thunderbolt that lasered, white-hot, through the pandemonium of air and water outside.

A slight figure sat up in the bed, a bright yellow comforter pulled up to her waist. She wore a different T-shirt today, this one emblazoned with a British ensign made up of colored rhinestones. Other than that, if you discounted the fact that she no longer appeared dazed and disoriented, Maddie Shepard looked little changed from the girl whose appearance quelled a riot the prior afternoon.

On the bedside table, I noticed a small tray with a glass half filled with cola, and a small plate littered with fragments of what looked like crackers. A miniature pleated paper cup, the kind hospitals use to distribute meds to their patients, lay casually crumpled alongside. A flat-screen iMac commanded an otherwise cleared desktop, but the clutter was across the room, on and around a graphic artists' table. There, a T-square clung to the slanted top, near a multitiered plastic rack that held a variety of X-acto knives and standing ranks of illustrator's pens in a full rainbow of colors. Sheets of paper, covered with a flowing abstract geometry, were corner-taped to the propped surface; others lay, balled and discarded, on the floor.

Aside from the obligatory teen-heartthrob poster, the hanging artwork was mainly home-done: the largest was on the wall opposite the bed, an intricate collage of news articles and photos carefully razor-trimmed into irregular shapes. These elements dueled with various other glued-on items of cryptic significance: an empty matchbook, its cover folded back; what looked like a pencil stub, splintered at its midpoint; a single plastic high-heeled pump that might have fit a Barbie doll. But centered in the artwork was an old-fashion skeleton key, itself entangled in a spider web of tangled and knotted string that stretched corner-to-corner.

Something glittered behind the web, and I leaned closer. My

own eye stared back at me from the fragment of mirror artfully concealed behind the radiating strands. The effect was somehow unsettling, as if I had a glimpse of some formless intimacy seen through a door intentionally left slightly ajar.

From the bed, the artist was watching me closely as I straightened.

"Hello, Maddie. I'm Lieutenant Quynn. I'm with the police."

"Hello." It was a small voice, but I could detect no wariness in it. I selected a chair from several pushed against the far wall and dragged it closer to her bedside.

"Quite a storm outside." I smiled. "I got pretty soaked."

Maddie nodded, but did not reply.

Now that I was here, I found myself ill at ease. I felt as if I had forced my way into a private sanctuary, one where my presence was both inappropriate and intrusive. There was much I wanted to know, but in my discomfort I was unable to frame even the most simple of questions.

Instead, I looked around the room as if admiring the decor, while Maddie waited, her eyes steady on my face.

On the dresser, a sky-blue cellular telephone stood at attention in its charger. The green LED on its keypad blinked like a distant navigational buoy, slow but regular.

"That has to be handy," I said, awkwardly. "I mean, to keep in touch with your friends."

"I guess," Maddie said. "Mostly, I'm supposed to check in with Dad when I'm out. He worries."

"I talked to your friend Wendy. She said you had just talked with your father when all this happened to you the first time."

"I guess. I don't remember."

"Does that happen every time? Not remembering, I mean. You know, when you have your visions."

Maddie hesitated, then spoke. "Do you have something with your name on it? Something I could see?"

I fished one of my cards from my wallet; it was damp, like the rest of the contents. I held it out to the girl, who took it and studied it for a moment.

Then her eyes rose to my face, her brows knitted as if in concentration. "I'm sorry. What did you say?"

"I asked how it feels when you have one of your visions."

Maddie shook her head slightly, but not as if in dissent. "It's . . . it's like I kind of go away for a while."

She frowned, the first time her expression had changed since I arrived. "No, that's not it, either. There are . . . patches. It jumps around, like a movie. I remember being someplace, then all of a sudden I'm someplace else."

She looked at me, a strangely intent expression on her face. "Does that make sense?"

"Do you remember going outside yesterday?"

She colored and shook her head.

"What about the messages?"

"They said I say things. My dad, and Sister Benedicta. That I describe Mary, and she talks to me and stuff."

"But you don't remember. Not any of it?"

Again, she shook her head.

"Did you talk about it to your Dad?"

"No," she said quickly. "I mean, he doesn't want . . . I . . . I don't want to."

"How about with Sister Benedicta?"

She shrugged slightly. "I guess. She's a nice person. She tells me about when she was in Africa. Stuff like that. And she likes to look at my artwork. She thinks I could make a living as an artist someday."

I nodded, but I was already thinking of how to word my next sentence.

"Maddie," I began, then took a deep breath. "Maddie, this is pretty important. I need to know about your hands."

She stiffened, and thrust both of her bandaged hands beneath the comforter, out of sight.

Had I been under oath and pressed by a particularly persistent interrogator, I would have said the response appeared involuntary—a fight-or-flight reaction that was outside the girl's conscious control. But that was only an opinion; it left unanswered any question as to its significance, or even its relevance.

"Maddie?"

"They keep bleeding," she said, her voice barely above a whisper.

"Do you know why?"

She shook her head.

"Do you think I could see them?"

"Why?"

I shrugged, hoping the gesture looked more casual than it felt.

"I'm a police officer. I've seen a lot of injuries in my time. Sometimes you can tell something about a wound just by looking at it."

"I don't want to take off the bandage."

"I know. But I wouldn't ask if I didn't think I had to."

For several seconds she did not move or react. Then, slowly, she took her hands from beneath the comforter. Without looking at me, Maddie peeled the strip of adhesive tape that secured her bandage. She pulled the gauze away in a straight line, and we both watched it unravel from her left hand until it fell away onto the bed. Twin padded squares of the same material, one on either side of her palm and both punctuated with a single brown-red dot, stuck fast to her hand like limpets.

Maddie held her arm out to me, as if offering to shake hands. I cupped her fingers and turned her palm up. As gently as I could, I peeled back the gauze pad.

I do not know what I had expected, or wanted. I may have been looking for justification, though whether of my skepticism or my conviction, I could not say. Maybe I hoped for a miraculous healing, to find Maddie's flesh whole and unmarked by any penetration, whether temporal or divine. At the moment I unveiled Maddie's palm, I truly did not know my own mind.

But whatever I had been hoping to see, it must not have been there. The disappointment I felt, so strong that it left me shaken, told me that.

Some of it must have shown in my face.

"What do you see?" Maddie asked. "Is something wrong?"

I made a show of turning her hand over, judiciously examining both sides.

"I'm not impressed," I said, making my voice mock-solemn. "I was hoping they'd look *really* gross."

I was rewarded with a tentative smile.

"It looks like the scab is broken, but I'd say you're healing nicely. Does it hurt?"

"Not much," Maddie offered. "Not anymore."

I replaced the pads and rewound the gauze around her hand. I kept my eyes on the task, but I knew Maddie was watching my face as I worked.

"All set," I said, and Maddie immediately slipped her hands back under the comforter. We sat like that for a moment, then I spoke.

"What do you think caused your cuts, Maddie?"

She did not respond.

"I talked to the doctor at the Emergency Room. Remember Dr. Shenker? He thought maybe you might have injured yourself. Could that have happened, Maddie?"

The girl still looked at my face, but not as if she was seeing me. It was somehow unnerving, but I plowed on.

"You're not in any trouble, Maddie. Things happen, and

sometimes they go farther than anybody expected."

There was no reply, and little change in her countenance; if anything, it looked even more intent and fixed than before. I put on my most understanding expression, and reached forward to pat the hand still concealed beneath the yellow fabric.

"Do you want to tell me anything, Maddie? Anything at—"

I stopped, suddenly aware that Maddie was no longer listening.

At least, not to me.

Maddie's lips began to move, a soundless conversation in which I played no part. Her eyes were open, wide and unblinking, and a cold pallor spread over her face. I rose, and bent close. The girl's pupils were broad black dots rimmed with only a hint of blue iris. She was still sitting upright, as if frozen, but when I pressed my fingertips against her throat, her pulse felt like a struggling, frightened bird.

I straightened at the same instant the door flew open, and the bedroom exploded in a harsh blue-white light. Before I could react, a hulking form had already rushed forward, holding a bright-burning row of three suns in his extended hands. He was followed by a second figure whose humped left shoulder looked, in silhouette, like a second head.

"Go tight, go tight! Frame on her face, Frankie!" I recognized Clipboard Woman's voice. "Don't lose this, dammit! Do we have audio?"

Vivid black shadows danced crazily around the room as the lighting technician adjusted his position, closer to Maddie's bed. I was bumped, hard enough so that I stumbled off-balance several steps to the wall, as the man with the videocam on his shoulder pushed past me.

Then Jack Reagan was there, moving as if he also had been pushed from behind. He pulled up beside the cameraman. For an instant he stood stiffly upright at Maddie's bedside, looking down as the girl's lips began to move even faster. Then, as if he had been prodded from off-camera, he abruptly bent and held the microphone close to Maddie's face.

"Who are you talking to, Maddie?" I heard Jack's voice say. "Can you tell us? What is she saying to you?"

I pushed away from the wall, only to be jostled again as Clipboard Woman pushed to the videographer's side. "Two-shot, Frankie," she hissed, an undertone in the room's clamor. "Get Reagan's face in the frame, too."

From the corner of my eye, I saw Roger Shepard framed in the open doorway. He looked as if he was in shock and unable to move. I pivoted back toward the bed, and the movement must have caught Jack's eye. His head turned, and we found ourselves looking into each other's face.

For an instant, there was no expression on his features. Then something changed in his eyes. Jack looked at the melee that swirled around him. He stared down at Maddie, or perhaps at the microphone that he still held close to the girl's lips.

As I watched, Jack seemed to shake himself, as if forcing himself to awaken from some dark dream. He straightened, and the hand holding the microphone fell to his side.

"Jack?" Clipboard Woman's voice was impatient, became insistent. "Jack!"

Then I heard Jack speak.

"No. I'm sorry. I can't do this."

He thrust the microphone into the hands of a startled Clipboard Woman.

Then Jack Reagan wheeled and pushed out of the room. In the sudden silence, I could hear his footsteps moving down the stairs.

For a moment, his video crew stared at the doorway or looked at each other, uncertain of what had just happened. Then another bolt of lightning crashed in the storm still raging outside, and it was as if the sound freed them from some spell.

"Keep rolling, Frankie," Clipboard Woman said, and shoved the microphone toward Maddie's bed.

"Turn it off or you'll be fishing that mike out of your ass," a new voice growled, and all eyes turned to Tito Schwartz.

Beside him, Roger Shepard broadcast equal measures of outrage and disbelief, very much the look of a man who had just realized he had been mugged.

"I got a press release for you jackals," Tito said, and it would have taken a foolhardy person to interrupt or object. "Mr. Shepard has had a change of heart. He's withdrawing his invitation, revoking his permission, whatever the fuck. In short, you have ten seconds to get the hell out of his house. I'll have that videotape, now."

"No fucking way," Clipboard Woman said. She turned to me. "We'll leave, but the tape is going with us. I know about him, and about you, too. This time, I'll sign the complaint personally. This ape *will* go to jail, and the network will sue him for his last cent."

"Yeah, I'm pretty scared," Tito said, and stepped toward the man holding the camera. I moved forward, between the two.

"What the hell are you doing?" Tito hissed in my ear.

"I don't like it, either," I said quietly. "But this won't help, Tito."

"Fuck that. It's my ass, Quynn."

I have no inkling what would have happened next, had Roger Shepard not made the whole question moot.

"Let them keep the damn tape," Roger Shepard said. "I just want them gone."

Tito stared at him; my own face probably looked as astonished.

"You heard the man," Tito said after a moment. "Score one for the sleazebags, I suppose."

"It's called the First Amendment, asshole," Clipboard Woman said. "The people have a right to the truth."

"If they ever get any," Tito said, "you geeks better find a deep hole to hide in."

CHAPTER 19

Roger Shepard eased his daughter back onto her pillow, pulling the yellow comforter up to her shoulders. Maddie's eyes had closed to slits and her lips had stopped their movement, but even in repose she still looked stiff and unnatural. Unbidden, an image of the girl flitted across my mind's eye: Maddie, locked in solitary confinement within a soundproofed room, unable even to pound on the walls to summon help.

After a few moments, Shepard ushered me into the hallway outside Maddie's room.

"You were right," he said. "I should have listened."

"Should I bring Sister Benedicta up here?"

"There's no need. Maddie will go to sleep soon." He shook his head, as if to clear from it a disquieting image. "She'll wake up in a few hours as if nothing had happened. At least she won't remember the way those vultures just . . . *came* at her."

"Is she like that each time?" I asked Shepard. "When she has these spells, I mean."

He did not answer immediately. I was not certain he would respond at all, and wondered if I had entered an area that Roger Shepard found too painful, or perhaps even too intimate, to reveal.

"This time her lips just moved," he said finally. "Usually, you can understand at least part of what Maddie is saying. The first so-called 'message,' all I could hear was something about babies, baby-killers. Everything else was just . . . noise. At least to me."

"The first time. That was the message the Centurions put on the Internet?"

Shepard nodded, his lips a tight line. "Those bastards."

"The Centurion's Web site was pretty specific about what Maddie said."

"Then their source heard a helluva lot more than I did." He blew out a breath, hard. "Look, Lieutenant Quynn. I've gone round and round with Sister Benedicta about this. There were two of us in with Maddie—Sister Benedicta and me. Sister Benedicta, she's a nun and a doctor. She claims she didn't say anything to anybody about . . . what Maddie said."

"You don't believe her, Mr. Shepard?"

"Somebody had to let it out."

"Could Maddie have done it?"

Shepard's expression was as if I had slapped him. "Are you insane? My daughter could not have—"

"Maddie is Internet-savvy; you said that yourself. And she was the only other person present."

"No. For God's sake, you saw what she's like when . . . no." He appeared to shake himself, then spoke with a voice again firm. "The good Sister works for her Church. I know they have their own agenda, Lieutenant. Priests, nuns—they report to somebody higher up, and I don't just mean God."

"If you feel that way, I'm surprised that you still allow her access to your daughter."

"If there had been any more 'mysterious' leaks, her ass would have been bouncing down my sidewalk. I told her that, too. Look—whatever political game her Church is playing, I'm convinced that Sister Benedicta has the best of intentions for Maddie's health. She's tended to my daughter almost around the clock since she arrived, even brought in another doctor. He may be a priest, but he seems competent enough. They say they want to help us. I believe them."

"But?"

He clenched his fists. "But nothing's been right since all this began. I can't find a way to make it better. You just saw the result of my latest attempt. It was a complete debacle."

Shepard's voice faltered, and I saw the futility in his expression. "I may have to institutionalize my daughter, Lieutenant. Take her away from this . . . this disaster. She's not getting better here."

I tried to find words that might comfort him. I tried to imagine what I would do in similar circumstances, and found myself completely at sea.

"I'm sorry, Mr. Shepard. I wish I could help."

"Yes. So do I." He looked away, toward Maddie's door. "I'm going to sit with my daughter for a while. Alone, if nobody fucking minds."

I watched him enter, close the door behind him.

When I turned, I found Tito standing a few paces away, studying me as if I had grown an extra limb.

"I swept out the trash," he said after a moment. "Thought you'd want to know your boyfriend's gone, too."

"Big surprise there," I said. "I expect he'll turn up at six o'clock, on the news. Jack got everything he came for. Another juicy story to put on the air."

Tito shook his head. "That's what I'm telling you. The lady with the potty-mouth was still looking for Reagan when I threw 'em out. Seemed pretty pissed off when she couldn't find him. They drove away without him."

"Damn," I said. "He's probably looking for some more dirt to put on the news. I'll help you search the house."

"What do you think I've *been* doing? Reagan split, Quynn. I saw the look on his face when he walked out of the kid's room. Like he'd had a batch of bad clams."

"It wasn't pretty in there. I felt like vomiting, myself."

"So maybe Reagan just had his fill of being a news-whore." Tito shrugged, watching my face carefully. "I mean, hound."

As if from a distance, I heard another rolling crash of thunder; the windblown rain still pelted the windows without mercy.

"Could have happened," I said.

But it did not sound convincing, not even to me.

I found Sister Benedicta in the kitchen, seated on a stool at a tiled counter. Missy was there, too, standing on the ceramic surface and licking the nun's extended fingertips. Both of them looked up as I entered, but only Missy appeared glad to see me. She wagged her stump-tail in greeting, then turned back to the attentions of her new friend.

"I guess all the excitement is over, Sister," I said. "Mr. Schwartz escorted the television crew out." I tried a smile, but the nun seemed immune to charm—at least, any that I possessed. "He says they were short a newscaster. Did Mr. Reagan come through here?"

"No."

"He may have left on his own. Has Missy been behaving?"

"Yes." She rose, her face still stony. "If you'll excuse me, I—"

"Sister? Have I done something to offend you?"

"I don't understand you."

"I'm a detective, Sister Benedicta. When I arrived, you brought me a dry towel and offered to feed my dog. Everything seemed fairly cordial between us. But right now, I'm detecting a distinct lack of warmth from you. Did I grow horns in the past half hour?"

If the look she gave me was an indication, I may have.

"Mr. Shepard said you insisted on talking with Maddie," she said, in a voice intentionally devoid of inflection.

"There was a TV crew waiting to see her. I wanted to assess her condition first."

"You interrogated that child, didn't you?"

"We spoke. I asked some questions. Of course. Why is that a problem, Sister?"

"Exactly what did you expect to hear from her, Lieutenant? Did you wish to have her speak of cherubic choirs, of angels and Madonnas flitting about her room? Or perhaps you are a skeptic. Did you wish to prove that Maddie is playing some complicated game, attempting to perpetrate an elaborate hoax?"

"I don't know. Which do you think it is, Sister?"

My rejoinder appeared to catch her by surprise. But only for an instant.

"You've honed your interrogation skills on the wrong kind of people, Lieutenant. Do you think that you can turn my questions back on me, and avoid answering them yourself?"

"Not at all, Sister. I really don't know what is happening upstairs. I hope you can help me."

"Why should I?"

"So I can help Maddie."

Sister Benedicta did not answer.

"What medication is Maddie receiving, Sister?"

"What business is that of yours, Lieutenant?"

"Is there a reason I shouldn't know?"

"Aside from a patient's right to confidentiality, do you mean?"

"I saw Maddie's eyes, Sister. Just before she slipped into a fugue state."

Sister Benedicta frowned. "You're speaking in riddles."

"She may have been going into a religious trance. But it would help me to know what she is receiving. Tranquilizers? Narcotic drugs, or pharmaceutical hypnotics? Is somebody feeding Maddie drugs, Sister?"

"Certainly not!" she flared.

"I saw the paper cup on her tray."

"Then you saw the multiple-vitamin tablet I placed in it,

Lieutenant."

"That's all you give her?"

"She is no longer being administered the antibiotics that the emergency room clinic prescribed. That regimen ended two days ago. Maddie is receiving no prescription medications at this time. And if you have any additional questions about Maddie's treatment, please address them to her father. Or bring me a court order."

At that moment, Roger Shepard leaned into the kitchen from the hallway outside.

"Sister, go check on Maddie, when you—" He stopped abruptly.

He stood in the doorway, frowning.

"What in hell is *that* doing in here?" Shepard demanded. He glared at Missy, then at me, his face flushed and angry.

But his reaction was mild compared to the effect his arrival had on the animal.

Missy had stiffened, staring in Shepard's direction. Her nose twitched once, twice; then from her throat came a sound, low but with an intensity that could have come from a much larger animal.

Missy stood on the counter, front legs braced as if to attack. She looked like a diminutive Hound of Hell as she growled at Roger Shepard, her pointed ears laid flat and her teeth bared.

"Oh, for God's sake. Did you bring that dog in here, Lieutenant Quynn?"

"I'm sort of baby-sitting. I'm sorry. She's usually pretty docile. I think you may have startled her."

"I'd appreciate it if you took it the hell off my kitchen counter, Lieutenant. In case you didn't know, food is prepared there." He turned to the nun. "Sister, look in on Maddie, if you're finished talking about us to the police. She seems agitated, I think. Don't do anything that will make it worse, understand?"

Without a word or a backward glance at me, Sister Benedicta departed.

I scooped up Missy and tucked her under the arm farthest from Shepard. She made no attempt to snap at me, nor did she try to twist from my grasp. Her muscles were tensed rock-hard throughout her small body. With a fingertip, I lightly stroked the top of her head. I felt the tension ease slightly as she pushed closer into the side of my chest.

But she did not cease her soft snarls until Shepard left, heading back toward Maddie's room.

CHAPTER 20

The storm blew out shortly after nine, tumbling over itself until it was far into the Gulf. There, the lightning lost its anger and turned playful; flickering tongues of fire in the inky distance lent a carnival air to the fresh-washed night back on shore.

As I drove home to the marina, I passed the usual post-tempest debris: downed electrical lines, corkscrewed tin roof panels, fallen limbs and shredded palm fronds, the occasional stretch of street flooded hubcap-deep.

But Nature also offered compensation for her ill-mannered tantrum. She had scrubbed the air free of the sweetish wet-rot that is the nighttime norm along the coast. The fast-food wrappers, forehead-crushed cans, torn plastic beach balls and other spoor routinely abandoned by vacationers had been flushed from roadsides and gutters by her deluge.

I pulled into the parking lot behind Conquistador's Landing. Under the night-spot's expanse of thatched roof, a band on the open-air patio was mauling Marley's "Stir It Up." Storm or not, the place was packed with drinkers, dancers and the occasional late diner. I parked my rental car, giving a wide berth to the collegiate-looking throng near the dumpsters; one of them was vomiting heroically as an enthusiastic gender-mixed crowd of supporters cheered him on.

Missy allowed me to carry her down the plank stairs that led to the marina. When we reached the crushed-shell pathway below, I set her down on the sandy margin. She sniffed the ground dubiously, then glared up at me.

"It's your decision," I said. "But I'm not getting up to walk you at midnight. And you better be boat-broken, too."

Afterward, she trotted down the middle of the path a few paces in front of me, hesitating only briefly when we reached the wooden pier. Her toenails tap-danced on the planks, a pleasant counterpoint to the slap of wavelets against boat hulls.

Then we were at my houseboat. I had turned a cabin light on before I left, and it cast a soft white glow through the pilothouse window. Every surface was shiny with puddled rainwater. I was relieved to see that the craft was riding normally at its mooring. Had the shore power failed, I was not confident my antiquated batteries were up to the task of running the bilge pumps.

I stepped aboard, and a second later Missy landed lightly onto the deck beside me. She followed me aft, waiting patiently while I checked the docking lines and adjusted the fenders against the boat's rubrail.

"Does it have a name?"

I looked up, and Jack Reagan was standing on the pier. He made an impatient gesture with the hand not holding the plastic go-cup.

"Your boat," he said petulantly. "It should have a name."

I straightened and brushed my hands against my slacks.

"It should have a name," I agreed. "I've been too busy to think up a good one. Do you want to come aboard?"

Jack sipped at the cup and looked pensive. Then he nodded sagely.

"Sure. It's not like I have anyplace else to be."

He put a foot on the deck, and the boat dipped slightly. I was just able to catch him by the elbow.

"Oops." Jack smiled sweetly. "Almost spilled on you."

"Don't you have a newscast to do?"

"Nope. Taking a sabbatical. Called in, left 'em a message at the newsroom." His voice dropped to just above a whisper and took on a conspiratorial tone. "Had four . . . five? . . . drinks up there—" he waved the plastic cup in the direction of the Landing, where the patio music now had shifted into Jimmy Buffet mode "—and this one makes . . . four. Or six."

Jack pulled his upper arm from my grasp and walked unsteadily toward the sliding door of the salon. He tugged at the handle with energy, scowling when it refused to budge. Then he straightened, waiting with an unsteady dignity as I unlocked it for him. He swept into the salon, stopping in the middle of the room.

"You stink, Quynn," Jack informed me. "You stink like—" he halted, as if none of the various alternatives he was considering was sufficiently heinous to complete his simile.

Then he gave a small shrug, and some of whatever was in the plastic tumbler he held sloshed over the rim. Jack looked at it, surprised and then pleased, as if he had forgotten what he was holding. He lifted the drink to his lips and tilted his head back in a long draught.

Too far. Again, I barely caught him before he completed a back-flip. I propped him up under the arms, and took the drink from his hand at the same instant that his knees buckled. Had he been a larger man, we both would have tumbled to the deck.

Jack slumped against my shoulder, bonelessly, his head back. His face was so close that I could feel his soft exhalations on my own.

"Poor little girl," he said, slightly slurring the last word. "Jus' a goddamn shame . . . poor little kid . . ."

Then his eyes closed and his head lolled forward.

Missy looked up at the two of us, an uncertain expression on her face.

"I should hang out a sign," I told her. " 'Open all night. Strays and newsmen welcome.' "

With effort, I half dragged Jack into the stateroom and tipped him into my berth, on top of the light blanket under which I usually slept. I covered him with another from one of the lockers, and Missy immediately jumped into the bed, burrowing alongside my unconscious guest. I left to the sound of soft snoring, and quietly closed the door behind me.

Out on deck, I settled into one of the canvas chairs I kept there. The fabric was still damp, and so was I, but I was too exhausted to care. I propped my feet against a deck stanchion, closed my eyes and listened to the music from Conquistador's Landing mingle with the other sounds of the night.

In a few minutes, I was asleep.

I awoke with a start. By my watch, it was after four a.m. The full moon was just past directly overhead, the featured player in a sky flecked with other luminaries, great and small. Somewhere, a mullet leaped and splashed.

I flexed my shoulders to drive out the stiffness of chair-sleeping. I inhaled deeply, drinking in the cool freshness and salt tang, when I heard Jack's voice nearby.

"Do you ever take this thing out on the water?"

Jack was standing at the railing, leaning into it and looking out over the harbor. He had apparently rummaged through my locker, because he was wearing a terrycloth robe that I recognized as my own. The robe was belted tight and only slightly undersized on his form—unremarkable, had the cloth been any color other than faded pink. It should have looked ludicrous, but I found the effect somehow endearing. For some perverse reason, this also made it appear far more appealing on him than it should have.

Jack's hair was damp, and I assumed that he had made use of my shower, too. I could not detect any ill effects from his earlier activities, except perhaps for the almost unnatural stillness of his posture and attitude.

"Sometimes," I answered. "The diesel has a few problems. I'm still working on them."

He whistled softly. "You're a mechanic, too?"

"When Pop and I moved down from Chicago, his first job here was on a shrimp boat. The owner let us live aboard for a while, in exchange for keeping everything shipshape. Grow up around boats, you kind of pick things up."

He nodded, as if I had verbalized some sage insight.

"But your boat will run?"

"Most of the time. No guarantee it will get you back."

"Getting back may not be my top priority, Quynn. Or may I call you Aria?"

"You'd be the only one who does. Or has, for a long, long time."

The comment brought a thin smile to Jack's lips. "Aria Quynn. That's an interesting combination. Aria means 'song,' doesn't it?"

"My grandmother's name was Aria Leonetti, second-generation Italian. My mother said she always wanted a namesake. When I was born, my parents fought over it. Dad tried to hold out for an Irish name. Mom won, more or less."

"Aria's a pretty name."

"Sure. Made my life tougher, though."

Jack arched his eyebrows in polite inquiry. "Sounds like there's a story there."

"Not really. I grew up in an Irish neighborhood in Chicago, South Side. All the girls were named Mary Kate, Mary Pat, Mary Margaret. Kids there, they kind of took my first name as an insult to St. Patrick. It took a lot of fistfights to convince them otherwise."

"And so you became Quynn. Just-plain-Quynn."

"That took longer. Around the neighborhood, most people

called me 'Little Quynn.' Lasted until I was twelve."

"Then what happened?"

"I got big. That came with a brand-new set of problems."

He grinned. "I'll bet."

"By then, my mother had died, and I had to figure out things sort of on my own. Anyway, when I turned thirteen Pop moved us down here."

Jack took a moment to consider that. Then he turned and folded his arms.

"So how about it, Quynn? How would you like to take me on a boat ride? A *long* boat ride."

"Maybe. Where do you want to go, Jack?"

"I don't know. Anywhere. How about some place where people don't point at me on the street. Pick a place where nobody watches television."

"What happened this afternoon, in Maddie's room?"

He shrugged. "It's hard to have to admit that you've become a bottom-feeder. It can ruin your whole day, you know?"

"Maybe you made the right decision. For what it's worth, I think you did."

Jack's lips did not quite smile. "You don't understand how it is in broadcast journalism, Quynn. There aren't a lot of second chances."

"I don't believe that, Jack. Not for someone with talent like yours."

"Talent," he repeated. "That's what they call the on-camera people, you know. As if we're born with some kind of special gift."

"I didn't mean to—"

He shook his head. "It's just a numbers game, Quynn. You start on the ass-end of the totem pole; a third-rated station in a third-rate market. Most of us never go any higher. You get a couple of years to make-or-break, then a new crop of eager j-school grads comes along and the ride is over. So are the dreams, if you still have any. Do you have a cigarette, Quynn?"

"Sorry. Gave them up a long time ago."

"Me, too. Years. But one would be good right now." Jack paused, again staring over the waters of the marina. "Anyway. So I was lucky, back when I started. I was given a few good assignments, and I thought up a few new twists that attracted enough attention. All of a sudden, I was in Atlanta, one step away from the top rung, and I had a good chance to make it. I *knew* I was going to." He turned, looked at me almost as if in challenge. "You know, at one point I had two of the broadcast networks interested in bringing me up?"

"I saw you work, Jack. I believe it."

He nodded, but not before he had turned away from my eyes.

After a moment, I spoke. "I never understood the drugs. It seemed . . . I don't know. Out of character for the man I saw on the screen."

His smile was sardonic.

"The man on the screen. I'm not sure I knew him all that well. He was somebody I ran into at work, I think. A guy who knew exactly what to do to get what he wanted. But I think he knew what lines he wouldn't cross, either. I'll tell you, Quynn—I wanted to *be* him."

"You are him."

"No. Not now, and maybe not even back then. Oh, there were times I thought I was. There was this fire I covered once—"

Again, he stopped. Again, I said nothing, waiting.

"Here's what I really was, Quynn: I was a guy taking a pretty wild ride. Part of the ride involved cocaine—for me, for my friends and even a few colleagues. It turned into a *lot* of cocaine. Toward the end, I'd sometimes be buying it in kilo-weight. Do you want to hear the whole sordid story?"

"Only what you want to tell me, Jack."

"Okay, short version. One night . . . morning, rather . . . I kept some pretty late hours during my heyday . . . I was pretty much wasted. I ran a light downtown and got myself pulled over." His voice turned rueful. "Not the first time, of course. Usually, the cop would recognize me from TV and I'd get a pass. A warning."

Jack shook his head. "That night I could tell it was going to be different, just by the way they were acting. When they told me to get out of the car, I panicked. Freaked out totally."

"It's okay, Jack," I said. "I know the rest."

Almost everyone did. Even in a town as jaded as Atlanta can be, it is high-profile news when a well-known TV personality careens wildly along Peachtree Street with police in hot pursuit. The incident and the events that followed put Jack Reagan into *People* magazine, as did his subsequent plea bargain. It also put him on a minimum-security prison farm for the full six months.

"It's been more than a year now. I go to my twelve-step group—I don't have to, it wasn't a condition of my release, but I do. No coke, no anything, not so much as a beer after work." Jack looked at me, head cocked. "So tonight I show up here, falling-down drunk. Why do you think that is?"

"You had a hard day. It happens, Jack."

"That's not the question. Why *here*, Quynn?"

The conversation was taking a turn I had not anticipated. I tried to make a joke of it.

"I live downhill from a pretty popular nightclub. You probably tripped on your way out, and it was a lucky roll to my doorstep."

"Nope. Try again. I think I came here with something else in mind."

"Be careful. I'm a married woman. Besides, you told me I stink. Twice."

"Are you married, Quynn? That's not what I hear."

"We're not together right now."

"So there's a reconciliation in your future?"

"There has been, before. This time, I don't know."

"But?"

"But I don't know."

"You like me, Quynn. A man knows when a woman likes him."

He had the grace to look abashed at the look I shot him.

"Okay, I admit we're generally clueless about this sort of thing." He paused. "So. Do you?"

"I like you, Jack."

"Well, here I am. And I'm reasonably sober."

"And I'm still a married woman."

"You're a strange lady, Quynn. You puzzle me."

"I believe I said the same thing to you."

We looked at each other for a long moment. I was very much aware of him, in ways definitely not designed to stiffen my resolve.

"So," Jack said finally. "I guess I better get dressed and go home. Can I call a cab to meet me here?"

"You'll have a hard time getting a cab in Spanish Bay at this hour. Why don't you go back below? Get a few more hours of sleep."

"Where will you sleep?"

I gestured around me. "The captain of a vessel is always on watch. Seriously, I'm comfortable out here."

"Really? It won't be . . . I don't know. Awkward?"

I tried to smile like an older sister, or an aged aunt, or just about anything else than how I actually felt at the moment.

"Not at all. Besides, consider poor Missy. If you were gone when she woke up, it might hurt her feelings. At least buy her breakfast."

"There's that," Jack admitted, and stifled a yawn. "Okay. I'll spring for bacon and eggs, for the three of us." He smiled, suddenly. "But it might ruin your reputation, if this gets out."

"Let's chance it," I said. "Life has been too quiet lately."

CHAPTER 21

I was in that twilight region between deep sleep and wakefulness, my eyes still closed and my feet still propped against the rail as I lay in the deckchair. I shifted slightly, and at that instant a projectile, small but with purpose behind it, struck me hard in the stomach.

My eyes jolted open at the impact, the shock and adrenaline rush turning my heart into a pounding trip hammer. Automatically, my right hand fell to my belt, seizing the butt of my pistol and jerking it half from its holster.

Then the weight shifted, prancing higher, and I found myself looking into the Doberman-like face of a miniature pinscher perched high on my chest. It took several tachycardiac seconds for cognition to kick in and the memory of my boat-guests to resurface.

I disentangled myself from Missy's attentions and placed her on the deck. She sat, less than patient, as I collected myself.

"We need some ground rules if you're going to stay here," I said to Missy, who cocked her head to listen. "I don't shoot you in my sleep, and you don't give me a coronary. Deal?"

It was early, but the sun was already warm on my face and forearms. Around me, the glory of a Northwest Florida morning was in full flower. The air, rain-washed from the previous evening's storm, was still fresh and clean, though it now carried a hint of salt tang from a light onshore breeze.

I became aware of the clamor of the harbor, which rolled like smoke across the water: the mechanical sounds of boat engines firing up and winches cranking at anchor chains, the people sounds of returning shrimp boat captains throwing friendly insults at each other or sport fishermen genially trash-talking as they passed billfish rods and bait buckets onto charter boats.

The sliding door to the salon was open slightly, and from inside the cabin I caught the scent of coffee brewing. I stood, stretching the kinks from the length of my body, and followed Missy inside.

There was a bowl of water on the floor of the galley, and from deeper inside the cabin I could hear the sound of the shower running, loud and strong and long. Cleanliness is a virtue aboard a boat, though water discipline comes in a close second. I made a mental note to top off my freshwater tanks after Jack's visit.

I glanced at the chronometer on the chart table: not quite seven-thirty. Third watch was almost ended, and if there was any fresh information on the shooting at Tito's I wanted to hear it directly from Elle Kvamme before she left. I fished my cell phone from its clip on my belt and flipped it open. But no little green light blinked its welcome. In the thrill of hosting two different species the previous evening, I had neglected to plug it into the charger.

I tapped a knuckle against the door of the head. Jack's voice came over the sound of the shower.

"Be out soon," he called. "Give me another ten minutes?"

"Take your time," I said through the door. "My cell phone's dead. I'm going ashore to check in with the office."

"Use mine," I heard him say. "On the table, next to the bed."

I almost missed it. Jack's phone was a far more sophisticated model than the one I carried, and I had no hint of whatever features it might contain in its silicon-chip microprocessor. It was also stylishly undersized, with a keypad small enough to make punching in the numbers difficult for fingers unaccustomed to them. I misdialed Elle's office extension twice before I got through.

It rang a long time, and I was about to give up when an impatient voice said, "Detectives. Sergeant Kvamme speaking."

"I want to report a crime in progress, ma'am. But while I was waiting for you to answer, the criminal and the victim both died of old age."

"You're a scream, Quynn," Elle said. "You want our premium service, fix it so your name shows on the Caller ID. When the only thing that comes up is a number I don't recognize, don't expect me to know it's my favorite shotgun-assault victim."

"I'm on a borrowed phone," I said. "But it's good to know I'm a priority. Especially now that the police have started screening their calls."

"Technology—gotta love it. So, Lieutenant, what can I do for you this fine morning?"

"Anything new on my shooter, or the car?"

"Nope. Nobody's shown up at any area hospitals full of holes, and nobody's found any bullet-riddled cars." Her voice took on a teasing tone. "Hey, Quynn, you sure you even *hit* the thing? C'mon—you can trust me. I won't tell the guys."

"When we get time," I said, "let's meet at the range. Bring your wallet, Sergeant."

Elle laughed. "No thanks. Mama warned me about ringers like you."

"Did anybody talk to the parolee?"

"Yep. Edward Tapley—Eddie to his friends, as if he has any—got a visit from his P.O. and me yesterday afternoon. Long drive in the rain for nothing. He was alibied up pretty good. Seems he spent the night in the hospital with a face that looked like ground beef. That your work, Quynn?"

"Do we have anything at all? There should be something

from the crime lab by now. Or the canvass . . . did we turn up a witness yet?"

"Sorry, Quynn. Lab's not real optimistic, and all the canvass found out was that people in that neighborhood sleep at night." I heard her yawn. "Unlike yours truly, the Queen of the third watch."

"Thanks anyway," I told her. "Your shift's over. Go home and get some sleep."

"Fat chance," Elle replied. "No rest for the weary. Interdepartmental request for assistance just came in, and I caught it. Just a couple of stupid files, but of course, nothing in the computer databank. I'll have to dig the jackets out of Records, by hand. That is, if there *are* any records on either of 'em."

"Put in for overtime."

"I wish," she said. "I'm already over the limit for the month. Cornelieus would have my scalp."

"Then I sincerely hope it's something interesting."

She snorted. "It's tagged as a missing-person case. Out in the county, but the *Federales* seem to have decided it needed their high-level touch. One of their people made the request."

I felt a stirring in a corner of my mind.

"What exactly do the Feds want?"

"Just a minute." I heard paper rustling. "Okay, here it is. First one—they're asking for the jacket for a Cabot, Harvey Thomas. Says he was born in Spanish Bay. DOB makes him, uh . . . thirty-six." There was a pause. "Huh. Feds want all the usual stuff—*plus* a photocopy of the birth certificate, if available. Guess I'm going to have to call the County Clerk's office for that."

"Who's the other file, Elle?"

"Same last name, Cabot. Might be the wife. Funny first name, though. Mar-goat. Y'ever hear of one like that?" There was a pause. "Quynn? Hey—you still there?"

211

"The 't' is silent. It's pronounced 'Mar-go.' Who made the request, Elle?"

"Just a min . . . okay, Justice Department guy named—whoa. I'm not even going to try to say *this* one."

"Let me guess," I said. "Zhang-mei. Howard Zhang-mei."

I rang off, knowing that I had just stumbled onto an important fact. But that was all I knew. Whatever else it meant, I didn't have a clue.

I had met only one Harvey lately, and I was relatively certain that the probation report I had seen on him had not listed his last name as Cabot. But it would have been too much of a fluke to think that there was suddenly an overload of missing persons named Margot-with-a-silent-t, and I had never been much of a believer in coincidence. It would have been interesting to confirm what the "C" in M. C. Mason stood for, but I was willing to wager that I already knew.

Obviously, Zhang-mei had discovered a far more intimate relationship between Margot Mason and my sparring partner Harvey than I had known existed.

It would be prudent to find out more.

I had no idea when Federal employees reported for work. The probability was that Zhang-mei was either still at his home, or at best fighting the morning traffic on his way in. But at the least, I could always leave a message.

I pulled Zhang-mei's card from my wallet, and with difficulty punched in the numbers on Jack's undersized keypad.

The phone at the other end rang twice, and I was handed my second major revelation of the morning.

"Ah, yes, I've been wondering when you were going to check in," Zhang-mei said, before I could speak. "I hope you have something good for me this time, Jack. Jack? Hello . . . are you still there?"

CHAPTER 22

In the backseat of my car, Missy stood on her hind legs and pressed her nose against the thin gap I had opened in the window. She sniffed with a mad abandon, and I could only guess at the smorgasbord of scents she was absorbing in the slipstream. Perhaps, for a human, it would have been akin to skidding along a heavily laden banquet table, mouth open wide.

As we circled the harbor, Jack snapped back the mirrored visor he had been using to examine the morning-after effects. I saw no significant damage, aside from slightly bloodshot eyes. He glanced outside, then swiveled to me.

"Where are we going?" he asked.

"Just a short detour. Something I want you to see."

"Ah. A surprise. I *like* surprises."

We drove on in silence, though Jack was anything but at rest. He punched through each of the pre-sets on the car radio, frowning at the selections. He rifled through the contents of the glove compartment, even scanning the rental agreement I had placed there. He shifted restlessly in the passenger seat, readjusted the seat belt, realigned the angle of the chair back. Several times, he reached back to pat Missy, who wigwagged her stump-tail absently as she continued to sample the outside atmosphere.

But I said nothing, and studiously avoided Jack's eye as he fidgeted.

I turned just before reaching the bridge that linked Oklaloosa

Island with the mainland, steering west on the parkway. Here, a great wall of high-rise condominiums blocked all but fleeting glimpses of the sparkling Gulf on our left. But to the right, on the side that bordered the Intercoastal Waterway and the waters of the bay, the older tourist courts gave way to rental townhouses and then to private residences of increasing affluence.

By the time we neared the end of the public roadway, the houses were truly estates, most of them gleaming white in the semitropical sun and topped with *faux*-tile roofs in various pastel shades and hues. I pulled off the pavement near one, the crushed shells of the shoulder crunching and popping loudly beneath my tires. Missy, sensing a rest stop, vaulted the seat into Jack's lap, where she perched impatiently.

I shifted into park and let the engine idle, and twisted to face Jack.

"We're here," I said.

He looked over the stucco wall that was just below the level of his window. On the other side of thirty yards of kelly-green Saint Augustine lawn, the graceful Moorish architecture seemed to rise from the landscape like a living entity. But its balance and symmetry did little to disguise the size of the structure, or the opulence with which it had been built. A Jaguar sedan the color of sea foam was parked outside the twin garages on the upward-sloping flagstone drive.

Jack studied the house for a moment, then turned to me and shrugged.

"Nice place. So?"

"Nice place indeed. There's a patio and pool behind the house, and a dock and boathouse on the Intercoastal. On the other side of that bay window is a formal dining room. The table in there seats fifteen, not counting the host. Island property is pretty pricey. Land values out here, you couldn't touch this place for less than three million dollars."

He tried an inquisitive smile. "Are you moonlighting as a real estate agent, Quynn?"

"Just making a point. You see, the man who owns this place used to be my boss. He was the chief of police before Cornelieus."

"Times sure have changed, Quynn. Now I wish I'd taken the civil service test."

"You'd be pretty disappointed. His salary was a matter of public record. Go back and check the minutes of the Spanish Bay City Council. You'll find out he never made more than eighty thousand dollars annually in any of the eleven years he headed up the force."

"I don't guess you're telling me that he was a very thrifty fellow."

"That's the way it used to be around Spanish Bay," I said. "Four years ago, things had become a little too blatant. A few of the younger turks in the police department did a little homework, off the books. Hardly scratched the surface. Even so, they were coming up with evidence of drug payoffs, extortion, connections with gambling syndicates. They didn't know who they could trust with the information. So finally they took what they had to the FBI."

The door to the house opened, and a stout figure in beach attire and sunglasses appeared. He was deeply tanned, a stark contrast to the full head of carefully combed silver hair on his head. I watched as he walked to the Jaguar and opened the trunk.

"There was a Justice Department investigation," I said, my gaze still on the man in the driveway. "The Spanish Bay cops agreed to go before a Federal grand jury and tell what their investigation had found. Ended up with their names in the headlines—usually not a good idea for a whistle-blower, but they figured they were protected. After all, they had the Feds on their side. People were talking about how racketeering indictments were about to come down, there were even rumors that some of the mid-level fish were about to turn state's evidence."

The silver-haired man had removed a set of golf clubs and closed the trunk. Without apparent effort, he hoisted the heavy-looking tournament bag and turned back toward his house.

Jack waited for several counts. "And?"

"And then it all went away, very quietly. It was a Presidential election year—you remember how tight that race was, particularly down here. All of a sudden, the votes our good-ol'-boy network controlled began to look very valuable to both sides. So word came down to make a deal."

I nodded through the windshield at the opulence on display before us. "Part of the price of dialing it all down was set by the man who lives in there. The Feds let him retire quietly. It was a pretty clear message to anybody else who might have been thinking about cooperating. Add the benign neglect from the prosecutors . . . well, it didn't take long for the case to run out of steam. No indictments, no harm, no foul. In exchange, they agreed to bring in somebody from the outside—the stated objective, of course, was to clean up the mess in the police department."

"So everybody ended up happy," Jack said, too brightly. "Why aren't you, Quynn?"

"In the interim before Cornelieus came in, the axe fell on every one of the cops who had gone to the Justice Department. They were hung out to dry. They lost everything, including any chance of getting a job in law enforcement anywhere else. Certainly, their chance of making a living in this area was over."

The man in the driveway had noticed us now, parked along the margin of his property. I imagined his eyes behind the dark-tinted lenses of his sunglasses, squinting in curiosity or, more likely, irritation. He had turned to face us now, shifting the big tournament bag to his left hand as if it was weightless.

"Why are you telling me this, Quynn?"

I forced my gaze away from the silver-haired man and found Jack looking at me intently. Whatever was in my expression made him frown, as if I had uttered something inappropriate or profane.

"I guess I wanted you to hear the story," I said. "In case you're ever tempted to make a deal with the local power structure, or perhaps with somebody higher up on the governmental food chain. It won't matter how smart you are. They're all part of an established system that will chew you up and spit you out without a second thought, if it serves their purpose."

Jack was still frowning, but his eyes had not left my face.

"When Cornelieus came in, some people hoped that had put a stake through the heart of that particular system, at least on the local level. Maybe we were overly optimistic." I shook my head. "I don't want to see it come back again."

"And you think it will," he said. "Or has."

"Old habits die hard. There's a man in the police department whose brother-in-law is a United States Congressman. The people behind him are the good ol' boys who used to run things under the old system. There are rumors the man with the brother-in-law is going to be our next chief of police."

The silver-haired man was walking toward us now, still carrying the golf clubs. He bent to look in Jack's window, and I pressed the button to roll down the dark-tinted glass. Missy squirmed in Jack's grasp, but made no attempt to escape, evade or attack.

"Can I help y'all with—well, I'm a sum'bitch. That *you*, Quynn?"

"Hello, Chief. I was just showing your house to my friend."

"That so?" He stared at Jack for a moment, then broke into a broad smile, his teeth shark-like and preternaturally white against his tan. "I'd invite y'all in, but we're late risers here." He chuckled. "And I've got me a guest inside who probably still ain't entirely decent, if y' get my drift."

"That's all right. We've got someplace to be. But it's a beautiful house."

"Well, maybe you gonna get one like it," he said, still grinning. "Someday."

"I don't think so, Chief. The price is a little too rich for my blood."

He looked at me, and I could have sworn that behind the sunglasses his eyes were crinkled with humor, or perhaps with something else.

"Yeah," he said. "Well, maybe so. Still, things have a funny way of happening, don't they? You never know. One day, you might wake up and just want something bad enough to take it." He stepped back. "Take care, y' hear? You, too, there."

As we pulled away in a great circle that took us back toward where we had come, I looked in the rearview mirror.

He was still standing there, his hand raised high over his head. It might have been a genial farewell, but for a reason I could not explain it looked much like a warning.

"Let's get breakfast," I said.

Beside me, Jack Reagan was silent, and now his eyes were hooded.

We ate at a bright-yellow Waffle House that had been at the foot of Brooks Bridge for as long as I could remember. Pop and I had come here regularly in the old days, and the cuisine was as close to home cooking as I knew. The restaurant catered to the casual walk-in trade, drawing from the high-rise condominiums and beach houses that lined the seaward side of the harbor as well as from the back-bay working docks.

As a result, the dining area was filled with an eclectic mix:

tourist families getting a jump on their day, and a variety of locals—most of them shrimpers, crabbers or nocturnal commercial fishermen stopping off after a long night of work out on the salt. Children squalled or pleaded; parents fussed or threatened; men in Morse Diesel caps and faded pocket T-shirts held cigarettes with net-scarred fingers and lingered over white china cups of coffee—all of it set against the sound of a jukebox playing a Tim McGraw country ballad.

I carried the paper sack outside, to where Jack waited at a round concrete table. I removed two paper cups, then pushed the bottom-heavy bag toward him. The aroma of hot coffee rose as I pried off the lids. Across from me, Jack arranged the foamed-plastic containers as if he was setting the table with fine porcelain.

By then, Missy had caught the scent of my seven-way hash browns. She came at a dead run from beneath the oleander bush where she had been stalking toenail land crabs and skinks whose speed had taunted the dog's pursuit.

I fished several chunks of diced ham onto a paper plate and bent to place it on the ground. They disappeared before I was more than halfway there. Missy bounced near my ankles, demanding another helping.

"You're going to make her sick," Jack warned, and cheerfully tossed Missy a corner of his toast. He saw the look I gave him. "It's only *bread*. To settle her stomach."

"Yeah, sure. That's different, then."

As I sat, he looked around. "This is pretty damned nice, Quynn. I don't do this often."

"You don't have breakfast?"

Jack kicked me lightly on the ankle. "I usually work the ten-o'clock broadcast, Quynn. I get in about midnight afterward. I don't see too many mornings, is what I mean." He smiled, the full-wattage version I had not seen for a while. "And I don't get to a Waffle House much, either."

"Now you know what you're missing."

"I do indeed." He scooped up a quantity of scrambled egg with his plastic fork and munched it with a distinct enthusiasm.

I studied him, trying not to appear I was doing so. I had much to think about.

When Howard Zhang-mei had answered my call from Jack's cell phone, for the first few seconds I had been too surprised to speak. I had hesitated only briefly, then pressed the disconnect button.

Almost immediately, the telephone had rung again. When I compared the number on its diminutive liquid-crystal screen with the one on Zhang-mei's card, it was obvious that I had inadvertently triggered a round of telephone-tag. A half dozen rings later, the phone went silent. Instead, a small mailbox had appeared in a corner of the screen, blinking inexorably.

I had squinted at the keypad until I found a button marked MENU; when I pressed it a list of options appeared. VOICE MAIL/PAGER was the second line, and I selected it.

Immediately, an alphanumeric line had scrolled across the screen: WE WERE CUT OFF. CALL ME BACK. H.

DELETE? the screen had offered, and I had selected it. But I also knew how temporary a solution that was. I had only postponed whatever would happen when Jack and Zhang-mei compared notes on the morning hang-up. He could call back at any time, and whatever advantage my new knowledge might provide would be lost.

But at the same time, I was strangely reluctant to break the temper of the morning; I wanted it to last, if only for a short while longer.

"Quynn?" Jack was frowning at me, his fork stopped midway to his lips.

"Sorry. My mind was wandering a bit."

"I said I'm going to have to find out if I still have a job." He shook his head. "I can always claim I had an attack of nausea. I'm probably safe."

"Do you still want it?"

He shrugged, but his eyes were no longer the eyes of the man who had, only a few hours before, talked about slow boat trips to parts unknown.

"It's what I know how to do," Jack said, and his words sounded defensive.

"I've seen you do it," I said with a nod. "You're good. You do your job very well, even when the way you're doing it is . . . kind of despicable."

He arched an eyebrow.

"I guess that's a compliment," he said slowly, and there was nothing defensive about his tone now. "But 'despicable' sounds pretty harsh."

"Why did you rush out of Maddie Shepard's room yesterday?"

"Touché. That was over the top, I agree. We shouldn't have gone after the interview that way. But it was only a lapse, Quynn. One instance of poor judgment doesn't mean I shouldn't tell Maddie's story."

"I'm not your conscience, Jack. Or your judge."

"Sure sounded like you were campaigning for one or the other, Quynn."

"I have my opinions, Jack. I think there are times when a person has to decide how far he's willing to go. There's always a line you simply don't cross."

"And—in your expert opinion—where is that line?"

"Maybe it's where you start betraying people. Or maybe it's when you start betraying yourself."

For a moment, Jack's expression was that of a person who

has just been slapped, hard and unexpectedly. Then his features narrowed.

"That's a pretty shitty thing to say, Quynn."

"Only if that's what you're doing. Is it?"

"I don't have to answer a question like that. In fact, I don't have to tell you a damn thing."

"Probably not," I agreed. "But I get the feeling that you're caught in the middle of something that you don't control. If that's the case, if you're being used or manipulated, I want to help you."

"I don't know what you're talking about," Jack said, but there was not the same force behind his words as before.

"What do you know about Howard Zhang-mei? His background, for instance."

Jack shrugged. "Up to a few months ago, Zhang-mei was an assistant U.S. attorney in Raleigh-Durham. I'm told he had the reputation of being rather . . . well, let's call it 'hungry.' According to the Justice Department grapevine, he's made a number of requests for a posting to Homeland Security."

"All of them denied," I said. "He told me the most exciting work he had been doing up there was tracing deadbeat dads. Don't you wonder why?"

"I understand that it's pretty political in the Justice Department. Maybe he made some enemies there. Of all people, *you* should know how that can happen."

"So he transfers from Raleigh-Durham to Mobile. At best, that's a lateral career move. More likely, a step backward. Why would an ambitious person do that, Jack?"

"Maybe he liked the climate here, Quynn. Maybe he wanted a fresh start, or followed a girlfriend who moved down here. There's a lot of things I don't know about Zhang-mei—or care about, either. What's your point?"

"Where have you been getting your information, Jack? For

your news reports, I mean."

"I don't reveal sources."

"Think about it. You were the first journalist to report that there was a link between Bobby Teasdale and the bombing in Spanish Bay. Ever since, it's been repeated by every reporter in the country, as if it was gospel. But what was *your* evidence, Jack? Who sold *you* on the idea that Teasdale is behind any of this?"

He glared at me. "I'll say one thing. My source on Teasdale has goddamn strong credentials. It's solid information, believe it. My source knows as much about the bombing and the sniper attacks as . . . as anyone could know."

I nodded, noting his stumble but saying nothing. As I waited, my silence seemed to pour gasoline on the fire of Jack Reagan's irritation.

"I have no need to prove anything, to you or anyone else. Check the transcript of the broadcast. There was a stated attribution for everything I reported about Teasdale."

"Yes. I recall that you attributed it all to 'highly placed sources.' But you never gave your source a name, or even an affiliation."

"Standard practice. I told you, I protect confidential sources."

"Makes it pretty hard to confirm, doesn't it?"

"You're accusing me of faking the quotes?" He was truly angry now. "I've never manufactured a quote in my life! I've never *had* to. I do my research. I find people willing to talk to me."

"Makes it easier when you don't have to name them, I guess."

"Go to hell, Quynn."

"I think you're wrong about Teasdale. I don't believe he's the bomber. I doubt that he shot DeBourche. If I'm right, ask yourself this. Why are some people so determined to put him in the spotlight?"

"This is your little fairy tale, Quynn. Why don't you tell me?"

"I don't know. Not yet. But if I'm right, somebody is using you to help set up Teasdale. Your source has a personal agenda."

"Are you back on that, Quynn? Well, here's a news flash. Most people have an agenda. I'm not ashamed of using the information I get from a source with an axe to grind."

"You said 'a' source, Jack. Are you counting on what one person chooses to tell you?"

"I'm not discussing my source, or sources. Not with you."

"I'm not asking much, Jack. Whatever he tells you, check it out independently before you go on camera. It could keep you from making a serious mistake."

"I've made mistakes before," Jack said. "One of them might have been coming to see you."

"You might discover that I'm the only person you can trust, Jack."

"I don't think so." He rose, smoldering. "Thanks for your advice. I'm late for work."

"I'll drive you."

"No, thanks," he said; his voice was level, but his eyes furious. "I think I'll find my own way. I've been doing that for a very long time."

He stalked off, leaving the remains of his meal on the table.

At some point during our discussion, Missy had taken cover under the table. Now she emerged, tentatively, looking first at the departing man and then turning to me.

I imagined I could read the question in her eyes, but it was more likely I was merely asking it of myself.

"Everybody sets his own line," I answered her. "And you always know when you've crossed it."

But I was not talking of Jack Reagan, and I knew it.

CHAPTER 23

As I had hoped, Elle Kvamme was still at her desk when I arrived. She was working at her computer, simultaneously talking into the telephone tucked against her cheek by a hunched shoulder. She looked up as I entered, and gave a double take when she saw what I was carrying.

I stood by her desk, waiting until she hung up.

"No," Elle said. "Isn't going to happen, Quynn."

"C'mon, Elle. You like animals. Everybody knows it."

"Which is why I've ended up with four dogs—*and* a husband who already thinks I'm nuts," she said. "Dave'll kill me if I even think about bringing home another stray."

"Missy's not a stray, Elle. She's just going through some hard times."

"I'm getting a reputation in my neighborhood. They expect to find my body someday, surrounded by stacks of old newspapers and covered with dog poop."

"Look at her. I'm trying to track down the owner. But right now, Missy needs help."

"Dammit, Quynn. *You* keep her, then."

"I can't leave a dog alone on my boat all day. With the schedule you and Dave have, somebody's always home at your place." I waited a count, then shrugged sadly. "Oh, well. I guess it's the county shelter, then."

"You bastard. That's not fair."

"Forget I asked, Elle. I shouldn't have imposed."

The policewoman looked at me, then at Missy's face. She sighed and shook her head.

"This is a temporary arrangement," she warned me.

"Just a few days, a week at the most. Any longer, I'll come up with another plan."

"As soon as you locate the owner, I'm off the hook."

"Absolutely."

"I mean it."

"I owe you one, Elle."

I patted Missy's head and passed her over to Elle. The animal changed hands without protest, and as she sniffed at her benefactor her stump-tail wagged—slowly at first, then with enthusiasm. Maybe she was simply picking up the scent of a confirmed dog-lover, maybe she was just becoming accustomed to meeting new people.

Elle made to hand Missy back. "Bring her back in an hour. Dave's going to freak."

"Go home, Elle. Your shift's over."

With the hand not holding Missy, she gestured at the cluttered desktop. "Can't do it. That file request from the Feds? There wasn't hardly diddly-squat, records-wise. But I still need to pick up that birth certificate."

"Let me worry about it, Elle. Consider yourself off duty. I'll make sure everything gets to the people who need to have it."

As I had expected, I didn't have to make the offer twice.

But as Elle turned to leave, Missy cocked her head to look back at me for a moment. I knew that I was re-routing my own emotion through the animal. Still, I imagined I saw something in her eyes.

It might have been an accusation.

As far as the official records revealed, Harvey Thomas Cabot had passed through the first two decades of life without attracting the attention of law enforcement—or, to all appearances, that of almost anybody else.

Elle had tracked down two news items from what was, in a more innocent age, called the *Playground Daily News.* There had been no birth announcement published, but a Harvey Cabot was mentioned as a fourth-grade finalist in a district spelling bee and a twelve-year-old "H. T. Cabot" had played second base on a team that had made it to the city's Little League semi-finals.

But aside from those two news articles, Elle's unpaid overtime had been a largely wasted effort. To be safe, I even rechecked the stack of old city directories and outdated telephone directories Elle had pulled from the department records room; no Cabots, Harvey or otherwise.

There was a scribbled note on Elle's pad, a local phone number and the words CO. CLRK/SKEETER J. I dialed the number and a bored voice with a peckerwood accent answered: "Registry. Mr. Jackson."

"Quynn, Spanish Bay Police. Is Skeeter there?"

"Speakin'."

"I'm following up on a birth certificate. A Harvey Cabot, middle name Thomas."

"Uh-huh. 'Nuther lady cop named Kvamme called about it."

I waited, but apparently that was the extent of it. "Okay. And?"

"And I got it right here."

"Good to know, Mr. Jackson. We're going to need a copy. A fax would be fine with—"

"Five dollars. Cash preferred. No checks."

"Beg your pardon?"

"Five dollars. That's what a certified copy gonna cost."

"Skeeter, did I mention I'm with the police? This is an official police request."

"Don't matter to the county. Want it, that's what it costs."

I took a deep breath, not for the first time contemplating the eccentricities of the Florida political patronage system. It was more than plausible that Skeeter Jackson was somebody's nephew-once-removed, or possibly the otherwise-unemployable second cousin of a deep-pockets campaign contributor.

I knew it was hopeless, but I tried again anyway.

"Put it on our tab. Send a bill to the Spanish Bay Police Department."

"Gotta pay in person. Cash preferred. No checks."

"I'll come over."

"Close here at two."

I looked at the clock; it was just after ten a.m.

"I'll be there in fifteen minutes."

It was actually less than that. The County Building was a short walk across the square from the Spanish Bay Municipal Center, and I made the trip at double time.

I took the elevator to the third floor, where I found an efficient-looking young woman sorting through a stack of what looked like old-fashioned punch cards. She looked up politely as I smiled across the counter.

"I'm looking for Skeeter Jackson. He's expecting me."

"I'm sorry. Mr. Jackson just went on break."

"I talked to him ten minutes ago. I said I was coming right over." I showed her my identification.

She nodded solemnly, but I caught a hint of a twinkle in her eye.

"It must have slipped Mr. Jackson's memory, Lieutenant Quynn."

"I guess I'll have to wait."

"Mr. Jackson's breaks usually last a while."

"When do you expect him back?"

"He's usually in by nine-thirty."

"I'm supposed to come back *tonight?*"

"Pardon me, I was unclear. Nine-thirty a.m." Now the twinkle was in clear display. "He's left for the day, Lieutenant. We won't see him here again until tomorrow."

She looked around, then leaned forward in a mock-conspiratorial manner. "If you've come to arrest him, Mr. Jackson has a standing tee-time at Sugar Sands Country Club."

"He's playing golf?"

"Mr. Jackson plays on a foursome with two of the other department supervisors here. Number Four is his uncle, Jeff D. Jackson. You might know him; he's been a county commissioner forever. By the time you get there, they'll probably be on the second hole."

"He has a file we need."

"In that case, maybe you should deal with me." She offered me her hand, arm extended over the counter. "Samantha Hatcher. I'm the associate registrar."

I shook her hand. "Are you anybody's niece, or second cousin?"

She laughed, a healthy sound full of pure amusement.

"Yes, but not in the way you mean. No political connections at all. But I have a masters degree in administration from Florida State University, and my BA was in government affairs. So I'm kind of expected to take up any slack that might occur around here." Her voice dropped a degree, becoming professional again. "Now, what file did you need, Lieutenant?"

I gave her the name, and she disappeared into an office. She emerged a moment later with a sheet of yellowed paper. It was a standard form, with CERTIFICATE OF LIVE BIRTH printed in baroque lettering across the top. The name that was typed in the first blank read HARVEY THOMAS CABOT.

But that was not what caught my eye. In the space reserved

229

for the mother, an uneven line of typewritten letters spelled out MARGOT CABOT. But across from it, the line meant for the name of the father was blank.

"Does this mean what I think it does?" I asked Samantha.

She turned the sheet on the counter and looked where my finger indicated.

"It's not all that uncommon in the old birth records," she said with a nod. "Girls have been getting themselves in trouble for as long as there's been two genders. Sometimes the baby was given the father's last name, if the mother was determined to show paternity. Doesn't look like she was, here."

"How likely is it that Cabot was a false name?"

"Well, that depends," she said. "In theory, the attending physician or midwife was supposed to endorse the accuracy of a birth certificate. In practice, especially in instances where the family might not want people to know—" Samantha shrugged knowingly.

I nodded.

"I'll need a copy of this, Ms. Hatcher," I said, and corrected myself. "Two copies. Both copies certified, please."

"Won't take a minute," she said, and took the original into the back office. When she returned, she handed me two letterhead envelopes, OKALOOSA COUNTY CLERK emblazoned in ornate script across the left corner.

I took a ten-dollar bill from my wallet and fished one of my cards from my pocket, then held both out to Samantha Hatcher.

She looked at the money, then at me. To my eyes, it appeared she was trying hard not to laugh.

"Thanks, but we don't accept tips here," she said. "My treat, Lieutenant."

I shook my head. "This is official business, Ms. Hatcher. Please put this on Skeeter's desk. I'm sure he'll be looking for the money."

Her answering grin was wide. "I'm sure you're right. He always is." Her voice became professional again. "Is there anything else we can do for you today?"

"Just tell Skeeter thanks for me," I said. "And would you ask him to send me a receipt? The address is on my card."

"I wouldn't hold my breath waiting, Lieutenant."

"Miracles can happen, Ms. Hatcher. Miracles can happen."

CHAPTER 24

Tito grunted, and took another bite from the belly-buster double cheeseburger he held in both his large hands. Then he scowled, in a way not intended as an endorsement of his menu choice.

It was still short of midday, and the lunchtime rush had not yet arrived. Maybe it never did, if the quality of food and service was any evidence. We sat alone at the counter, close to the air conditioner that jutted from the wall.

The unit gurgled and rattled, and its tired exhalation was only slightly cooler than the air outside. But the noise it made gave us a measure of privacy from the counterman who leaned against the wall, idly thumbing through the morning paper.

"What are the chances that this Harvey Cabot guy is the same Harvey you messed up in that bar?" Tito asked.

"The gender is right," I said. "But that's about all. According to the parole file, the guy I tangled with is named Eddie Tapley, age twenty-three. He did a year and a half as a guest of the state, up at Port Léon Prison Farm. Possession-with-intent, paroled two months ago. Tapley's not our Harvey Cabot."

"And?"

"And so I have a mystery here. According to the birth certificate, Harvey Cabot was born in Spanish Bay thirty-six years ago. After that, he turned into the original Invisible Boy. Except for a couple of old newspaper clippings, there's virtually nothing in the system on him. Tapley grew up in Birmingham;

he has a very colorful juvenile record. Minor stuff, but it goes all the way back to junior high school."

"So Tapley's not your guy. Why's that a problem?"

"I keep tripping over Howard Zhang-mei. He's running the bombing investigation. He takes over the Margot Mason disappearance. Now he's hunting for what appears to be Mason's illegitimate son—somebody named 'Harvey,' which just happens to be the name Tapley was using."

"That's it? Pretty thin soup, Quynn."

"Call it a gut feeling, Tito."

Tito avoided my eyes, and took another pass at his cheeseburger.

"Could come from eating this crap," he said, and tossed the rest of his sandwich onto the tabletop. "You know much about identification theft?"

"Some," I said. "Probably not enough. Mainly about the wrong people using somebody else's credit card numbers."

He snorted. "Tip of the iceberg, credit cards. I told you about the case I turned over to Interpol, the bookie? You get people who know what they're doing, they can literally take over your whole life. They can buy cars, houses, stocks—hell, for all intents and purposes, they *become* you. They want to, it can go on like that almost indefinitely."

I frowned. "Until you start getting the bills, you mean."

"If that's the game they're playing, sure. But say a person has a good reason to become somebody else, permanently. These days, just flashing a phony driver's license won't do it. You need a complete history to step into—a lifetime of schools you've attended, jobs you've held, marriages, banking records, medical and credit histories. Too complex to fake, and too many computers have it all in their archives.

"So you get the documentation you need—dumpster-dive somebody's trash, or follow the mailman around and go through the letter box. All you need is a Social Security number and a driver's license whose numbers match up. Next, you apply for a credit card or a minor loan—small amounts, because it's not the *money* you want. It's building your new identity."

"And that's it?"

"You set up a safe address where the bills go, one of those places that'll rent you a mailbox, maybe," Tito said. "Now you have a street address, see? You make sure you pay the bills on time, retire the loans ahead of schedule. Long as the real guy doesn't get an overdue notice or a call from a bill collector, you can be his financial doppelganger for a long, long time."

"What happens when he looks at his credit report?"

"Hell, most people never see their own credit report, not unless there's some kind of problem. But say he does. So what? Guy sees a few minor loans, all of 'em paid off. Worse case, he maybe bitches to TRW about how they mixed up his records."

I shook my head. "It's interesting, but it doesn't give me anywhere to go. No judge will authorize a data search with what I have now."

Tito shrugged, trying to appear nonchalant. "I could run the Cabot name through some Internet sites I know. Not strictly legal, but—I've kind of been doing a *lot* of that lately." He tried to look contrite, and failed. "Amazing, the kind of crap you turn up on people that way."

"I don't know, Tito." I shook my head in frustration. "Harvey Cabot's a phantom. Margot Mason's missing, maybe dead. Right now all I really have is Eddie Tapley."

"So have somebody pick up the guy, bring him in for a little one-on-one. Better yet, do it yourself."

"That's what I had in mind. But Eddie is tied in with the Centurions of The Lord. With their leader missing, they might be a little jumpy."

"Those assholes? They only *play* at being soldiers, Quynn."

"Still, I could use somebody to watch my back."

"Sounds like common sense."

"Problem is, I don't want to advertise that I'm looking at Eddie Tapley. Cornelius ordered me off, and Beaulieu is aching to catch me with my panties down some way or other. If I bring in backup from the department, it's bound to get back to one of them."

Tito looked sidelong at me, then his features brightened. "Ah-ha. Be like old times, right? Might even be fun to—dammit, don't give me that look, Quynn." He raised his palms, a gesture of surrender. "Okay, I'm just along for the ride. I'll just stand there, see how a *real* cop works."

"Remember that," I warned. "This is nothing like old times. Do you hear what I'm saying, Tito?"

"Yeah, yeah, yeah," Tito replied, but his voice was still happy. "Don't worry, partner. I won't squeeze the Charmin."

The probation report on Eddie Tapley gave us an address in a district zoned mainly for commercial operations. He lived in what once had been a mom-and-pop tourist court, the kind that thrived in years gone by. Then the major hotel chains had arrived in Spanish Bay to build their pleasure palaces hard against the Gulf, and places like this found themselves adrift in a red-ink ocean.

It might have been inviting here once, even homey. Now, large sections of the stucco had flaked away, exposing the water-stained concrete block construction. Sandspurs grew in abundance in the otherwise barren soil.

Tito pulled his vintage Eldorado into a Winn-Dixie parking lot across the street. There, the midday sun pressed down mercilessly. Above the asphalt, the superheated air undulated like the hallucination of a psychotic. We stopped at the far end of the lot near the architect's sole concession to greenery, a dusty Brazilian yew that offered little more than a semblance of shade.

By some miracle, a slot under it was open, blocked only by an empty shopping cart crosswise in the space. I opened my door, intending to push the cart aside. But before I could step outside, an elderly man wearing a green Winn-Dixie apron and a matching baseball cap was already there.

He watched, a genial expression on his face, as Tito parked.

"Nice car," the old man said when Tito beeped the door lock. "What you got there, a '65 'Dorado? Special Edition?"

"Close," Tito said. "She's an SE, but she came off the assembly line in 1967. Hey, I bet you owned one like it; probably bought it new. Am I right?"

The old man shook his head. "Always wanted one of 'em, 'fore I retired."

"Sell you this one, for the right price."

The old man laughed. "Hell, on my damn pension? I got to work stock boy at Winn-Dixie or learn to like dog food." He looked at Tito's car again and suddenly grinned wide. "But even an old man can dream. Y'all have a nice day."

We crossed the street, threading our way through the noontime traffic. Tapley lived in a second-floor unit, and as we walked along the open balcony there was only the occasional sound of life from inside the various apartments. Few pedestrians were in evidence, driven inside or to air-conditioned autos by the heat of the day.

At Tapley's door I rapped loudly, waited, tried again. No response.

Tito pressed his ear against the metal door.

"Nothing," he said, and gave me a significant look. "Guy's not home."

Tito leaned over for a moment, studying the lockset.

"Shaeffer," he said cheerfully. "Show any Shaeffer a lockpick, damn things just about give up and open themselves."

He pulled a small leatherette wallet from an inside pocket. In it was an assortment of probes and flat-strips, each neatly secured in its own loop. Tito selected one and bent to work.

"Damn it, Tito," I began, but before I could complete the sentence the lock clicked and the door cracked open.

"Oh, grow up, Quynn," he growled, but there was an unmistakable ebullience in his tone. "When did you ever learn anything on the wrong side of a closed door?"

"This is an illegal search. No matter what I find, it's inadmissible."

"I won't tell anybody if you don't. Worse comes to worst—for the record, I'm a witness. I'll testify the door was wide open when we got here." From another pocket, he produced two sets of latex gloves and handed me a pair. "Shall we?"

After a moment, I snapped them on and followed him inside.

It was a typical motel layout that had probably rented as a double room. There was a television on a corner bracket high on the wall. A sink was at the far end of the unit, next to an open door that led to a toilet and standup shower. The bed was unmade, and old newspapers and magazines were strewn around the room. A hotplate, shiny with grease, shared a shelf with a stained coffeepot.

Tito had gone ahead of me and was looking down at a scarred table.

"Well, well," he said. "What have we here?"

Amid the mummified remnants of take-out meals, snippets of small-gauge wire littered the tabletop. I saw pliers and a tube of cold solder, still uncapped. A twelve-pack of AA batteries had been ripped open and gutted, empty.

And then, under the table so that it blended with the shadows, something else caught my eye; Tito and I saw it at the same moment. It was a torn wrapper, stiff with wax and dusky green in color, perhaps the size of two soap bars placed end-to-end. I lifted it to my nose, and despite the odor of my latex gloves I could detect the chemical tang that the paper had absorbed.

"Plastiqué," I said. "My guess is Semtex." I replaced it, careful to position it where it had lain.

But Tito looked less pleased with the fruits of our break-in than I had expected.

"Something's big-time screwy here, Quynn," Tito said. "This guy's got a parole officer who could walk in any time, with no notice. Why the hell would he be running a bomb factory in his own crib? And then he just splits, leaving all this evidence right in the open? Doesn't make sense."

"Unless he knows he's not coming back," I said.

We checked the closets and drawers. They were all empty, stripped clean.

"No personal stuff on the counter," Tito observed. "He's cleared out."

"I think it's time we left and locked the door behind us," I said. "We were never here. I'll call Tapley's P.O., tell him I want to interview Tapley with him present, and get him to meet me here ASAP."

"I take it you want me gone."

"You might be hard to explain if anybody wants to start asking questions."

"Yeah, you're right. Too bad. I enjoyed it. For a while there, almost felt like I was back on the job again."

We left carefully, trying to look as casual as any two people who had knocked and found nobody home. I stopped near the entrance to the Winn-Dixie.

"My cell phone didn't get charged last night," I said. "I'm going to call Tapley's parole officer from a pay phone and wait for him here."

"You can use mine," Tito offered.

"Too many people have Caller ID," I said. "Anyway, it's time for you to head over to the Shepard house. Go on, get out of here. Say hi to the rioters for me."

Tito headed for his car, a long walk across hot blacktop. I turned and went into the grocery.

But I was only a few steps inside when I felt a hand on my forearm. It was the elderly man in the apron and cap who had admired Tito's Cadillac.

"That guy talk to your buddy about buying his car?" he asked.

I frowned, puzzled. "Beg your pardon?"

"Right after you two walked away, guy came over to look. Can't blame him none; it's a beaut. I tole him the owner was talking 'bout selling. Fella sure seemed to like the car."

"What guy?" I asked, and startled myself at the intensity I heard in my words. "What was his name? What did he look like?"

"I dunno," he said. "Short, but bulked-up—muscles, you know? His face was all tore up."

I stared at him, feeling a sudden chill. "What did he do?"

"I tole you," the old man said. "He checked out your buddy's car. Walked around it couple times, you know? Seemed like he was pretty interested. Even crawled under to look at the—hey, lady, what's the matter?"

But by then I was moving, pushing through a knot of stock boys loitering near the line of carts, skirting an elderly black woman who seemed not to notice my haste, bumping against a burly man in madras shorts and a Harley T-shirt hard enough to knock him against the wall. Then I was past the electric-eye doors and into the bright sun outside.

It dazzled my eyes, and it took me a moment to orient myself. Squinting, I turned in the direction Tito had gone, toward where he had left his vehicle. Incongruously, part of my mind registered heat, noting with a distant awareness how the sun-baked asphalt scorched the soles of my feet through my shoes even as I sprinted across the parking lot.

Then I saw movement to my right. By instinct, my head snapped toward it.

Amid the sea of mostly unoccupied vehicles, a man sat alone in a parked car less than thirty yards away. My vision was partially blocked by the other autos. Even so, I could see that his bruised face was staring intently through the windshield in the direction of Tito's Eldorado. The driver's side window was partially opened, I noted. An object protruded through it, a thin shape that reflected sunshine along its length.

Then Eddie Tapley shifted slightly, and his eyes dropped to something he held in his lap, out of sight. His shoulders moved, as if he was adjusting whatever the shiny chrome antenna served.

Still running, I veered toward where Tapley was parked. My pistol was out and in my hand now, coming up in my extended arms. Other cars still blocked my line of fire. Only the top of Tapley's head bobbed in and out of my sight picture, but I had no time to slow to steady my aim.

The angle was such that in my peripheral vision I could see Tito, half a football field away. He was a dozen feet from the Eldorado, extending his arm as he aimed the keychain remote.

Then something made Eddie Tapley look up. He saw me, saw the weapon I held, and even at that range I could see his eyes widen. My aim was still partially blocked, and I swerved to the side to get a clear shot.

At the same instant, I shouted a warning.

"Tito!" My voice burst forth pitched shrill and high; it might have been a scream. "Bomb! In the car!"

Tapley was looking down again, and I had no more time. I skidded to a stop, with a clear corridor to my target now. As if by its own accord, my Smith & Wesson locked firm on target. Tapley's head was centered post-and-notch in my gunsights.

"Tapley! Show me your hands! Do it *now*—"

But I was too late.

Tapley's shoulder dropped, and an intense white light erased the shadows of the midday sun. As my pistol bucked hard against my grip, I felt heat on the side of my face.

An instant later, the concussive blast reached me.

I was crouched low in a shooter's stance. That, more than anything else, shielded me from most of the force. But around me, car windows shattered inward an instant before the roar of the explosion reached my ears.

I remember for a long moment pressing close against metal, the side of a car, my eyes squeezed tight against a confused discordant wailing. Some of it came from dozens of cars around the parking lot, their alarms triggered by the blast.

But even as I rose and rushed toward the fiercely burning hulk of what had been Tito's Cadillac, I realized part of the screaming that filled my ears was coming from deep inside me.

CHAPTER 25

The next half hour is still indistinct in my memory, a kaleido-scopic blur of shouting people and ambulances and frenzied movement from parking lot to vehicle to hospital. I remember the details well enough, but not as if I had experienced them personally. It was as if, dispassionately, I had watched individual scenes in a particularly poorly edited film.

In contrast, I remember the smells as stark and distinct—first the smoke, acrid and foul, later the mingled odor of diesel and blood in the ambulance. Finally, an air-conditioned reek that was at once both antiseptic and yet somehow unclean, the unmistakable bouquet of every hospital.

I forced my way onto the ambulance that transported Tito, standing in a half crouch with one hand against the roof bracing myself against the mad bouncing. There had been no attempt to stabilize Tito at the scene, and in itself that was a prognosis of his condition. During our six-minute transit to Spanish Bay Memorial Hospital, the EMT twice employed the electroshock paddles in a desperate bid to jolt Tito's heart back into sinus rhythm.

Then we were there, skidding to a halt as the twin doors but-terflied open in an explosion of sunlight. The sudden brightness dazzled my vision, and by the time I could again see clearly the attendants had bustled the wheeled stretcher inside the emergency entrance. I started to follow, but strong hands seized my upper arms and steered me instead to the ER waiting chairs.

I had not been there more than five minutes when another ambulance squealed to a halt at the door, disgorging its own bandage-swathed cargo amid the choreographed ballet of different medical-crisis team. The draped form was rushed into an ER suite that adjoined the one where Tito had disappeared. Immediately, a uniformed officer who I did not recognize took up position outside the suite's door.

He felt my gaze on him, and acknowledged me with a slight inclination of his head. But when I approached, he shifted enough to signal that I could not pass.

"That my guy?" I asked, and was surprised to hear my voice unsteady.

"Yeah," he said, then lowered his voice. "Nice shooting, Lieutenant. Bastard took it through the temple. Organ donor now, looks like. Better 'n he deserves, what he done."

Gina Schwartz arrived moments later, flanked by two Spanish Bay cops, one of them a female officer. Gina spotted me and pushed past the nurse administrator to where I stood. Her eyes searched my face intently.

"Oh, God, Quynn. How is he?"

"I . . . it doesn't look good, Gina. He's hurt pretty badly."

"Oh, God," she repeated.

I forced the words past my lips. "I did this to him, Gina. The bomb was meant for me, not . . ." I faltered, and it was a moment before I could try again. "This was my fault."

Her eyes were closed tightly, and I thought for a moment she had blocked out my words. But when I opened my mouth to speak again, her hand shot out and took my forearm in an iron grip.

"The best time of his life was when you two were partners," Gina said. "He wanted to be a cop again, Quynn—he never stopped wanting it, ever."

Just then the door flew open and they wheeled Tito from the

emergency room, a corps of scrub-suited residents and nurses moving at an awkward run toward the elevator that led to the surgical suites. I had only a momentary glimpse of my friend as he passed, a crimson-stained form motionless on the gurney. Tubes and conduits looped from various monitors and hanging IV bags, an inexorable web that had ensnared Tito at its apex.

Then the nurse administrator was there, a plastic clipboard in her hand. With her was another person, a squat man in blue scrub pants and a white lab coat. He needed a shave, but his hands looked solid and competent.

"Mrs. Schwartz, I'm Doctor Panjaniti. I'm the attending physician. Your husband requires immediate surgery. We'll need your consent."

In a flash, the nurse had swept Gina away, down the hallway in the direction Tito had been taken. The physician moved briskly toward a door that led to the stairwell. He studiously ignored my presence beside him, until finally I took his upper arm in my grasp.

"Is he going to die?"

"Are you a relative, madam? You heard what I told Mrs. Schwartz."

"I need to know, Doctor. He's my partner. My—" I groped for words I could not find, words that would make the physician understand.

"As I said, he's heading into surgery," Panjaniti said. Then his features softened and he lowered his voice. "Look, I do not know why the man is still alive. Most people with his injuries would have died at the scene. Am I being clear enough for you? Now, I have to scrub in. Pardon me, please." He pulled his arm from my grasp and trudged up the stairs.

I had just made my mind up to follow when Chick Cornelieus appeared at my shoulder.

"Quynn. Are you injured?"

I shook my head, and realized that for some unknown reason the question infuriated me. "Tito is hanging on by his damn fingernails. When the bomb blew, he—"

"I know. Let's sit over there."

We settled into an unpopulated corner of the waiting area, and I saw more officers take up position to keep away any interlopers. Cornelieus leaned forward in the chair, his forearms on his thighs supporting his body weight. He seemed to gather himself before he spoke.

"What happened, Quynn? From your viewpoint."

"I went to Tapley's apartment. He must have spotted me in the parking lot. I suppose the temptation was too much for him to resist."

"The Winn-Dixie people maintain video surveillance of their parking lots. We'll know more after we review the recording."

I nodded tightly. "Everybody is videotaping everybody else these days, it seems."

"You're sure Tapley was after you, not Schwartz."

"I knew Tapley, he knew me. We had a bit of a history. I roughed him up, humiliated him in a room full of people. He had a bomb and saw a chance for payback."

"So he blows up the wrong guy?"

"For all he knew, I was coming back at any minute. Then he saw me drawing down on him and panicked."

Cornelieus considered that for a moment, or perhaps he was simply granting me time to anticipate his next question.

"Why were you there, exactly?"

"Why the hell do you think? I wanted to try to develop a lead on whoever took the shot at me."

As I spoke, Cornelieus lips had pulled tight. Still, he waited, as if knowing I had more to tell him.

"Tapley's also the only link I had to M. C. Mason and the Centurions."

His eyes closed, then slowly opened again. "So it was just bad luck that you crossed paths in the parking lot. You haven't talked with him since the two of you tangled?"

"I didn't talk with him, no. By the time I spotted him, the son-of-a-bitch already had his finger on the detonator. I wish to hell I had dropped the hammer on him then. Instead, I let him see me."

Cornelieus nodded, but not as if he had heard my words. Then, "Tapley is flat-lined. No brain-wave activity, clinically dead. I assume you already know that."

I remembered the sight picture that had centered Tapley's forehead, but I said nothing.

"He had a toy walkie-talkie from Radio Shack. The kind they sell in pairs."

"The other one was wired up to a blasting cap and a half kilo of Semtex."

"That's what we figure," Cornelieus said. "Seems like a lot of trouble to go to, just to even the score for a beating."

"He had some other plan for the bomb, Chief. This was impromptu. He saw me and used the weapon he had with him."

Cornelieus nodded. "That's the other thing. There was a shotgun in the trunk of his car. Twelve-gauge pump, fired recently. It makes Tapley look awfully good for the shooting at Schwartz's house."

"A shotgun. Why didn't he use that, instead of a damn bomb?"

"No shells in the gun or the car. I guess he forgot to pick up more ammo."

"I wish to hell he had."

Cornelieus waited for me to say more, but I had nothing left to give him. Or so I thought, until he asked the only question that really mattered.

"What was Schwartz doing there, Quynn?"

"I asked him to come. He was watching my back."

Cornelieus sighed audibly, a long exhalation that betrayed weariness, and perhaps whatever emotions he was trying to hold in check.

"Why involve Schwartz? Why a civilian?"

I could not look at my superior. "I wanted . . . deniability, I guess."

"To deny what, exactly?"

"I don't know. Whatever it took to get a few straight answers."

"For God's sake, Quynn."

"It gets worse, Chief. The reason I knew Tapley had a bomb? I broke into his apartment."

"You did *what?*"

"Eddie Tapley was connected with the Centurions of the Lord. With Mason missing, he was the only lead I had."

"Was Schwartz behind this?"

"It was my idea. Tito waited in the hallway while I went in."

"What in hell were you thinking, Quynn? It's all a Federal terrorism investigation. I thought that I was clear. You are not—*we* are not involved."

"Every time I accept that argument, Chief, somebody else dies."

"You're on awfully thin ice already, Quynn. Don't say anything you're sure to regret."

"Somebody better say it, Chief," I said. "Since the Feds arrived, Howard Zhang-mei has been working overtime to sell the lone-lunatic theory. The bombing that killed Tara, the sniper attack on DeBourche, M. C. Mason's disappearance—each time, Zhang-mei takes over the case and marks it up to the same guy. Bobby Teasdale's no criminal genius, even if the Centurions of the Lord have made him their patron saint."

"Tell me how any of that justifies an illegal entry-and-search."

"Everything that's happened is linked together, Chief. Even

the so-called 'miracle' with Maddie Shepard connects into the Centurions somehow. Why is everyone trying so hard to pretend differently?"

I took a deep breath and tried to sound analytical, if not reasonable. "What I did was inexcusable. But God help me, now we have a plausible reason to doubt that Teasdale acted alone. One way or the other, the bomb in Tito's car puts a definite kink in Zhang-mei's portrait of Bobby Teasdale as a one-man terror ring."

"Not good enough, Quynn. Not for what you did to get there."

"I did what I thought was necessary."

"That's the problem. That's the problem, exactly."

He stood, and for the first time I noticed that he looked even more pale and gaunt than I was accustomed to seeing. "I don't want you to say anything more—not to me, not to anybody. I'm sorry about Schwartz. But as of this moment, you're suspended."

"If that's how you really want to handle this," I said. "But it's not going to make the problem go away, Chief. There's something rotten here. We both smell it."

"I'll arrange for you to make a formal statement later, probably tomorrow. Think about what you want to say—for the *official* record. If you know a lawyer, call him."

But before I could respond, a voice came from behind us.

"Now *that's* a fine idea, Chief Cornelieus. Let's call it 'Option One.' Option Two is busting her ass on Federal charges, right here and now."

The expression on Howard Zhang-mei's face was composed enough, but his words were clipped and angry.

Cornelieus turned to him. "This is an internal police matter, Mr. Zhang-mei."

"Oh, I think you're wrong there. What this is, is *me*—looking very upset because Quynn blows my investigation to hell by playing Wonder Woman."

He did not wait for either Cornelieus or me to respond.

"I've just been shown some really interesting video footage, Chief Cornelius."

Cornelius frowned. "Winn-Dixie was going to provide their tape to us before—"

"Winn-Dixie, hell. I'm talking about the video surveillance the FBI was conducting on one Edward Eugene Tapley." Zhang-mei spat the name out as if the taste of it was foul. "You know, I expect lowlifes like Schwartz to step in the crapper on a regular basis. What the hell, we were an eyelash away from busting him on Federal computer-hacking charges. But imagine my surprise when the playback shows Schwartz breaking into the residence of a suspect the Federal government had under surveillance, and this time, his accomplice is a law enforcement officer."

He shot a thumb in my direction. "Your girl here takes a damned nice photograph."

I felt Cornelieus' eyes on me, but I could not make myself look at his face.

Zhang-mei turned his attention to me. "Now, all of this is a problem for *me,* what with how courts look at evidence that's potentially been tainted or even planted outright. But it's also felony B&E, and that makes it a far bigger problem for *you*—oh, and for Schwartz, too. If he lives long enough to be indicted."

"Now is not the time to have this discussion," Cornelieus said.

"I disagree. It might be in the best interests of everyone concerned if the Lieutenant and I talk this out. Privately." He smiled tightly. "Who knows? We might even come up with an Option Three that makes *all* of us happy."

Cornelieus stared at him for a long moment, his brows furrowed. Then he turned to me. "It's your decision, You don't have to talk with him, Quynn. I'd advise you against making any statement whatsoever."

"Don't worry yourself, Chief. I'm suspended, remember?"

Zhang-mei took me by the elbow and led me past the nurses' station, then through a glass door into a room stocked with linens and supplies.

"You've been extremely stupid. Even if you dodge any formal charges, you're a blink away from unemployment. Normally, that would bother me not at all. But I don't relish the thought of you—all of a sudden, with no restraints whatever—crashing into the scenery."

"You have something to say to me, Zhang-mei?"

"Sure. I may have given you the wrong idea a few days ago. If it sounded as if I was encouraging you to poke around the bombing, or anything else with a Federal label on it—well, let's say just I did not express myself clearly."

"Moira Osterholm thought it was clear enough."

He raised his eyebrows. "Is that so? Well, perhaps she misunderstood also. I'll make it clear now. We'll handle it from here, on our own. In the interests of . . . let's call it 'professional courtesy' . . . we don't splash your little black-bag entry all over the press. *Capice?* That'll give your friend Beaulieu and his Congressman brother-in-law one less bullet to shoot at Chief Cornelieus."

"Despite what happened today, you're sticking to the story that Teasdale bombed the clinic?"

"I can accept a two-man conspiracy, Teasdale and Tapley, and that fits the situation just fine. Oh—and before you ask, we found Teasdale's fingerprints all over Mason's place. Makes that one kind of an easy call, too."

"And the sniper attack? Still Teasdale?"

"No new evidence there. He looks very good to me."

"Come off it, Zhang-mei. You're working awfully hard to

make the facts fit one suspect. I want to know why."

"You're rather out of your depth here. Surely you sense that?"

"Tell me something. Did you send Jack Reagan out to see me last night, or was that his idea?"

It took him aback, but only for a moment.

"Don't look a gift horse in the mouth. In any event, why would it matter?"

Zhang-mei, a genial smile on his face, waited for me to respond.

But I was in no mood to debate, even had I been able. A taut elastic sinew, by now almost a physical presence inside my skull, torsioned itself even tighter. I took a step toward the door, but Zhang-mei shifted to block my exit.

"Just so we're clear, Lieutenant. If you try to interfere again, I'll make sure that you're placed under arrest. If Cornelieus is too shy to act, I'll find some Federal charges that will work just fine. Believe it, that would just be the start of your troubles."

"Do what you have to do," I said. "If you're going to have me arrested, do it. If not, get out of my face."

"You really don't want me as an enemy, Quynn," he said softly. "Trust me, it would not be a good move."

Without doubt, he was right. But I no longer cared.

I started to push past him to the door, but once more he moved to block my path. He looked at me, his chest so close that it brushed the tips of my breasts. But I said nothing, and a thin smile crossed his lips. The smug satisfaction that I read behind his eyes was the tipping point.

The too-tight band inside me snapped.

As if by its own volition, my left hand shot forward. Fingers and thumb formed a pincer that thrust deep into Zhang-mei's throat and closed in an unyielding grip around his windpipe. Immediately, his mouth fell open and his eyes opened wide.

I dipped slightly, thrusting my shoulder into his chest and

pushing hard with my legs, slamming him violently back against the wall once, then again. I held him there with the weight of my body leaning in. With my free hand I slapped away his clawing fingers as I squeezed infinitesimally harder. The message was clear. Immediately, Zhang-mei's own hands fell away in surrender and his struggle ceased. In response, I eased my grasp on his airway enough to permit him a thin, wheezing inhalation, then another.

Whatever was in his eyes now contained no measure of conceit. Zhang-mei stared at me as if I was an unrecognized life form, alien and unmistakably dangerous.

"I'm tired," I said, leaning close to his congested face. "I'm tired of playing whatever game this is. I'm tired of seeing the people I care about hurt. I'm tired of being manipulated and lied to. But most of all, I'm deadly tired of *you.*"

"You're insane," he rasped, and even so I could hear his fury. "You've assaulted a Federal official. You'll be lucky if—"

His words stopped abruptly when I squeezed again.

As if someone else controlled my actions, I glanced past him. The nearest person, a nurse studying a computer monitor at the station, was a dozen or more feet away and on the other side of the door. Neither she nor anyone else within view was looking in our direction.

The temptation was so enormous that it startled, then alarmed, me.

Some of what I felt must have shown on my features, because Zhang-mei started to struggle once more. This time, he flailed at my arms and kicked out at me. I must have been close to crushing the brittle cartilage of his windpipe, and it was only that realization that dispelled the dark compulsion that had held me in close embrace.

I released my hold, and Zhang-mei slid down the wall. He sat on the floor, legs splayed. As he stared up at me, his lips moved like a fish wrenched from the water and cast far up on the bank.

Whatever terrible force had come close to possessing me was gone now, but in its aftermath I could feel the muscles in my thighs tremble.

"Don't come near me again," I said to him. "Don't even let me see you again. The next time, I don't think I'll be able to stop."

I stepped over his legs and left.

But I did not get far before the world caved in.

As I passed the nurses' station, I became aware of a commotion down the hallway. It was the tumult of voices, several of them talking at once. But above them rose a sudden cry that, in its wordless despair, filled me with dread.

I broke into a run, oblivious to anything in my path. I was vaguely aware that Cornelieus had reached out to seize my arm, and that I had wrenched myself from his restraining grasp. Down the hall, Gina Schwartz was already being helped into a room by a taller figure who was half supporting her.

I pushed past people I might have known, thinking to follow; but at that moment, my focus was caught by a man who stood unnaturally still, watching me approach. He still wore the pale-blue surgical scrubs I had seen him in earlier, but now they were spotted and stained. Close up, he smelled of copper pennies and disinfectant.

I halted before him, but when I opened my mouth no sound emerged.

If my paralysis was an attempt to stop time, to keep the fearful words from being said, it failed utterly.

"We did everything we could," Dr. Panjaniti said to me. "I'm very sorry."

CHAPTER 26

I half expected someone to intercept me as I left the hospital—a delegation of my police brethren, perhaps, or maybe one of the walkie-talkie-equipped security guards who I envisioned memorizing my description, thoughtfully provided by Howard Zhang-mei. Perhaps I even hoped for a confrontation, prayed for an opportunity to vent my murderous sorrow with the relief of raw physical violence.

One guard eyed me with serious intent in the lobby, or I thought he did, but he only nodded to me, a sympathetic response to whatever he read in my features, and I pushed through the revolving door and into the sauna outside.

I crossed the parking lot under a blazing orb bright and merciless, so searing that I did not know if my eyes squeezed tight against its light or to fight the tears that burned equally hot. I knew I should go back, that I should comfort Gina and receive comfort in return.

But I might as well have willed myself to fly.

Instead, I forced myself to keep walking, stumbling half-blinded on asphalt that scorched the soles of my feet inside my shoes. I had no plan or destination, save to flee my pain and my guilt.

Luck was with me. Near the outpatient entrance, a taxi had just disgorged a gray-faced man wearing a stained Thompson collar. I slid in. The windows were tinted almost opaque, turning the interior dark as cobalt, and chill with the sterile exhalation of the vehicle's air conditioner. I pulled the door shut behind me, as if I was closing my own casket.

"Just go," I told the driver. "I don't care where."

We wandered across town, an aimless meandering. We passed bay-front townhouses and high-rise condominiums along the Gulf, their lush landscaping tended by acolytes in shorts and dirty T-shirts. We drove by ramshackle shotgun shacks, their roofs rusted to the color of dried blood and shaded by an overgrowth of palmetto and pines, where people holding oversized bottles of malt liquor stared at us with hooded eyes. In our directionless roving, we transected the breadth of Spanish Bay, both geographical and sociological. At one point, I realized that we had driven within a block of the house I had only recently shared with Ron. This time, I felt only an odd detachment at the fact.

After his initial tentativeness had passed, the driver kept up a nonstop chatter: gasoline prices, local politics, whether there were more tourists this year than last and whether this was good or bad. To each topic, I responded briefly or not at all; either way seemed fine with him. He did not mention sacred apparitions or violent death, nor did he speak of betrayal or truths concealed, or any of the other thoughts that swirled dark across my mind.

We drove for more than an hour before I finally gave the driver an address. Fifteen minutes later, he pulled up in front of the Spanish Bay Municipal Center.

In an odd gratitude that I did not understand myself, I overtipped him as I left his cab.

I had not been at my desk for more than a few minutes when Cornelieus appeared at my elbow. I ignored him, instead pretending to concentrate on the computer screen on my desk as it spun up into life. He reached across to the console and pressed a switch; at once, the screen display faded and died.

"My office, Quynn. I don't want to do this out here."

"No need for formalities, Chief." My eyes were still on the now-dark screen as I opened the top drawer of my desk. Inside, my badge and ID lay next to the Smith & Wesson, still in its pancake holster.

"I'm sorry about Schwartz," Cornelieus said, his voice low. "I know how close the two of you were. But you're still suspended."

"If that's your decision. I made a mistake, Chief. But you're making a bigger one."

"You made the mistake when you decided to write your own rules." Without fanfare, he reached into the drawer and removed the badge and weapon. "If there's any personal property in your desk, take it with you now. I'll let you know when we schedule the formal hearing."

He walked away, and my eyes flickered right and left. The whole exchange had taken only a minute and had been so deftly handled that none of those working around me seemed to have noticed my transition to quasi-civilian.

I stood, but I did not take Cornelieus' advice. There was nothing I needed from my desk. I could detect no odd looks, whether of sympathy or simple curiosity, from any of my fellow officers in the Detective's bureau. It was proof positive that Cornelieus had not yet relayed word of my suspension to my colleagues. Good. I no longer had my badge and my sidearm; but until word got around of my new status, I was not completely without official resources.

I left by the front door of the bureau. Then, instead of turning toward the main exit, I headed directly to Records, where a rail-thin black woman in a sergeant's uniform scowled at my request.

"Dammit, Lieutenant. What the hell's wrong with the computer on your own desk?"

"C'mon, Rosa," I said. "You know the story around here. Systems people say I can't get the monitor replaced for another week."

"Those lazy dickheads," Rosa muttered, grudgingly acknowledging solidarity against a common enemy. "Okay, okay, use the damn terminal in the file room. You need any of my hard-copy jackets, you call *me*. Don't you go rummagin' around, makin' no mess back there, or you and me gonna go *round* and round."

When I had pulled the jacket on Eddie Tapley after our barroom confrontation, I had accessed the salient facts about him. But as with any story, there are always levels deeper than the digested version. Under the surface were the details, and it was here that the devil was often to be found, smiling scornfully at anyone who tapped the source.

It took me a while to call up everything that various law enforcement agencies had compiled on Eddie Tapley, including the computerized case notes that had been keyed in by the various officers who had investigated or arrested him over the years. Most of it was both predictable and routine.

But some of the notations were cryptic, penned in the manner of a street-wise cop who knew that what he wrote might someday be the object of a defense subpoena. These were careful to merely imply culpability or involvement, though if one had learned how to decode the dialect they were often more revealing than a body-cavity search. I focused on these as I scrolled through Tapley's detailed rap sheet.

Tapley was twenty-three, and much of the official record up to age eighteen was sealed under statutes that applied to most juvenile crime. But in the five years since he graduated to adult-offender status, the pattern of Tapley's life was clear and writ-large in his file. Even if I had not turned him into a potential organ donor, it is doubtful that he would ever have been a candidate for the Mormon Tabernacle Choir.

Drugs—both using and dealing—formed the core of his criminal profile. From the files, I discovered that he was considered a probable participant in a methamphetamine ring that a county sting had broken up three years before. He had escaped arrest and prosecution there, mainly by luck and the inclination of all States' Attorney offices to concentrate on the bigger fish.

But the close call had not encouraged him to Bible study. There was an addendum, this one an interdepartmental advisory from an informant for the Texas Rangers. The note linked Tapley's name to a gang of El Paso bikers who were smuggling drugs, prescription and otherwise, in over the Mexican border. The author of the report speculated that, with the increasing anti-terrorist police presence, manufacture of a number of the drugs were shifting to garage laboratories in the U.S., particularly in Louisiana and Florida.

There followed a long list of suspect pharmaceuticals, along with the street name of each drug. I scanned through it. Despite my experience, I found myself still astounded at what people insisted on ingesting regularly. A few of the substances were highlighted in yellow, and a footnote defined these as increasingly common to spawning sites that drew the young like moths to flame. Listed were nitrous oxide, crystal meth, several formulations of Ecstasy; gamma hydroxybutyrate, AKA "Georgia Home Boy" or "Liquid G"—

I frowned suddenly, something stirring deep in my memory.

I found part of what I was looking for in the case notes of Tapley's most recent arrest, the one that had sent him to Port Léon for felony possession of illegal substances with intent to distribute. In the write up, a Spanish Bay undercover investigator had fingered Tapley at one of the better-known rave clubs that lined the harbor. He had been arrested in the parking lot, a moment after he had concluded a cash transaction with two males, aged seventeen and fifteen respectively.

Tapley had slammed his car trunk shut when the halogen beam jack-lighted him and his customers. But after he was taken into custody, the trunk was pried open and inventoried. Among the contraband entered into evidence was a glass half-gallon milk jug, more recently refilled with what the inventory described as a clear, syrupy liquid.

When it was tested by the State Crime Lab, it was found to be a particularly refined form of gamma hydroxybutyrate.

I pulled the telephone closer and dialed an internal number. But when a voice answered "Narcotics, LeFeberre speaking," I hung up, unsure of the wisdom of broadcasting my presence in-house. Instead, after a moment's consideration, I punched in the number for Spanish Bay Memorial Hospital and asked for the emergency room. There, after telling a receptionist what I wanted, a familiar voice sounded in my ear.

"Shenker here—you got the Superdoc, at your service."

"Dr. Shenker, Lieutenant Quynn. We spoke a few—"

"Yeah, I remember. The Shepard girl. What, she turning water into wine now?"

"I need some information," I said.

"If it's about the guy who got blown up, all I know is what I hear through the grapevine. He had three of the hottest surgeons in the South up to their elbows in various parts of him. But, hey—the kind of massive trauma he came in with? Miracles are kind of in short supply, unless you count the Shepard girl. What, you knew him?"

"I'm calling about something else," I said, trying to keep my voice even. "Refresh my memory. Gamma hydroxybutyrate. Club drug, isn't it?"

Shenker snorted loud through the phone I held to my ear.

"If by that you mean, 'do a lot of spoiled-punk weenies use their allowance to buy it at joints where the music shatters glass'—" Shenker laughed, but not with amusement. "Then, yeah—it's a club drug."

"Do you see a lot of cases?"

"Depends what you mean by a lot. Here, we get maybe a half dozen GHB cases a month, more during spring break season. Nasty stuff, Lieutenant."

"What are the effects?"

"A low dose, GHB can make a kid feel like half a dozen beers, minus the bladder load," Shenker said. "Higher dose, you get your primo-grade hallucinations before you blink out into sleepy-time land. *Very* high dose—or when you mix-'n-match with booze or other drugs—there's erratic heart and breathing rates, blood pressure goes up right off the chart, then suddenly plummets and you probably black out. A pre-lethal coma, we call it."

"Do adults use this stuff?"

"I've never had one come in any older than twenty or so. They usually show up in my ER on weekend nights. If they're lucky, their friends walk 'em in. If they're less lucky, they get carried here. If they're crapped out of luck altogether—well, we had two DOA in the past year or so from GHB overdoses."

"What constitutes an overdose?"

"You mean how much by volume? Varies from individual to individual, and a lot depends on whether the guy who made it knows his trade. But even with the top-shelf stuff, there's a damned fine line between getting to a euphoric state and blacking out, maybe forever. GHB is a bitch to control. It's hard as hell to know if you're taking too much."

For a moment, I was silent. I pondered what Shenker had told me, and tried to fit it all into the crazy-quilt patchwork of guns and bombs and armed radicals in which Tapley had wrapped his recent life. But if there was a logical place where it all jigsawed together, I could not find it.

Then, as if to fill the dead air, Shenker spoke—and in doing so, provided the key.

"What, you bust some pimple-faced snot trying to get laid?"

"What makes you say that, Doctor?"

"GHB is a drug-of-choice, if date-rape is your thing," Shenker said. "It's odorless and tasteless. The little bastards slip it into the victim's drink, then they slip 'it' into an unconscious girl. Budding necrophiliacs, you ask me."

"Rape loses its allure when the police show up the next morning."

"For these whack-off artists, that's the beauty of GHB," Shenker said. "See, even in moderate doses one of the side effects is amnesia. The victim wakes up—well, it's a bunch of bits and pieces. The hallucinations tend to merge with snatches of what's actually happening to her; you end up with one confused, spaced-out victim. Reality takes kind of a backseat to the delirium—that is, if she remembers anything at all. Usually, she won't."

I said nothing for a moment. Then, "How quickly does it take effect?"

"It's pretty fast-acting," Shenker said. "On an empty stomach, maybe fifteen minutes or so to get the full effect."

"What if you've just had something to eat?"

"No more than a half hour, even with a full belly. But Lieutenant, most of the creeps who use it to get laid don't exactly treat their victims to dinner first."

"I'm thinking of something lighter," I said, remembering a small bedside tray with a half-filled glass and a saucer littered with fragments.

I thanked Rosa, who responded with the ill grace of the overworked everywhere. She did not look up as I left, but I still waited until the door had swung shut behind me before turning left, toward the doorway that opened onto the courthouse parking lot and my rental car.

But as I reached for the crashbar of the frosted-glass door, it swung abruptly away from my hand and I found myself face-to-face with Elle Kvamme. Her face was puffy with lack of both sleep and makeup, but her eyes were alert as she looked into mine.

"Huh," she said. "Cornelieus said he was calling me in because you were off the roster."

"I'm taking a few days. Personal leave."

Elle looked at me, not unkindly. "That so? Way I heard it, Quynn, you didn't have much say about it."

"Sorry you have to take up the slack for me, Elle."

"*Que sera.*" Her voice lost its careful nonchalance. "Damn, Quynn, I feel like hell about Schwartz. He was always decent to me, you know?"

"He knew you were a good cop, Elle."

"Radio news also said a detective at the scene capped the bomber. How are you makin' it, Quynn?"

"I've shot people before, Elle."

"Still."

"Nobody ever deserved it more than this guy."

She nodded. "You want, Dave probably wouldn't mind some company." She smiled tentatively. "Give you a chance to say hello to that beast you fobbed off on me. She's already got the other mutts hiding under the sofa, by the way."

"Thanks. I may take you up on it later."

"Do it. I get off duty, we can all burn some steaks, open some beers, talk until dawn."

"I'll try," I said, and saw her reaction. "No, I really will try."

Elle nodded as if she believed me. Then, "That birth certificate? Did you get—"

"Went over there this morning. Picked up two copies." I did

not mention they were both still in my pocket.

"Damn," she said. "I was going to ask if you got my message."

"What message?"

"I called your cell phone. Turns out, the Feds didn't need the information after all. Guy with the Chinese name even called me at home to cancel the request." She caught my expression, and looked apologetic. "Hey, Quynn—try checking your messages more often."

A good idea. I borrowed Elle's phone and keyed the number of my voice mail.

The first message was Elle's own. The second, an extended period of background ambiance that was tantalizingly familiar, but too indistinct to identify. It ended with the audible click of a receiver being replaced on a phone cradle.

But it was the third voice mail message, in a voice unmistakably female, that held my attention.

"Hello . . . hello?" There was a pause, then a sound as if someone had steeled herself a deep inhalation. "What you asked. About . . . about all this?" This time, the dead air was longer. "I want . . . I *need* to tell you something. But I have to know if—" Then the connection had abruptly gone dead, as if someone had slammed a door on her own painful resolve.

She had left no name, but even over the cell phone, I recognized the caller.

It was the recorded voice of Maddie Shepard.

CHAPTER 27

In my dark night of the soul, when I had made my nocturnal visit to Tito's house, both of us had believed that Maddie Shepard was the focus of a tug-of-war between forces who wanted to use her—but in a figurative manner, to further some political or social agenda.

That night Tito had said to me, "Don't let them use that girl." Of all that I had heard, experienced or deduced since then, that statement alone stood clear. It was as close to a deathbed request as Tito would ever make. Protecting Maddie Shepard was the only unambiguous mandate I had left, and I seized upon it like a nonswimmer cast into dark waters far offshore.

It was almost two-thirty when I pulled up at the Shepard house. There were already some small groups standing on the sidewalk or leaning against the concrete Jersey barriers that still herringboned the street. Judging by the placards and the occasional banner I saw, both sides of the abortion debate were prominently represented.

But the mood today was quiet, almost somber; perhaps the news of the morning's violence had struck some sense of propriety even among those whose beliefs drove them to fanaticism. I did not perceive the same impression of menace that had erupted into violence only two days ago. There was the occasional catcall or obscene gesture between individuals; still, even these seemed somehow dispirited—perfunctory, rather than the prelude to religious warfare.

I walked across the spacious grounds, and finally found Jesús Castile in charge, briefing a handful of men clad in the uniform of Tito's security force. When he saw me approach, he broke off the discussion and jogged to meet me halfway.

"Lieutenant Quynn. Is it true?"

I nodded my head. "He didn't make it, Jesús."

"Shit. We heard you shot the *maricon* who did it. Is the son-of-a-bitch in hell yet?"

I was silent, and Jesús did not press the issue. For a moment, we stood without speaking.

"I guess you talked to Mrs. T out at the hospital," Jesús said at last. "How's she holding up, Lieutenant?"

"Gina is a cop's wife," I said, and realized that I was stating a fact. "She never stopped being one, just like Tito never stopped being a cop."

My words seemed to make sense to the younger man. He nodded, and his gaze swept around the Shepard grounds and adjacent street.

"Shit," he said again, and raised his eyes to mine. "What in hell do we do now? Without Mr. T, all this just seems—"

"You do what Tito would have done. You do the damn job, Jesús. You don't get the luxury of feeling sorry, either for Tito or for yourself." I caught myself. "I'm sorry, Jesús. It's just that . . ."

"Don't sweat it, Lieutenant. It's okay."

"Tito told me that you're his top man. He thought the world of you."

"Means a lot. A helluva lot. Thanks."

We were both without words for what seemed like a long time.

"About today," Jesús began, speaking slowly. "If it's okay with you, I got my guys deployed along—"

"Change of plans, Jesús," I interrupted, and nodded toward

the residence. "I'm going to be inside. I'd appreciate it if you didn't bring up that fact, when my replacement arrives."

Castile was looking at me thoughtfully.

"Uh-huh. Anything I should know, Lieutenant?"

"I've been pulled off, Jesús. Suspended. The fact is, you'll be taking a chance if you help me."

He searched my face, as if looking for a revelation that would make everything reasonable, if not a matter of logic. "C'mon, Lieutenant Quynn. You gotta tell me why I should."

"I can't think of a reason if you can't. Either way, I'll still be inside."

Jesús Castile inhaled deeply, and blew it out in a sibilant *sotto vocce* I took to be an obscenity. Then he raised his eyes to meet mine, and his gaze was steady.

"You came by, told me about Mr. T," Jesús said as if reciting from a textbook. "After that, I don't know where the hell you went."

The door to the Shepard residence was unlocked when I tried it, a welcome breech of security. After my last visit, I didn't care to contest my entry with Sister Benedicta, and this time I did not have Missy along to vouch for my good intentions.

The foyer was empty, though I could hear muted activity elsewhere in the house. I checked my watch; almost three. I still had some time. Under the established pattern, Maddie's apparitions occurred at or around four. Given the time required to take effect, it was still too early for anyone to have slipped any drugs to the girl upstairs.

If, in fact, that was what was happening at all. If it was not, then the most optimistic outcome was that my present suspension would be made permanent.

I was surprised at the extent to which I did not care.

As quietly as I could, I crossed the foyer, toward the stairway that led to Maddie Shepard's room.

"If you're looking for Mr. Shepard, he went upstairs a few minutes ago to visit with his daughter."

The voice came from the study, and it belonged to Sister Benedicta. She sat near the telephone stand, and I noticed that her chair had been arranged to command a view of the hall. By her feet was an oversized suit bag and a nylon valise, its sides bulging. It seemed far too much luggage to have packed for an overnight visit to Atlanta.

"I'm here to see Maddie. After that, I have a few questions for you."

She raised her eyebrows at that, but when she spoke it was on a different subject.

"You asked about what happens when Maddie has her spells. What exactly did you see yesterday, Lieutenant?"

"I think you know. What is the proper term, Sister? Trance? Fugue state?"

She ignored my tone. "But nothing you would term . . . inexplicable. In the natural course of events, that is."

"You're the expert on miracles, I thought. Isn't that why you're here?"

"Nobody is an expert on such occurrences, Lieutenant. That's why they're called 'miracles.' " She shrugged, self-deprecating. "In any event, if you have anything to ask me, you'd better do it now. I'm only waiting to see Mr. Shepard. I want to thank him for his hospitality."

I frowned. "You're leaving?"

"I've overstayed my welcome." Her voice sounded nonjudgmental, carefully neutral. "I fear that Mr. Shepard and I are not of compatible natures."

"Who'll treat Maddie now?"

"Mr. Shepard made that very clear. It is no longer my concern." There was a steely light in her eyes I would not have cared to have aimed in my direction. "In any event, I've completed what I came here to do."

"Really," I said. "You consider the girl cured?"

"An odd choice of words, Lieutenant. Am I to assume you are not one of those who consider all this a miracle?"

"In all seriousness, Sister, you're still talking about miracles?"

"Wouldn't it be nice to believe in them?" She smiled as if she was agreeing with something I had said. "However, whatever I might say on that subject will be included in my report."

"What happens then, Sister? After you make your report, I mean."

"That's not my call, Lieutenant Quynn. People far more distinguished will make those kinds of decisions."

"Advise them not to move too quickly, Sister."

"They'll move as fast as they wish to move. Why the attitude, Lieutenant?"

"If anyone is thinking to exploit Maddie, to use the media to milk mileage from what's happened to her, they might get a lot more exposure than they expect."

"Why would we want to 'exploit' the girl?" Benedicta asked.

"You may think you can replace some of the bad press your people have been getting for the past couple of years. A girl who converses with heaven might be quite an asset, if you need a new plaster saint."

Now there was no mistaking her amusement. "Lieutenant, humor me—are you a Catholic?"

"That's not relevant."

"I see." The nun was silent for a moment, as if marshaling her forces. "Nonetheless, you seem to think that if Maddie's experience is declared a miraculous event, there would be some benefit to the Church. Am I accurate?"

"Your Church wants a figurehead for its campaign to repeal the abortion laws."

"Well, Lieutenant, that's incredibly insulting. Not to mention exceedingly naive."

"Maddie's tailor-made for your purposes. You've made certain of that."

Benedicta cocked her head, and the amusement had disappeared from her manner. "To the contrary, Lieutenant. If anything, Maddie would be a catastrophe for any such movement."

"Educate me, Sister."

"You claim not to be a religious person. Fine. Then stop trying to look at all this as a religious issue."

"It's not one?"

"It's far more than that. It's a question of social policy. A great many people are asking if the United States should stand for murder-on-demand of innocent children."

"Murder. You use that word far too freely, Sister. Don't presume that you speak for me, nor for women in general."

"Ah. So you are pro-choice, Lieutenant?"

"I'm a woman. I've seen what happens when a woman is forced to bear an unwanted child. I've also seen what they'll do to keep that from happening."

"That speaks to the presumptive rights of the woman. It ignores the rights of the unborn."

"At this moment, Sister, I'm more concerned about the rights of Maddie Shepard. I won't let any of you use her as some kind of symbol to advance your own political cause."

"You are remarkably ill-informed, Lieutenant. Dangerously so, when it comes to analyzing the political interests of a church you appear to have abandoned."

The nun read my expression, frowned impatiently and tried again.

"With all due respect, Lieutenant Quynn, wake up. *Roe vs. Wade* will come before a Supreme Court in the very near future.

The chance that it will be overturned is great indeed. That is not seriously disputed by either side in the debate. I wish the Catholic Church could claim credit, but no single church or religion is strong enough to have done that alone. Behind this movement are many people who hold many different politics and theologies—some of which are wholly incompatible with any other. What they have in common is a recognition of right versus wrong, as it relates to *this* issue."

"That's an appalling thought," I replied. "I don't particularly relish the concept of an American Taliban, made up of a coalition of the righteous."

"You already live in a dictatorship," she countered. "How do you feel about living under a dictatorship of the politically correct?"

"And you believe that your side will win."

"I don't know. But if *Roe v. Wade* is overturned, the political agenda of the entire country will shift. The so-called 'modern conservative movement' is a coalition made up in large part of people who were mobilized by the issue of abortion. There are other issues, certainly—but reaction to *Roe v. Wade* helped create the conservative social movement of the past three decades."

"Which tried to turn back the clock," I said, "on feminism, sexual freedom and freedom of choice. I'm sorry, Sister, but I've never had a lot of patience for social Luddites. People who believe the world is flat are bad enough. It's worse when they insist it's a sin to think otherwise."

"I won't argue over anything as facile as the labels you chose to employ, Lieutenant," the nun said. "In certain ways, you seem an intelligent woman. So you tell me. Remove *Roe v. Wade* from the equation, and what happens?"

"Abortion would no longer be considered constitutionally guaranteed," I said. "I'd assume some states would restrict, even abolish abortion rights. There would be increased pressure for abolition of abortion at the national level."

"Very perceptive, Lieutenant Quynn. I think your assessment is quite likely accurate."

"And your side wins."

"Politicians don't think the way you or I do. For conservative candidates, it would no longer be just a question of defending *limited* restrictions on abortion. They would have to state clearly whether they were willing to send women and their doctors to prison for infanticide. Think, Lieutenant Quynn—for those who 'won' with the end of *Roe v. Wade,* would that be that good or bad?"

"Sister, why don't you tell me?"

"The liberal faction would move quite quickly to encompass the moderates—all those appalled by the 'extremism' of the conservative political-religious base. Very quickly, the conservative movement would find itself losing ground in every key state. Any chance at winning the presidency would be gone, at least for a generation. There would be political chaos for years."

"What has this to do with Maddie, Sister?"

Benedicta leaned forward, intent. "Try to understand, Lieutenant. The *last* thing the Catholic Church would want is to have the pro-choice movement thought of as some kind of religious crusade, particularly one orchestrated by us. Put it another way. To 'manufacture a saint,' as you put it, would be stupid. It would be incredibly divisive. It could ignite a firestorm among the various political factions that today are only at an uneasy peace with us, and with each other."

"You want the result but you shrink from the blame," I said. "You take a lot on yourself, Sister. You and the others who want to turn back the clock."

"So you are pro-abortion, Lieutenant? In your profession, I would have expected you to have more respect for human life."

"Maybe I believe that a woman has the right to choose

271

whether she will become a mother."

"The woman who chooses abortion doesn't cease to be a mother," Benedicta retorted. "She simply becomes the mother of a dead baby."

"In your view, perhaps. In the ideology you'd like to impose."

"In *truth*, Lieutenant," Benedicta said. "This truth is a particularly painful reality. When a woman has an abortion, *something* dies. Try as one might to deny it, deep inside we all know it's a human life."

"Not everyone believes that, Sister."

"Do tell, Lieutenant Quynn. A day ago you quoted Thomas Aquinas on the concept of natural law. The instinctive knowledge all humans carry inside them."

"So?"

"So I've spent a large part of my life talking to women who have had abortions—hundreds of them, on both sides of the issue. The overwhelming majority of them manifest a profound sadness, a heartfelt misery, when they discuss it."

I felt my anger rise, despite the knowledge that my reaction was as personal as it was rhetorical. "And how is that proof of your argument?"

"Do people experience regret when they have a mole removed, or when a cancerous tumor is surgically cut from their bodies? If one truly believes that a fetus is merely an inconvenient lump of tissue, why would there be so much sorrow even years after the event?"

"That's rather simplistic, isn't it?"

"No. It's only simple—as in 'plainly evident.' What should surprise you is how many of these women turn to drugs or alcohol abuse, uncharacteristic sexual promiscuity, or some other self-destructive behavior after exercising their 'choice.' The myth of 'choice,' indeed. Is it so difficult to see that they're self-medicating? Punishing themselves?"

"Are you speaking as a physician or a nun now?"

"I was a physician long before I took the vows to become a nun, Lieutenant."

"Then you should know better than to make moral assumptions about why people do what they do."

"Open your eyes. Can you not see that each of these poor women has become another victim of this carefully packaged lie, this politically correct evil?"

"It continues to bother me that you throw the word 'evil' around so easily, Sister."

"I was once a missionary, in Africa. Before I became a nun, I was a lay physician there. I ran a mission hospital in Rwanda when the Hutu tribal faction massacred *eight hundred thousand* Tutsi tribesmen in a matter of just a few months. I have seen death and disease and all manner of human misery and sin, so don't presume to define 'evil' for me, Lieutenant Quynn."

"In my experience, Sister, people create their own definition of evil. It doesn't have to mirror reality, as long as it reflects their own prejudices or fears. It's the same basis children use to manufacture the monsters that live under their beds."

"Monsters exist. I've seen them, as I'm sure you have in the work that you do. They live among us, and they prey upon our weaknesses. Today, more than ever."

"You know your dogma well, Sister. A few days ago, I heard M. C. Mason make much the same arguments. The two of you would be a very effective debating team."

"Despite the gulf between us as to the morality of violence, the Church and Mason's Centurions both recognize abortion as intrinsically evil."

"You have one advantage the Centurions don't. You can play the miracle card, even if it ruins a young girl's life. Is that your plan, Sister?"

"I say again, it's not my decision to make, Lieutenant."

My voice rose.

"That won't wash, Sister. This is all tied in somehow to the Centurions and the violence they preach. I won't let you stonewall whatever you know. Not when people are dying."

"I can't help you, Lieutenant. Why can't any of you understand that? I've said the same thing to Mr. Shepard, to Mr. Zhang-mei, to Mr. Schwartz—"

"Tito Schwartz was killed earlier today," I said, and the nun's face froze in sudden shock. "A Centurion set off a bomb in his car. Tito died without regaining consciousness."

"I'm sorry," she said. "I didn't know. My God. I didn't know."

"I'll ask you again. Is your Church going to declare all this some kind of supernatural occurrence and use Maddie to hype your headlines?"

There was an extended silence as my gaze bored into hers, but I could detect no deception or artifice in them.

"I cannot divulge the specifics of what I will report to my superiors, Lieutenant," she said finally. "But I can tell you this, as a matter of Church dogma and of my own personal conviction. The Mother of God simply would not urge people to murder any human being—not abortionists, not anyone."

It was my turn to frown.

"You think that the girl is pretending to see and hear these . . ." I stopped, not certain what word to use.

"I don't believe Maddie Shepard is pretending anything," Benedicta said.

"Then what is your explanation, Sister Benedicta?"

"Open your ears, Lieutenant. I don't *have* any answers to share. How do you prove a negative? By saying 'It's not a miracle because I don't believe it's one'?"

"That is the nun speaking, Sister. What does the doctor say?"

"For the love of God, Lieutenant. I've tended that girl, spent hours—days!—talking with her. How can I know the difference anymore?"

Her words were still heated, but her attitude was that of a woman adrift. I saw the realization of what she had said cross her features, and it shocked both of us into an extended silence.

"Well, there you have it," she said, finally. "Consider the case of a nun, a religious person who has been ordered to look for a natural explanation for every event in Scripture." Her face twisted into a rueful expression. "You know the story of Jesus' torment in the Garden of Gethsemane. How a sweat of blood ran down his face as he prayed to be spared the death he knew was imminent?"

"Yes."

Benedicta smiled, characteristically wry. But now there was a measure of pain in it that I did not understand.

"The medical term is 'hematidrosis,' you see. It's uncommon, but by no means undocumented in medical literature. For a certain percentage of the population, extreme stress can cause the small blood vessels near the sweat glands to rupture. The result is, literally, a sweat of blood. For these people, it's not a miracle. It's simply a medical condition."

She took a deep breath. "During Maddie's episodes, we've monitored her vital signs, of course. Not always, but often enough to provide a pattern. At those times she becomes very agitated and her blood pressure rises significantly. Enough so that the wounds in her hands can open and she begins to bleed."

The nun grasped my forearm, as if she felt the need for me to understand a critical point.

"For Jesus, was it a miracle or merely the physiological re-action of a man who knew he was about to be betrayed, to be executed in a particularly hideous manner? Or was it both? One could ask the same questions regarding Maddie Shepard."

Again, I saw the strangely sad smile.

"My job demands that I become a professional skeptic, Lieutenant. I can't think of a faster way to endanger one's faith. You find yourself questioning every core value, every belief you started out with."

Her voice faltered, and for a long moment her eyes locked onto mine. "I suspect you know exactly how that feels, don't you?"

When I did not respond, she nodded as if I had confirmed some deep-seated secret for her.

Then she said, "Does it matter, in the end? Maybe all I do, by dissecting such things, is to endanger my own soul—or worse, that of others—by engendering a futile doubt."

"Everybody has doubts, Sister. You deal with them. And you try to do the right thing, despite the doubts."

"Yes, I'm sure. Absolutely, that's the only course possible for us."

Sister Benedicta glanced at the oversized watch on her wrist, and stood like a person who had made a decision. "If that's all, I'll say goodbye now, Lieutenant Quynn. I wish we could have met under different circumstances."

"Aren't you going to wait for Shepard?"

"There's no real need for me to see him again." She swung the bulky suit bag over her shoulder and hefted the valise. I moved to help her, and she waved me off with her free hand. But at the doorway, she turned back to look at me.

"I'm sorry about Mr. Schwartz. He seemed a good man."

"He was, Sister. Better than any of us deserved."

I waited for more than ten minutes after the nun left, occasionally wandering to the window to look outside. More people had arrived, and the banners of both sides of the religious–political divide were again being raised.

I could see Jesús Castile moving among his men, forming

them up along the property line and at the foot of the drive. Among them, I picked out the tan uniforms of the Spanish Bay police detail, standing in knots of two or three; even at this distance, they appeared uncertain as to their own roles. There was still no sign of Jesse Beaulieu, though the hour for today's miraculous visitation was close at hand. Nor had Roger Shepard come downstairs.

I lingered by the window for a few minutes more, then stepped into the hallway, listening for any sign of my host. But there was nothing, not even when I found myself at the foot of the stairs that led to the family quarters. It was far too quiet—as if derelict, completely abandoned by any living entity, human or divine.

The thought sent a chill through me. Without knowing why, I climbed the stairs, moving slowly and careful to keep my own steps in the center of each riser.

The door to Maddie's room was slightly ajar. With my fingertips, I eased it open.

Empty.

Inside, the yellow coverlet had been thrown back as if in haste, exposing sheets that were wrinkled but cool to my touch.

The closet was filled with girl-clothes, shoes, various other items; on the dresser, a hairbrush, comb and other personal items lay in precise alignment. The cell phone I had noticed on my first visit was still in its stand, and the battery icon indicated that it was fully charged. Nor did it appear that anything obvious was missing from the dresser drawers.

But there was a tray on the bedside table, on it a single wet ring of condensation.

I knelt, peering into the wastebasket next to the drafting table. There I found what I sought. Amid pared strips and curlicues of colored paper, shards of glass that once might have held a soft drink lay broken and wet upon a shattered saucer.

What looked like a saltine cracker was inside, too, soggy and dark with the spilled cola it had absorbed.

And then I heard footsteps behind me, moving fast.

Before I could turn, Roger Shepard was upon me, his face crimson and his eyes those of a wild creature. He seized me by the lapels and hauled me bodily to my feet. Before I could react, Shepard's open hand had swung in a wide arc, catching me on the side of the face with a sound like that of a pistol shot.

"You bitch!" Shepard said, his voice a hiss. "Tell me where she is, damn it!"

He drew back his hand again, but I stepped inside his arc and clipped him, burying a hard right hand just above his belt-line. It staggered him, and I took the opportunity to seize his outstretched arm. I twisted it behind him, levering the wristlock painfully high and pinioning his body close against the wall.

"What have you done with her?" Shepard demanded over his shoulder, and this time his voice was a hoarse rasp. "Where have you bastards taken Maddie?"

I stared at him, uncomprehending.

Shepard surged backward, trying to break my control-hold. Again, I thrust him hard against the wall.

"Calm down, Mr. Shepard. *Talk* to me, damn it! What's happened to Maddie?"

His eyes squeezed tight and he took a great, shuddering breath. When he looked up to refocus, it was as if he was noticing my presence for the first time.

"She's not in her room. I can't find her anywhere." His features were stony and accusatory. "She's not in the house. You—*they*—took her, you damned bunch of—"

"When did you . . . concentrate on *me*, Mr. Shepard! When did you last see her?"

"I don't know. Fifteen, twenty minutes ago. I took up her

afternoon snack, and she was working at her graphic-arts table."

I pulled him away from the wall and pushed him roughly into a chair. "Stay there, Mr. Shepard. No, *don't* get up—don't make this more difficult. I don't want to hit you again."

I rushed downstairs and flung open the front door, scanning the knot of security guards at the front of the house. One of them, a large man with a faded USMC tattoo on his sun-reddened forearm, looked up in surprise.

"You," I said. "Do you know who I am?"

"Sure, you're Lieutenant—"

I steered him by the elbow down the hallway and into Maddie's room.

"Stay here until I come back, or until Jesús Castile tells you differently," I told the guard. "Keep him here. Neither of you leaves this room until I say so."

I retraced my path back outside, where the rest of the door security was standing uncertainly, aware that something had happened inside. Jesús Castile was not among them, but I spotted him near the head of the circular driveway. I waved him over, and whatever he saw in my gesture brought him at a dead run.

"Secure everything, Jesús," I said. "Pass the word: lock it all down. Nobody enters or leaves the property. Roger Shepard says he can't locate the girl."

"Oh, shit." Castile lifted his handheld radio and spoke into it, his voice low and urgent.

We searched the house, floor by floor and room by room. But in the end, all of our efforts availed us nothing.

Maddie Shepard was missing—gone, without a trace.

"It's after three o'clock, Lieutenant. You think she's out there somewhere, maybe going to talk to the crowd again?"

I shook my head. "I don't think she just walked out this time.

If she's not inside, somebody took her. Who do you have on the gate?"

He keyed his radio again. In less than a minute, a stocky man in the forest green of Tito's security firm was standing with us, breathing heavily from his run up the driveway.

"The Shepard girl," Jesús said. "Did you see her today, Frank?"

"That why you had me runnin', in this kinda heat? Damn, Jesús, you coulda asked that on the radio instead of—"

I took the guard by the upper arm. He winced, as surprised as I by the intensity of my grip.

"Has anybody left the grounds in the past half hour?" I demanded.

"Just the Sister," Frank said. "You know, that Sister Benny-something. One's been nursing the kid. Didn't know they let 'em drive cars." He turned to Castile, his voice defensive. "I was tole keep people out. Nobody said nuthin' about keepin' 'em *in*."

Jesús's voice was calming. "You're not in any trouble, Frank," he said. "We just need to know when the Sister left, okay?"

"They drove outta here . . . I dunno, maybe ten minutes ago."

"What do you mean 'they'?" I said.

"They always travel in pairs, ever notice?"

CHAPTER 28

There is a routine to all modern law enforcement, and few systems are as rigidly efficient as what occurs with the report of a missing child. A sequence of carefully planned steps are set into motion, immediately and automatically; there is little time wasted and even less left to chance, if only because the stakes have proven to be so high, so often.

In the case of the missing Maddie Shepard, a part of that translated to the arrival of a three-car convoy of Spanish Bay detectives and technicians only minutes after I punched in 9-1-1 from the phone in Shepard's study. Tires squealing, the cars pulled into the driveway past the startled crowd outside, which parted like the Red Sea before the screaming klaxons and flashing lights.

Jesse Beaulieu was in the lead car. Before the vehicle had crunched to a stop, he already had one foot on the ground. A moment later, he burst through the front door like a home invader, and scowled darkly when he spotted me. Then, without comment, he pushed past me.

In his wake, half a dozen officers carrying oversized bags and cases trooped into the foyer and down the hall. As Beaulieu turned into the study where Shepard now waited with my ex–Marine guard, two of them disappeared into the front room. The others headed for the upper floors, taking the stairs two steps at a time. A moment later, the reflected flash of a photographer's strobe lit the walls, again and again.

I gave my statement to a uniformed officer I knew only slightly, one eye on the study door, watching for Beaulieu to reemerge. Even so, I was startled when he suddenly appeared at my shoulder.

Without preamble, he spoke. "You again."

"The girl's missing, Jesse. This isn't the time."

"Whatever. He said you talked with the nun. What did she say to indicate she was going to pull this kind of shit?"

"Nothing. Mainly, we were discussing politics."

"Sure you were." His voice was hoarse and tight, most likely with the effort he was expending to restrain from throttling me.

"Benedicta said she had overstayed her welcome. That sounds to me as if she didn't leave by her own choice."

"Shepard claims he ordered her out."

"Why, Jesse? He says Benedicta leaked word of Maddie's so-called message to the Centurions. What made him act now, if he didn't throw her out back then?"

Beaulieu shrugged impatiently, as if waving off my concern as irrelevant. But I had made a point, and he knew it.

"The room she used here is cleaned out. Nothing left to tell us where she went, or why she took the kid."

"Benedicta had luggage with her, Jesse—several bags, two of them sizable. She didn't appear nervous to me."

"You have a point to make here?"

"If somebody's planning an abduction, I don't see them taking along all their stuff, let alone getting into a debate with a cop just beforehand."

He grunted in what might have been agreement. "Shepard also says you're somehow mixed up in his daughter's disappearance."

"Are you asking me a question, Jesse?"

Beaulieu did not reply immediately. When he did, his tone was flat and deliberate.

"We've put out an all-points-alarm on the nun's car, and the State is issuing an Amber Alert on the girl. Find a place, sit there. I might have a few questions in a while."

For the next quarter hour, I did just that, too well aware of my own uselessness.

Several voices rose outside the front door, loud enough to turn heads of those around me. It was loud enough to draw a scowling Beaulieu from the study. His first guess was the same as mine.

"No reporters," he growled to the uniformed cop who had taken my statement. "Keep 'em away from the house until I say different."

But at that moment the front door opened, and I turned to see Moira Osterholm surveying the room as if she was memorizing its layout. She had two neatly dressed young men in tow. Without a word the trio crossed the foyer until they stood nose-to-nose with Beaulieu.

"Where is Chief Cornelieus?" Osterholm demanded.

"Having a relapse," Beaulieu said, and my head snapped up at his words. "You can probably reach him at his doctor's office. I guess you think you're taking over this one, too."

By the look Osterholm gave Beaulieu, she might have been examining a particularly pungent variety of pond algae.

"I am not here for that," she said. "Not as long as it is being dealt with adequately by *local* authorities."

Osterholm turned her back to him. She scanned the room until her gaze settled on me. She pointed, and the two FBI agents stepped forward. They took up positions flanking me, and at her gesture each took a solid grip on my biceps.

"What in hell are your priorities?" I said and felt the hot flush on my face. "Maddie Shepard is—"

"I am aware of the situation," she interrupted. "You will come with me, Quynn."

"Am I under arrest?"

"Not at present."

"Then we have nothing to discuss." I shook one of Oster-holm's contingent loose from my arm; in reaction, his companion's grip tensed. Of its own volition, my newly freed hand tightened into a fist.

But before the situation could escalate into violence, Oster-holm's voice cut through it like a whip.

"Let her go," she said to her underling; then, her tone chill, she addressed me.

"I assumed you might still have an interest in Maddie Shepard's welfare."

"What do you want?"

"A moment of your time. In private."

CHAPTER 29

We marched to the formal dining room in an unintentional lockstep; Osterholm had that effect on people. At her gesture, my two bodyguards released their hold on me at the entryway. One of them shut the double doors behind us as we passed through.

Inside, eight chairs were arrayed around a table polished to a mirror finish. Osterholm took the one at the table's head and motioned me to sit at her right.

"What's going on, Moira?"

Osterholm lifted her chin to scrutinize an impressive chandelier centered over it, tapped a sensibly square-cut fingernail against the polished wood grain. In a personage less stoic, it might have been called a display of discomfort. In Moira Osterholm, it surprised me.

"My office has developed information that we believe has relevance to domestic-terror activities," she said finally. "It is extremely sensitive in nature. You would be required to maintain it in strict confidence. Do you wish to hear it?"

I felt my body stiffen.

"Uh-huh," I said. "For no particular reason, you want to give me confidential information from a Federal investigation. Are you just wearing a wire, or is all of this being recorded on videotape, too?"

"You have been suspended by your department. An official of the Justice Department would like to see you in a Federal prison and your scalp hanging in his trophy case. It is no secret how Jesse Beaulieu feels about you. Unless I have missed something, you are running short of friends these days." She saw my face change and raised her palm. "A poor choice of words, Quynn. I am sorry about Schwartz."

"Get on with it."

She leaned forward, her elbows on the table, and I had an urge, sudden and incongruous, to correct her manners. "If I provide this information, you will treat it as strictly confidential," she said. "Agreed?"

I nodded.

"First, does the name 'Harvey Cabot' have any significance to you?"

"Should it?"

"Only if you are the Spanish Bay officer who visited the County Records Department earlier today and left with a copy of Cabot's birth certificate. If not, you should be aware that someone who fits your description is using your identification. Must we play these games?"

She waited a few beats, then continued.

"There is a Harvey Cabot who is on record as having violated an order of support issued in North Carolina. Presumably, he fled across state lines. I say 'presumably' because there is no record of his arrest—or, in fact, any official record of his current whereabouts. I am interested as to why you found it necessary to obtain information on Cabot's birth, Quynn."

"Is Zhang-mei wondering about that, too?"

"That is the point of this conversation, Quynn. Howard Zhang-mei has not yet been informed about your interest in Cabot, or of any efforts you may have made to learn more. I would prefer him not to find this out . . . *prematurely,* as a result of some action you might feel compelled to take."

I kept my face impassive, but it was an effort.

"Zhang-mei made a backdoor request to my department for any information we had on Cabot," I said. "Then he changed his mind and withdrew the request. A few hours ago at the hospital, Zhang-mei made it clear that he didn't want me looking into Bobby Teasdale, Margot Mason, or anything else connected to these killings."

"And that struck you as unreasonable?"

"He threw in a few threats, too," I said. "They seemed out of proportion to what he wanted from me. It made me a little curious."

She nodded. "And?"

"And I did some digging. I'm fairly certain that Cabot is Margot Mason's son. That is your point, isn't it?"

"Interesting subject, this issue of parentage," Osterholm said. "In the past few days, Zhang-mei has been rather actively engaged in researching the same subject. Or at least, getting others to do it for him, as he did with your Sergeant Kvamme."

A light went on in my head. "You've tapped his phone."

"In point of fact, no. Our electronic-surveillance warrant covers only Mr. Reagan's telephone—specifically, the cell phone he carries." She made a face at my look of astonishment. "Read the Patriot Act, Quynn," she said. "This is a terrorism-related case. Mr. Reagan seems extraordinarily well informed about certain . . . *confidential* details."

"Are you saying that Jack Reagan knows about Cabot?"

"Not necessarily. But *you* were using Reagan's phone when Kvamme spoke of Zhang-mei's request."

Osterholm waved away any comment I might have made. "Suffice it to say that we did find something interesting when we processed Cabot-comma-Harvey through the computers." She rummaged deep in her bag, finally producing several sheets of tractor-feed printout.

"What is it, Moira? Put that away. I don't need to see it, just *tell* me."

"The computer came up with a seven-year-old case in North Carolina," she said. "Anne Sikora, age twenty-three, had divorced one Harvey Cabot, age listed as thirty-seven, the year before."

"Sikora. Not Cabot?"

"Common-law wife, recognized as legal in North Carolina. Ms. Sikora never bothered to change her name on the paperwork while she was with Cabot. Afterward, it seems likely she was trying very hard to forget she ever heard the name."

"Why?"

Osterholm looked up at me. "There were allegations of abuse—severe physical abuse, including sexual maltreatment, supported by medical evidence presented at the divorce hearings."

"So Harvey Cabot rapes and beats up women. Interesting, given his mother's politics."

"You will find this even more interesting, Quynn," Osterholm said. "In the divorce petition, Ms. Sikora listed her profession as 'obstetric-surgical nurse.' After the divorce, to supplement her income she took a part-time job at a family planning center."

Now she had my full attention. "They do abortions there?"

Osterholm nodded. "Apparently, that was enough to get Ms. Sikora's name listed on one of those Internet Web sites that opposes abortion. North Carolina State Police has a folder full of threatening letters, incidents of harassment—all aimed at people who were on the same list."

"Have you spoken with her yet? What does she know about her ex-husband's whereabouts?"

"Once we had the Cabot link, we took a deeper look at her," Osterholm said. "The divorce wasn't the only record we found, Quynn. The other one is dated a year later. It lists an Anne Marie Sikora, age twenty-four, as a murder victim, shot at long range by an unknown gunman."

This time, I did not protest when Osterholm produced a color photograph from her bag. She pushed it across the table to me, and I looked at a studio image of a woman with prominent cheekbones and auburn hair that fell to her shoulders. She wore a wide smile for the camera. A nose that might have once been broken and set badly gave her an air of wistful vulnerability.

"The case is several years old, but the files still list it as 'active,' " Osterholm said. "Except it's not a North Carolina State case. It's one of ours."

"When? When did all this turn into a Federal investigation?"

"The same question occurred to me." She pretended to consult the papers she held. "On the day of Ms. Sikora's death, the case was declared under Federal jurisdiction in accordance with the anti-terror provisions of the U.S. Patriot Act."

I realized that my body had tensed. "Who made the call?" I asked. "I don't mean the FBI case officer. Who was the supervising attorney assigned from the Justice Department?"

She nodded, as if she were the teacher and I an unexpectedly apt pupil, and I knew the answer before she spoke.

"There are not many people named 'Zhang-mei' working in the Justice Department, Quynn."

CHAPTER 30

Jesse Beaulieu eyed me narrowly, then switched his glare back to Moira Osterholm.

"Bullshit," he said, his voice wary.

"You can appreciate this better than most people," I said. "Given what you're trying to do to Cornelieus."

"When a Federal official acts in an unusual manner, we do not dismiss it lightly," Osterholm said. "I believe that there is a disquieting pattern of behavior here. Surely you've noted his propensity for assuming jurisdiction over so many investigations?"

Beaulieu snorted. "Be hard to miss that. Most of them have been mine."

"I relay this to you in confidence," Osterholm said. "We believe Mr. Zhang-mei may have an interest in . . . *shaping* the outcome of those investigations."

"So what's all this have to do with a missing girl?"

"You're aware that statements attributed to Maddie Shepard were displayed on the Web site of the Centurions of the Lord? As a group suspected of involvements in acts of domestic terrorism, they—"

"I know about 'em. How's the girl involved?"

"At present, that is unclear. But Howard Zhang-mei took pains to find out more about Maddie Shepard and her so-called 'apparitions.' He tried to involve Lieutenant Quynn in finding out more, in a clandestine manner."

"Say that I agree to cooperate. What do you want me to do?"

"You work the incident for what it is—a child is missing," she replied. "That has not changed. You have your team here. Go through the full drill." Her voice hardened. "When Zhang-mei demands the information you have on the girl, and he *will* make that demand, you will comply. But you will make available to him only the information I have authorized. I will provide you with certain details that will provoke him to act in a way that will make his culpability clear."

Beaulieu digested this for a moment.

"Let's cut to the chase—you want my help to take down your boss."

"I am asking for your assistance," Osterholm said, her tone careful. "And for your discretion."

Beaulieu eyed the Federal agent for several seconds, and I could see he appreciated the irony involved.

"Uh-huh. Here's the deal. I do this for you, I want something back. This comes out the way you expect, there'll be news-papers and TV all over it. So, you tell them I helped you make the case—no, wait. I want you to say that I was 'instrumental.' And you say it a *lot*. Deal?"

"If you cooperate," Osterholm said dryly, "I will reciprocate."

"And I get any assistance I request from you on finding the Shepard girl. But I'm in charge, and I *stay* in charge."

"Agreed," Osterholm said. "Under the conditions I stated."

"There's one more condition," I said. "You give me something to do here, Jesse."

For all the effect my words had on Beaulieu, I might not have been in the room.

"Quynn's suspended," Beaulieu said to Osterholm. "One of the few things Cornelieus ever did that I agree with."

"I have made certain promises to her," Osterholm said. "Again, in exchange for her cooperation."

The light came on, and Beaulieu chuckled. "I get it. You promised her a Federal job, didn't you?" He turned to me. "You're smarter than you look, bailing out before I get a chance to fire you. But that doesn't mean I'm going to—"

"She can federalize your case, Jesse," I warned him. "She can cut you out completely. Or she can make you a hero in the news media."

This time, Beaulieu's head snapped sharply toward the Federal agent. Osterholm nodded, her features serene.

"Moira would rather have me inside the tent peeing out, than the other way around. You might want to think about that too, Jesse."

"Enjoy yourself now, Quynn. Your time is short around here."

"Either way, you want the girl safe first," I pressed, as though I was convinced Beaulieu's priorities placed that objective on the same general plane as his own ambition. "Get Cornelieus on the phone, Jesse. Or your brother-in-law, if you'd prefer. They'll both tell you to let Osterholm call the shots on this."

"Exactly how do you help me, Quynn?"

"Benedicta has been living in this house for almost a week," I said. "She's had to have some outside contact, maybe someone who has an idea where she is now. Get Shepard's permission to review his telephone log."

"Then what?"

"Then I'll do it," I said. "I've traced phone records before."

When we left the dining room, Shepard was waiting. He charged across to us like an enraged bear and stood in front of me, his face tight.

"Did she tell you what she knows?" Shepard demanded, his gaze not leaving my face.

"Calm down, Mr. Shepard," Beaulieu said. "Quynn had nothing to do with your daughter's disappearance. We've ascertained that as fact. The nun acted on her own."

"Why would Sister Benedicta—"

"We're working on that," Beaulieu said. "We need to go over your phone records."

"What?" Shepard frowned. "Why?"

"Because I want to know which phone-sex hotline you use, okay?"

Osterholm overrode Beaulieu's version of diplomacy. "It could help find someone who has information, Mr. Shepard. Perhaps Maddie telephoned a friend. We will not know until we examine the call list."

"There *is* no friend. You said the nun took her."

"Then maybe *she* called somebody," Beaulieu said. "Look, Mr. Shepard, I can get the information another way, but we're wasting time if I have to get a warrant. Do we have your permission to review your telephone usage records or not?"

Shepard hesitated a beat, then waved his hand in what looked like impatience. "Yes, certainly, if it will help get my daughter back."

"All right, then. Get on it, Quynn."

Telephones and communications equipment had been set up in the dining room, as well as tape equipment and a direct line to the phone company; any incoming calls could be recorded and backtracked to its point of origin almost immediately. At least, that was the theory. In practice, I had seen the system fail too often to have an excess of faith in it.

It took only minutes to route the formal request to the correct supervisor at the telephone company. It took even less time to set up for the "phone dump"—a download of Shepard's record of incoming and outgoing calls—onto the portable PC where I sat.

I booted the reverse-directory software, into which I would manually type each number. The number-for-name cross-check would provide the identity of each recipient.

Across the room, I saw Jesse Beaulieu at the center of a knot of tight-lipped officers, some in uniform and others plainclothes. They were gathered around a new arrival, a younger woman who pecked at her laptop's keyboard with serious intent.

At that moment, Roger Shepard entered the room. He balanced a stack of plastic cups in one hand, a large thermal carafe in the other. As I watched, the detective accepted the carafe and the cups. I glanced over to the far corner where Moira Osterholm stood, a plastic cup of coffee in one hand and the other pressing her cell phone to her ear.

The download moved slowly. I was still waiting for the transfer to end when a hand entered my field of vision and placed a large foam-plastic cup on the tabletop, dark and steaming and smelling of coffee.

I looked up into the face of Roger Shepard.

"It's fresh. I thought you might want . . ." he began, not meeting my eyes. Abruptly, and to my surprise, he lay his hand on my shoulder. It felt oddly intimate, almost possessive.

"Lieutenant Quynn, I . . . I apologize for the way I acted before. I don't usually . . ." Shepard closed his eyes and took a deep breath. "I know you're all trying to help."

He looked across the room. When I followed his gaze, I found Jesse Beaulieu looking back at us, his features characteristically stony.

"I want my daughter back, Lieutenant. Find her. Please."

Before I could respond, Shepard spun on his heel and left.

The coffee was good, strong and fragrant. I drank deeply of it, anticipating the caffeine rush.

By the time I put the cup down, the phone record listings had popped up on my computer screen. I scrolled down the list, hoping to find some pattern or logic to the various area codes and numerals.

And then it was there.

I found it near the end of the list—immediately above my own 9-1-1 call: a seven-digit number, a local call. Even without cross-checking, I knew whose number it was. Only recently, I had used Jack Reagan's phone to call it.

Then I saw the time the call had been made, and the realization of what that meant must have shown clearly on my face. Osterholm saw my expression change and walked quickly to where I sat, her own half-finished cup of coffee forgotten in her hand.

"What is it, Quynn?" she demanded.

"Zhang-mei," I said. "Someone in this house called his cell phone forty-seven minutes ago. That would be just about the time Sister Benedicta left with Maddie."

I looked at Moira Osterholm.

"She's taking Maddie to him."

"That makes no sense," Osterholm said. "Why would Sister Benedicta want to deliver the girl to Zhang-mei?"

"Sister Benedicta called him," I insisted. "When you two came out here, the first time, did you notice Zhang-mei talking to her? Alone, without you?"

Her expression was my answer.

"Zhang-mei likes to establish 'informal' relationships," I said. "He made one with me, and another with Jack Reagan. Why wouldn't he make one with the nun who was watching over Maddie?"

I could almost see the wheels turning inside Osterholm's mind, weighing and analyzing.

"Why is Maddie Shepard important to Zhang-mei?" she asked.

"Assume that Zhang-mei knows we've identified Harvey Cabot," I said. "He'll know that it's only a matter of time until we trace Cabot's relationship to M. C. Mason, and link it to the sniper attacks and the bombings here. Zhang-mei's involvement in the North Carolina investigation will become known."

"That case is already a matter of record," Osterholm objected. "The Shepard girl is irrelevant to any of this, aside from her name appearing on the Centurion Web site."

"Not just her name—her *words* appeared there." I heard the obstinacy in my voice. "That's the connection. Someone leaked Maddie's statements to M. C. Mason. Whoever did so had to have a reason."

"Clearly, the nun shared Mason's anti-abortion views."

I shook my head. "Benedicta told me that making Maddie an anti-abortion icon would be a setback for the pro-life movement. I believe she was telling me the truth, as she saw it."

"If not Benedicta, then who?"

"I don't know, Moira. Roger Shepard told me that he and Sister Benedicta were the only two present when—"

I stopped abruptly. For a long moment Moira Osterholm and I stared at each other.

Then she turned to the taller of the pair of agents. Like well-trained guard dogs, neither had left her side.

"Get Shepard in here," Osterholm said to one, and he moved to obey. To the other she said, "Locate Howard Zhang-mei. I do not want to speak with him, but I want to know where he is. Be discreet."

But within minutes, it became obvious we had acted too late.

When we searched the house, Roger Shepard was nowhere to be found. As for Zhang-mei, he was not in his office; nor did he respond to calls to his cellular telephone.

"Shepard bolts." Beaulieu shook his head, his features furious. "You say you can't locate Zhang-mei. That makes three missing persons. You've been playing me, and I want to know what's going on. *Now.*"

Osterholm ignored him. "A father would not slip away from his home while his daughter was missing," she said to me. "Not unless he has an idea where she might be."

"But if you assume Shepard knows that the nun is taking Maddie to Zhang-mei . . ."

Moira Osterholm saw it at once. "Shepard knows where they are, and he's going there to recover his daughter."

"So what?" Beaulieu demanded. "Even if you're right, nobody has a damned clue where they're going to meet."

"Somebody might," I said. "I think I know who to ask."

CHAPTER 31

I tried Jack Reagan's cell number first. It rang the requisite half-dozen times before switching to his recorded voice mail. I punched in the number of his station's newsroom, identified myself to a bright-voiced receptionist and asked for Jack. There was a pause of several seconds, then the receptionist was back on the line. This time, her voice was reserved and carefully correct.

"I think I better take a message, Lieutenant."

"I know he's screening my calls," I said. "This is not a personal matter. It's police business, and it's urgent. It's critical that I talk to Mr. Reagan, *now.*"

"I'll try. Hold please." An incongruously cheerful tune played for several long moments before the melody broke in mid-note.

There was no preamble. "What do you want?" Jack said flatly.

"I need your help. It's vital that I find Zhang-mei."

"Try his office, Quynn. Call his cell phone. You know the number. I understand that you called it earlier today."

"Jack, where is he?"

"I'm a journalist, not Howard Zhang-mei's appointments secretary. So if there's nothing else, why don't you go stuff yourself?"

"Stop it. Where would he go to meet someone he doesn't want to be seen with?"

"Why should I know that, Quynn?"

"There's no time for this, Jack," I said. "You've been meeting with Zhang-mei on a regular basis. I need to know where."

"I'm hanging up now . . ."

Across the table, her own handset pressed against her ear, Moira made a low noise that might have been a growl. Her expression was tight as a clenched fist.

"This is Moira Osterholm, Mr. Reagan. You know who I am. Do you recognize my voice?"

"Yes."

"If you have the information Lieutenant Quynn requests, please provide it immediately."

"I'll make you a deal, Agent Osterholm. Tell me why you want it. Better yet, tell me why you don't already have it, and why it is so important. And I mean on the record, not for background. Then maybe I—"

"Mr. Reagan, we have three missing persons, two of them female, one a minor child. I do not care what arrangement or deal or exchange you may have made with Howard Zhang-mei. If you know where he is, or where he may be, speak now."

"Is it Maddie Shepard? Has someone taken her?" Jack's voice was still insistent, but now his excitement gave it a new edge.

"This isn't a damn news story, Jack," I said. "Maddie's missing. Sister Benedicta may be taking her to Zhang-mei. If I'm right about him, they're both in danger."

"Exactly what are you trying to pull now, Quynn? Remember what I said about revealing sources? Do you think because you say it's so, I'm going to believe that Zhang-mei is—"

"I can prove Zhang-mei is dirty, Jack. I'm convinced he's connected to the killings."

"Are you out of your mind? He's with the Justice Department."

"So am I, Mr. Reagan," Moira Osterholm said. "Does that tell you something about the urgency of this request?"

There was an extended silence on the line, moderated only

by the buzz of newsroom activity in the background.

"I know Zhang-mei was your source, Jack," I said. "On Teasdale, on Mason's disappearance, on every aspect of what you reported about the killings. On me, even."

"You're sure that—"

"He provided the leads; you told the story that he provided, that he wanted on the air. The trade-off was that you got it first, as an exclusive. The rest of the news media took it from there."

"He was in charge, Quynn. I believed what he told me."

"That's not important, not now. Zhang-mei's not familiar with Spanish Bay. He'd need someone to suggest a quiet place to meet. Someone who knew the area, Jack."

"Quynn, I—"

I glanced at my watch. Almost a quarter hour had passed since Shepard had fled the house.

"Please. Just say it, Jack."

He took a deep breath, then plunged ahead. "Last spring, I did a story on the decline of shrimping along the Gulf. I taped a stand-up on location at a shut-down processing plant, off Stevens Inlet."

"I know the place. Delstone Fisheries. It's been out of business for years."

"The old ice plant, Quynn, down by the pier. That's where we'd meet."

CHAPTER 32

We left in Moira's car, a solidly built Ford sedan. Moira Osterholm buckled herself into the driver's seat, and I braced myself as the spinning tires spat gravel and crushed shell as we rocketed down the drive.

I glanced behind us. Jesse Beaulieu had stepped outside, alone. I expected him to sprint to his own vehicle, if only to pursue for himself whatever glory he could salvage from the debacle.

Instead, Jesse slowly descended the stone steps, half stumbling near the bottom and barely saving himself from a tumble. He reached the pavement and steadied himself, his stance wide and careful of his balance.

As I watched, I felt my jaw drop in astonishment.

Beaulieu lifted his hand as if in a cheerful farewell, as if we were departing guests from a successful dinner party. I could have sworn there was the shadow of a goofy, cocked smile on his face.

"How long?" Osterholm demanded from the driver's seat, and when I turned her eyes were grim on the road ahead. "Damn it, Quynn—how long since anybody saw Shepard?"

"Twenty minutes," I said, checking my own safety belt as she held down the horn. It scattered the group of protesters—pro-life, by the placards that they dropped in their haste—who blocked our path to the street. "Less. He left the coffeepot near the door, Moira. It was almost empty, but still warm."

301

We bounced over the curb and onto the pavement, and I tried to ignore the breakneck speed at which we were traveling. Moira drove as if possessed by some fierce, raging phantom.

Delstone Fisheries was on the southern edge of Spanish Bay, a lingering remnant of the commercial fishing industry that supported the region before tourism and Yankee retirees created a new economic base. It was a roundabout trip that took us past cinderblock one-rooms and tourist cabins converted to Section 8 subsidized housing. Many of the lots we sped past were choked with weeds and clinger vine and festooned with the burned-out hulks of abandoned cars and black-plastic bags of garbage.

"Turn here," I said, pointing.

We skidded into a cross street, and Moira cut hard onto a two-lane that led toward the saltwater. Its cracked and buckled macadam still showed hard use by overloaded short-haul transports and refrigerated sixteen-wheelers. Ever since the fishery had closed a decade before, most of the road's traffic came from weekend boaters with trailers, looking for an easy access to launch or haul out.

Some of these were already on the road, traveling in both directions. Moira threaded around them, slowing only when necessary and using her horn liberally. We did not speak.

Finally we reached an open stretch, clear and straight, and I felt the car leap forward again. We were almost there. In the middle distance ahead, on the far side of a cluster of gray concrete buildings with rusty sheet-metal roofs, I saw the twinkling sparkle of sunlight on water.

"Look out!" I shouted, and Moira swerved back into our own lane. We barely missed an oncoming sedan in the oncoming traffic, its horn Doppler-ing angrily as we shot past.

"Oh, wow," said Moira Osterholm. "That was a *close* one."

I stared at her in surprise. Instead of sounding shaken, her voice was that of a woman enjoying herself immensely. She glanced at me, sheepishly, as if I had caught her in a *faux pas.*

"Sorry," Osterholm muttered, but she did not slow the vehicle.

And then she giggled.

"Watch the damn road," I heard Moira say, and by the expression that crossed her features she appeared surprised to have spoken aloud.

For reasons I did not understand, it seemed incomparably hilarious to me.

Osterholm glanced at me and made a face.

"What?" she demanded, trying to sound stern. "Why are you grinning . . . like . . . like . . . a loon . . ." She snorted, and dissolved in laughter again.

We swerved again, this time scraping loudly against a BMW parked at the curb. Moira was clutching the wheel with both hands and had pulled herself forward so that she was almost leaning over it. As I watched, she squeezed her eyes tight and shook her head as if to clear it.

She turned toward me and I saw her lips move, but I heard nothing, not even the sound of the car's engine or the wind that I knew rushed past outside the window. I was dimly aware that the light had changed, too. The bright Florida sunlight had muted, and the objects it illuminated were somehow hazy and indistinct.

As was I. I knew that I was awake, aware of my surroundings. But I also could feel myself waver, as if I was on the brink of . . . of . . . of *not* . . .

"Moira? *Moira!*"

She snapped upright, startled, and for an instant the look of alarm froze on her features. Then her face slowly relaxed again, and a new expression, distant and vacant, slipped over her features. Her eyelids fluttered, then closed. Her head drooped until the chin rested on her chest.

I grabbed the wheel and leaned closer, my belt tightening against my torso as I reached across to her. Moira's eyelid seemed somehow elusive, and it took me several tries to thumb it open. But when I finally succeeded, her head snapped up again and she slapped my hand away. She wrenched the wheel from my grasp, and once more we swerved madly before she regained control.

This time, the giggle I heard was my own.

I was drifting in an odd sort of twilight, my head nodding and my eyelids heavy as a guilty conscience. Oddly, all seemed fine and mellow in my universe; even the pressure behind my temples, which I otherwise would have defined as painful, seemed an acceptable state. But I was unable to focus my attention on any line of thought. After a few seconds, my thoughts would start to stray, a gradual process that saw them end as erratic and wildly random.

Then I sensed the car turning sharply, accompanied by the squeal of abused brakes. I was thrown forward against the suddenly unyielding embrace of the shoulder belt as the car bounced hard and came to a stop.

I snapped back to a pale imitation of awareness, like a man jolted awake just as slumber reaches out to claim him. We were outside what looked like a warehouse, near a secondary concrete ramp that led to a side entrance. On the squat, silo-like structure, in faded blue paint I could make out the words DEL-STONE FISHERIES.

I pushed the button that retracted my window, fighting a sudden wave of nausea. The smell of salt and decaying fish rolled in, and it triggered the reflex. I vomited through the half-open window, a spasm violent and extensive. A bitter tang filled my mouth, metallic and tasting of copper.

And of coffee.

From close by in the front seat, a thin keening wandered up and down the scale, punctuated at regular intervals by deep rasping. I forced my eyelids open again, and peered toward its source.

Osterholm was slumped against the driver's-side door, her eyes squeezed tight and her right palm slapping against the steering wheel, again and again. For a moment, I thought she had somehow injured herself. Then the sound began again, this time louder, and I recognized what it was.

Moira Osterholm was singing.

I shook her shoulder, hard. It did not stop the singing, but her eyes opened to thin slits. I shook her again, and raised my voice to be heard through her song.

"Moira—wake up."

It had all the effect of commanding the tide not to rise. I tried again.

"We've been drugged, Moira. By Shepard . . . in the coffee . . ."

With the hand not beating out the rhythm, she pushed away my own from her shoulder. Then she took a lung-filling breath and her singing rose in volume.

I fumbled with the seat belt awkwardly. My fingers seemed as nerveless as cucumbers, an observation that I may have made aloud.

Either way, it caused a bubble of mirth to rise inside me, like hot magma rising in a volcano. Instinctively, I knew that to give way to it would be to surrender the few vestiges of rationality I still held, but as the seat belt latch continued to resist my efforts, that seemed to me increasingly less important.

It took an eternity to find the buckle's clasp, working with fingers that felt the size of sausages.

Then I was free, and pushed open the door. Moira had brought the car to a crooked halt, one wheel atop the concrete curbing. A few feet away, a ramp way zigzagged in a downward slope, and I pushed away from the car toward it.

The ramp was chipped and cracked, and rusty stains marked where the steel reinforcing poked through the crumbling surface. I stayed close to the handrail, which flexed under my weight. But somehow it held through the first two switchbacks down which I stumbled.

As I rounded the corner to the next level, I saw a bundle of stained gray rags dumped carelessly on the pavement, unremarkable to my eyes even as litter.

Until it moved, a fitful stirring its only sign of life.

I staggered on legs that felt alien to my body and knelt next to the nun. The gash on Sister Benedicta's forehead was deep and ragged, and blood flowed copiously. As I fumbled for a handkerchief to press against the wound, her eyes fluttered. They opened, focused on my face for a moment. Then her gaze shifted to the handkerchief I held, and her eyes went wide in alarm.

"No! Don't!" Sister Benedicta said, and pushed away my hand with surprising strength.

I shook my head to push back the encroaching fog and tried again to stop her bleeding. She twisted her head out of my reach.

"You must not, Lieutenant! My blood is—no, not without gloves to protect yourself." She snatched the handkerchief from my hand. Clumsily, I helped her guide it to her forehead, and pressed her hand tight against it.

"Sister," I said. "Where is Maddie?"

The nun squeezed tight her eyelids, though whether in pain or with the effort to focus herself on the question, I could not tell.

"We were . . . we were waiting for Mr. Zhang-mei," she said. "Maddie began to . . . she became disoriented. I was trying to help her back to the car when . . ." Her voice faltered, and I saw her command herself to remain conscious. "I heard footsteps."

"Who was it, Sister? Zhang-mei, or Shepard?"

But now she was losing the battle. "It was . . . I don't know . . . he took Maddie . . ." Her free hand fluttered, gesturing down the concrete walkway.

"Stay here, Sister. I'll get help."

But when I rose to my feet, the world flip-flopped and ratcheted sickeningly in and out of focus. I swayed, almost falling. When my vision cleared, everything appeared in too-sharp contrast, distorted in perspective. I felt an irrational desire to weep, then to giggle madly; I may even have done so. In an act of sheer will that was the most difficult thing I had ever done, I made myself stagger forward in the direction Sister Benedicta had indicated.

I do not know how long I stumbled along. I must have fallen at least once, because at one point I noticed the blood welling from the heels of my hands. It took a surprising effort to make myself stop looking at them and to continue my halting pursuit.

And then I rounded a corner of the walkway, toward the front of the building.

Less than a dozen yards away, Howard Zhang-mei was half dragging, half carrying a slight figure in a nun's habit. One of his arms was hooked under her waist, holding her tight against his side. In the other hand, he held a blue-steel revolver.

At that moment, the nun slipped from his grasp, falling heavily to the walkway surface. As Zhang-mei muttered curses that were surprisingly distinct in my hearing, the figure rolled faceup, and I recognized Maddie Shepard, her features slack and void.

I steadied myself with a hand against the rough concrete, squeezing my eyes shut in an attempt to clear them of the wavering lines that blurred my vision. When I tried to open them, it seemed to take a great effort.

Maddie lay where she had fallen, unmoving save for the mad fluttering of her eyelids. After an initial attempt to pull her to her feet, Zhang-mei thrust the revolver into the side pocket of his suit jacket. Then he bent at the waist, locking both of his arms under Maddie's, and began to half lift, half drag her inert form toward the car.

A dozen yards. An infinity to cover before Zhang-mei looked up, saw me and shot me. In my condition, it was a low-odds bet. Far better were the odds that it was the only opportunity I might have. I bent to a low crouch, swaying as if drunk, and pushed forward toward the pair of them.

He spotted me before I had taken more than two unsteady steps. Maddie dropped again to the pavement, her head bouncing with an audible *thonk*, while Zhang-mei clawed to pull his weapon.

And then the pistol was free, rising as he leveled his aim at me. Even as I lurched forward toward him, I saw the cylinder rotate into battery.

The gunshot was a painful detonation that I felt as well as heard, a flat concussion that echoed as a sustained ringing inside my head. I could not tell if I had been hit. The rational part of my mind stood to the side, aghast at the prospect of almost certain death and too numb with the effects of the drug to register any pain. My legs pounded forward, as if on auto-pilot.

He had time to fire again. This time I was close enough to feel the hot spatter of burning gunpowder tattoo my cheek and the forearm I raised to protect my eyes, an instinct that was as automatic as it was futile.

And then I was on him, my left hand clamping down on the cylinder of the revolver to prevent another shot as my shoulder smashed hard into his chest. As we fell, I tried to lock my right arm around his neck, but I was far too slow. Zhang-mei twisted in my grasp, fighting to free his pistol at the same time he turned to drop, knees first, atop my chest.

The impact, multiplied by Zhang-mei's weight, exploded the air from my lungs. That, and the agonizing pain from my breasts, sent a pinwheel vortex of white-hot meteors across my vision. I fought back the blackness, and swung at him with my free hand—an incredibly slow, looping punch that he avoided with ease. His answer was a fist hard against the side of my jaw, then another with the same hand, this one striking high on my cheekbone.

I grabbed at him, but Zhang-mei surprised me with his agility. Despite the grip we both struggled to keep on the weapon, he twisted out of my reach and pushed himself to his feet.

The position gave him additional leverage. I felt my torso lift from the ground, my arms straining above my head and both hands now locked in a desperate grip around the revolver's cylinder. We were frozen in that position for a long moment, both of us straining for possession in a lethal tug-of-war.

Then his weight shifted and my back thudded to the pavement. Before I could react, his leg snapped forward and a scuffed Oxford shoe mushroomed crazily in my vision.

The kick smashed viciously against the side of my head. There was a white-hot, pinwheeling flash across my vision, and in the strength-sapping pain of it I felt only dimly Zhang-mei wrench the revolver from my grasp.

And then my vision cleared, and he was standing above me, the weapon's bore a yawing cavity that opened into eternity, dark and empty. Zhang-mei's face was impassive, devoid of emotion as he thumbed back the hammer and sighted down on my forehead.

Perhaps someone more courageous would have looked back at Zhang-mei, would have coldly held the eyes of death in her own stare. For myself, I felt my own lids drop and squeeze tightly closed.

I heard the gunshot as if from a distance, though in reality it must have been close by: a thunderclap that echoed from the surrounding walls.

But there was no crushing impact, no sensation of bullet coring deep into my skull, and it was the curiosity of what had not happened, more than any sound dimly heard, that snapped my eyes open.

What I saw was Zhang-mei staring above and beyond my supine form. As I watched, his face changed into an attitude of utter astonishment. Only then did I realize it was not the pistol he still held extended at me that had fired.

The next shot was also strangely muffled and flat, but that too was not what was remarkable.

Instead, whether by the effects of whatever drug I had ingested or from simple shock, I found myself transfixed by an abrupt slow-motion puckering of Zhang-mei's coat sleeve.

As if in a dream, I watched the fabric flex inward, rippling like a rock thrown into a pond. Then a ponderous outward explosion of red mist and cloth fibers burst from the other side. The impact flung Zhang-mei's arm in a graceful arc, and in my peripheral vision I saw the pistol spin unhurried from his hand, as if he had agreed to cast it aside in a show of good sportsmanship.

I must have blinked, an interminable stretch of time, for when my eyes next opened an eternity later, Zhang-mei was already halfway to his car, his shattered wrist weeping dark crimson despite the tight lock of his other hand on the wound.

Then, as if he had been conjured from the air itself, Bobby Teasdale stepped over me.

He worked the bolt action of the hunting rifle he held, an awkward movement that sent an empty brass cartridge spinning away, sparkling in the sunlight. Bobby looked down at me and his lips moved. The sound was eerie, like that of music played at a fraction of normal speed, and I could not discern his words. He grinned, suddenly, then snapped home the bolt and followed in Zhang-mei's path.

In the few seconds it took me to push myself to my hands and knees, Zhang-mei reached the car he had left at the curbside. Even at that distance I could see him fumble one-handed with his keys. He wrenched the door open and slid into the driver's seat.

The world around me was spinning again, but my hearing had cleared enough to hear the car door slam.

I was almost standing when Teasdale skidded to a halt twenty yards from the vehicle. Once more, he raised the rifle to his shoulder and sighted in on the man behind the wheel.

"Here's some more, you lyin' cocksucker!" I heard him shout.

But before he could fire, an intense white flash suddenly ignited inside the passenger compartment. Then, as if disdainful of the ability mere metal and glass had to contain its power, it burst through into the open air with the triumphant roar of a demon escaping from hell.

The wave of superheated air washed against me, knocking me backward several staggering steps. I thought to move forward, to where Teasdale had been, but some other instinct drove me instead to lurch in the direction I knew Maddie Shepard lay. I stumbled against her inert form.

But I could no longer see her—or, for that matter, anything else.

The full force of the drug I had been fighting swept over me. With my last conscious thought, I dropped onto Maddie, shielding her just as the debris from the explosion began to rain around us.

The world swirled sickeningly, folded in upon itself. I clutched at Maddie; together, we were falling, a cartwheeling plummet down a tunnel gray and claustrophobic. I fancied that we were dropping toward a single bright pinpoint of light, but one which seemed to recede as fast as we approached.

There must have been more, for I am told that when we were found, I was walking down the centerline of the street three blocks away, an unconscious Maddie Shepard cradled in my arms. They say I spoke words that made no sense, and that I fought the first efforts by the paramedic who found us.

But I can remember nothing of it. Nothing at all.

As it turned out, that was a foretaste of the next few hours.

I do not remember arriving at the hospital. I have no memory of the treatment I received. I do not even recall being asked questions, insistent and urgent, by investigators from both the Spanish Bay police and the FBI. Despite their best efforts, I could not even recall the precise location where I parked my rental car, let alone the tag number it carried.

By the time investigators obtained that detail from the rental company, established that I had indeed driven it to the Shepard residence, and found witnesses among the bystanders who saw Shepard drive off in it, it was too late to put the information to any productive use.

Still, it was not for lack of trying. For hours after the explosion that killed Howard Zhang-mei, patrol cars in Spanish Bay and the surrounding counties crisscrossed the area looking for my car, but to no avail.

In the end, it was Jack Reagan who provided us with the footnote we had not found ourselves. He had arrived at the fishery with his crew, trapped on the wrong side of the police barricades and too late to do more than videotape the clouds of smoke boiling into the sky. But broadcast news is a hungry beast, and Jack was no neophyte at finding ways to feed it. Even more relevant, he had not forgotten the lesson he had learned in front of an ATM several days before.

Back at the station, Jack went to work, digging through his files until he uncovered the notes from his original story on the closing of Delstone Fisheries. Among the snippets of information had been the name of the mega-corporation of which Delstone had been a subsidiary.

He had backtracked, had worked the line of contacts and sources until he had found the corporation's vice-president of risk management, and through him the regional security director. From the former, Jack picked up several interesting facts about standard insurance requirements; from the latter, he learned about the value of the security cameras that most corporate-liability policies insist remain active on otherwise shuttered operations.

The rest is, literally, history—though of a decidedly contemporary variety. The footage was broadcast first on both Jack's station and countless times thereafter on both YouTube and the full range of "most wanted" tabloid TV.

On the exclusive footage Jack Reagan obtained, we found definitive proof that Roger Shepard had stolen my car—had, in fact, driven it from his home to the meeting place Zhang-mei had so preferred in his private meetings with all those with whom he had conspired.

The stop-action video shows Zhang-mei's car arriving, shows him exit the vehicle. Then, moving like a mechanical toy, the Justice Department prosecutor scurries out of frame. For several minutes, nothing happens. Then, suddenly, a red car pulls alongside Zhang-mei's Lexus, and we see Roger Shepard emerge. He circles the Lexus once, then ducks low out of sight. He reappears, dusting his hands, and drives past the bottom of the video screen.

Again, time passes in the oddly comic compression of the medium.

Without preamble, Zhang-mei enters the frame in a stiff-legged gait. He opens the door, an effort made awkward with the wound to his arm, and climbs inside.

An instant later, the entire scene is hyper-exposed by the flash of the explosion. For the next few seconds, the image is jumbled and pocked by lines of static. When the image steadies, the shot is framed at a crazy angle.

But the show is not over, not yet.

Even as the flames boil skyward in the foreground, the observant viewer catches movement in the top corner of the screen. Here, a Pontiac that might be fire-engine red has lurched into motion. A secondary explosion, most likely the gas tank, again blossoms white like a giant lily unfolding and scrambles the screen once more.

By the time the picture is again visible, the Pontiac is already fishtailing down the road. The last shot shows my stolen car careen around the corner in a cloud of dust, its spinning rear tires spitting shell and gravel behind the vehicle.

And then it had disappeared—and along with it, so did Roger Shepard.

CHAPTER 33

The next time I saw Moira Osterholm was on the day of Tito's funeral, when she was among a small contingent of tight-lipped men and women whose attire and attitude marked them unmistakably as Federal agents.

It was a graveside service, in accordance with Tito's expressed wish, in a cemetery where the irregular ranks of headstones were shaded by tall oaks and broad-limbed pecan trees. Many of the markers predated the Civil War; Tito's closest neighbor, according to the weatherworn inscription, had fallen at the Battle of Cold Harbor. It seemed a long time ago—yet not so, either, not here.

Osterholm and her fellows stood separate and apart from the main body of mourners, most of us Spanish Bay cops or Okaloosa County deputies. It may have been a display of fine delicacy, a nod to the unspoken manners of the situation. More likely, it was born of an unconscious acknowledgment of the distance between our stations.

Whatever *bonhomie* had been established by the effects of Shepard's drugs had vaporized like a puddle under an arid sky. Osterholm's attitude and expression was all business now. Once during the services our eyes met and locked inadvertently. Her chill stare offered no apparent recognition, and I returned it with an equal lack of warmth.

I stood with Gina and Victoria Schwartz. Elle Kvamme and her husband were behind us, with Chick Cornelieus and Lincoln Jabbar close by. They wore stiffly starched dress uniforms, as did the other local law enforcement officers who had come to pay their respects. From some of these, I caught the occasional dark glower at Osterholm's delegation, and knew that I was not alone in remembering how Tito's police career had ended.

Finally, a piper in Black Watch tartan played a dirge, discordant yet achingly mournful. It was followed by "Taps" played by a Marine bugler accompanied by an honor guard in full dress blues.

Afterward, as I stared emptily at the casket wherein my best friend rested, Osterholm appeared suddenly at my shoulder. She spoke past me to Tito's remaining family.

"Mrs. Schwartz, Ms. Schwartz. I'm very sorry for your loss, both of you."

Gina nodded, but Vic stared straight ahead as if she had not heard the words. Then, abruptly, she pivoted from us and walked stiffly away. She stopped at a group of people, roughly her own age. One of them, a tall boy in a light sports jacket, wrapped his arms around her. Vic buried her face in his shirtfront, and even at the distance I could see her shoulders shake in uncontrollable sorrow.

Moira Osterholm's voice brought me back to the moment.

"Quynn, you have not returned my calls."

"No."

"I need to speak with you."

"No."

"This involves Schwartz. It might make a difference in how you want your friend remembered."

"I wouldn't pretend a concern for Tito, if I was you," I said. "I haven't forgotten what your people did to him, or to a half dozen other former Spanish Bay cops who thought they could trust your organization. You might want to forget all that history, Moira; I won't."

As I had spoken, the FBI agent had colored. It was slight, and in a face that otherwise remained outwardly unshaken. But it was enough for me to see that my words had not gone without effect.

"Listen to her, Quynn," Gina interrupted, her hand on my forearm. "She's already talked to me. You need to hear her."

We walked to a stand of live oaks, where the three of us stood in a tight knot under its beard of Spanish moss.

"Okay, I'm listening. What do you have to say, Moira?"

"I believe we have established a motive in the death of Tito Schwartz."

I stiffened, glaring in sudden fury at the Federal agent.

"I know why Tito died. Is this what you call—"

"Quynn," Gina said. "It's not what you think."

I turned my eyes from Osterholm to Tito's widow, then back again.

"Say what you came to say, Moira."

Her purse hung over a shoulder. This one was more formal than her usual handbag but still oversized enough for the .40-caliber Glock I knew it held. From it, she produced a large Manila envelope, the kind that closes with a string clasp.

Inside was a sheaf of computer printouts, but what caught my attention were two letter-sized transparencies on top, each dappled by rows of black hash marks of varying width and spacing. There were no labels, but on each someone had used a black marker to hand-letter a nine-character code along the lower right corner.

"These are—" she began.

"I've seen DNA test sheets before."

"Compare them," Osterholm said, unruffled at my tone.

I superimposed the transparencies, and held them so that the cloudless sky served as a backlight. A clear majority of the black marks aligned with each other. Only a relative handful did not match, and most of these were in the areas where one or the other of the plastic sheets had an empty space.

"For what concerns you, the most important genetic markers are here—" She reached across to touch the tip of her finger to one block of markings, then to another several rows down. "—and here. Both are an exact match. In combination, they indicate the existence of a relatively close intra-family relationship. The fact that both the subjects tested are female makes it conclusive."

"You're saying that these women are blood kin. Who are they, and why should I care?"

"Seven months ago, M. C. Mason had bunion surgery," Osterholm said. "As a matter of surgical routine, a sample of her blood was cross-matched. We obtained a sample and had a DNA test performed. The sheet on the top is hers."

"And the other?"

"That one was somewhat easier to acquire," Osterholm said, and I could have sworn I heard an uncharacteristic bantering behind her words. "There has been quite a bit of it showing up lately, hither and yon."

"I don't have the patience for riddles right now, Moira."

"It came from a bandage, Quynn. We took it from a trashcan behind Roger Shepard's home."

Moira Osterholm waited a count. Then, inappropriately for where we were, she frowned with impatience. "Think about it, Quynn," she said. "Who has been shedding blood around the Shepard residence?"

I stared at the DNA sheets, then at Osterholm.

"Edward Tapley was the assassin in a conspiracy to commit homicide, but he was not the primary conspirator," Osterholm said. "Tito Schwartz was murdered at the direction of Harvey Cabot, AKA Roger Shepard, to prevent Schwartz from revealing his actual identity."

"Tapley didn't even know Tito," I said. "He had no motive."

"But Shepard did," Osterholm said. "Look at the printouts. *Look* at them, Quynn."

"She's telling the truth, Quynn," Gina said. "They came from Tito's computer."

"The top sheet is the original credit check Mr. Schwartz ran on Shepard," Moira Osterholm said. "It came up clean, and Schwartz accepted the assignment,. But something must not have felt right, and he went back for a second look. That's when he began to find holes in the story Shepard had given him. So he dug deeper."

"Tito enjoyed the chase," Gina said. "You know that, Quynn. He said it made him feel like a cop again."

Moira was silent for a long moment. When she again spoke, her face was stony.

"For whatever reasons, he started running Shepard's data through a number of Internet snooper sites. I told you, Quynn—we track activity on those Web sites. Schwartz's inquiries ended up on Zhang-mei's desk, and Zhang-mei tipped Shepard."

"Why?"

"We are going through Zhang-mei's files, looking at his computer," Moira said. "We are finding indications that Zhang-mei was using Shepard, or trying to use him, as his own private informant inside the Centurions. He was very ambitious, Quynn."

She examined my face, and her lips tightened in what looked like exasperation. "Schwartz was a bulldog. Shepard knew that, sooner or later, he would figure out the Cabot linkage. That made Schwartz a threat."

"No—Tapley pushed the button, not Shepard," I said; for reasons I did not understand, my voice sounded petulant and insistent, as if I were a toddler being deprived of a favorite toy.

"Where do you think Shepard obtained the GHB he used on us, and on his daughter?" Osterholm demanded. "They were working together, Quynn. Tapley went to prison for dealing drugs—specifically, gamma hydroxybutyrate. Shepard knew him long before that—he was in the Centurions when Shepard showed up the first time. We've established that. The timeline is firm."

"The bomb was meant for *me*, Moira."

She shook her head, but it was Gina who responded.

"It's okay, Quynn," she said. "Tito doesn't need you to save him anymore."

I could think of no response to make. For what seemed like a long time, I gazed out over the sun-dappled cemetery, listening to the faint murmurs of the breeze through moss and leaf. When I finally turned back, I felt on me the gaze of the woman who had shared my best friend's life.

I tried to return her smile, and failed utterly.

"So, what do I do now?"

"You know what Tito would say. He'd tell you to start saving yourself."

CHAPTER 34

Once, on a vacation trip to South Florida, I sat on the stern of a trim Hattaras cruiser owned by one of Ron's many cousins. Raul chartered out his boat for a living—mainly to fishermen, though I suspected that he was not adverse to offers that involved a nocturnal run in a darkened boat loaded with illicit cargo. It would all have been the same to Raul, as long as the customer paid well and in cash.

We had motored east for several hours from Marathon Key, cutting a wide wake through a sea that had metamorphosed from pale green to a deep, rich cobalt. Raul had cut the engine, and we were drifting north on the invisible river of the Gulf Stream.

The day was sunny, the waters impossibly blue and sparkling. A thin band of white paralleled the western horizon, perhaps the reflection of tropical light from whatever shoreline lie there. Only a mild chop marked the ocean—that, and the occasional porpoise that would surface an arm's length away, sighing as if recalling some ancient regret before an arching dive took it back to the other half of its universe.

It was an idyllic scene, the stuff tourist postcards always try to capture and usually fail. The master touch was a bulky flight of three pelicans, ten yards off our beam and only a few feet above the water. They glided past in a line so geometrically flawless they might have been bound by an invisible cord.

And then the surface exploded, and a flash of gray-and-white emerged and disappeared so quickly that, had I blinked, I might have missed it entirely.

As it was, I might even have believed I imagined it had it not been for the pelicans. Already, they were clawing for altitude, veering sharply in opposite directions from the return wash of the splash that bubbled white against the blue water.

Except now there were only two.

Ron's cousin grinned at the expression I must have worn.

"Sometimes," Raul had said, "the sharks, they get a taste for something different."

There was a metaphor there, and it was one that my profession had never let me forget. But never had it been more vivid in my mind than now, as I turned my replacement rental car into the driveway of the house where Maddie Shepard waited.

I pulled closer to the covered portico of the Shepard house than I had on other visits. The devout and their politically active counterparts had long departed, moving on to other ideological battlefields. The gauntlet of security had also gone elsewhere, and this time there was only a single guard at the door. He was dressed in the forest-green uniform of Tito's firm, and dark circles of sweat looked like the shadow of folded wings under his arms. He lifted a hand in greeting as I stepped from my car.

"Hey, Lieutenant. Pretty damn hot today, ain't it?"

"Hello, Frank. Anything happening here?"

The guard shook his head. "Nah." He winked. "Ain't no miracles to report, that's for *damn* sure. Dunno why Jesús's keepin' me 'round here."

Frank peered at what I carried in the crook of my arm and laughed. "That suppose t'be a dog? Thought you was holdin' some kinda stub-tail rat." He extended a finger to the Mini-Pinscher, which Missy licked with unseemly exuberance.

"Careful—she's a police-issue trained killer," I said, and Frank grinned back at me. "K-9 officers carry them concealed in an ankle holster, just for emergencies."

Inside, Sister Benedicta greeted me with polite reserve. In contrast, Missy was welcomed with an enthusiasm usually reserved for visiting Pontiffs or returning prodigals, and returned the emotion by yipping and squirming in delight.

The bandage was still high on the nun's temple, a corner of the adhesive tape showing under the edge of her starched wimple.

"How is she, Sister?"

"Physically, there is no evidence that her health is at risk. At present, it is impossible to know. GHB is a street drug, and there is little research on the effect of long-term exposure to it. Thanks to that man, Maddie had been ingesting such filth for at least six months—possibly on a daily basis."

"What does she remember?"

"Of her father's abuse? Like most sexual abuse victims, any damage to her physical health is but the tip of the iceberg. The psychological damage is compounded in cases of incest. But it is no doubt quite severe, and in Maddie's case most likely magnified by the fact of his disappearance."

"Doesn't she realize what kind of monster he was, Sister? Does she understand that we believe he killed his own mother?"

"Maddie has been told that M. C. Mason was her grand-mother, Lieutenant. Whether the full implications of that have registered with her—" The nun shrugged. "Maddie has been abandoned by the only parent she has known for some years. For a thirteen-year-old girl, that is devastating. In her case, she believes that her father has left not because of what he has inflicted on her, but because of her efforts to free herself of his abuse. She is conflicted by feelings of guilt, relief and shame— the latter, because she has just begun to realize all that has been done to her."

"It might have gone on a lot longer if you hadn't been here," I said.

The nun made a gesture that might have been assent, but said nothing.

"Sister, I have a confession to make—rather, an apology. I thought you were responsible for faking Maddie's visions. I had no inkling of what was being done to the girl. You were able to see what I completely missed."

"You were able to see the evil in Mr. Zhang-mei when I could not, Lieutenant. For that, both Maddie and I owe our lives to you."

"I should have seen it earlier, Sister. I've known more than a few bad people in my life."

"So have I, Lieutenant Quynn," she said. "For many years I was assigned to mission work, in Africa. I was there during the genocidal massacres in Rwanda. As for detecting the signs of severe sexual abuse, I had only suspicions at first. Give me no credit, Lieutenant; it should not be so difficult to recognize such symptoms." She fixed her gaze steady on me. "At least, not when one has also been the victim of the same affliction."

I had no words to respond, but Sister Benedicta read my thoughts as if by intuition.

"At Ntarama, we set up a medical aid station in the rectory," Sister Benedicta said, as if she was making a formal report to a supervisor. "The first night—there were dozens of injured people, Lieutenant. Both adults and children, most of them beaten severely or bearing wounds inflicted by machetes. We tried to bring the children into the church itself, but of course there were too many of them. And the Tutsi families that were still intact wanted to stay together, out on the grounds of the compound.

"For several days, they poured in. The children, many of them, had even brought their school homework. We found a handful of Rwandan teachers to hold classes. One of the Tutsi Sisters was in charge of setting up communal kitchens, and the tribal councils had designated men to dig latrines and construct what shelter could be made."

She seemed to remember that I was there and nodded as if she had successfully argued a point. "Really, for having almost six thousand persons inside such a small enclosure, it was quite well organized. You might have thought we had decided to create a small, vibrant city there. Nobody expected that we would all be trapped there.

"On the third afternoon, they came. The Hutu militia had explosives and they blasted gaps in the red brick walls. Our people were screaming, everyone running to and fro within the compound grounds, trying to get away. But the militia was shooting and throwing grenades into the crowds. Then the civilian mobs burst in, thousands and thousands of them pouring through the rubble. They had machetes, axes, knives . . ."

"Sister, you don't have to—"

"Many of the women and girl children were raped first, but that was only incidental. The mobs really only wanted to kill. And they did. Five thousand Tutsi men, women and children died in the church compound. Only a handful survived, most of them horribly wounded. Left for dead.

"What was five thousand, out of eight hundred thousand persons murdered? Or the tens of thousands of orphans? Or the slow death of so many women raped? You see, Lieutenant, I have kept up with the reports. Sixty percent of those raped at Ntarama were infected with AIDS."

She read my expression unerringly.

"I'm one of the luckier ones," she said quietly. "You see, in the Western world we have access to the drugs that slow the progress of HIV. Most of the others who were infected that afternoon have died of the disease long before now, while I continue to enjoy a relatively low viral load."

"I'm sorry, Sister."

"I do not seek sympathy. I tell you this only to let you know that I have seen the result of hate and violence, Lieutenant. I have no wish to see it happen again, whatever the 'cause' it promotes." She smiled thinly. "Besides, it is what brought me to my calling, both as a psychologist and as a nun. Just as the evil you have known led you to yours, perhaps."

We were silent for a moment. Finally, the sense of obligation that weighed on me won out.

"When we last spoke, Sister, I came on way too strong. I think you should know it wasn't aimed at you, not directly. I came here, and there was Maddie. I was seeing a lot of . . . uncomfortable parallels . . . between her life and mine."

"Lieutenant Quynn, what you think is—"

"I ran pretty wild as a kid, Sister," I said, overriding her words. "About age fourteen, I decided to do whatever I wanted to do. My mother had died the year before, and I guess my father saw too much of her when he looked at me. He found it too painful, I suppose. Or maybe he was pretty much sunk in his own problems by then, and raising a daughter was too difficult. It hurt me. My reaction was to hurt him—or *somebody*—in turn."

"Adolescence can be a difficult time, Lieutenant. Particularly for one so young and without the guidance of a mother."

"It was more than that," I said. "I read once that the only thing no human being can endure is a conviction of his or her own inexplicable worthlessness. So I went out to give my worthlessness a reason. I chose drinking, and sex with people I didn't know or particularly like."

I shook my head. "There was no shortage of men who thought that was a fine idea. I spent a lot of time riding in cars with them, going to the kind of places where nobody much cared about a man being with a minor girl. Usually we'd end up at a motel. I saw the inside of a *lot* of motels in those days.

"I had a few false alarms. The first one scared the hell out of me. After two or three—well, at that age, you start to think it can't happen to you. Then it did. I was sixteen. The father was thirty-five, if I guessed the right guy. Either way, he offered to pay for the . . . procedure."

"And you agreed."

"Not at first. I had been brought up to believe it was wrong, a sin. As was the act that caused it, for that matter. But ultimately—yes, I did it."

"Why, if I may ask?"

"Fear, mostly. Even with how things had become, I just couldn't let Pop know what I had been doing." I shrugged. "Or maybe I just didn't want to look into his eyes and see what I had become. Funny thing is, I know that he would have loved me no matter what. So I took the money, and I had my abortion.

"Here's my point, Sister. Having that abortion gave me my life back. It changed who I was—no, that's not it. It changed who I was turning into. It was my second chance. I had nearly destroyed *me*, Sister. I would have, ultimately. I know that for a fact."

"You made your decision, Lieutenant. And you live with it."

"It's not the best memory I carry around. But I can't say it was the worst, either."

I looked at her and heard the challenge in my own voice. "So there it is. That's why we're on different sides here, and we always will be. What do you say to that, Sister?"

"Nothing original, I'm afraid," Benedicta said. "Hate the sin. Love the sinner. That's good advice for all of us."

We stood without speaking for a moment, a silence punctuated only by the high-pitched chirps of ecstasy that the nun's attentions elicited from Missy.

"What happens to Maddie now, Sister?"

"They have located Maddie's aunt," Sister Benedicta said, addressing me but with the rest of her attention again focused on the canine crooked in my arm. "The mother's sister. She has a home in Seattle, and arrangements are being made for Maddie to live with her."

"Sister Benedicta . . ." I stopped, not certain how to ask. "The lab tested the crackers and soft drink we took from Maddie's wastebasket. There was no trace of GHB, or any other drug. But at the ice plant, she was obviously . . . disoriented. In a trance."

The nun nodded, her expression calm and patient.

"It also raises a question about the day when Maddie left the house and spoke to the crowds outside. GHB begins to act no more than a half hour after being ingested. Roger Shepard was away—at least, he was not here during that timeframe. On that day, he did not have access to Maddie."

Sister Benedicta's eyes searched my own.

"Lieutenant, what are you asking me, precisely?"

"I don't believe you did anything wrong, Sister. But I'm looking for answers."

"Then I'll answer as a doctor. Was there a delayed reaction, a flashback caused by the aftereffects of the drug? It is possible; we don't know. Could it have been a psychotic event, a disassociation episode? We don't know. How much of Maddie's behavior was caused by the drug and how much by the pathology of the horrific abuse she experienced at the hands of her father? I don't know. We may *never* know. But however it happened, Maddie's presence did stop violence that day."

"No offense, but that's not much of an answer."

"There is another explanation, of course," Sister Benedicta said. "But I would be answering as a nun."

"About the stigmata, Sister. Did she hurt herself?"

"Again speaking as a doctor, I would consider it possible—perhaps even likely. In a disassociative state, it's not uncommon for people to injure themselves. Plus, abused girls often engage in 'self-cutting,'—an act which psychologists say makes them feel that they have some control over their victimhood. Maddie's wounds are clearly consistent with that profile."

I nodded, surprising myself at the effort it took to hide the sharp disappointment I felt.

"I need to talk with her. There's too much I still need to understand about all this. You can be present, if you wish."

She shook her head. "She seems to trust you, Lieutenant. I do, also. All I ask is that you not press her any harder than you must. Shall I watch our canine friend while you visit?"

I smiled. "Actually, Missy here is one of the items on the agenda."

Upstairs, the smell of contact cement was strong in Maddie's room; the tang of it was sharp and chemical, not unlike that of a pistol recently fired.

Maddie was seated on a high-backed stool when I entered, her back to the door as she bent low over the graphic artist's table I had seen on my first visit. Her palms were still wrapped with white gauze, but the bandages appeared less bulky than previously. The floor around her was once again a riot of litter: crumpled balls of construction paper of various hues, thin curlicues of razor-trimmed pasteboard, the random pile of balsa shavings and the occasional tangle of discarded string.

At last she turned, looking at me with solemn eyes. On the wall behind her, the enigmatic construction that had captured my curiosity on my first visit framed her as if she was one of its elements.

"Hello, Maddie. I'd like you to meet Missy. I thought we

could talk, the three of us."

I put Missy on the carpeted floor, and she immediately dashed to where Maddie sat. Before either of us could react, the dog had vaulted into the girl's lap and stood on its haunches, high enough to flick a pink tongue against the tip of Maddie's nose.

Maddie burst out laughing, a clean and healthy sound that seemed to surprise all of us in the room. It was a pleasure to hear it come from her.

"Is she yours?" Maddie asked, twisting and turning her face in a game of tag-dodge in which Missy willingly joined.

"That's one of the things I want to talk about," I said, as Missy again scored wet points to Maddie's loud delight.

But the laughter did not last long, and as Missy calmed, the solemnity I had seen when I entered returned to the girl's manner. She appeared as if she was waiting, anticipating the footfall outside her door that her experiences had taught could only augur ill.

Missy had settled into Maddie's lap, content in the manner of all undersized creatures who sense they have found sanctuary.

I sat on the edge of Maddie's bed, the yellow comforter soft and yielding under me, and gestured at the project my arrival had interrupted.

"Go ahead, if you want. Will it bother you if we talk while you work?"

"I'm almost done anyway." She pivoted on her stool back to the table, Missy still perched on her thighs.

I watched while Maddie aligned the pieces with a straight edge, then used an X-acto knife to carefully razor away the trimming. It looked like a process that demanded precision and seemed to engender a fierce focus from the girl. She was lost in concentration, and after a few minutes I was not certain if she remembered that I was still in the room.

Finally, she carefully smoothed the pieces down on the backing and turned to face me. Again, I noted the surreal stillness of her posture, and in a *gestalt* leap I guessed at the nature of it.

"I don't have any news about your father, Maddie. That's not why I'm here. I just wanted to see how you are doing."

The girl said nothing, but her shoulders slumped as the muscles relaxed. Deep inside her eyes, I saw what I read as relief.

She rolled Missy onto her back and began to tickle her belly, smiling again when one of the dog's hind legs began to twitch in a mad canine step-dance.

"They found my aunt Tessa," Maddie said, in a tone meant to sound casual. "I talked with her. On the phone. I guess I'm going to live with her, in Seattle."

"Is that okay with you?"

Maddie shrugged. "I don't know anybody there."

She was making a conscious effort to sound nonchalant, so I followed her lead with my next words.

"Dogs can be good company on a trip. I was wondering. Do you want to take Missy along?"

From her perch on Maddie's lap, the subject of our discussion wig-wagged at the mention of her name.

"With me? To Seattle?"

"If your aunt doesn't mind feeding two growing girls, she's all yours."

"I can *keep* her? Really?"

I nodded mock solemnly. "I already talked it over with Missy. We decided it was in the best interests of all concerned."

I reached out and scratched behind the dog's ear, and was rewarded with a mad semaphore at her opposite end.

"I've heard good things about the Pacific Northwest," I said, probably to both of them. "Lots of trees, and the summers aren't as hot as here. I think you'll like it out there." I shot Maddie a stern look. "But we ought to negotiate visitation rights, in case I ever get out that way."

Her eyes were down, looking at Missy; but I saw the smile flicker across her face.

"She sounds nice."

"Huh," I said. "Wait until you hear her when she's hungry."

"Aunt Tessa, I mean. She said I could bring all my stuff."

"That's good."

"I guess," she said. "I remember her, a little. From before my mother left."

"They probably look a lot alike. Being sisters, I mean."

"I don't know. I don't remember a lot about my mom. Dad never wanted to talk about her much."

"You said that your mother left, Maddie. Was it maybe the other way around? That your father came for you and the two of you left?"

Maddie's response was a small shrug.

"I'm not trying to pry, Maddie," I began, and stopped at the look I received. "Okay, maybe I am. But I have a good reason. We need to find out why all of this happened. If you'll trust me, maybe we can."

But the girl said nothing, and for a moment I thought that my visit had been a selfish indulgence, an attempt to lay to rest my own demons by tracking the genesis of Roger Shepard's twisted odyssey. Whatever answers Maddie might possess, I had no right to demand them from her.

Then Maddie began to speak, her voice a low, noncommittal monotone that I suspected was her own attempt at self-preservation.

"Some people hurt her," she murmured. "She died."

"Did your father tell you that?"

Maddie nodded. "He came and got me and said they wanted

to hurt us, too. So we had to change our names and move away."

"That's how you came here, to Spanish Bay."

"It was just him and me, after that. It was a secret."

"You had other secrets, too, didn't you?"

"No . . . I don't know. I . . . I don't want to talk about that."

"It's okay, Maddie. You don't have to."

Maddie watched me from her seat at the graphic-arts table, one hand stroking Missy.

"Maddie, remember when you called me? You left a message. You said there was something you needed to tell me. You hung up before you said what it was."

Again, there was a long silence. Again, when Maddie finally began to speak, at first I thought she had decided to change the subject.

"I read that when people dream, they let loose all the bad things that are in their heads—the things they don't want to see or do or think about, not in real life."

"I've heard that."

"Do you think it's true?"

"Sometimes, I suppose. A man named Freud wrote a lot about what dreams mean. I'm not an expert, Maddie. But what you're talking about—I think he might have called it 'letting go of an unconscious repression.' " She screwed up her face as if I had spoken in pig Latin. "It sounds worse than it is. All it means is that in your dream, your mind lets you think about stuff it covers up when you're awake."

She thought about that for a moment, the solemn look back on her features.

"I dream a lot, Maddie. But I can't remember much about them when I wake up. Do you?"

Maddie's voice was strained and low. "It was a horrible dream. I'd pray and pray and pray that I wouldn't have it." She looked up at me. "That worked, sometimes."

"What did you dream?" I asked, but Maddie shook her head fiercely. I thought it was a refusal, particularly when her next words seemed disjointed, out of sequence.

"I saw the light blinking, so I checked." She sounded suddenly defensive. "Sometimes there *was* a message that would be for me."

"Sure," I answered, not wanting to chance saying more.

"It was a lady's voice," Maddie said. "I thought she just had the wrong number. She talked for a long time. You know, saying how she wanted to see him, and stuff like that."

"She wanted to see your father?"

"I thought. But then she started calling him Harvey."

I trusted myself no more than a slight nod. "The lady would, like, get mad. She'd shout things, mean things. Then she'd cry, and she wasn't so mad anymore. She called him 'baby boy,' and talk about how sorry she was. It was really sad."

The girl fell into a silence that seemed to stretch forever.

"Maddie?"

"She said she had pictures of him—of *both* of them, and she would make sure everybody saw them on the Internet," Maddie said, and as if that breached the floodgates, her words began to pour out faster and faster. "She said they had done an awful thing, disgusting and frightful *animals*. Him and . . . the girl. That's what she called her. The girl."

Her voice took on an eerie quavering quality that, to my ears, mimicked a voice I had heard before. "The girl sinned, Harvey. You both sinned when you helped her murder the innocent. Hell, Harvey . . . hell is forever . . ."

Maddie suddenly looked stricken, and her voice again became her own. "But it was worse, worse than she knew, because . . . because even animals . . . I can't say it, I can't even—"

Her face froze in mid-sentence, mouth open and eyes focused a thousand meters distant. I had seen those eyes before, on others who had gazed with horror into their own pit of fire, deep and unquenchable.

But before I could move to comfort her, once more the words tumbled from Maddie in a torrent.

"And . . . like, they were walking and people were shouting and holding signs . . . and he had his arm around her shoulders and made . . . made her go inside and they took away what she wore and put her on the table—"

Maddie stopped speaking abruptly, as if a switch had been thrown.

Sometime during her rush of words, she had stopped petting Missy. Now the dog moved on her lap, pushing her nose insistently under one of Maddie's still-bandaged hands. Finally, slowly at first, one hand began again to move, softly caressing the soft coat of the dog. It seemed to comfort both of them.

"She was describing *my* dream," Maddie said, her voice barely above a whisper.

"Did you find her Web site, Maddie? Did you send her an e-mail about your dream?"

As if in a dream now, Maddie nodded, her head barely moving. "She said . . . she said it was a sin, what happened. She said it made every mother weep. Even God's mother." A sob racked her body, and I moved to rise.

But before I could stand, Maddie's eyes opened wide in alarm. She flinched, drawing back as if she had been threatened. I settled back immediately, my hands palm-out as if to demonstrate that I meant her no harm. My smile was intended to be reassuring, but I doubt that Maddie even noticed it.

She was gazing at my hands, fixed on them as if they had been conjured from the air. She remained like that for several seconds, though it seemed to last far longer.

"It's all right, Maddie. Everything is all right now."

There was no response, not for a moment. Slowly, her body

calmed. Her eyes shifted to my face. I saw recognition in them, and then something else.

Before I could say more, Maddie pivoted in her chair, turning her back to me. I stood, watching as she pulled open the desk drawer wide. It hung up on its brackets, and Maddie gave it a final tug that freed it from the desk. The drawer was empty. She reversed it in her hands. With the back facing her, she peeled off what looked like a strip of masking tape.

"Here," Maddie said, holding it out to me.

I took it, and when I turned the tape over something small and metallic glinted in the pale light of the room.

I examined it gingerly, careful not to disturb the small brown flecks that adhered both to the inch-long strip of tape and to the object of Maddie's confession. Nor did I want to add any of my own. The small triangular blade still looked razor-sharp, despite the faint stains along its length. Some of the blood had dried inside the machine-stamped letters on the inch-long steel, and the word X-ACTO stood out in sharp filigree.

"If you put it between your hands and push hard, it doesn't hurt all that bad." She held her palms together to demonstrate; to me, her joined hands took on the aspect of prayer.

I smiled, as if to encourage her. "And that's how you made your hands bleed, all those times?"

"Only twice," she said, in a small voice. "I swear. At the mall, and when Dad made me show him what I had done. All the other times, they just started by themselves. I don't know how."

I nodded. "Why did you do that, Maddie? Help me understand."

"I just wanted somebody to see," she said, and her face collapsed like wax melting from a taper. "I just wanted somebody to *help*."

"We're going to get you help, Maddie," I said. "I promise."

★   ★   ★   ★   ★

But I had one more stop to make, and it took me back to a world of antiseptic smells and enigmatic sounds which the past two weeks had made all too familiar.

This time I had to drive the sixty miles to Mobile, where the government maintained a secure medical-treatment facility for Federal prisoners considered high-risk. Moira Osterholm had called ahead, and within minutes of my arrival I was standing over a figure whose hands, arms and facial features were obscured by layers of bandages. But his eyes were visible through the gauze, and when I had entered the ward they had watched my approach with an unsettling intensity.

I pulled up a chair close to his bed, as if I was an old friend invited to share confidences. Teasdale lay motionless, and I had the feeling that both of us were acutely aware of the chromed chain that led from the bed's railing to the manacle around his ankle.

"I know some of it already, Bobby. I'd like to hear the rest from you."

Teasdale eyed me narrowly. "Yeah? Way I hear it, you don't remember most of it no-how."

"I remember that I'm in your debt, Bobby. You saved my life. I'll do whatever I can to help if you go to trial."

" 'If.' " He snorted. "Sure. That Chinese guy had such a hard-on to put me in jail, he was walkin' around bowleg."

"Zhang-mei's not walking around at all, anymore. He's no longer your problem, or anybody else's. Whoever planted the bomb in his car made sure of that."

"You gonna try to put that on me, too, huh?"

I shook my head. "No. You're not a bomber, Bobby. Not a shooter, either. You're just a man who tends to trust the wrong people."

"I ain't gonna trust *you*, that's for damn sure."

"I think I can prove that you didn't shoot the nurse in North Carolina, Bobby. If so, it would be hard to convince anyone that you were responsible for the DeBourche shooting or the abortion clinic bombing here. I've already told that to Jack Reagan, by the way."

"Yeah? Then who you think done it?"

"I think it was Roger Shepard—Harvey Cabot, if you want to use the name he was given at birth. But you knew about that, Bobby. Am I right?"

He was silent for so long that I did not expect him to respond. But his eyes were sharp and calculating. Finally, his lip curled in a manner meant to be cynical.

"Bullshit. Every damn thing you said, just bullshit to mess me over more. Well, you can all go to hell. I ain't sayin' *nuthin'*."

I gestured at the television set, mounted high on the wall. "It was on TV at noon. If you don't want to believe me, watch it on the news this evening. I'll come back tomorrow, or the next day. But the wheels are turning now. If you have anything you want to say, this is the time to do it."

He eyed me narrowly.

"You ain't lyin' to me? You swear? I wanna hear you say it."

"I'm telling you the truth. You have my word on it. I want to help you, Bobby. You told me you didn't kill anybody; I believe you. Maybe you're guilty of other offenses, I don't know. If you are, a court may take into account that you were being hunted for crimes you didn't commit. You had to survive somehow."

I leaned forward, my voice and features earnest. "Help yourself. I think we can make most of this go away. At the least, I can try to help you get reduced jail time, possibly in a minimum-security facility. But you have to give me something to work with."

His tone was wary. "I ain't gonna sell out the people what helped me, past three years."

"Tell me about the rifle. I know it wasn't yours, Bobby."

He shook his head once, and his gaze slid away from mine.

"Then talk to me about Margot Mason, Bobby. She's dead. Nothing you say can hurt her now. C'mon, Bobby—help yourself for a change. She got you mixed up with all of this, didn't she?"

"You don't know nuthin' about her," he said, and his voice was hot with sudden outrage. "Miss Mason, she was a *damn* fine woman. She was real good to us—me an' the other folk in the Centurions. Took care of all of us like we was her own."

When I did not respond, a look of exasperation crossed his face.

"That Tapley guy you wasted? He got outta the joint, he had *nuthin'*. Lotta people in the Centurions, they wanted to toss his ass back on the street, him selling drugs like that. Miss Mason took him back in, cleaned him up. Treated him like he meant something, like he was a man. Gave him a second chance. You think he got that from anybody else in his damn life?"

"Probably not. But Eddie Tapley was the same guy who rigged up the bombs Shepard used at the clinic. They tried to hang that on you, Bobby."

"Miss Mason didn't know nuthin' 'bout that. Don't try to tell me she did, neither."

"I saw how she picked Tapley's clothes, dressed him, combed his hair. And when he needed an alias, she told him to call himself 'Harvey'—the name of the son that she abandoned right after he was born. Doesn't that strike you as just a little odd, Bobby?"

He shrugged. There was anger in the gesture, along with something else to which I could not quite put a name. Briefly, I wondered if Margot Mason had attempted to superimpose the name of her lost son on more than one of her charges. But I also sensed it was not the time to ask, either.

So I waited.

But when Teasdale spoke, it was not to answer the question I had posed.

"She din't abandon the kid. Hell, she was a kid herself. You don't know shit about it, just like you don't know shit about her."

"Then tell me, Bobby."

"Why? You ain't gonna listen."

"I told you, I know some of it already. The Centurions were her family. You especially, I guess. The two of you were pretty close, weren't you?"

"Treated her a damn sight better than that son of hers," he retorted.

"Help me understand, Bobby. Help me see how all this happened."

Teasdale was silent for a moment. But when he began to speak, he started at what I am sure he thought was the beginning.

"All over the country, people'd send her pictures. From them abortion places—you know, to put on the Internet. This one packet, they was from right here in Spanish Bay."

I nodded, remembering the digitized faces of women trying to push through gauntlets of anti-abortion protesters. Most had looked scared and harried and utterly alone, even those who had clung to the arm of a friend or companion. More than a few had appeared dazed, disoriented by the tumult that swirled around them. I imagined that Maddie Shepard, likely dosed with GHB, had fit seamlessly into this picture.

"Miss Mason seen him takin' the girl in, and knowed him right off," Teasdale said. "Even after all that time. 'Bout broke her heart, her own boy decidin' to walk that path."

"Are those your words, or hers?"

"She tole me 'bout it—gettin' into trouble all them years

back, havin' a li'l baby she had to give up. Tole me how she cried when she let 'em take him off. Said she wanted to lay down and die, herself."

"Where did they take her son?"

"Into the damn system, where'd you think? Foster homes, at first. She'd find out where, just 'bout the time they'd move him to a new one. Kept track of him, best she could. Sometimes she could leave stuff for him—candy, toys, whatever she could afford. Them days, you give up a kid you din't have no right to it no more. She was tryin' to figure out a way to steal him back and take off. Then, kid gets to be maybe nine or ten, he got adopted for real. Miss Mason said after that, she couldn't find him."

I stitched a doubtful look on my face. "And then, twenty-five years later, she recognizes him from a snapshot? That's a stretch to swallow, Bobby."

"I say that? You don't wanna listen, get on outta here."

"It's your story, Bobby."

"Damn right. Four, five years back, she says, this guy shows up at her place. Clean-cut, dressed all fancy—talks real good, too. Tells her he found out he was adopted, so he's out looking for his 'natural' mother, name of Cabot."

Teasdale held up his hands, palms out, and rolled his eyes heavenward in sarcasm. "Hallelujah—he's Harvey, her kid. Takes him in, goes out and just 'bout slaughters the fatty lamb for him. Turns out he got hisself a degree from some dipshit college somewhere, so she lets him handle a bunch of the money the Centurions had raised. Mostly cash, a'course."

It fits, I told myself. As Roger Shepard, he was in business as an investment counselor.

"Guess she figured him to take over for her some day." He pulled a face. " 'Cept it turns out the sorry bastard don't believe in nuthin', 'less you count his own sweet self. Cocksucker looted whatever he could steal, then took off."

This time I frowned and put skepticism in my voice. "I suppose some people might just let it slide, being ripped off like that. But the Centurions don't strike me as turn-the-other-cheek types."

"Sure she covered for him," Teasdale said, not meeting my eyes. "Ain't that what a mother supposed to do?"

"Okay. So Harvey Cabot disappears, again—until he shows up in a photo going into a Spanish Bay abortion clinic."

"Yeah—'cept he was callin' himself 'Shepard' by then."

"How did Mason track him down after she saw the photos? Roger Shepard struck me as a pretty smart man."

"Half-smart, maybe. Goes to the trouble givin' a fake name and payin' cash to them baby-killers, but still drives there in his own damn car. Don't even think to switch plates on it, even when he knows people taking pictures there. You got a tag number, only 'bout a million ways to get a name."

"So Mason just called Shepard for a little mother–son chat."

"Hell, you think she didn't *try?*" Teasdale said. "Son-of-a-bitch wouldn't even talk to her on the damn phone. Not 'til she tole him she knew what he done." Improbably, a thin smile flitted across his features. "Played back his message machine *that* night, betcha he 'bout shit a brick."

"What did she tell him, Bobby? 'All is forgiven, drop by for a visit sometime'?"

Teasdale let out his breath in a long, disgusted exhalation. "See, you don't get it at all. She said he didn't come see his own mother, fine—she'd fix it so he could damn-well dial up on the Internet and watch himself helpin' some poor li'l girl kill her own baby. Maybe let all those rich guys he worked for see it, too. Tell you what, *that* brought him 'round her place fast enough."

"Were you there when they talked?"

"Nah," he said as if he had made the offer and it had been declined with little grace. "But she tole me 'bout it afterward. She was still coverin' for him—sayin' how the girl was some neighbor tramp, how she was older than she looked, how her Harvey weren't even sure the baby was his anyway."

He snorted. " 'Bout turned my stomach, her makin' up excuses for pond scum like him. Like he weren't a growed man who knowed it was wrong to mess with girls that young."

"When did all of this happen, Bobby?"

"Month ago was when she got the pictures. Took her maybe two weeks to find him, then get him to come by."

"The next week, Maddie Shepard starts to have visions in a shopping mall. A few days later, a bomb goes off at an abortion clinic. Then the sniper attack on Dr. DeBourche. A pretty busy month, Bobby."

"You got a point you tryin' to make?"

"How much of this did you know when you came to my boat?"

"None of it, but I wouldn't of tole you if I had. Hell, only reason she tole *me* was—" He stopped abruptly, as if some inner failsafe mechanism had engaged.

"Be smart, Bobby. Tell me now."

"Night it all happened, we was watchin' TV together, me and Miss Mason," he said. "Figured we see what kinda new lies that damn Reagan asshole was gonna make up 'bout me." He shook his head. " 'Stead, they showed that story about the girl with the hands. Middle of it, I turn and Miss Mason—well, she's just starin' at the TV. I thought she was havin' a stroke or somethin'."

Teasdale looked at me steadily now, and in his eyes I saw a terrible knowledge that I imagined was now mirrored in my own.

"Guess that's when she found out the girl was her granddaughter," he said quietly. "His own damn kid. The one he was takin' in for the abortion, I mean. And she knowed, then—if he'd lie 'bout who the girl was, he probably lied 'bout the rest of it, too. Even 'bout who got that poor girl in a family way. Miss Mason knowed it all, then."

"And that's when she told you the whole story."

"It was like once she started, she couldn't stop all them words from comin' out. I wanted to go out and kill the son-of-a-bitch, right then; 'least tell a couple of the other Centurions, let them handle things. Miss Mason wouldn't let me. Guess even knowin' about him being a daughter-rapin', lyin' thief weren't enough."

"You never told anyone, Bobby. Why not?"

"She made me swear." His head tilted back, and he stared at the ceiling. "Probably don't matter now, her being dead and all."

He was silent again, this time for so long that I thought it was the end of his story.

But then he spoke again, and I understood that there was one final footnote to his story, a dark denouement that must have torn down the last illusion that Margot Mason might have held about the infant son she had carried so briefly, so many long years before.

"Night I was on your boat, I come back to her place afterward," he said. "Found all her computer stuff busted up. Them files, the one she kept pictures in—they was gone, too. Miss Mason ain't there, but there was blood all over her kitchen floor. Dirty bastard come there and kilt her, his own mother.

"Figured I better get my ass outta there 'fore he comes back, or sends the law. Pried up the floorboards where she'd hid my stuff for me, and got me one helluva surprise. 'Long with all my things, there's a huntin' gun in there. A Remington."

Teasdale fixed me with his eyes. "I ain't no fool. Right off, I knowed it was the gun that kilt that abortion doctor here, probably the nurse what got shot out in 'Carolina, too. Nobody else knowed about the floorboard hidey-hole. Ain't but one person coulda put it there."

Then he shrugged, as if he had come to terms with a betrayal that had been the last act of a woman who had been the only mother he had known.

In the end, faced with a choice between the son she had borne and the surrogate she had created, Margot Mason had made her final, possibly inevitable, choice. She had carefully placed the evidence that would shield the one by condemning the other.

"I don't blame her none," he said. "Blood's thicker 'n water. I knowed that. Hell, for sure I knowed *that.*"

Then, despite whatever private promise or resolve he had made to himself, Bobby Teasdale turned his face to the wall and began to cry.

CHAPTER 35

"She was trying to *frame* Teasdale?"

Jack's voice was incredulous, though how much of it was real and what percentage was an interview technique, I still could not say.

I took my time to answer, savoring the day.

We were at a table under the shade of the thatched roof at Conquistador's Landing, where Jack was nursing a tall club soda.

From where we sat, I could look out over the harbor below as the charter boats headed for the pass. As usual, late-summer vacationers were still braving the elements. Nearby, a family of four was leaning over the railing, their skins cherry-red and painful looking. But it was comfortable here, on the covered patio, and a breeze redolent with the fresh smell of salt from the nearby Gulf moderated the typical August heat and humidity.

There was a large mug in front of me. The beer that filled it was ice cold, and I could smell the lime, tart and pungent, that I had squeezed into the creamy white foam atop it.

I tested it with a sip, then nodded.

"That was the plan. Ballistics confirmed that the rifle was the weapon used in the DeBourche shooting. It also matches the one in North Carolina, three years ago."

"What about evidence? Teasdale's fingerprints?"

"Covered with them, but they were all fresh. The evidence techs are willing to testify that it had been wiped clean earlier, probably with a terrycloth towel. So Teasdale takes the trouble to wipe a gun clean, then handles it without gloves? What's wrong with *that* picture?"

"Well, he was going to shoot Shepard."

"If Teasdale was the cold-blooded killer he was reputed to be, he could have taken Shepard down at his house. Even the way he felt by then, Bobby didn't have it in him to murder anyone in cold blood. Instead, he follows Shepard to the meeting with Zhang-mei." I grinned. "And lucky for me that he did."

"But there was something else, wasn't there? Something that would have linked Teasdale to the rifle if you had found it still in her apartment?"

"Yep. Trace Evidence recovered three hairs from the blanket that was wrapped around the rifle. DNA matched them to Teasdale. Three hairs, in an otherwise freshly washed blanket. Again, a cynic might be tempted to think 'planted evidence.' But with everything else that had been stacked against him, it probably would have been enough to get a jury to convict."

"I can't believe it," Jack said. "I mean, she treated Bobby Teasdale like a son."

"She already had a son," I said. "The rest of her 'boys' were just substitutes. Even Teasdale, despite the fact she had been protecting him for more than three years."

"It's still pretty damned cold, Quynn."

"She was a pretty cold woman. Mason was even willing to use her own granddaughter by posting a faked 'message' on the Centurion's Web site. Though whether to punish her son, or to force him to come back to her . . . well, maybe even Margot Mason didn't know for sure. But any way you write it, she sacrificed Teasdale."

Jack paused, lost for a moment in thought. Then, almost imperceptibly, he lifted a shoulder in a slight shrug. "Maybe she was just being realistic, Quynn."

"Most of the groundwork had already been laid," I agreed. "Thanks to Zhang-mei, Teasdale was already the people's-choice candidate for the crimes. All Mason did was make the decision to go along. She was providing physical evidence that would protect her Harvey—or her Roger, if you want to go by the name he was given—when Zhang-mei helped him get into witness protection."

"Poor guy," Jack said, and I knew he was not referring to Shepard.

"Yeah. Poor guy. Teasdale had one thing to hold on to, and it turned out to be an illusion. Lot of that going around, it seems."

"Quynn, I get the sense that you're depressed about proving Maddie's 'miracle' wasn't one."

"A little, I suppose."

"Come on—that's the job you have. It's what I do, too. We're supposed to separate the lies from the truth, and let people know which is which."

"People need to believe in something, Jack. Sister Benedicta told me that one of her worst fears was that what she did was undermining the faith of others. I feel the same way about all this."

"Poor Maddie."

We sat in silence for a while, but it was not an uncomfortable one.

"The man should burn in hell, Quynn. Don't you want to make him pay for all that he did?"

"Not my concern," I said. "The Feds came in and took over the case."

"Yeah. And how do you feel about that?"

I shrugged and hoped it did not look as evasive as it felt. "Makes sense, with Shepard on the run. He could be just about anywhere in the country by now."

Jack frowned, as dissatisfied with my answer as was I. "Seems to me you might want . . . I don't know. Something. Closure, perhaps."

"I don't know what that is."

"Oh, for crying out—"

"Look, if he's alive, I want Shepard caught. But if you're asking whether I want some kind of payback . . . well, revenge won't bring back Tito, or Tara Kinsey, or any of the other people Shepard killed. It won't undo the damage he did to his daughter, either."

Jack had the grace to let the subject drop.

I looked at him closely and laughed out loud. "You already know all of this, don't you? You're letting me talk, so I'll relax and spill something good for you."

He grinned. "You have to start watching me on TV. I had all this on last night's news, Quynn. Okay. Give me something I don't already know. Pretty please."

"How about this? Those pictures Margot Mason had of Shepard at the abortion clinic? Zhang-mei sent them to her."

Jack's eyes widened. "No," he said, his voice incredulous; but I had learned not to fully trust my reading of his reactions.

"The FBI sealed his office and his house," I said. "They found a digital camera in his bedroom. A memory stick—that's a digital storage device some digicams use—was in his desk drawer. It was loaded with shots of Shepard taking Maddie inside DeBourche's clinic."

"I can quote you? I want to use this tonight."

I laughed. "Call your buddy Osterholm. I'm sure she'll confirm, for the record."

"Why would Zhang-mei send them to Mason?"

"Best guess, Shepard was continuing to refuse to play mole with the Centurions. He wouldn't even contact his mother. It must have made Zhang-mei furious. He most likely thought this would force the issue. I guess he was right." I took another sip.

"Fair's fair. You tell *me* something I don't know."

"They tracked down the man whose identity Harvey Cabot stole," Jack volunteered.

"T. Roger Shepard of Houston, Texas," I said. "Works at a college there. He never had a hint."

"A lot of people don't," he said, and it was my turn to let it pass.

"Anyway," I said, "if our Mr. Shepard is alive, he'll show up eventually. His face is all over Fox News *and* CNN."

"I had the story first," Jack said too quickly. Then, to his credit, he looked abashed as I grinned across the table. "Well, I did. An exclusive."

"You are clearly a rising star these days," I said.

"Moira is being very cooperative. She's given me one or two heads-up calls."

"Fair's fair, given your cooperation to help make the case against Zhang-mei." I chuckled. "Is there really a videotape of Moira Osterholm singing?"

"Maybe." Jack grinned. "It helps that all this makes Osterholm come off like Wonder Woman with a badge." His gaze slipped away to look out over the harbor's waters. "Did I mention that I've had calls from a few news directors? One of them is from a network owned and operated in Chicago."

"Good for you. Does this mean you're heading for the Windy City?"

"I'm thinking about it." He looked up and studied me closely. "Quynn, did you get anything out of this?"

"Well, Jesse Beaulieu seems to have reconsidered his career plans. I guess the powers-that-be decided dumping Chick Cornelieus would have been a touch too high-profile. It's hard to downplay how Shepard doped the larger part of law enforcement in Spanish Bay right under Jesse's nose. Add that to the incident at the Marina, and it doesn't exactly put Jesse—or his brother-in-law, the Congressman—in the best light."

"Shooting off guns in a crowded marina is usually considered poor community relations," Jack said. "Especially in an election year."

"Uh-huh. Any idea who leaked *that* story to the newspapers?"

Jack looked wide-eyed and innocent. "I've told you before. Newspeople don't reveal sources."

I laughed.

"Aside from that, I'm not being charged for the B&E at Tapley's place. Osterholm even gave me the videotape."

Jack snorted. "The *only* copy?"

"Maybe Moira Osterholm will tell *you*. Do you want to ask her for me?"

Jack shook his head, and his demeanor turned serious. "Actually, I only want the answer to one question, and that's the one Moira won't discuss in any kind of detail—at least, not with me."

"Where is Roger Shepard?" I said, and he nodded. "I wish I knew, Jack. Shepard seems to have dropped right off the face of the planet."

"Do you think he's dead? You've talked with her about this. Admit it, Quynn."

I took a deep draught of my beer and did not answer immediately.

"Moira Osterholm wonders the same thing," I said after a moment. "He was in Zhang-mei's car long enough to plant the bomb. One of the current theories is that Zhang-mei met with Shepard, who realized the game was up. So he killed the man to remove the only witness who could link everything together. Then Shepard goes off to find a quiet place in the backwoods to kill himself."

"You don't seriously believe that?"

"Manhunts are based on the fact that few criminals have

either the patience or the resources to hole up and wait, Jack. They're most vulnerable when they turn rabbit. On the move, almost invariably somebody sees them, recognizes them—that, or they call attention to themselves through their need for food, shelter or transportation." I shrugged. "At least, that's what the cop textbook says."

"So Moira says there's no evidence to indicate Shepard's still alive."

"Yep. And I'm sure that she's telling the truth."

But Jack either sensed the ambivalence in my response or had come to know me too well.

"You don't believe it," he repeated, and this time it was not a question.

"He's disappeared before, Jack," I said. "With a monster like Roger Shepard, it's safer to keep an open mind."

CHAPTER 36

It was almost four weeks before we had any new answers.

By then, most of the national media had turned its collective attention from the events in Spanish Bay to matters of greater import: in Washington, a congressman from one of the Northeastern states had the poor judgment to initiate a relationship with one of the more ambitious interns in his office. He compounded that mistake by penning a series of letters to his young mistress that discussed, in graphic detail, their encounters in a motor lodge just outside the Beltway.

Three months later, he tried to break it off. The woman-scorned went public with the letters, thereby laying a scent trail that ensured the undivided attention of the tabloids, both print and broadcast versions, as well as a significant number of the more traditional news outlets.

There was neither miracle nor murder involved this time, but illicit sex has always been a reliable fallback when catering to a fickle mass audience.

As the weeks had passed without sign or sighting, what had begun as merely one theory among many had assumed the status of fact: Roger Shepard was dead. Shepard's body had not yet been recovered, but that was the kind of afterthought that mattered little to anyone except his daughter and possibly a few of us in law enforcement who remained skeptical. We were initially humored and finally dismissed as hopelessly out of touch with reality.

Among those in the know, it was generally assumed that Shepard's mortal remains would show up eventually in an advanced state of decomposition, much as had the body of his own mother.

Two weeks after Tito had died, an alligator poacher had noticed a bundle of rags entangled in the sawgrass deep in the backwaters that fed Spanish Bay. He had poked at it with the same bamboo lance he used to prod 'gators into the open, and what the various swamp predators had left of M. C. Mason did a slow roll to stare at him through empty eye sockets. Worse still was the gaping wound that stretched from high on the left of her throat downward past her windpipe, a ragged, lop-sided leer. The poacher later confessed that he had almost fallen from his aluminum flatboat.

The discovery of Mason's body had at last laid to rest a persistent rumor that had circulated among the Centurions: that Margot Mason was still alive, still planning the anti-abortion campaign that had driven her for more than three decades.

Later that same day, on a seldom-used fire trail not far away, searchers made a second discovery. It was the sedan that I had riddled with bullet holes on a night that now seemed to me long ago. But there was no body in it, and the only bloodstains were in the trunk, along with a bone-handled carving knife. The blood was Margot Mason's, and the knife matched others in a set from her kitchen.

By now it was late September, and the summer season had ended. Aside from the influx of the college-aged on weekends, the sugar-white beaches were again the province of older couples, some of them early-arriving snowbirds and others part of the growing cadre of year-round resident retirees. Among the working locals, not even Spanish Bay's upcoming annual bill-fishing rodeo caused more than a ripple among people who had counted up the season's take and now wanted only to settle back for a few months of tourist-free living.

I also took the interval as a respite, using the comp time I had accumulated to work aboard my floating home. I had traced most of the electrical problems, replacing the moth-eaten wiring with marine-grade conduit. I had retired the bank of deep-cycle storage batteries that had already been ancient during the Clinton Administration. With my new on-board power supply, I was starting to feel confident that the bilge pumps could at least handle the seepage normal to all vessels.

But the diesel still befuddled me, in an increasing variety of problems.

It stubbornly defied my ongoing attempts to diagnose its fickle nature. Whenever I fired it up—whether for an extended trip up the Intercoastal or even for an afternoon's float to the shallows in the lee of the harbor bridge—at some point the engine would invariably cough and sputter to an evil-smelling halt. It was scant comfort that, after a period adrift that ranged from a few minutes to a half hour, I could usually coax it again to life.

I checked and rechecked pressure and fuel lines, replaced jets and filters and ports, calibrated compression ratios—all to no avail. But regularly losing power and steerageway was a Damocletian sword I was determined to sail out from under.

But crawling around my diesel had revealed an even worse problem. I had probed the rubber and steel fittings that held the engine to the hull. On two of the four mounts, the screwdriver had pushed easily into what should have been solid metal. What I had taken for the surface rust and corrosion common to all metal fittings in marine environments was far more advanced; at minimum, I was looking at a major repair bill in the very near future. The discovery had done little to improve my outlook on life.

I was working in the cramped engine compartment, half twisted around the transmission box, when I heard footsteps tap across the deck above. Before I could extricate myself, a familiar voice called down the companionway.

"Hey, Quynn—anybody home down there?"

I emerged, wiping the grime from my hands, as Jack Reagan leaned in from the deck. He was dressed in a bright yellow Polo shirt and cargo-pocketed khaki shorts. A pair of expensive-looking sunglasses was pushed high, an amber-lensed crown on his close-cropped hair.

"I thought it was about time you made good on your promise," he said, then looked at the oil and grease that streaked my face.

"I'm playing with the raw-water cooling system," I began, and stopped at the look Jack gave me.

"Uh-huh, whatever that is," he said. "So how about it? Want to sail me around on the big blue sea?"

"It's a little brisk out on the Gulf today. Storm's coming, probably by late tonight. Waves already kicking pretty high out there, especially for a houseboat."

His face fell. "So, no way?"

"The bay would be choppy, too. Still, not as bad as out on the big salt, I guess."

"Look, Quynn—will the boat work or not?"

"As always," I said, "I can sail you out. As always, there's still no guarantee I can sail you back in."

"I'll chance it if you will. See—I brought sandwiches."

I lined up the bow on the sandy spit that formed the seaward side of the harbor passage, a tricky S-shaped cut that provided scant clearance for two vessels to pass in it. It helped that the tide was running in. The clear Gulf waters had already flushed the murky harbor, making the sandy white bottom easy to see from where we sat at the high bridge atop the superstructure. Despite the freshening breeze, it was too nice a day to steer from the inside conning station below.

"Friends of yours?" Jack asked, looking past me to starboard. From a few feet away, almost close enough to touch, the usual crowd milled about on the boardwalk dock. They smiled and waved at us as we eased past.

"Everybody gets that treatment," I said, and lightly tapped my air horn. "People just like watching boats go by."

We passed the docks and entered the sinuous channel cut. I eased the throttle forward slightly to increase steerage and made a half turn of the wheel. A fisherman—a boy, rather, in faded cutoffs—stood a dozen feet away on the packed sand with a casting rod in his hand.

He started to lift a hand in greeting; then I saw him frown. Over the rhythmic gurgling pop of my engine, I could not hear what he shouted. When I waved, he shook his head and jabbed his finger to the stern of my boat. I feathered back the throttles a hair to reduce the wave to a minimum, and shot an "o" with thumb and forefinger through the open window of my bridge.

And then we were past, into the clear water of the cut that linked the Gulf with the waters of Spanish Bay. I eased the throttle forward and was relieved to hear the engine answer smoothly. I cut the wheel against the tidal current and settled on course.

But I could not shake the image of the boy, his finger pointing to the stern of my boat.

"We may be dragging a docking line in the water," I said to Jack. "Last thing we need is a line wrapping around the propeller. You better take the wheel."

"Yeah, right. And do what with it, exactly?"

"See that green daymarker? Steer a course that—never mind. Just keep us straight for a minute while I check aft. Try not to hit anything that looks expensive."

"Go to hell, Captain Bligh," he said, and I laughed as I gave him the helm.

I descended the ladder from the upper bridge into the main salon, still grinning, and felt the vibration of the engine as I crossed the deck.

Outside, a cruiser passed, heading in the opposite direction toward the open Gulf, and as we crossed its spreading wake my boat rolled right, then back again. I tight-roped toward the sliding glass door. Distracted by the need to maintain balance, I noticed too late that it was partially open.

There, on the teak sole, were a set of wet footprints.

At that instant, something hard jammed against the back of my head.

"Nice day for a boat ride," the voice of Roger Shepard said into my ear.

CHAPTER 37

Shepard walked me awkwardly across the rolling deck, back to the ladder. At his direction, my fingers were intertwined on top of my head. The barrel of his weapon lightly brushed the nape of my neck.

Once, I pretended to stumble, thinking to bring him close enough for a counter-move, but Shepard was either too experienced or too canny. Instead, I was rewarded with a sharp rap behind my ear, hard enough to draw blood.

"Quynn?" From the bridge above, Jack was still trying to sound mellow, but I could hear the edge in his voice now. "We're getting kind of close to that green thing. You want to get up here and drive, dammit?"

"I'll shoot you, and then him." Shepard's voice was low, but also somehow conversational. "Or you can do what I say and both of you may even survive. At least, for a while longer."

"What do you want, Shepard?"

"Tell him to cut the motor," Shepard said. "Then say to come downstairs." He read my expression immediately. "You don't want to test me. Do it."

"He won't know how." I gestured forward, at the conning station. "I can do it from down here."

Shepard watched from a careful distance as I eased the throttles back and shifted into neutral. I locked the wheel amidships and turned to him. As we lost headway, the houseboat began to wallow clumsily in the choppy waters.

"Hey," I heard Jack shout. "Whatever happened, I didn't do it. Quynn!"

"Now," Shepard said, "call him."

I did.

When Jack's feet appeared, Shepard shifted the pistol to him, though his eyes remained on me. The message was clear, and I stood immobile as he descended to the salon deck and turned.

"I thought you were kidding about all the problems this tub—" Jack stopped in mid-sentence. I saw his eyes flicker between Shepard and me, weighing the situation. There was nothing of fear in his face or his manner, although I was not certain the same could be said of me.

"Mr. Shepard, I'm Jack Reagan. Do you remember me? We've wondered where you—"

"Shut up. You're a cop, Quynn. Where do you keep your cop stuff?"

He rummaged through the drawer until he found my handcuffs, and tossed them to me in an easy underhand. "Right wrist, Quynn. Thread the other end through the ladder, then on your guest."

I did that, too.

Shepard checked the cuffs, then moved past us to the conning station. As I watched, he tried to turn the spoked wheel. It did not budge.

He turned to me. "I don't have time for games."

"Release the wheel-brake," I said. "The lever on the right."

He did, then pushed the throttle and shift quadrants forward; with one hand holding the pistol, he spun the helm to starboard until it bounced against the stop.

Too hard, and too much throttle. The propeller cavitated, spinning wildly in the underwater void and causing an alarming thudding and vibration until the blades finally found water. With the rudder hard over, the stern swung tightly. Shepard overcorrected, and we cut a serpentine wake for the several seconds it took him to regain steerage control.

Even in the relatively protected waters of Spanish Bay, he was an obvious novice at boat handling. Nonetheless, the course he settled on was taking us down the channel toward the open sea.

We churned ahead through Spanish Pass into increasingly restless waters, but the real pounding began when we rounded the breakwater and entered the Gulf of Mexico. With a lighter hand this time, Shepard turned the wheel to a west-by-southwest heading, angling away from the coast.

He waited at the helm for several minutes, his eyes flickering between the compass and the retreating shoreline. Then, satisfied, he locked down the wheel and eased his way along the bouncing deck to where Jack and I stood.

He grinned hugely, though I could detect little humor in it. "I suppose you're wondering why I called this little meeting today. I actually came to see you, Quynn. And, of course, to borrow your boat. Mr. Reagan is an unexpected bonus."

"You're making a stupid move, Shepard. Do you know how easy it is to track down a boat on the open sea? This is Florida. The Coast Guard has had a lot of practice doing it."

"Yes, I've noticed there's no longer a problem with drugs or illegal immigrants getting past them anymore. Give it a rest, Quynn. Nobody's looking for your boat, or for you. In the unlikely event they're still looking for me around Spanish Bay—which I doubt, given the attention span of modern law enforcement—who'd guess I'm here with you?"

I did not answer.

But Jack leaned forward, as composed as if he was working an interview in his station's studio.

"Mr. Shepard, you've been able to elude a nationwide search for weeks. You've shaved your head. It appears that you've lost weight, too. I guess that's why nobody has reported seeing you."

He smiled engagingly, bringing his most potent weapon to bear. "Quynn says you'd have been caught if you had been on the run. So, where *have* you been hiding?"

Shepard ignored him, instead addressing me.

"How about *you*, Quynn? We may have a long trip ahead of us. You've had time to think about everything that happened. Don't you want to ask me something? Clear up all the areas you still don't understand?"

"Not particularly. You're a monster, Shepard—a multiple-murderer, a homicidal brain-melt who killed his wife and own mother, who drugged and serially assaulted his own daughter. I'm not especially interested in the self-justifications of a twisted freak of nature."

He nodded judiciously, as if pondering a point of debate that I had made. Then the hand not holding the pistol shot out to the side and locked hard around Jack's lower jaw.

It must have hurt. I saw his eyes water, but they stayed fixed on Shepard's face. He glanced at Jack almost fondly, then turned his stare back to me.

"Mr. Reagan might disagree, I think. He might think that a 'freak' certainly could have something of interest for him." He squeezed harder, and this time Jack's eyes closed tight and a small tight sound escaped him. "Or even *show* him, if I feel the need to do that."

"Okay, Shepard, I'll play. I figure you hid somewhere in Spanish Bay. How did we miss finding you?"

Shepard released his grip on Jack's face. As he pulled away, the paper-white marks his fingers had left were clearly defined on the newsman's flesh.

"Have you ever noticed how a lot of your elderly cripples live by themselves? You have to admire the plucky old farts—living like that with all the problems they face." Shepard passed his hand over his shaven scalp. "Guy I found was handicapped *and* bald. I guess you could say he didn't have any luck at all." He laughed, and the sound sent a chill through me. I had no doubt as to the fate of Shepard's host.

He stitched an intent expression on his face. "Interesting fact about the handicapped, Quynn. Did you know they can still get groceries delivered? They make a call, leave some cash on the porch in an envelope. Never even have to leave the house."

Shepard smiled. "As long as the neighbors see a little activity every now—well, you know, people only look at the wheelchair. They don't really see the guy who's sitting in it. And hey, it's not hard to roll yourself onto the porch every now and then."

He nodded, as if to encourage additional inquiry.

"You're doing fine, Lieutenant. Don't you want to ask me more? From the beginning, for example?"

I forced my voice to sound level, even a touch annoyed.

"I know a lot of it already, from talking to Zhang-mei's former colleagues," I said. "I've guessed most of the rest."

"Fire away, Lieutenant. Let's hear what you have."

"Both sides were protecting you," I said. "Your birth-mother, out of whatever misguided mix of love and guilt. Zhang-mei, because he saw you as the chance to make his bones."

"*Protecting* me? The son-of-a-bitch was trying to blackmail me," he said and chuckled.

I shrugged, as if to concede the point. "The beginning, then. In North Carolina, Zhang-mei catches the case of one Harvey Cabot—to him, just another no-account, wife-abuser who fled across state lines. Pretty routine stuff, mostly; but then, Zhang-mei had been mostly working low-level fugitives—skips, deadbeat dads—for several years. He tracks Harvey to Spanish Bay without much trouble."

"I wasn't trying too hard to hide, either." Shepard's voice was still genial, but I caught the undercurrent of offended pride in it. "Don't give the little bastard too much credit."

"He finds Harvey had been working right in the headquarters of the Centurions of the Lord, which the Justice Department has listed as one of the most active anti-abortion groups around. Bells ring, lights flash. To Zhang-mei, it translates as 'career maker'—if he can turn Cabot into his own mole inside the Centurions."

I looked at Shepard. "But Harvey Cabot had already left town by then. Next thing, Cabot's wife is shot dead back in North Carolina, and the evidence points to anti-abortion extremists. Zhang-mei is no dummy. The timing seems a little too convenient, especially when he finds out that Harvey Cabot is back in Raleigh. I guess he picked up enough evidence to guess the truth. It should have stopped there. With Cabot put away for killing his wife, this would have had a happier ending. You would have been in jail by now, probably awaiting execution."

This time, Shepard's laughter was genuine. "Happier for some, maybe. I wouldn't have enjoyed that at all."

"And it wouldn't have gotten Zhang-mei what he wanted, either. So instead of charging Harvey Cabot, he makes an offer. Not only will he let you slide on the murder, he'll make sure you and your daughter get brand-new lives. All you have to do is agree to go home to Mom, inform on the Centurions. I'm guessing he didn't know you had looted their treasury, but that's a minor detail. Zhang-mei was counting on a mother's love for the prodigal son."

I looked up at my captor. "Here's one of the places where I'm a little unclear, Shepard. A deal like that—relocation, new identities, the whole nine yards—well, normally that means involving the Witness Protection program. But Zhang-mei decided to freelance it, on his own."

Shepard just smiled and said nothing.

"My guess is that he didn't want to share you. You were his

ticket to the anti-terrorism big leagues, as long as you stayed his own personal source. Am I right?"

Still smiling, Shepard dipped his head in mock humility.

"Or maybe it was just being realistic. A cold-blooded, sniper-murder of a wife and mother—by a man who had already committed incest on the daughter he had now reclaimed? Zhang-mei knew a grant of protection didn't have a chance in hell of going through. Some things turn the stomach of even the Justice Department."

Shepard's smile had turned frosty, but he remained silent.

"So Zhang-mei arranged for another suspect," I said. "Enter Bobby Teasdale, a small-time con with a big mouth, and the bad luck to have made blowhard statements about abortionists. How am I doing so far, Shepard?"

"Slick," he said. "Very slick, Quynn."

"Teasdale gets elected everybody's favorite hate-crime sniper, and Cabot becomes Roger Shepard. A new name, a new city, some help with references—everything he needs to set himself up to look like a successful businessman. Even the money you took from the Centurions. You had it all—and with Zhang-mei in so deep, compromised—well, you could welsh on playing the mole for him."

Despite myself, my voice trembled with the rage I had sought to conceal. "And you had Maddie. We know what you were doing to her. Were you worried she'd see how sick you are, and tell somebody who'd believe her? Somewhere along the line, you found out about GHB and what it did to short-term memory. The molestation continued, but with a new twist."

"Molestation," he said, his voice dripping scorn. "You don't believe it, but it was a good life. For both Maddie and me."

"I believe that *you* believe it," I said. "But I've heard it before. A lot of sexual deviants feel the same way about their victims. You impregnated her. Then you aborted her child, and killed innocent people to cover it all up. Along the way, you turned Maddie's mind into emotional rubble. Add it up. You're nothing special, just another sick son-of-a-bitch. And that's the book on you . . . *Harvey.*"

"I love my daughter, Quynn. I really do."

"Sure."

"My mother abandoned me. I went back for Maddie."

"You went back to kill her mother. You went back because you're a pedophile who targeted his own child. Does that sound like father-of-the-year material?"

Shepard's eyes blazed, then the veil fell again. He studied me for a moment, as if considering response or rebuttal. Then he shrugged, as if further discussion was irrelevant.

"Well, we'll see," he said, and his tone was now confident.

"Maddie's out of your reach now, Shepard."

"Oh, I know where Maddie is," Shepard replied. "In fact, I've always wanted to visit Seattle."

"She won't go with you. You'll never have her again."

"Want to bet? I'm her father, Quynn. One way or another, she'll do what I say."

For the next three hours, we pounded farther away from land. Shepard's fit of *bonhomie* apparently had passed; he spoke seldom, and then usually in monosyllables. For the most part, he busied himself searching through the various lockers around my boat. Inside and out, the deck was now cluttered with my clothes, books and papers, and assorted nautical gear. He went through the signal-flag rack and even rummaged in the hinged compartment on the aft sundeck where I kept the half dozen life jackets on board.

By the course he had set, he could be going anywhere. Mexico was a possibility—Shepard could easily parallel the U.S. coastline, ducking back to land for fuel and provisions in the guise of an offshore cruising boat-bum. Of course, on such a trip he would have no use for extra passengers; the deep water into which we headed had served often enough as an unmarked grave.

Jack and I, linked together at the wrists, experimented with various positions until we found one where neither of us risked dislocation or gangrene. We too spoke little; there was little to say.

As outlandish as it sounds, I even dozed.

I opened my eyes to a semi-darkness and the steady rumble of a diesel engine, a throaty mechanical throb that played in counterpoint to the one in my own skull.

The weather had worsened. Despite the clear night, the northerly winds whipped the Gulf into deep troughs and steep moving peaks. A full moon lay low in the sky, a dramatic white globe that turned the troubled surface into a living creature of light and shadows.

I fought down a wave of nausea. It might have been the inevitable byproduct of being too long belowdeck on a moving vessel. More likely, it was fear. I glanced toward Jack. His eyes were closed and his breathing a soft rasp; he too had surrendered to sleep.

But something, some irregularity, had roused me.

Shepard was standing at the conning station, both hands on the wheel. He was studying one of the gauges, the frown on his face exaggerated by the shadows cast by the lighted instrument board. The effect was one I remembered from childhood, when we would hold a flashlight under our chins to create the face of a monster.

At that moment, I heard it again—felt it, rather. The throb of the diesel missed a beat, coughed raggedly before it resumed its pulsing rhythm. But the RPMs had changed, slowed. I watched Shepard touch the throttle, tentatively push it forward to regain engine power. It was a logical act, but the wrong one. Whenever I had tried it, trying to trace the demons that possessed my boat's mechanical heart, the engine had rebelled and jolted to a stop.

As it did now.

"I hope you know about diesel engines, Shepard," I said. "I've been trying to find the problems with this one for months."

He turned, one hand clenched around the wheel for support in the pitching seas.

"Fix it."

"Give me that pistol. Then I'll try."

"Stand up."

I shook my head. "Take a look around, Shepard. How long do you think we can wallow in this kind of sea before we break up and sink?"

"Do you think I won't shoot you? *Both* of you?"

"We're dead anyway," I said. "You don't leave witnesses."

Shepard pulled himself closer until he stood over Jack. He cocked the revolver and placed it against his temple, then looked at me.

"Do you think I'm sane, Quynn?" His voice was calm, even serene.

"No."

"I think you may be right, but I'm not completely sure. If I kill Mr. Reagan here, right now—if I blow his brains and blood all over you—that would prove it once and for all. Wouldn't it?" He arched his eyebrows. "Shall I? Or would you prefer to put the question off for a while longer? It's really up to you."

"Let him, Quynn," Jack said. "Let him shoot." His words were clear and distinct, but there was an underlying tremolo that indicated the effort it had taken him to keep them so.

"That's one vote counted," Shepard said, still as if conversing. "Two out of three wins it."

He waited a few seconds, looking at me. "Alright, then," he said, and his arm stiffened.

"No," I said. "I'll do what you want."

He handed the key to Jack, standing aside as he waited for the newsman to unlock my cuff. I rose with difficulty, a result of both the unsteadiness in my cramped legs and the wildly erratic rock and roll of the boat itself.

We worked our way aft toward the engine compartment, Shepard careful to keep Jack between us, holding him by the handcuff that still dangled from the newsman's wrist. I slid the salon's glass doors open, and a maelstrom of wind and water greeted us.

The engine access was a hatchway perhaps four feet square in the center of the sundeck. I freed the safety latches and thrust it aside, then lowered myself inside.

It was cramped for three people, even with one of them tight against the hull. There, a large seacock that fed water to the engine cooling was bolted solidly to the bulkhead. Shepard snapped the free end of Jack's cuffs to the cast-bronze intake, flush against a rubber hose as long and as thick as my forearm that led to the engine block.

"Get to work, Quynn," Shepard said. "I want this thing running again."

He watched me work, wedging himself against the pitching of the craft. His back lay solidly against the rough fiberglass hull, and a shoulder pressed against the gritty rust of the engine mounts. The revolver in his hand was steady, again aimed at me.

Engine repair is a dark science, a magic born of tiny screws, improbably undersized springs and fickle electrical contacts, all bound together by tolerances measured in millimeters. It is an alchemy difficult to summon at any time; when waves and gale-force winds rage, it can be close to impossible.

It was hot here and smelled of raw fuel oil, which did little to quell the churning in my stomach. Carefully, I worked my way around the bulk of the engine in a kneeling position, my hands gripping the still-warm engine block to steady my balance. My previous repair attempts had ruled out the obvious: fuel and air manifolds were clear, and the compression levels that ignited the oil/air mix were within the proper range. I had checked the fuel for water contamination, bled the system for bubbles, switched out an infinity of filters.

I tried to look like I knew what I was doing. The truth was that I had no idea why the engine stopped, this time or previously. I had even less insight into why it would finally restart, as it always had before.

Again, I pulled the intake jets and cleaned each; again, I adjusted the screws that controlled the pressure, volume and ratio of air and fuel. Finally, I wiped my hands on my thighs and looked at my captor.

"I have to try it now, Shepard. To fire it up, we have to go back inside to the conning station."

"Okay. Let's go."

"Give me the handcuff key."

"Mr. Reagan stays here. Marching the two of you back and forth provides too many opportunities for mischief."

"I'm fine, Quynn," Jack said. "Really. Go." His eyes flickered almost imperceptibly to the pipe to which he was shackled. It happened so quickly that I thought I had imagined it. Perhaps I had. If Jack had devised a plan, I did not see what it might be.

The trip back to the shelter of the cabin took longer this time. The winds were stronger and the waves even higher. I fell twice, catching myself on hands that found the deck beneath the wrist-deep cataract of seawater that washed from bow to stern with each breaking wave. Shepard made the passage without mishap, the beneficiary of the free hand he kept tight on the railing.

We were both drenched and dripping when I stood at the controls. There, I went through the start-up checklist: switching on glow plugs, priming the fuel feed, setting the throttle and mix. It was an anticlimax when I thumbed the starter switch and heard the engine turn without firing.

"Not there yet," I said, my knees flexing as a particularly rogue wave tumbled under the hull. It was accompanied by a gust of wind that threw a torrent of foam against the windward glass, for a moment obscuring the outside world as if a blanket had been thrown over our vessel. Then the gale ripped it away, leaving only the blur of salt spray to streak the glass.

"I'm losing patience, Quynn. That means you and your friend are running out of luck."

I had no answers; he was right, in every way I could devise.

But as we fought our way back to the engine compartment, Jack was already at work, giving us one chance more.

In Shepard's absence, he had worked the handcuff past the bronze inlet pipe, over the stainless steel clamps that attached it to the thick rubber hose. Now, as the open hatchway came to view, Jack was standing, his feet braced on either side of the seacock—pulling, straining, his face a tight grimace and his free hand locked around his shackled wrist to bring to bear the strength of both his arms.

And the rubber hose was flexing, pulling upward, tearing away from the three-inch bronze fitting. Even as we watched from the deck above, a first jet of seawater shot from the splitting rubber—thin, but with force behind it.

Shepard realized the danger in the same instant. He aimed at Jack from a yard away, the cylinder of the revolver already turning and the hammer rising. I saw it start to fall at the same instant that I flung myself against his body.

The detonation pressured my eardrums painfully, but there was no time to do more than register that fact, or anything but the death grip I had taken on Shepard's gun arm. We fell through the open hatch into the engine compartment, crashing painfully to the rough fiberglass hull.

The momentum of my attack drove him back, both of us stagger-stepping and clawing at the other. Locked together, we rolled across the deck.

I felt a knee snap-kick into my stomach and the gut-twisting pain rocked me. But I could not let go of my adversary, and we crashed against the bulk of the engine block in a painful impact that I felt through his own body. I heard the barking gasp as his breath exploded from him. I twisted hard. The pistol fired again, then once more before I levered it back and smashed it sideways against the hull. I felt the gun bounce against my shoulder as it flew from his hand. It slid into the space beneath the engine block, out of reach.

I hit him high on the cheek with a short left hand, then followed with a crossing right to his jaw. But he blocked my finishing punch and hammered an elbow against the side of my head. Simultaneously, he wedged his foot against my chest and kicked me away.

From the corner of my eye, I saw Shepard scramble crabwise until he reached the engine. He sprawled, groping beneath it with a desperate urgency. When his hand emerged, it held the pistol. He pointed it at my face, and a slow smile lit up his features.

Then the world tilted crazily, turning us almost ninety degrees and flinging me like a rag doll to the deck. It was a massive wave, primeval and without mercy. The entire vessel groaned at the impact of it. I could hear things snapping and breaking throughout the boat.

The din of it all was tremendous. Even so, it was dwarfed by the explosive crack as the weakened engine mounts parted and tons of metal shifted, slid and broke free a few inches from where I lay.

But louder still was Shepard's scream, cut horribly short by the crash of the engine atop his chest. It was replaced by a ghastly gurgling moan that rose and fell again and again.

The wave's impact finished Jack's work for him. It toppled Jack backward with a force he could not have mustered alone. He bounced to the deck close to me, one end of the handcuffs attached to his wrist and a torn length of rubber hose still locked in the other.

From the now-unrestrained seacock gushed a flood, a torrent, an unstoppable deluge. It had the force of a fire hose in it, pulsing unchecked through what was in effect a three-inch opening to the sea.

"Good God, Quynn," Jack said. "Is this thing sinking?"

"We have to get out—*now.* Can you make it to the hatch?"

We half carried each other up the steepening incline, the roar of the wind and water now accompanied by the irregular sound of my boat's imminent destruction. At the hatch, I motioned Jack to go first, watching as he hoisted himself up to the open deck above.

Jack leaned back, extended a hand. I looked through it, then behind me.

"Don't do it. Quynn, get out of there. Come *on!*"

"Find a life jacket and put it on. Then get off. I'll meet you in the water." I saw his expression. "I will. Now *go,* damn it!" Another blackwater wave washed over both of us. When I looked again, he had disappeared.

The water was already at Shepard's ears when I turned back, and rising fast. Adding to it was the seawater now also cascading down over the rim of the hatch. We could not have had more than a few inches of freeboard left before it was completely submerged.

Another wave loomed high, broke over us. For what remained of the stern, itself burdened by the now-unstable weight of the diesel, it was the death blow. I heard Shepard cry out once more before it was drowned under the wash of dark waters, filling and then overflowing the confinement where the trapped man lay.

I had an instant's awareness before the wave struck, a pulverizing force that seemed alive and vengeful. A part of the hull collapsed inward beneath my feet, tried to swallow me. I clawed forward, but it was the solid wall of water that hurled me, spinning, from the engine room to the open sea. My flailing arms found a deck railing and locked around it. When I opened my eyes I was surrounded by water dimly lit by a poisonous green glow. An agonizing pain stabbed inside my ears, and I realized the surface was already a dozen feet above me, receding fast.

I still do not know why I kicked my way back to the engine hatch. I can find no rational explanation for hauling myself back inside, or for expending strength and my remaining air while I strained against the engine block wedged against a still-struggling form.

At some point, perhaps recognizing the futility of my act, I switched my grip to Shepard himself. But even with both hands wrapped around his chest and my feet braced against the bulkhead wall, I could not free him, nor even move him an inch. That knowledge came simultaneously with another realization: the fingers that had first clutched me, then clawed at me in desperation, now had ceased to move at all.

And I had no air left in my lungs. Only fire filled them now, and my mind screamed at me to inhale, to relieve the raving need—with *anything*, even the water around me, cool and dark and deadly.

I turned and pulled myself out, a frenzied hand-over-hand

struggle in translucent waters that roiled and churned in the convulsions of my dying boat. As I cleared the hatchway, my foot snagged a tangle of docking line, jerking me to a halt. I worked with frantic fingers, made clumsy by the imperative to find air, to breathe.

By the time I freed myself, the quicksilver ceiling seemed an impossible distance away.

Just then, the hull twisted and fell away beneath me even faster, and I felt the suction of it—a sullen, greedy strength that spun and tumbled and tugged me down again, back toward itself.

For an instant I caught a glimpse through the still-open engine hatch. Framed in it, wide-eyed and with his mouth open in a scream that would last forever, Roger Shepard stared out. I fancied I saw his eyes change, fix on me in either accusation or in a final, fearful entreaty. But that must have been my imagination, a delusion made manifest by oxygen starvation.

Then my boat—Shepard's tomb—began its corkscrew dive into the trackless depths, down to the darkness where all our monsters dwell.

As if freed from a spell, I clawed toward the surface, already aware it was too far, much too far. A single shimmering dot that had to be the moon was my only bearing. I pulled with locked throat toward it, on and on.

I was near surrender, reduced to a feeble thrashing that gained no purchase against the death grip of the sea. It was then that a hand seized my wrist. At the same instant, I broke through into a blinding world of light.

In a great, shuddering gasp I tasted air.

When my vision cleared, I was looking into the face of Jack Reagan. He was wrapped in an oversized vest, bulky and bright-orange, salvaged from the flotsam pitching and bobbing in the rough seas around us.

I was without strength. My eyelids drooped, fell shut, but I felt Jack against me as he moved and arranged my body. I felt myself held tight in his embrace, then felt his legs clamp around my waist. At one point, I opened my eyes. Jack's face was inches from mine, and the expression he wore was composed in equal parts of forced humor and real concern.

"Don't worry, Quynn," Jack said, just before another wave broke over us. "You're safe. See, I *know* you're a married woman."

And that was how they found us, almost fourteen hours later.

Sometime during the night, the seas had calmed to a light chop. At dawn, an infinity of sparkling rubies spilled from the red-orange disk that muscled itself above the horizon. I recall seeing a pod of dolphin swim past, whistling and popping as they slipped sinuously in and out of the twin worlds they inhabit. By then, it had been my turn to don the life vest while Jack dozed fitfully.

Our salvation arrived at mid-morning. It came in the form of a chartered deep-sea fishing boat that initially passed a half mile distant, then suddenly heeled in a long, graceful curve toward the speck of orange and yellow that bobbed in an otherwise empty sea.

AFTERWORD

On a bright afternoon a week before Christmas, I found myself standing over the grave of my best friend. The rectangle that marked the boundaries of his final rest was still bare and fresh-looking, as was the simple marker that Gina and Vic had insisted upon. It was a simple brass plaque inscribed with his name, the appropriate dates of birth and death, and three words: "Husband. Father. Friend."

It was seasonably chilly, though the snowbirds from more northerly climes found it mild enough to amuse the rest of us by donning shorts for their golf games and walks along the beach. They may have been right, even wise, to extend the season so. Here, under the now-leafless oaks and pecans, it was easy to regret the sunny days we have squandered, to lament how few summers are allowed us.

The death of Roger Shepard had been a minor news sensation for a few days, extended somewhat by the fact that a minor celebrity—one of their own—had been involved. I had watched two or three of the interviews done from Jack's hospital bedside. In my opinion, none of them had been as good as the original, which featured Jack in effect interviewing himself on the circumstances of his abduction, hostage ordeal and ultimate rescue. It had been picked up by the network, and mentioned in the *People* article that ran the following week.

I had been allowed to retreat from that spotlight, a slow fade into the semi-obscurity of a reinstated local cop. Jack granted me that courtesy, though I was still not certain if it was a display of his own sensibilities or of his own ambitions.

In any event, the exposure had tipped him over the top. I had already received a Christmas card from him, postmarked from New York and tastefully embossed with the peacock logo of his new employer. Jack had signed it, but there was no personal note. Perhaps I should have been hurt—but after all, I was a married woman.

There had been other Christmas cards, too. One from Gina and Victoria Schwartz, an understated Nativity, signed by both. Chick Cornelieus sent one, the same card that went to all active and retired members of the Spanish Bay Police Department; a handwritten note inside included the address of the Minnesota clinic where he was undergoing the latest of his treatment therapies.

Another card arrived from Belize, where Ron was wintering with yet another of his new friends. The "wish you were here" struck me as particularly inappropriate, under the circumstances. But the divorce papers are still un-filed, by either of us, so perhaps the conclusion to that story remains unwritten, too.

I also got a calendar from my insurance agent. No note there, either.

I received only one real letter, and that one was mailed to me from Seattle. It was four pages in length, single-spaced. Along with it came a photograph of a girl with happier eyes than I remembered. She was holding a small black dog. In the background was a snow-covered mountain range framed by a sky so blue it looked like cobalt.

I have had no word from Sister Benedicta, but that came as no surprise. She had not struck me as a person to whom sentimentality came easily, or whose fears or beliefs or rationalizations could be contained within the constraints of any card.

In that—and, I suspect, in much else besides—we have a great deal in common.

ABOUT THE AUTHOR

E. L. Merkel is the author of *Final Epidemic,* a Barnes and Noble national bestseller, and *Dirty Fire,* a critically acclaimed mystery set in Chicago. Merkel spent more than a decade as a journalist, newspaper columnist and investigative reporter, and for several years has served as co-host of a nationally broadcast talk-radio program. Merkel is currently working on *Fire of the Prophet,* a contemporary suspense-thriller.